ARTEMIS

By Philip Palmer

Debatable Space
Red Claw
Version 43
Hell Ship
Artemis

PHILIP PALMER

ARTEMIS

www.orbitbooks.net

ORBIT

First published in Great Britain in 2011 by Orbit

A CIP catalogue record for this book
is available from the British Library.

ISBN 978-1-84149-945-1

Typeset in Garamond by M Rules
Printed and bound by CPI Group (UK) Ltd, Croydon, CR0 4YY

Papers used by Orbit are from well-managed forests
and other responsible sources.

MIX
Paper from
responsible sources
FSC® C104740

Orbit
An imprint of
Little, Brown Book Group
100 Victoria Embankment
London EC4Y 0DY

An Hachette UK Company
www.hachette.co.uk

www.orbitbooks.net

To Bess

Preface

I was fourteen years old when I first read Artemis McIvor's account of her life and times. It was a wild and rambling tale and it seized my imagination. These are quieter times, and we look back in awe at the great history of our civilisation, in all its absurdity, barbarity, and cruelty.

The book I read was somewhat erratically edited, and in publishing this new corporeal edition[1] we considered very carefully whether to delete some of the interpolations from this unnamed and now forgotten scribe before eventually deciding to retain them. However, readers should be aware that large sections of McIvor's manuscript were excised by this editor for reasons which in the eyes of posterity appear spurious; and all these deleted sections have now been lost. And, apparently, McIvor herself showed no interest in revising her manuscript, even when the charges against her were dropped.

So this is the story of Artemis. She was not a revolutionary, or an idealist; she was merely a survivor. But we salute her spirit.

Henry Exon, publisher-in-chief of
Heritage of Humanity Books

1 A beaconspace edition will also be available, but the editor's original hyperlinks are no longer valid.

Publisher's Note

The events described in this volume predate the planetary carnage wreaked by the entity known to history as the Hive-Mind. In consequence, several of the planets named by Dr McIvor no longer exist.

The following text is unamended from the original highly amended first edition, published by Way Out of Orbit Books.

Edited Highlights[1] from the Thought Diary and Beaconspace Blog of Dr[2] Artemis McIvor[3]

BOOK 1

REVENGE[4]

1 Very heavily edited in fact. My goodness! By the time I excised the worst of the scatology and the extremest of the rants, this shrank from nearly half a million words to just slightly more than one hundred thousand words. – *Ed.*

2 Artemis was indeed awarded a PhD in History and Politics from the University of Rebus at the age of fourteen. – *Ed.*

3 Professor John McIvor is a great hero of mine; please disregard the slighting references to him in this text. – *Ed.*

4 I have been asked by the author to issue the following warning:

"If you are reading an illegal download of *Edited Highlights from the Thought Diary and Beaconband Blog of Dr Artemis McIvor* please stop. OR ELSE."

Considering the contents of the story which follows I would, if I were you, heed this advice. – *Ed.*

Chapter 1

Prison Break

"Fuck you," I said, then walked into the kitchen. Picked up the mug of scalding hot water. And threw it over my own face.

It hurt. A lot.

I could feel my skin melting.

I began to scream.

Let me back up a little. Who was I saying "Fuck you" to? Why throw boiling water over my own face? And why was I screaming like a bratty little girl? (I can, I assure you, take a lot more pain than *that* without whining about it.)

To know all that, you'd have to know why I was in the high-security wing of the Giger Penitentiary on the arid wilderness that is Giger's Moon, in the midst of the greatest prison riot of all time.

It's a long story. I'll tell it when I'm ready. For the moment just stay with the basic facts. Boiling water, melting face, girly screaming from me. And then Teresa Shalco running after me, shouting "Bitch!" and "Whore!" and other such expletives, before punching me viciously and knocking me to the ground.

I wept and huddled, playing the helpless victim. And Shalco

screamed a great number of mostly unfounded insults at me, whilst savagely kicking my prone body. It took three DR dubbers to pull her off.

It was all going according to plan.

Giger's Moon – I'm digressing now, bear with me – is a boon to lovers, if you happen to live on the planet of Giger.

The Moon is a third of the size of the planet it orbits. And thus appears to Gigerians as a glorious silvery orb that fills half their night-time sky. Its surface is scarred with cliffs and craters that cast dark shadows which, to the imaginatively minded, resemble the faces of mythical beasts. There are ruined cities up there too, and eerie ziggurats made of solid metal which have no discernible function, like desk ornaments the size of skyscrapers. All products of the mysterious alien civilisation that once dwelled there.

And – I love this bit! – Giger's Moon is believed by most Gigerians to have an aphrodisiac effect that is in inverse proportion to its size.

In other words, when there's a full moon, the hearts of lovers will beat just a *little* faster.

When there's a half moon, lust starts to really stir.

And when the moon is a thin crescent – oh boy!!! – shameless and indiscriminate carnality ensues.

Which I guess is why they call it the Horny Moon.

No one knows how Giger's Moon became a barren wilderness. Or why its original three-legged five-headed inhabitants fled. Or where those strange denizens of Giger's Moon went *to.* Or indeed (okay, I admit I'm the only one who wonders this) whether they wore hats on any or all of their five heads.

Nowadays, the Brightside of Giger's Moon is a vast Industrial Zone. And the Darkside of Giger's Moon is where they house the Penitentiary. It is the second largest prison in the Solar Neighbourhood, after Pohl Pen. It houses recidivists and sociopaths and stone cold killers. As well as all those generals and soldiers and Corporation lawyers who were so astonishingly evil they couldn't get pardoned in the round of judicial amnesties that followed the Last Battle.

Security here is formidably tight. No one has ever escaped from the Giger's Moon Penitentiary.

Until now.

"Keep your head still," said the doppelgänger robot, and I kept my head still.

The DR sprayed my scalded face with healant, and it stung like fuck. I could feel the skin becoming stiff, and I knew that in about forty-eight hours my burned flesh would start to regenerate.

"My eyes!" I whined, "I'm fucking blind!" I wasn't, in fact, but the dubber operating the DR was too dumb to know that. His silver-skinned robot-puppet shone its torch in my eye and my pupils didn't dilate; and the idiot at the controls thought that proved something.

"Shackle her," said the DR, and the two other DR-dubbers put magnetised shackles on my arms, pinning them behind my back. Then they did the same with a bar-shackle around my ankles. Then they fastened an explosive collar around my neck and strapped me to a trolley. They were taking no chances.

Teresa Shalco, meanwhile, had fucked off. Even though she was the aggressor and I the victim, no one attempted to arrest *her.* Because she was the *capobastone*, and hence the Boss of this entire fucking prison, and was hence pretty much untouchable.

The lead DR wheeled me on my trolley down the Spoke. Past the R & R rooms. And past the F Spoke cells and through twelve sets of force fields, until we reached the Outer Hub where the prison hospital was located.

"What have we got here?" said Cassady briskly – that's Cassady Penfold, hospital trusty, five-foot nine, ruby-haired and, oh, my lover – as I was wheeled into the receiving area. I groaned and raised my head and looked straight at her. Cassady, bless her, didn't flinch at the sight of my melted face.

"Gang violence," said the DR. "Burns on face, torso injuries, big mouth."

"Can we use cosmetic rejuve to restore the skin texture?" said Cassady, in her usual gentle half-murmuring tones.

The DR was silent a moment, as the dubber at the other end of the virtual link considered this question. Although in truth there wasn't much to think about. Waste high-quality cosmetic rejuve on a *recidivist*? "No," said the DR.

Then the DR picked my stretcher up with one hand with effortless strength and dropped me on to a bed. I groaned, trying to sound as if I was in agony and filled with abject despair at having forever lost my lovely looks.

The agony part was real enough.

"Anyone else to come?" asked Cassady.

"Nope," said the DR, and then the light went out of its eyes and it was motionless.

Now there were only two of us with functioning minds in the reception area. Me and Cassady.

The hospital reception was a large oval room with a mirrored ceiling (don't ask me why, but it made looking upwards a dizzying experience) and a hexagonal purple and green virtual array hovering at its heart. It also had the standard SNG pale-pastel walls of the kind that always made me want to blaze away with a projectile gun full of primary-coloured paints. And there were of course, carefully embedded in the walls, micro-cameras that covered every single area in the room. But it was a fair bet no one in the surveillance centre was looking at us. Not *now.* Not with all the shit that was going down.

"The riot's started?" asked Cassady.

I consulted my retinal display. "You bet your arse," I confirmed.

There are, so I am assured, not that I give a damn about such things, many cool things about me.[1]

Such as for instance, my hair. Which is long and lustrous and, these days, vividly yellow-blond.

And the fact I have a scary stare that can terrify the toughest of tough guys, even though I am slight and girlish-looking.

And the many augments which my paranoid mother built into my DNA, which give me all kinds of amazing superpowers.

And my personality, which has been described by friends as "acerbic" and "sarcastic".[2]

And my philosophy of life, which many feel is "immoral" and "vile", but is based on a principle of savouring every moment to the full regardless of consequences.

But the coolest thing about me by far, in my view, is the fact that I am the daughter of an archivist.[3]

Yeah, I do mean it. That really *is* cool.

For you see my father, from an early age, taught me all about *databases*. Their architecture, their hidden byways, their lockouts and encryptions, their base codes, their security protocols. Almost all databases you see are built on the ruins of their

1 I met the author several times during the editing of this book, and I can confirm the accuracy of this self assessment. She is, indeed, exceedingly cool. And courteous too. I recall how she complimented me on the niceness of my cardigan, which was at that time almost brand new. I also admired her lustrous blond hair; but I did not, however, thankfully, witness the "scary stare". – *Ed.*

2 I can, I fear, also confirm this! – *Ed.*

3 Professor John McIvor, with whom I have a beaconspace friendship of long duration. – *Ed.*

predecessors. So most systems can be decrypted if you understand the *archaeology* of that database.

It helps, too, if you have a Rebus chip, as I do – it's a small addition to the standard brain chip implant, which allows me to directly access databases from any quantum computer brain in shortband range.[4]

This is why I spent a year on Giger. Staring up, every night, at the Moon. (Which is how, by the way, I learned at first hand, and – oh boy! – *often*, about the Horny Moon phenomenon.)

Dekon is the name of the QRC on Giger's Moon. It's linked of course to Ariel, which is the name of Giger's own planetary computer. (Or possibly Ariel is a clone of Dekon?)[5] I spent the aforementioned year finding a way to explore the dusty corridors of Dekon's mind. And when I succeeded, I set up a permanent data-pathway into my implant.

Now at any moment, night and day, I can conjure up a living map of the entire prison. I can see which Spokes are locked down, which force barriers are on Red Setting, and where the DRs are patrolling.

And this was what (lying on a trolley in the hospital reception area, flanked on all sides by pastel-coloured walls, face burned off, next to my red-haired lover Cassady) I could now see. A prison in crisis. Inmates rioting and attacking DRs and smashing "hidden" cameras ('cause everyone knows where those fuckers are). And then DRs being unleashed *en masse* from the Spoke Storage Bays to contain the riot. General chaos in the A, B, C, D, E and F Spokes, and the Outer Hub. In short, a prison riot.

This of course was why the doppelgänger robot in the hospital reception area had been switched off. The human operator was needed elsewhere.

4 All true. Rebus is aeons ahead of other planets when it comes to the accessing of data. – *Ed.*

5 The latter hypothesis is correct. – *Ed.*

Meanwhile, as I was witnessing the riot in my mind's eye, Cassady was unfastening my shackles and explosive collar with the electronic lock-decoder I had purchased some weeks before. And when I was finally free, she passed me a roll of toilet paper. I grimaced.

Time for the next stage in my plan.

I am not, repeat NOT, providing any visual or tactile details about what occurred during this next stage of this escape plan.

Suffice it to say: I took the toilet roll. And staggered to the john.

Once there, knowing I was unobserved, I wept hot tears on to my scarred cheeks at the thought of – things that had happened some years before. Bad experiences that were the motive for – but we'll get to that.

Then I stopped weeping. Got a grip on myself. Covered the toilet bowl in plastic film. Swallowed six laxatives. And awaited the results.

And a little while later I had a scrubbed-clean cylindrical package of mouldable organic explosive. Enough to blow up a skyscraper.

I should add that this wretched thing had been there, concealed in the deepest recesses of my colon, for nearly six months. That is what I call forward planning.

Let me go back in time a few months, and tell you how I first met Teresa Shalco. That *capobastone* bitch who beat me up, remember?

It was my first day in Giger. I'd been through all the scanners. They'd x-rayed and ultrasounded me; and had missed the bomb up my arse, and the bone-claws embedded in my hands. And they'd also DNA'd me to confirm I was who I said I was. Which in fact I wasn't. DNA archives are so fucking easy to hack! So, officially, I was Danielle Arditti. Psychopath. Serial killer. Assassin.

Then they dressed me in a purple overall and I stood in the Holo Hall and listened to Prison Governor Robbie Ferguson explaining the rules of the establishment. No drugs. No drink. No sexual molestation. No gang lingo. No murdering other inmates. No fomenting rebellion against the democratically elected government of the Solar Neighbourhood. Oh, and this was the absolute killer; moral rehabilitation classes were compulsory.

Fuck! I'd rather be beaten and hosed down with cold water.

After the bullshit briefing, I went to the inmates' bar and got slaughtered on cheap rum.[6] And, when in my cups and dribbly with rage, I vowed to kill the entire fucking Parliament of the SNG. Shalco heard me at the height of my rant and laughed. She told the barman to give me a free drink, grinned at me, and eyed me up.

"Danielle," I said, introducing myself ritually, despite my drunkenness: "*vangelista*[7] of our Beloved Family. I respect the authority of the Clan."

6 From this it may be deduced that the no drinking rule was not strictly enforced. – *Ed.*

7 In a long digression, which I have deleted, Artemis explains the origin of the Clan hierarchies, which date back to nineteenth century Naples. (Naples is a city on Earth.) In brief:

Capobastone is the boss of bosses, the equivalent of *capo di tutti capi* in the non-Neapolitan "Mafia" clan.

The *cardinale* is the religious adviser to the *capobastone*, and will generally possess psychic powers, or will at least claim so to possess.

The next in command are the five *quintini,* who report directly to the *capobastone.*

At the next level are the *vangeliste*, who are senior gangsters of extraordinary ruthlessness, who have to swear by their personal god (as allocated by the *cardinale*) to dedicate their life to crime.

Shalco held out her right hand. Her middle finger was a stump. I kissed the stump.[8]

"Do you fuck girls?" she asked me. I grinned, but shook my head. I didn't, then.

"Shame." She grinned back. She had an infectious grin. "How's the booze?"

"It's, um." I took another sip of the free booze she'd given me. It was whisky, not rum. Richer and more wonderful whisky than I'd ever drunk before.

"Four-hundred-year-old malt," Shalco informed me.

"They spoil you guys."

"I have some contacts."

The prison bar was in the gym. Some nutjobs were chinning up and lifting weights around us. And then Shalco introduced me to Bargan Oriel, who was playing solitaire at a table, while drinking a six-hundred-year-old bottle of port.

Oriel was Shalco's *quintino.* He was a thin man, with a vulture's beak nose, and a piercing stare. (He had two artificial eyes, I later learned.) He'd been *quintino* of the New Earth Clanning, which was comprised of seven planets in the Alpha 4 sector of the Solar Neighbourhood. His boss, Trajo Marol, had been a legendary monster, responsible for organising massacres on behalf of Gamers on an awe-inspiring scale. Marol was killed resisting arrest, despite having been slipped enough sedatives to put a buffalo to sleep. Now *that* was a story.

Below this is the rank of *santista.* These are often elderly Clannites, who have a largely supervisory role. It's possible to go from *cammorista* to *vangelista* in one step, if you earn enough money or kill enough people.

Then *cammorista.* The *cammoriste* will run all the street rackets and in the old days would deal directly with fabricator staff who were stealing from the Corporation.

And finally, *piccioto*, or more formally *piccioto d'onore*, the lowest rank. A *piccioto* is sometimes called a "button man", whether male or female. Their main job is to beat, bully, murder, intimidate, or make coffee. (Coffee is taken seriously in the Clan; it is rumoured Clannites have 400 different words for "coffee", the only one of which I know is "latte".) – *Ed.*

8 Elsewhere, in one of the other sections I have deleted, Artemis explains that kissing the finger stump is a sign of respect from a junior to a senior Clannite. – *Ed.*

Anyway! Oriel was a quiet man, who exuded an aura of control freak. He was however very charming to me, offered me some port, and told me a series of very funny stories about his life on New Earth III.

I disliked him immensely. He had a knack of pitching his voice so low you had to lean in close to hear him. He was impossible to interrupt, because he left such huge pauses you could never be sure he'd finished speaking.

And he was, like so many of these guys, enveloped in self-love. I mean! If he could have fucked his own arse, he would've done.

Shalco, by contrast, was exceptionally likeable. She was a big woman – tall *and* broad – with an appealing extrovert personality, who took her power for granted. I'd heard good things about her from the Clan scuttlebutt sites. She was considered to be fair, and generous, and at times merciful. Though she was, of course, a Boss, and it goes without saying that Bosses have to be tough.

And oh yes, she *was* tough.

The DRs broke up the party at nine pm and escorted us to our cells. I was in cell 2333x. The x meant it was on the twenty-fourth floor of the cell complex. The hardglass lifts carried us up twenty at a time. A DR ushered each of us into our cell, and closed the door behind. The doors were heavy and metal and slammed loudly when they were shut. That was for effect.

I was drunk and cheerful. It had been a sociable evening. In the course of it, I'd met a few old friends. Though they didn't recognise me of course, because I was taller and black-haired (not blonde) and somewhat bigger busted when they knew me. And my eyes then were brown, not blue. And my face, of course, was quite different. My body language was maybe similar, though I'd worked hard at that. And my voice – well. The timbre had changed. And I'd altered the rhythms of my speech, and of course my favoured catchphrases. No more "Yo' mollyfocker" as a term of endearment. I missed that. It was a phrase that had once defined me.

The cell was small. A bunk, a toilet, and three hangers for

clothes. I had three sets of purple overalls, in case I fancied a change. One pair of black shoes, no laces. There were still bracket marks and screw holes on the hardmetal floor, where the torture bench had been removed and replaced by an actual bed. The ceiling was slightly curved. It was like living inside a tin can. There were no books on the shelf, which by the way was a breach of my human rights.[9] And there was no mirror, which was also a breach of my human rights. The walls were not soundproofed, which meant I could hear the prisoners in the neighbouring cells wanking, or talking, or even fighting. This also was a breach of my human rights.

There is a four-hundred page SNG Act of Parliament[10] outlining in some considerable detail all the human rights which even the scummiest and most evil prisoners are deemed to possess. I found it hilarious. Human rights! What the fuck *are* those?

At three am the doors of all the cells were opened. And, or so I assumed, the corridor and cell cameras were all switched off. I stayed put. I heard the movement of prisoners outside. The chatter of conversation, the casually muttered asides, the occasional burst of subdued laughter. And after a while I heard, as I had been warned I would hear, the sounds of rape.

It went on all night long. The victims, I knew, would all be non-Clan. Hence, fair game. Some of them would be young – men and women in their early twenties. (Younger prisoners had their own juvenile wing.) And it was part of Clan culture that in prison the powerful should always abuse, sexually and in other ways, the less powerful. It was considered a form of redemption, believe it or not – a way for Clannites to reassert their lost authority. It was a credo that disgusted me, and which I had always failed to comprehend. But there was nothing I could do about it.

9 As decreed by the SNG Parliament, in its Human Rights Acts Section 445, paras a) to v). – *Ed.*
10 I've just told you about this. – *Ed.*

I'd covertly marked my door with a finger-scratched "V" as the DR had paused before ushering me in to the cell. V for "*vangelista*". It meant I was exempt from assault. My icon of protection.

So I stayed in my cell. I listened to the screams and groans which filled half that long night. I did not sleep. It brought back memories. But they were memories that I did not wish to endure, so I forced my mind to be blank.

I can do that, you see. I can make my mind entirely blank.

Remember this was not, none of it, my fault. Nor was it my responsibility.

So I blanked it out.

I slept for about two hours, which was all I needed. At five am the prisoners returned to their cells and the doors were closed. At seven am the doors opened again and we all filed out and queued for the elevators.

The view on the way down was disorientating. The cell blocks formed a vast tower at the centre of the prison, with the elevators on the outside. Beyond the circle I could see the Spokes which were the work and recreation areas. Beyond them, I could see the wilderness of Giger's Moon, grey and wasted behind the impermeable hardglass walls of the biodome.

I shared an elevator with nineteen other inmates, one of whom was a seven-foot giant. He stood very close to me, and leered down. "You missed a good night last night, *vangelista*," he said, grinning.

I ignored him.

"Maybe tonight?" he offered.

I ignored him. The lift stopped. The DR stepped out.

I elbow-struck the giant in his ribs, breaking several. "Speak," I said quietly, "when you are spoken to."

The other inmates shuffled around us to conceal the brawl from the DR's view.

The giant grinned at me. His teeth were large and ugly. "You aren't allowed to do that, *vangelista*," he said. He was in pain, obviously, but you'd never have known it from his tone of voice. "I have the protection of the Clan."

I stared at him, scarily.

After fifteen seconds, he flinched.

I walked away. That round went to me.

I went to breakfast. It was synthesised mulch. The dining area had clearly once been a recreational area for dubbers. Because in the old days, the prisoners here weren't given food, they were just injected with nutrients. I could see the outlines where a swimming pool had been filled in. White lines demarcated a former baseball pitch. They'd been a sporty lot, those old devils who once had run the Giger Dungeon.

Teresa Shalco joined me at my table.

"Just to outline the rules," she said cheerfully, as she sat down.

"Fuck you."

"Whatever your status elsewhere," she continued softly, "you have to earn it here. *Capisci?*"

She beamed nicely at me.

"*Non capisco.*"

Shalco continued to smile, but she didn't mean it.

"First and final warning," she whispered.

The following night the same thing happened. The footsteps, the doors opening, the howls of pain and regret.

At one point, I went out on to the landing and tried to differentiate between the howls of pain. To locate the worst and most terrible howl. When I had done so, which took a long while, I walked down the corridor and entered the offending cell.

"No more," I explained.

There were three of them engaged in the atrocity. They stared at me in astonishment. Appalled at my effrontery. Shocked at my stupidity.

Then they came at me.

I smashed heads. I broke bones.

Then I dragged the unconscious bodies out and dumped them in the corridor. And returned to the cell to see how the abused prisoner was bearing up after his ordeal.

He was bearing up, in my view, remarkably well. The prisoner was lean and young, and he grinned at me with open relief. "Thank you," the prisoner said. "That was well – fuck. Thank Christ it's over."

I shrugged.

"They'll make you pay for what you just did, you do know that?" the prisoner added, sorrowfully I felt. He was young, but he clearly knew the way of the world. Later, I learned his name: Tomas.[11] But I never actually got to know him.

"Whatever," I said.

I went back to my cell. I waited.

No one came for me. They were waiting for permission.

The following night, they had their permission.

I sat on my bunk in my cell and waited. I heard the footsteps outside the door. I heard the murmur of voices, cursingly vowing to "split my arse" and "rip my tongue out of my

11 Tomas Macinley, formerly a fighter pilot in the Corporation Navy, occupied a cell on Artemis's tier, and this was without a doubt he. Tomas was released after the riot, in which he played no role, and is now a school teacher on Gullyfoyle. – *Ed.*

mouth" and other such grisly pledges. And I heard the handle turn.

But it did not open. The door had been locked by Dekon, acting under my instructions. Thus over-riding the earlier "unlock" signal sent by the corrupt dubber who allowed this nightly anarchy.[12]

I can do that, you see. I'll explain how later.

Banging and shouting followed, and continued for some time. But the bastards couldn't get in. And eventually they lost interest. My lynch mob dispersed and they returned to their cells.

I hugged myself with delight – I love such moments of elegant victory – and then I slept.

Teresa Shalco joined me at breakfast.

"Who the fuck *are* you?" she marvelled.

I shrugged.

"You know that," I said calmly. "You've spoken to my people on Ariadne?"

Ariadne was the planet where the real Danielle Arditti had served the Clan.

"They say you're dead."

"I don't feel dead."

"They say you're a bitch."

"They got that right."

"You're in the Clan, okay?" Shalco told me patiently. "So you have to accept my authority. If you have a beef with your fellow prisoners, come to me. But don't take the law into your own hands. Nothing happens without my permission, that's the way of our Family, am I right, *vangelista*?"

12 Names and addresses of prison officers at such facilities remain confidential. – *Ed.*

"It's too loud. The stuff they get up to. I can't sleep."

She sighed, as a mother might sigh when her child has been a scamp. Shalco had a warm and comforting presence. It was tempting to yield to the allure of her maternal loveliness. But I reminded myself she was a Boss. Hence, evil and dangerous scum.

"There's only one way out of the dining hall," Shalco warned me. "You have to pass through a womb to get from here to the rec hall. And you *have* to go to the rec hall, because the DRs won't let you stay in here. Oh, and by the way, the cameras will be turned off."

"I guessed something like that might occur," I conceded.

"Your best bet is to stay here," Shalco said, kindly. "Let the DRs come for you. If you refuse to obey an order they'll detain you. You'll go into solitary. Best place for you."

"Why are you telling me this?"

"Hey, you're a nice kid," said Shalco. "I don't want to see you hurt."

I finished my coffee. It was, frankly, awful. "I'll be going," I said.

I got up. All eyes were on me.

I walked down the metal staircase and handed in my tray.

All eyes were on me.

I walked towards the exit door that was the only way out of the dining area.

All eyes were on me.

I entered the womb. A womb, by the way, is a rounded corridor of a kind you only ever see in prisons, with sealable hardglass gatewalls at each end. When the gatewall at one end closed, the gatewall at the other end would open. Like an airlock.

This womb was wide, as broad as many actual rooms. The sidewalls and ceiling were grey, unpainted – no pastels here. And at the far end of the womb, I could see a mill of prisoners peering through the hardglass to witness the violent altercation that was about to take place.

There were six of them in the womb with me. They weren't even attempting to conceal their evil intent. They just stood in the centre of this grey cage, ominously, waiting for me.

Seven Foot Giant was one of them. He carried a knife the size of a scimitar. I guessed it had been built in the workshop, out of stolen hardmetal.

His companion, who I mentally dubbed Big Ugly Motherfucker, was shorter, but just as broad, with a leering expression and bad skin.

And then there was Big Black Bald Guy, a black man with a shiny bald head and a body-built physique. He wore a vest so I could admire his bulging arms and his tattoos of women with breasts like moons.

And there were also two female Noirs who stood like shadows, dressed all in black to complement their jet black eyes, effortlessly graceful. They were clearly ninja-trained, and were eerily focused.

And finally Three Eyes, another giant, six-and-a-half foot high, with three eyes. That meant he was from Golgotha, there's a fad for it there.[13]

Three Eyes carried a baseball bat with spikes.

I glanced behind me. The rear gatewall was now sealed. No going back. Shalco had already warned me the cameras would be out of action. There was a window in the middle of the corridor, and through it I could see a DR store cupboard. But those DRs were all switched off. So, it was just me and them. One against six. I've had worse odds.

Though not often, and I didn't always win.

"Kiss my finger," I told the six mollyfockers, calmly and quite politely.

"I scorn your authority, bitch," said Seven Foot Giant, which was the gravest of insults for someone of my (alleged) Clan rank.

13 True. – *Ed.*

"Does your penis," I asked, still using my calm and polite voice, "look really odd? I mean, disproportionately small, compared to the rest of your lumbering frame?"

"I scorn your authority," he repeated.

"And how do you cope with doors? I mean, do you have to like *stoop?*"

"I scorn your authority, and call upon you to defend it," he said for the third time, clearly struggling to keep himself in check. But these proprieties have to be observed.

"I defend my authority," I said, and that was the cue for the fighting to begin.

Ten minutes later I walked out of the womb into Spoke A.

My shoulder was stiff, from throwing a really awkward punch. My ribs hurt. My hands hurt. And I had the mother of all headaches. But, of course, I acted as if nothing untoward had occurred. I walked into the Spoke A rec room and picked up a magazine and started to read it. It was a geek mag, full of racy images of ion drives and rocket engines, with a little section on how to solar surf, and a centrepage spread about building up abs without rejuve.[14]

Half an hour later a platoon of DRs arrived to arrest me for my breach of prison discipline. They stomped me through the Spokes, manacled and collared, their blank silver faces conveying all the contempt and rage that their human handlers could muster.

In the scuffle which had preceded this moment, I had managed to cripple and kill all six of Shalco's crew. Seven Foot Giant now had a broken skull and no eyes, and was

14 Despite extensive research, I have not been able to identify this magazine. There are, however, many like it in the marketplace. – *Ed.*

admitted to the prison hospital with no heartbeat either.[15] Oh, and his scimitar was broken. I had kept a shard of it as a memento. The other five were battered, broken, and also dead.[16]

None of them were true-dead, however – I was too skilful for that. And there was no camera footage of the fight of course. But dozens of prisoners had watched the combat through the hardglass doors, and clearly one or more of them had been coerced into stoolpigeoning.

And so now I was due to endure a month in solitary confinement, as my punishment for fighting other prisoners without sanction, and with excessive force.

I was looking forward to it.

You see, these days I get twitchy and restless when there are too many other people around me. I prefer wide open spaces; or failing that, small cramped spaces, and my own company. I'm sorry, that's just the way I am. These days.

Besides, I needed to recuperate. My hands were badly bruised, though the knuckles were unbroken. My skull however was fractured. And at some point during the fracas I'd been stabbed in the liver. But my healing factor had already kicked in. In a few weeks I would be, as my father used to say, much to my irritation, "as right as rain".

You know, that phrase used to drive me mad!

One time, when I was a kid I mean, I burst into tears in front of my father when he was putting me to bed. And my father had looked at me in horror. Until, much to his relief, he realised he had the solution to my problems. An aphorism! "Go to

15 Prison hospital records confirm that Marshall Jo Shane, an extremely tall felon who was a diagnosed psychopath, was admitted with these injuries on the day to which Artemis refers. – *Ed.*

16 Prison hospital records confirm this. The five other prisoners were: Lucius Mantian (black skinned, depilated scalp), Jana and Jora Priash (ninja-trained Noirs who were sisters), Andrew Jones (a large man of little aesthetic appeal, with a skin condition), and Jonjo Jesus, a three-eyed Golgothan. – *Ed.*

sleep," he had told me, with a big smile on his face, "and in the morning, you'll be as right as rain."

Hey! I don't know why I just told that story. Not very relevant, huh?[17] Move on, Artemis, tell the tale.

So, long story short: I was feeling pretty good about myself after the fight in the prison womb. My reflexes hadn't let me down. My fighting skills were still second to none. Only the thin red line on my throat betrayed how close I'd come to being decapitated and thus experiencing true-death in those first muddled lightning-swift moments of the *mêlée*.

Picture it:

There I am, licking my lips anxiously, fear in my eyes, as I walk towards Seven Foot Giant and his ugly pals. They read my seemingly fearful body language and they relax, just slightly. Enough to give me my edge.

Seven Foot Giant lunges first, trying to impale me with his sword. So I duck down low, come up with a punch to the ribs. His sword's backswing catches my throat a nick and I see a spurt of blood – yeah, that was the worst moment. But I give his body a tug and momentum propels him onward and the sword takes a slice from the skull of Big Black Bald Guy.

More blood spurts, but not mine this time. Seven Foot Giant is wheezing, the broken ribs have punctured his lung and I'm behind him and I leap up and catch his head in my hands and twist to one side. Broken vertebra, and I've managed to gouge his eyes out too. He falls like a building being demolished and I push off his body and fly up in the air and kick Three Eyes with both my heels on his chin. The impact rocks me, but it rocks him even worse. That's Big Black Bald Guy down, Seven Foot Giant down, and Three Eyes dazed and confused. Big Ugly Motherfucker, however, is biding his time. He will be trouble, I predict.

17 No, it's not. – *Ed.*

Then the Noirs come at me. They are elegant and achieve perfection in their every graceful movement. By contrast, I am a savage pit bull hound at bay. Elbows and heels and head butts, those are my weapons of choice. I keep it close, their finesse doesn't get a look in. I break their skulls because I know their sinuous bodies will constantly evade me. But grab a head with both hands and butt it and you can't miss.

The head butts hurt me like hell – that's when I broke my own skull – and it sure ain't *kata*. But the Noirs are down and weeping now.

Then Big Ugly Motherfucker makes his move, and he is fast, very fast indeed. His punch misses my head by a fraction, and I know that if his fist had connected my skull would have exploded. But it didn't, and it doesn't, for I am even quicker than he is. And I keep moving and snap back, and deliver a punch to his balls and an elbow strike to his head. This slows him down considerably. Then I punch him in the chest and his heart stops and he dies.

As he falls, his ugly face is consumed with disbelief. Here is a man, I guess, who has never lost a fight before.

Three Eyes is still in the fight though, as is Seven Foot Giant, despite his terrible injuries and his blindness. But that's to the good, 'cause he's just lumbering around now, getting in the way of the unconcussed fighters. I fall on the floor and weave like a snake and flip Three Eyes and Seven Foot Giant off their legs then savagely strike and kill them when they're down.

The Noirs are also back in the fight but slower now. And I get faster and my form becomes perfect. I am a *karate-ka* with open hands and a mind empty of confusion now. This bit would look beautiful if you could see fast enough to follow the different moves. Knife hand, claw thrust, side kick, roundhouse kick, kick-while-leaping, somersault, body twist, the whole repertoire. Savage strike to the face of the assailant in front, duck and weave and backheel to the rear to smash the head of the mollyfocker behind. Then repeat. And repeat, and repeat.

And then, like shadows struck by sunlight, the Noirs are no more.

Ten minutes five seconds, and the fight is over. At the end of the combat, I am still standing and they are all clinically dead, but kept brain-alive by the oxygen capsules in their brains. There are stars in front of my eyes, and my heart is pounding so fast I fear I will stroke out.

Then I press the button for the gatewall to open and I stroll, as I've already said, through.

My trial was brief. I wasn't allowed a lawyer. The holo of Prison Governor Ferguson appeared, heard the charges, and passed the sentence. One month's solitary to cool me down, plus twenty years additional moral rehabilitation therapy. (Yeah, that last bit really *did* scare me.)

As they dragged me to the Solo Cells, I howled in triumph: "VICTORY!" So the whole prison block would know what happened.

But then my troubles really began.

I had thought, you see, that it was all going to be plain sailing once I was in solitary. I would take my supposed punishment, actually a holiday for someone like me, then re-emerge refreshed and ready for Phase 2 of my plan.

I didn't think I would actually be *punished* by the prison authorities. It didn't, for pity's sake, even occur to me that such a thing might happen.

Because those days were gone! Or so I had been told. And so it was declared on all the news portals, and in the prison documentation. The days of beatings, sensory deprivation, brainthrashing, and cruelty beyond belief. The days of the Corporation regime, when Giger was a dungeon, not a prison.

THESE days every prison had a Specialist in Prisoner Welfare advising the staff on how to respect the human rights of the scumbag inmates. Even major infractions of the rules – drug-dealing, rape, murder – were liable to incur the mildest of sentences. A telling off. A brief period of solitary. A few more ghastly mornings sitting in a circle with fellow sinners repenting and vowing to be more empathetic from now on. But nothing that's actually going to hurt.

Thus, I had reasoned, all I had to do was tough it out for a few weeks. Sit in a cosy cell playing mental chess with myself. Then when I emerged I'd be Queen Bee of Giger. My rep would be secured. And I could do my deal with Shalco, prior to launching my escape bid.

That, as I say, was the plan.

They didn't bother with shackles. They didn't even slo-mo me. They just led me into the punishment block; and then they attacked me.

The blow was fast. I didn't even feel the air behind me stir and suddenly I was on the ground, bleeding from my ears. My skull was fractured in several more places. I could hear a roaring sound, like the wind whistling through my eye sockets. I got to my feet. The DRs took a step back. One of them had blood on its metal fist.

"Cruel and unusual punishment," I told them coldly, "is now barred under the laws of the SN Government. It is also an offence to—"

All three DRs moved, but this time I was ready for them. I threw one DR against a wall, struck the second in the neck, dislocating its power supply. And failed to see the sucker punch from the third.

I went down. A powerful hand picked me up.

"You can't do this," I explained.

And then a fist hit me in the face. And all the cheek and jaw bones whose graceful harmony of parts made me look like *me* were shattered and crushed by a single violent robot's punch. The DR smiled, an eerie silver smile, and opened its mouth. In the mouth were metal fangs. I groaned inwardly.

I tried to strike back, but the DR caught my hand and broke my fingers so I could not make a fist. And then it—

No more.

I took a beating, that's all that needs to be said. Every bone in my body was broken. Then acid was poured upon my body. Then the sprinkler came on and sprayed salt water on my flesh-less dying carcass.

But none of this really happened. It was all in my mind.

What *really* happened was that I was led, shackled and hobbled, into the punishment block; and at some point during my journey a sedative dart had been injected into my body, causing me to lose consciousness and wiping my short-term memory.

Then my body was taken to the lab and wired up to the brainthrasher. The reality simulation machine that is used to administer violent punishments to criminals and rebels alike.

They used to call it the "brainwiper", and it can indeed be used for that. To erase memories, to rebuild personalities by implanting false experiences. But more usually it's used to inflict pain. A myriad types of pain. Pain so intense that the hapless offender will (out of sheer despair and desperation) find remorse in his or her black soul, and henceforward turn over a new leaf. Only to find that the pain does not cease. Repentance is not an option.

It's torture without physical damage. There's no limit to the amount of agony you can inflict on a victim, because THEY CANNOT DIE.

Within thirty seconds of taking that first punch, I knew this was a simulation, and so I settled in to endure it.

But it took longer, much longer, than I expected or could endure.

Time manipulation, you see, is the cruellest of tricks. If you can alter a person's inner chronology, then a second can be made to last an eternity.

In reality, I spent only two days in the brainthrashing device. That's how long it took them to realise their error. And that's not long at all, not really.

Because, fortunately, help was on its way. For the moment I'd concluded the fight with Teresa Shalco's goons, I'd sent a signal via my Rebus chip to Dekon, alleging malpractice at the Giger Penitentiary. Alarm signals had been sent to the SN Government. And this meant the Recon Committee would soon be on the case, anxious as always to protect their precious 'human rights'. This was my failsafe strategy – for I've always been cautious to the point of paranoia when I know my arrest is imminent.

And thus, it only took two days for the Recon Committee to come to my rescue. Two days! Before a doppelgänger bureaucrat touched down and ordered my release.

But in my mind, those two days were two hundred long, terrible, agony-filled years.

I used all the survival tricks I had learned in my time with Baron Lowman to ameliorate my agony. I blanked out the world, and all my sensations. Dwelled upon my happy memories. Schemed terrible revenges. Conjured up music in my mind. Tried, quite simply, not to actually *mind* what was happening, as the hallucinations became increasingly more vivid and painful and gothically brutal.

Eventually, as I was being quartered – my legs and arms wrenched off my body by straps fastened to a wheel which was being turned by my OWN BLOODY FATHER – the pain suddenly stopped.

"You're free to go," said the DR and I realised I was sitting in a chair fastened to wires. The DR unhooked me. I tried to stand, and then I swooned.

Yeah I did. I actually passed out, aka fainted, aka "swooned".

Being flogged, hung, drawn, eviscerated, quartered, and feeling the heat from the flames which are roasting your flesh – it can really take it out of you.

I swaggered into the rec room in Spoke A. An old looking guy with a bald head and facial wrinkles eased up to me.

"Take a seat," he said.

"I'm fine," I told him.

"Take a seat."

He had his hand on my arm. He eased me over to a bench. I sat down. I felt my vision start to swim. I wanted to cry.

"Head up, look proud, don't let the bastards get to you," the old guy said.

"I'm fine."

"You're not fine. You look like shit. Don't let the Clannites see you like this. Take a minute. Take ten. Eat this."

He passed me a square of something brown. Chocolate. I ate it. It tasted of nothing. I remembered the taste of ash. I remember eating my own—

No! I forced myself back into present reality.

"Who are you?" I asked suspiciously.

I ate a bit more chocolate. This time it tasted more like chocolate. A lifetime of memories came flooding back. I'd eaten this stuff before. Hadn't I?

But . . . when? I couldn't remember.

"My name's Billy," said the old guy. "I'm a trusty. I've been where you've been."

"My name is—" I said, and realised that I had forgotten the details of my assumed identity.

"I know who you are."

That made one of us.

"Billy, will you—?" I said, and couldn't think of the next word.

He waited patiently.

I shook my head. I couldn't remember the words. Any words.

He offered me a glass of water. I sipped it. It refreshed me.

I felt a surge of delight. *That* was what I had meant to say. I had been thirsty, and wanted a drink.

I sipped again.

"Who are these people?"

Billy had led me through wombs and rooms that I didn't recognise, into a dining hall I had never seen before. A high vaulted chamber where silent men and women sat, staring into the far distance.

"Political prisoners, by and large," said Billy.

"There are no political prisoners," I said scornfully. "Not any more. They were released after—"

"Some of them wouldn't go." Billy nodded at a old grey-haired man with blind staring eyes. "Carter Broderick. Leader of the June Revolution."

I stared at the old blind man.

"Broderick is dead," I said, stunned.

"That's the story that went out on the news."

"*That's* him?"

I stared at Broderick. He stared back at me. A stare that haunted me for years after.

"Two hundred and fifty years in the brainthrasher," said Billy. "There's not much of him left. But that's him."

"Is he bitter?"

"Beyond bitter."

"Mad?"

"Beyond mad."

"He's a hero," I said. "A genuine hero. Some say greater than Flanagan."

"Flanagan was a chancer. Carter Broderick was an idealist."

"You followed him?"

The bald guy laughed.

"Nah. I fought him. I was a Space Marine. I served the Corporation loyally."

"So what are you doing here?"

Billy spat. An affectation of his. "I served the Corporation loyally," he said bitterly. "A lot of us ended up here, after the Last Battle."

"There were amnesties, weren't there?"

"Not for the ones like me. Not for what *we* did."

I looked at Billy again. He was old and had skin that was weathered and worn, but he carried himself with the special grace of the true warrior.

"Were you a Soldier, with a capital S?"

He glared at me.

"Nah. Wash your fucking mouth out. I was a volunteer. Not a zombie. I made my choice, and stuck with it. We all did. Back in those days."

"Why are you helping me, Billy?"

"It's what I do," said Billy, grinning shyly. "I help people, if I think they can help *me* in some way."

"In what way?"

"I want to escape."

"Escape is impossible," I explained.

He grinned at that.

"You don't need to be so fucking coy," he said, "There's no surveillance in this room. It's considered to be a breach of their human rights. These aren't prisoners, you see. They're just – well, they just won't leave. So you can speak frankly. Will you take me with you?"

"What makes you think I'm planning to escape?"

"I know. I know your sort. And I know what you did to those guys. You're on your way out of here, and I can help."

"I don't need help."

"Of course you need help." Billy smiled. He was holding something back.

"Give," I said.

He gave: "They're planning to kill you tonight," he said. "Shalco and her people. In your cell. They've bribed a dubber. A DR will come into your cell at midnight and force your tongue down your throat. They'll call it suicide."

"How do you know?"

"I'm the lookout."

This was Billy's story.

He really *was* an old-timer. He'd been a green recruit during the Loper Insurgency, and a veteran with fifty years experience when Earth was invaded by Peter Smith. He'd fought, of course, on the losing side, but quickly switched allegiance.

Billy was a hundred and twenty-five years old when America rebelled. He was at the Siege of Beijing. By the time he was two hundred, he'd quelled forty-five uprisings and was awarded a Purple Heart after losing his legs and eyes in the Belt War.

Billy was the laconic sort. "What was it like?" I asked him one time. "Serving the Galactic Corporation?"

"I didn't," he said. "I worked for the army."

"You served in the Marine Corps. The Marines were fully owned by the Galactic Corporation."

He shrugged at that. "I worked for the army. I did what they asked me to do."

"You never had, like, moral qualms?"

"Nope."

"Never?"

"Never."

"How many people did you kill, Billy?"

"We don't keep score. It's not a game."

"Ball park."

He thought about it. "Couple of million," he hazarded.

"Couple of million?"

"Not counting entire planets. Just enemy combatants killed in action."

"*Millions*."

"You asked for ball park."

"I did," I conceded.

Billy had been a doppelgänger rider and pilot. One of the best.

This was after he'd lost his legs and his eyes of course. His army insurance covered the cost of limb and organ rejuve. But that meant ten years with stumps, walking in an exoskeleton, viewing the world through artificial eyes, before the legs and eyes grew back. But he was still fit for virtual duties.

The truth, you see, and ignore whatever you've heard elsewhere, is that doppelgänger robots really AREN'T that scary. They're strong, for sure, and vicious, without a doubt. But also slow. Operated by amateurs and volunteers with no real idea how to fight. *Most* of the time.

But for the serious action engagements, in the days before Soldiers were bred, the doppelgänger department used crippled and aged Marines to ride their robot bodies and spaceships. That's how they enforced order on the ten thousand and more colony planets in which the Corporation held the majority shareholding.

"What was it like?" I asked.

Billy smiled. Memories of his doppelgänger days always lit a spark in his soul.

"It's like," he said, "being God."

"In what way?"

"In every way."

"Where did you serve?"

"Cambria. Gullyfoyle. Pohl. New Earth. Weisman. Juno. Too many to name. All the trouble spots. We allowed an asteroid to hit Pixar, so we could re-terraform it and turn it into a theme planet. And Cambria had a big rebellion. The colonists lived underground, they came swarming out to attack the doppelgängers in their castles. I led the commando squad there. I could operate fifty, sixty robot bodies at once. I was stronger and faster than any human, because of my robot body. And smarter than any human, because I was a *Marine*. And I couldn't die. I fought wars, and I won 'em, sometimes single-handed. It's Marines like me that held the Galactic Corporation together."

Yeah, I have to concede, he wasn't *always* laconic.

"Cambria is where they raped the colonists," I said. "The DRs. Ritual rape, once a year. I read about it. There's a whole body of work about it."

Billy shrugged, and spat on the floor. Spitting, I realised, was his way of saying, hey, the fuck, did *I* make the universe?

"That happened lots of places," he said, "not my fault, not my responsibility. That was the Gamers. People paid the Corporation for a chance to do that shit. We stood guard, we didn't pay no one, we *were paid*. There's a difference, okay?" He stared at me belligerently. "I never raped no-one, not as myself, not in any robot body. I draw the line at that. I fought, I killed; that's all."

"But you quelled the rebellion. You made it possible for—"

"Don't get philosophical on me."

That was Billy's response to everything. He didn't like to think too deeply about things.

I liked Billy.

But the truth is, he was a monster. A mass murderer. A warrior who had helped sustain the most evil regime in the history of mankind.

That's why he was in Giger. He was past redemption. But he had a simple code: do what you do 'cause it's what you do, and do it well. That's all that mattered to him.

Billy wasn't, in my view, a bad man. He wasn't, in any sense, evil. He just lived by his code. Never looked outside it.

I know a lot of people who are like that.

Me, for instance.

That night the DR came to kill me.

I didn't sleep at all of course. I just lay down in my bunk, allowing my muscles to relax, gathering my strength for the fight to come.

I had locked the door. But I knew that wouldn't make a difference. You can't keep DRs out of a prison cell; they have a shortband lock-override facility. Even I couldn't lock the door against them.

I had also turned the light off It was pitch-black, and I had my eyes closed. So that I could focus on sounds more intently.

There were no screams of pain that night. No one left their cell. Everyone knew what was going to happen.

So I waited and listened, in the pitchest of darks.

Then the cell door opened, soundlessly. Except no movement is truly soundless.

The DR entered, pacing forward slowly on its metal feet.

Again barely any sound was made. But my heightened hearing could hear the CRASH CRASH CRASH of footsteps.

Then the DR lunged and stabbed at my bunk but I was no longer there. I was clinging to the ceiling by my hands and bare feet, using my fingerspikes and heel spikes to grip the hard-plastic.

I had my eyes wide open now, and with my night vision I could see the robot's spectral silhouette. A body shaped like a human being but seven foot tall and with two extra arms fitted to cattle-prod inmates.

The DR looked up and saw me roosting like a bat, and abandoning all pretence at stealth it fired two plasma bolts up at me.

But I was in mid-air. Leaping, arcing, turning. Then I swept down with my two fingerspikes extended and slit open the machine's metal head. Then landed on its back and burrowed a finger into its electronic brain.

My two middle fingers, I should explain, are built up of erectile bone. They are undetectable to scanners. But when extended, they form a cutting tool of remarkable sharpness. DRs are designed to withstand bullets and missile blasts of less than six krismas. But if you have a tool sharp enough, you can open 'em up like a tin can. So I gouged and dug, and eventually plunged my right fingerspike into the main control chip and scattered the circuits with surgical precision.

The killer robot was turned into useless scrap in moments.

Then I got back into bed and waited for the next one. It never came.

In the morning the DR carcass was silently removed.

And I was called to see the Deputy Governor, Sheila Hamilton. Escorted by DRs. Led to the Holo Hall, where the DG's image glared at me with contempt.

I raised the middle finger of my right hand to her. Without the fingerspike extended.

"I wanna make a complaint," I said truculently.

"You destroyed a robot officer!" she said accusingly.

"It was trying to kill me," I countered.

"That's impossible!"

"Then what," I asked gently, "was it doing in my fucking cell?"

She had no answer to that.

Two days later the Recon Committee representative returned and interviewed me. I told him that the DR had attempted to kill me in the night, and that I'd acted entirely in self defence. I also explained that all the prison officers were being bribed by the Clannites who ran the prison. Giger was utterly corrupt, I told him.

My story was believed. The prison was fined for failure to exercise its duty of care towards an inmate.[18] I was even granted privilege points. redeemable at any point between now and the expiry of my sentence. These entitled me to extra hours in the gym, and additional time with my moral therapist.[19]

Yeah, my heart skipped a beat at THAT bit of news.

That's the story of how I killed a DR, single-handedly, and with no weapons aside from my claws. And it's all true, just the way I told it.[20]

But did I mention how afraid I was that night? How terribly and soul-quakingly afraid?

Yeah, okay, I was warned in advance that the DR would come for me. And yeah, I was ready for it.

But even so, I was terrified.

18 Prison financial records confirm this. – *Ed.*

19 There's no documentary evidence for this, but it is doubtless true. – *Ed.*

20 I have not detected a single significant factual error in Dr McIvor's account, much as I have striven to do so. Her opinions, however, are often extremely tendentious. – *Ed.*

I wasn't afraid of *dying*, get that, okay? Death holds no terrors for me. That's the way of my kind. People like me, the gangsters, the criminals, the killers for hire, we hold to the Viking way. We don't believe in death and glory, like the Soldiers, we just don't cling to life. That's what makes us so very good at killing others.

No. I was afraid of failing *in my mission*.

'Cause I knew I would only have once brief moment in which I could disable the robot's brain. And I knew that if I fucked it up, I would be killed outright. True-dead killed. And in consequence, my revenge would be aborted. My reason for living, my reason for *being*, would be gone.

That was my fear. The fear that when my moment came, I would be proven unworthy of it.

And this isn't, I hasten to add, me bragging in reverse. I'm not one of those warriors who coyly admits she *sometimes* feel fear, knowing damn well that most ordinary citizens are shit-scared *all* the time. I hate that kind of mindfuck – the false modesty *shtick*.

No, what I'm saying is that I feared I would fail and hence prove unworthy – because it's happened to me before. Not often – only once in fact – but it's happened.

And I can still remember, with a terrible vividness, the occasion when that occurred. When my life was destroyed because of my astonishing, pathetic failure to act. I could have fought! Or tried to escape. *But I failed to do so*. Inertia had possessed me.

And I know that such a moment of weakness could occur again. Easily. And that awareness haunts me like – well, like nothing at all I can think of. It just haunts me, and renders me permanently afraid.

Anyway! I just thought I should mention that. So you know the truth about me. My inner fears. My weaknesses. All my frailties. I owe you that, okay?

But even so – despite my soul-quaking fear – I fought and

killed the evil, gigantic doppelgänger robot with nothing but my bare hands and claws.

How fucking cool was *that*?

"Teresa," I said.

Shalco stopped, and stared at me.

We were in the prison yard. Every prison has a yard, but this one was bleaker than most. A narrow walkway on the outer edge of the spoke. There was rough gravel underfoot. The space wasn't wide enough to play a game of football, even if the dubbers had had the wit, or the generosity, to give us a ball. And outside – nothing but bleak airless wilderness. The craters and mountains and empty dust-strewn landscape of Giger's Moon.

And that's where I called out Teresa Shalco, *capobastone* of Giger Pen.

"You look like shit," she said. She was smiling again, looking like everyone's favourite momma.

I knew her history. She'd run the Russian gangs on the planet of Gorbachev. Everyone who knew her spoke highly of her fairness. She was cruel, yes, a killer, yes. But fair. You couldn't ask for a better Boss. She'd been ideally suited for the role of liaising with the doppelgänger ruling élite on her home planet. Because everyone trusted her, and yet she could kill without conscience.

And in fairness, she'd done a good job, back there on Gorbachev. Okay, many died because of her, but they would have died anyway. At least she organised her people into some kind of civilisation. She was a collaborator, for sure, but back in those days, the ones who didn't collaborate were either dead or trapped in Giger and places like it with their brains burned out.

All that was the ancient history about Shalco. Right at that moment, however – prison yard, airless wilderness stretching out eerily beyond, me staring nastily – the issue was that Shalco was the top bitch here. And it was my job to goad her into losing control.

"You ran to Mummy, did you?" I sneered. It was the gravest of allegations. That she had informed on me to the prison authorities.

"Never," she said coldly.

"You told them I killed that robot."

"It was obvious," she said politely, "that you killed the goddamned robot. It was in your fucking cell!"

"Kiss my finger," I said and held out my middle finger. She stood still, stared at me. This was sacrilege; for me to do this to *her.*

I laughed. Turned my back on her. And walked away.

I could feel her hatred burning after me. But she daren't attack me. Not here. Not in front of the DRs. So she had to let my insubordination ride.

Shalco was of course diminished by my actions. She had lost status in the eyes of all who saw us together. Which was only two or three people, but they all had big mouths. And so, sooner or later, to redeem her honour, she had to fight me *mano a mano.*

Either that, or acknowledge that I was the new leader of Giger Penitentiary.

Prisons are like cities. The rules are the same. The hierarchies are the same. It's just the quality of the booze that's different.

And I know what I'm talking about here, right? Cities and prisons, I know 'em both.

(I'm digressing here, by the way. Stick with me, I like to

snake my way around to the point. In fact, I remember one time.)[21]

Anyway, back to the actual digression.[22]

I killed three *piccioti* in the ensuing brawl. That made *me* a *picciotto*. And a legend. I was seventeen years old, in biological terms, by that point. No longer a child. But still – yes, still – a virgin.

So I knew about prisons. And I knew how to work the system in Giger. Swagger, brag, taunt, and build a myth. That way, I would be top bitch in no time.

What's more, Shalco's people on the outside had access to my criminal record, which was dark and devious. I was, supposedly, a psychopath, and a multiple murderer.

In reality, I *was* a multiple murderer, and quite probably a psychopath to boot.[23] But my fake criminal record had different victims listed, and different motives. And I have to say, this girl I was pretending to be – Danielle Arditti – was a total fucking monster. In the old days she'd have been executed, or

21 This is a digression within a digression – *de trop!* – so I've edited it out. – *Ed.*
22 I've edited this out too. It's quite an enjoyable but rather bloodthirsty and graphic account of Artemis's arrival on Gullyfoyle, as a naive sixteen-year-old girl (not counting the two years in hiber). The gist of her tale, which I've excised, is that she'd gone into a bar, bright eyed and bushy tailed, and had become extremely drunk. Then she fell in with some bad company and got even drunker. And then a very bad man had taken her back to his room where he attempted – with the assistance of several large companions – to rape her. This was a mistake because Artemis, possessed as she was of exceptional augments and remarkable martial prowess, killed them all with her bare hands. The would-be rapists were however Clan-connected, so Artemis was subsequently arrested and convicted of murder and spent a year (the maximum term for murder in those days) in a Gullyfoyle jail, where she learned about prison hierarchies and how to play the system, which is the point of this anecdote. To clarify the chronology for the benefit of inattentive readers: on her release from prison at the age of seventeen, she became a barmaid, and that part of her story will be recounted later. Since none of this is directly relevant to the main narrative I have junked it all and picked up the story at the point where Artemis survives an attack by some thugs in prison, namely on the line: "I killed three *piccioti* in the ensuing brawl." If you don't read footnotes but had merely continued reading the text, you might have found that segue somewhat confusing; but that does rather serve you right! – *Ed.*
23 Not so. Artemis feels remorse for some (though not all) of her many killings, which psychopaths would never do. – *Ed.*

promoted to Admiral in the Cheo's Navy. These days, lifetime incarceration is the preferred way of dealing with nutjobs like her. Or rather (since she was dead) me.

Two days had passed since I'd offered my finger to Teresa Shalco. I lived those days with my senses at their highest pitch. Expecting a knife in the back. Or poison in my food. Or – well, the possibilities were endless, and I was alert to them all. But I'm a hard girl to ambush. And my taste buds are pretty acute – another genetic modification – so I can detect most poisons in my mouth before I actually swallow them.

But my point here is – you don't know what it's like to live like that! In a state of constant fear. Worried that everyone who passes by may be plotting murder. Afraid to take a shower in case it will be the setting for a brutal execution. I took to carrying a sharpened chess piece as a weapon. I knew that everyone in the prison was my enemy and I lived every moment in terror.

No, you don't know what that's like.

It's *great*. It's the adrenalin rush to beat all adrenalin rushes. I have no fear of death, you see. And that liberates me. It allows me to be truly alive.

Bargan Oriel came to see me, and offered a deal.

"Back down," he suggested. "Go on one knee, kiss Teresa's finger stump, beg for her forgiveness. And then it'll be fine. She'll forgive you."

"And in return?"

"There is no 'in return'," Oriel said coldly.

"I capitulate, she grinds my face in the dust. *That's* your deal?"

"Pretty much," Oriel admitted. "Take it or leave it."

"I leave it."

"You're a foolish girl, Danielle," Oriel told me.

I seethed at that – I hate being 'girled' – and resisted an urge to beat his face to a pulp.

"How *exactly* am I a foolish girl?" I asked Oriel, with a girlish flick of my hair, and a girl-like twinkle in my girl-sized eyes.

"You could be a *vangelista* in Giger," he told me, in the same patronising tone. "I have the power to acknowledge your status. But you have to stop rocking the boat."

"And if I don't?"

Oriel sighed. His face assumed an expression of patient forbearance. "Then bad things will happen to you," he said.

"Bad things have already happened to me," I said lightly. "I'm used to it."

Oriel eyed me up. It was a possessive glance. This was clearly a man who had owned a lot of slaves and fucked a lot of whores in the course of his long and badly lived life.

"The entire prison population," he pointed out, "answers to the *capobastone*."

"How would *you* like to be *capo*?" I asked him, and for a moment Oriel's eyes lit up. I could see his excitement, his almost sexual longing for power.

Then he came to his senses.

"Is this your plan?" he asked, with open scorn, though, at the same time, barely able to conceal his greed. "You're trying to launch a coup? You want *me* to be the next boss?"

"Maybe," I said, just to taunt him.

Sweet Shiva! It was like offering raw bleeding meat to a jackal.

The hooded expression returned to his face, eventually. "I am loyal to Teresa," he said, in brittle tones. "Totally loyal."

He was scared of me now. He'd guessed that I was playing a dark game. Either on my own behalf. Or, more likely, for Teresa Shalco, acting as an *agent provocateur* to lure him into being disloyal. I could be *her* way of testing *him* – by setting *me* up to provoke *her*, and then suborn *him* into treachery.

This entire complex chess game unfolded in his mind in an

instant, and now he had me marked as a real threat to his life and power.

None of it was *true* of course. But that's the great thing with paranoid people. You just have to give them a hint, and they create their own mad conspiracy thriller in their heads.

"Tell Teresa I want to see her," I said, and Oriel flinched. Only the five *quintini* were allowed to call Shalco by her first name.

"She won't see you," he said.

"Then send her a message."

"What's the message?"

"'I challenge thee.'"

Oriel went pale.

I looked at his eyes. I could almost hear the thoughts whirring. Should he pass the message on or not? If he didn't, he might be failing some kind of test. If he did—

"I'll tell her that," said Oriel calmly, and I knew he was planning how he would seize power if and when I defeated Teresa Shalco.

We met in the rec room of A Spoke.

This was one of the few public areas in the prison which hadn't been attacked by the SNG interior designers. Instead of wishy-washy pastel coloured walls, there were jet black walls with, if you looked closely enough, dried blood stains. There was a stench of defeat and decay here. And it was the biggest rec room in the prison, more an amphitheatre really, with tiered seating. I didn't know what the former prisoners of Giger had done in this place, but it was a fair bet that death was involved. Maybe gladiatorial games? Or eviscerations and executions?

We had a full house. Every seat was occupied, and Shalco's goons were acting as stewards. I was wearing a T-shirt and joggers. Shalco wore an old vest, with a slogan on it (DEATH TO MUTANTS, which I assumed was the name of a band or a TV show, though I didn't know for sure).[24] Her arms were bare and muscular. Her brown hair was tied back in a ponytail. She was a big woman, but I could see now how little of it was fat.

Shalco had the right to choose the manner of combat, and had elected to wrestle me. I would have a preferred a sword fight – for with a blade in my hand, I'd have defeated her easily. Boxing would also have favoured me, because of my speed and grace and skill. But wrestling was Shalco's game. She'd been a pro fighter before she became a gang boss, and had won her partial freedom after sixty successful bouts to the death. And she still kept in shape.

She was about six feet four inches tall and I was five-five. She was built like a barn, and I was slight and slender. It was, on the face of it, a complete mismatch.

Oriel clapped his hands once and we circled each other.

I kept my hands high, boxing style. Shalco let her hands drop to her side, swaying as she first moved towards me, then stepped away. Her strategy was clearly to get me in a death grip. If she did, I doubted I could break it. I knew she was also augmented, and I'd heard she could bench press an army jeep.

I moved in fast with a flurry of punches and Shalco tried to catch me in a bear hug but I fell on the floor, slipped under her open legs, stood up, and toppled her.

She did a back somersault and landed on her feet and turned to face me. Fast and graceful, as well as powerful.

I threw a roundhouse kick at her head and it connected. But she caught my leg as I drew it back and now she had me. She

24 It's a band, famous briefly on Shalco's home planet of Gorbachev, of very little musical merit, but Shalco had a sentimental attachment to them because she had copulated with both the guitarists whilst she was a young and impressionable "rock chick". Prisoners at Giger Penitentiary were not of course allowed to wear their own clothes, so Shalco's adoption of the T-shirt was an infraction of the prison rules. *Mano a mano* fights to the death were also banned, under Prison Regulation 4 a (iii). – *Ed.*

twisted the leg and yanked and tried to pop it out of the hip socket. But my body bent like softplastic and I spun around and landed a two-fist strike to her face, breaking her nose.

She lashed out with an elbow strike to my face and the pain hit me. Then she threw me across the arena towards the ring pillar. I spun in the air and avoided a face-first collision with the metal post.

I got back on my feet and somehow Shalco had me in a neck hold. She really was fast. I forward rolled, as she broke my larynx, and then I turned and punched her between her breasts to stop her heart.

It didn't work. She grabbed me by the throat and began strangling me. I activated the oxygen capsule in my brain and pounded her arms which were like granite. She jackknifed me over and pinned my shoulders to the floor. Oriel began the count.

I jolted my body and threw Shalco off me. She flew about five feet in the air and I could see the look of total astonishment on her face. She'd had no idea I was so damned *strong.*

She recovered fast and turned the fall into a parachutist's controlled landing. But I leaped and grabbed her arm and spun her round and threw her to the ground and pinned her. Oriel counted it. Eight, nine, ten. First pinfall to me.

Shalco got to her feet, snarling. She'd never lost a wrestling bout, and she didn't like the way things were going. And so she lost her temper and came at me hard, with forearm strikes and vicious leg swipes.

I avoided them all, dancing around her, not hitting her but making her feel slow and old. Then I grabbed her in a hammerlock and twisted until I could hear her shoulder pop.

"Submit," I whispered.

She didn't. I knew she never would. I let her go and as she experienced a moment of joyous release I leaped across her body and spun her over then pinned her in a *la magistral.*[25]

25 For explanations of these wrestling terms with animated images, click here. – *Ed.*

Second pinfall to me.

Shalco got up, then simply leaped up in the air and landed on me. It felt as if a truck had descended from the clouds and crashed upon me when I had been out for a stroll anticipating mild rain. I'd no idea a human being could leap so fast, or fall so hard. Then she pushed up with her hands and flew upwards with arms outstretched and fell with what seemed like preternatural speed and landed upon me a second time.

This time, it felt like the truck's lardarse older brother had landed on me.

She raised herself up a second time and this time tried for a cradle pinfall, but I kicked free and rolled away. But she got me in a killer neck grip and whispered to me: "Let's deal."

I turned my head and looked into her eyes, which wasn't easy considering the agonising position I was in, and I nodded. But I couldn't speak, because she'd shattered my larynx, so I authorised a shortband MI transfer and spoke into her mind.

"*What can you offer?*" I said.

"*Anything. What do you want?*"

I told her.

Then I threw her off me and we battered shit out of each other for another hour and a half before I allowed her to pin me three times in a row.

What the hell – there was a crowd, they deserved a decent show.

That night in my cell I sat immersed in agony. It would take weeks for my throat to heal. Weeks too for my bruised limbs to stop hurting. I feared there was internal bleeding too. And my head hurt. One of those really painful headaches, you know? The kind you get when someone very strong punches you in the face a great many many times in a very short period. *That* kind of headache.

But I was happy. Because the entire landing of the cell block was silent. The doors had not opened. There were no footsteps outside. There were no groans and screams and howls of pain. There were no atrocities at all that night, nor would there ever be again. That was my deal with Shalco: she stopped the rapes.

There were twenty-five other landings in Giger of course. And what happened on those other landings would continue to happen. That wasn't part of the deal – I knew I dare not ask for *that* much. So it was a partial victory. Bad stuff was still happening in Giger – but at least it wasn't happening near *me.*

All this, I should point out, had nothing whatever to do with my real reason for being in Giger Penitentiary. It wasn't part of my plan. This was just, well, something I felt I had to do.

The plan itself was far simpler.

I needed Teresa Shalco and her fellow Clannites to help me escape. They had the power. They had the prison officers in their pockets. And they had access to illicit contraband of all kind – including weapons and bombs. The only reason they didn't try to escape themselves is that, well, frankly, life for the Clannites at Giger was cushy. They had all the luxuries they could desire.

And they also had all the freedom they needed, or were used to. Because, of course, all the Clannites had been raised on slave planets. Captivity, for them, was just the way life was.

So they weren't *desperate*, as I was. Which is why I needed to incentivise them. By telling them about the horror that was soon going to be inflicted upon them.

And so that was my next task. To tell Shalco and her Clan leaders about the coming of the Exodus Universe.

I had a great job in the Giger Penitentiary. I worked in the prison library. What a joy *that* was!

Hey guys, bear with me here! This does connect up with the story, eventually.[26]

I loved the work, because I adore books. More than anything. And I mean, literally, anything. Does that sound strange to you? A killer and a psychopath who likes to *read*?[27]

I had paid heavily to get assigned this plum job. And during my time in Giger, I'm proud to say that I made some major improvements to their prison library system, mainly by re-cataloguing the entire collection on saner grounds. In other words, by genre and category rather than by a) date of publication or b) how much the librarian liked the book.

The library itself was a wood-lined room with hundreds of desks each with its own virtual screen and limited access to the remote computer's archive of books. If you had a personal reader, you could down the book and read it in your cell. But most users of the library sat at the desk and watched the book unfold in front of them in mid-air.

But when I say, "most users", that didn't exactly amount to a whole lot of people. The library was not a popular destination. Reading, after all, was considered in these space-faring times as being, well, archaic, and odd. Whereas on Rebus, books were a way of life.

And the prison library's book collection was, in truth, pretty pathetic. No science fiction. No heroic fantasy. No finely crafted contemporary novels about cultural mores and the state of

26 It does, which is why I've allowed this digression. – *Ed.*

27 Not really Artemis. In fact, it makes me think that – sorry, I"m talking aloud here. I do that, sometimes, when I'm reading. I answer the author's rhetorical questions, I shout out advice to the protagonist, and I— Sorry again! This is not meant to be about *me*! – *Ed*

society (thank the gods for small mercies!). No satire. No poetry. It was almost all emotionally gentle and well-intentioned pap. Fictional tales of nice people learning to be nicer.

In other words, crap.

But I, of course, could burrow deeper, with the power of my Rebus-chipped thoughts. So I "stole" several thousand volumes from the libraries on Giger and elsewhere, stored in the computer's deep memory, to supplement my already vast implant library. Classics of literature from the nineteenth and twentieth and twenty-first and twenty-second and twenty-third and twenty-fourth centuries, as well of course as the great works from more recent centuries. Some were books I had read in the course of my boring childhood on Rebus. Most were books I always felt I should read. So I sat in the library and read them in mid-air, or downed them on to my personal mindslate to read at leisure in my cell or in the rec rooms. (This is how I developed a reputation for being a mad staring person.)

I also – this gets us back into the story – used my Rebus chip to down the Solar Neighbourhood Government ultra-confidential report[28] into the prison population problem. It was a bona fide report, I didn't have to fake anything. All I changed were few words – "possible" became "definite", "eventual" became "imminent".

Then I gave the download to Teresa Shalco and Bargan Oriel.

And I let them simmer.

They were appalled at what they read. And they swiftly realised it would mean the end of their whole way of life.

28 I've read this report. It makes for chilling reading, and of course, prepared the ground for the subsequent Exodus Laws. Although, on the other hand, what *else* are and were we supposed to do with these truly evil people? – *Ed.*

For crime was about to be banned, totally and for ever.

This was a wild and crazy time, remember. The cork had been let out of the bottle and the genie was – whatever the fuck, let that metaphor die – it was a time of anarchy and gang violence.

It was forty years now since the death of the Cheo. That had brought to an end the longest Dark Ages in human history, according to some historians.[29]

Other historians,[30] however, continued to argue these had been the Good Old Days. They argued that, because of the Corporation's libertarian polices, great works of art and wonderful acts of planetary engineering had been created. New planets had been colonised and terraformed. Rejuve had been perfected. Fabricator plants had been improved to such a degree that quality furnishings and beautiful designer clothes could be generated by self-replicating machines at next to no cost. And all in all, the quality of life for the few had been unsurpassably good. So did it really matter if billions of people on the colony planets lived in slavery and degradation?

I mean, what can you *say* to that kind of logic? How fucking stupid is – don't get me started!

Back to the point. In the "good old days" of the Corporation, the Earthian citizens routinely committed appalling crimes against humanity, and massacred alien monsters by the trillion.

But there was no crime, as such, back then. For why bother to break the law, when *obeying* the law was a better option for any greedy bastard with a soul of direst malignity?

There *was* rebellion, of course, and dissent, and liberal protest.[31] But all those who defied the authority of the state in however minor a way were executed without trial. Or tortured,

29 In particular, Brosnan, Ennis, Goddard, and Mohammed. – *Ed.*

30 See in particular, Fleischer, Camre, Bamborough and Thomas. – *Ed.*

31 See *The History of Dissent during the Year of Corporation Hegemony* by Professor Gillian Tobin (Way Out of Orbit Books; for a discounted edition, click here). – *Ed.*

horribly, in dungeons like Giger.[32] Lawyers[33] became a rarity, since there was literally no fucking justice in the world.

Now, however, supposedly, it is all different.

For in the years after the Last Battle, democracy has come to human-habited space. There's an incorruptible police force. There are fair laws. Peace and harmony reign. In theory.

In practice, however, there are a hell of a lot of very evil people out there. And so slowly the new rulers of humanity were realising they were fighting a losing battle. I read an academic paper about it: "*The Process of Moral Relativism; How Ten Generations of Human Beings Have Become Acclimatised to Evil.*"[34]

It's scary, you see. If you live within a system, you absorb its values. Peer pressure can, I kid you not, create entire regiments of psychopaths. Let me give you one word to prove my point: *Kristallnacht.*[35]

None of which, of course, explains me – my murders, robberies, all the other stuff I've done – 'cause I'm the exception to the rule. I live in a system and I *defy* its fucking values.

Back to the report. It showed that prisons cannot cope. Brainwiping is proving less and less effective, blah, blah. And so a new solution has been found. Transportation of all major felons to terraformable planets in the farthest reaches of our universe, well away from "civilised" folk.

A thousand planets have already been identified. And the quantum teleportation technology needed to transport millions – no, not millions, *billions* of criminals is already in place.

32 See *Prisons and Dungeons Through the Ages* by Professor Wexford Gillingham (Way Out of Orbit Books; for a discounted edition, click here). – *Ed.*
33 See *Best Lawyer Jokes* ed. Rutherford Green (Way Out of Orbit Books; if you want to buy it, click here though personally I think you'd be wasting your money). – *Ed.*
34 See *Journal of Moral Crisis in the Modern Age,* vol. 4,344,333,222 , pp. 45–94. – *Ed.*
35 See *The History of World War II* by Professor Mark Jones. – *Ed.*

"What's the catch?" asked Bargan Oriel.

I could see it appealed to him. The idea of getting out of prison and having his own planet, nay, his own *galaxy.*

I sighed. This was going to be tricky to explain.

If you want a physics lesson, ask a physicist. I'm just giving you the bare outline here, okay?

The slang term for quantum teleportation[36] is "the fifty-fifty" – because, duh, it only works fifty per cent of the time. When it does work, it instantly teleports human beings any distance you like into the far reaches of space. It works for space ships too. Fifty per cent of the time.

Those aren't great odds. In fact, the odds are worse than they sound. For it may be that every colonist on a fifty-fifty ship survives the journey through entangled space but the ship's hull becomes, for whatever random reason, porous. In which event, you will *all* die.

So that's the catch: a toss of a coin will determine whether you live, or die in appalling horror and bodily incertitude.

Despite these crap odds, as I patiently explained to Oriel and Shalco, there's already a volunteer scheme in place. But the Reconciliation Committee now have a plan to make the whole thing compulsory.

By teleporting entire prisons.

Well why not? Size isn't an issue. If you can teleport a colony ship, you can do the same to a self-contained domed community. There are no dubbers inside a dome like ours – all the prison officers and the Governor himself are safely outside in their vast Home Dome, several miles away from the

36 See "The Principles of Quantum Teleportation" by Dr Mark Ruppe, Dr John Bompasso, and Professor Jean Everett, *Quantum Stuff,* vol. 3,344. – *Ed.*

Penitentiary itself. And of course, every prison has an energy supply and fabricators and oxygen synthesisers, and all the other gadgets you need to sustain a civilisation on a new planet. So you can simply teleport the prison on to an alien world, and let the scum inside cope as best they can.

What a great plan!

This news was not, however, well received by Shalco and Oriel. They still expected to get their freedom in due course, once their bribes kicked in. And they didn't care for the idea of their survival being subject to the whims of the quantum-teleport process.

And so their rebellion sprang up; and thus was born the great Giger Prison Riot.[37]

Plans of the prison were downed by me from Dekon's mind and printed up for Shalco and Oriel to consult. Knives and grenades were smuggled in with their food packages. And the boxes which contained the food were dismantled to reveal hard-plastic components which, when carefully re-assembled, became mortars and plasma guns and force field jammers. And, as I pointed out to both Oriel and Shalco, the DRs all carry weapons, and *are* weapons. Their arm cannons and laser-eyes could be cannibalised to form the armoury for a mob of angry prisoners.

I suggested a date for the riot too. 1st June. That's when the prison was due to dematerialise, according to my modified research documents. At 14.00. Two weeks hence.

And those two weeks had passed. It was now the 1st of June.

Hence, the boiling hot water in the face, the girly screaming, and the riot.

37 See *Hell Erupts: The Story of the Giger Prison Riot* by Sheila Hamilton (Way Out of Orbit Books; click here), and by the way, this book was ghostwritten by me!. (Hamilton was Deputy Governor of Giger before she was shot and almost killed in the riots). – *Ed*

I half-wish I had been there, in the main body of the prison, to see the violence erupt. Though I read plenty of accounts of the violence in the months that followed.

Here's my favourite:

Failed Escape from Giger's Moon

Government sources indicate that a small number of recidivist prisoners incarcerated in the Giger's Moon Penitentiary staged a violent protest which was swiftly subdued. Considerable damage to prison property was caused, and the cost of repairs and replacement of equipment and furniture will be charged to the offending prisoners to be redeemed via work in lieu.

An official of the Solar Neighbourhood Government has exclusively told this news portal: "This was a brief and regrettable lapse, which was quickly rectified. The public can be assured that there was never any chance of these wrong-doers escaping and returning to their life of crime."

However, in a wholly unrelated incident, the Governor of Giger Penitentiary Robbie Ferguson was fatally injured during a training exercise.[38]

Well I mean! Whatever the fuck happened to the fucking gutter press? That's what I want to know!

There was a time when journalists would have had a field day with a story like this. Mobs of violent prisoners smashing DRs!

38 © Giger Times. At the inquest into Governor Ferguson's death, however, the forensic team concluded that death was caused by two exploding bullets, one in his body, whilst he was working in his office. Prison authorities claimed live explosive ammunition was commonly used in routine staff training exercises. This apparently was believed by the credulous jury and a verdict of Accidental Death was recorded. – *Ed.*

Attempting to flee to the planet of Giger via the space elevator in the Industrial Zones! They almost succeeded too. All the prisoners needed was for someone on the outside to open the prison doors, and to provide them with the transport they needed to reach the space elevator on the Brightside and hence, achieve their freedom.

That someone was me.

Oops!

Go back to where we left off.

There's Cassady and me, in the prison hospital, as the riot erupts in the main prison block. She's looking tense. And I'm looking – well, I'm looking at *her*, to be honest, transfixed by her beauty and her loyalty, as we wait impatiently for Governor Ferguson to open up the air vents.

And then he did! Four vents opened up in the wall of the corridor that led to the hospital's operating theatre. The atmosphere in the corridor starting gushing out; and before long the air in the entire hospital wing was being voided. The same thing was happening all over the prison. This was the prison authorities' secret weapon – for if you deny oxygen to the prisoners, all and any riots will soon come to an end.

But we'd *anticipated* this of course. Dekon, after all, knew all the prison security systems; and Dekon was under my control. Thus, all the ringleaders of the riot were equipped with oxygen cylinders to allow them to breathe in a vacuum. And the rest of the mob could[39] take refuge in the rec rooms, which had been been made air-tight by us; and there they could wait, breathing slowly to conserve the oxygen, until the vents were closed.[40]

39 And did. – *Ed.*
40 Which also occurred. – *Ed.*

And, as part of my augments, I had an oxygen capsule in my brain; while Cassady had an oxygen tube, stolen from the infirmary, through which she could breathe freely.

So when the vents opened and the air gushed out, I was entirely unconcerned. I simply stepped forward and packed all four vents with mouldable explosive and stood well back.

The wall exploded. I had my eyes closed to protect them from the flare. When I opened them again, I saw that the explosion had left a large gaping hole that opened out on to the planet. Then Cassady and I ran out into the icy airless nightmare that was the surface of Giger's Moon.

And for twenty appalling seconds it was incredibly fucking cold. But we ran and we ran, for eleven long and terrible yards.

Until we reached the force field corridor. The one that linked the prison with the Home Dome. It's invisible of course. But not to me, because I could see a blueprint of the prison in my visual array, courtesy of Dekon. Reality and map fused in my eyes, and we ran fast, and found ourselves in a zone of warm air and breathable oxygen.

And we carried on running. The corridor of breathable air was unpredictably winding. If you stumbled on it by chance, you'd have no hope of staying within it. But my mental map continued to show me the way, and we sprinted the three miles from the prison to the Home Dome with relative ease.

When we got there Cassady took my hand in hers. We looked at each other. We had what I guess you'd call a "moment".

The moment ended. We looked at the Home Dome. It was painted a faint gold hue, and was beautifully inlaid with patterns copied by archaeologists from the alien manuscripts left behind on Giger's Moon millions of years before. No one had ever translated this language. The hieroglyphs might, for all anyone knew, have said LITTERBUGS WILL BE PROSECUTED. But there was something haunting about the alien words etched on the hardmetal dome.

Then I mentally projected the access codes of the door and we were through.

We walked into a convention of burly Soldiers. Well, three of them anyway. They were passing the time in the way that brainwashed Soldiers generally do – namely, standing to attention whilst swapping grisly anecdotes about the many ugly alien fuckers they had killed.

And, naturally, they looked up as we blundered through the airlock, frozen and purple-overalled and clearly in the wrong place.

Within less than an instant their implants would have told them that we were not prison staff or authorised civilians and must therefore be escapees.

Although that was pretty fucking obvious – purple overall = convict, guys!

The three of them reached for their guns.

Cassady shot at two of them with her home-made anaesthetic gun, with dazzling speed, and almost hit them both. Whilst I took a deep breath, and went to work.

It was a brutal hand-to-hand encounter and I very nearly lost. But I had speed and surprise on my side, plus an airlock wrench. Afterwards, we stripped two of the bodies, dressed ourselves as Soldiers in body armour and shit-for-brains scowls. and proceeded onwards, at a brisk military walk.

I could now read the blueprint of the Home Dome itself in front of my eyes as I walked down the corridor. The shuttle bay was far down the corridor to the left, the Governor's office was to the right. We carried straight on until we reached a large armoured door behind which, I knew, we would find the doppelgänger berths.

I tried ordering the remote computer to open the doors; no chance. I had considerable influence over Dekon, but I could not over-rule her high-security protocols. So I used the last of my mouldable explosive on the lock. We stood back. It blew. The door slowly slid open.

Inside was a dormitory full of dubbers in trance, thirty or forty of them in all.[41] They were wired up and slackjawed, a couple of them were dribbling. Oh, and there were two guards as well, but we took them down fast.

The prison officers were inhabiting the bodies of the doppelgänger robots who were subduing the riot in the prison.

I watched the warring dubbers for a few moments, fascinated to imagine what was happening at the other end of their virtual link. Each of the forty-five[42] prison officers was, I guessed, inhabiting five or more robot bodies at a time. There were twelve female dubbers, eighteen male, and two herms. A couple of them were bodybuilders, but most were just ordinary joes, and janes. But in their virtual selves they were all-powerful robot monsters!

And to me they looked like – not that I'd even seen such a thing – a gang of teenagers having simultaneous wet dreams. Their bodies twitched uncontrollably, they groaned and grunted with effort as their robots bodies punched and kicked and shot prisoners.

"Danielle," Cassady warned me, and I stopped trying to imagine that which I could not see.

I disconnected the power, by smashing the wireless hub beneath a floor tile. And watched with delight as the dubbers

41 Forty-five unconscious bodies were recovered from this room, plus two dead body-armoured guards. – *Ed.*

42 Artemis had clearly counted them by this point. – *Ed.*

woke up one by one. Only to be sent back into somnolence by Cassady and her dart gun.

Then I dug deep into Dekon and tried to capture control of the DR network. I did this by attempting to persuade her that I was authorised to replace the now-unconscious prison officers. She knew of course that wasn't true – Dekon had seen with her own camera-eyes what I had just done. But – how can I explain this? If you're a computer, you're not truly in control of your own mind. You are the slave of your sub-programs. It's a strange—

Enough of that. You don't need to know what it's like to be a sentient quantum computer. But trust me – I *do* know.

So I dumped one of the dubbers out of his chair and sat down. Cassady wired me up. Dekon finally gave me access to the doppelgänger robot network. And then Cassady took a gun and aimed it at the door in case the DRs or dubbers came upon us.

And then I became the doppelgänger robots. Not just the ones in the prison, those in the Home Hub itself. There were six hundred of them in all.

I became six hundred Mes!

That was far more Me than I could deal with. So I deactivated the four hundred and eleven DRs in the prison. The riot was now over; our side had won. Shalco and the others could proceed with the next stage in the plan, namely breaking out of the prison and escaping to the planet of Giger. All I had to do was drive the lunar buggies across to them remotely, and then open the doors of the prison dome.

First, however, I closed the air-vents in the prison dome, and seeped an atmosphere back in. I didn't want anyone asphyxiating if there was a delay.

Then I accessed the control nexus that would let me open the prison doors and allow Shalco and her gangsters to escape.

And finally, I took control of the doppelgänger lunar buggies; sixty in all, enough to take the entire escaping prison population and convey them to the Brightside space elevator.

Then I hesitated.

And I left the doors closed.

And I left the armoured buggies parked.

I betrayed, in other words, Shalco and all the other prisoners who had put their faith in me.

What can I say? I do that sometimes.

"All done," said Cassady.

"All done," I said wearily. I always found this process tiring. Because I'm not a computer hacker, I'm an emulator. I emulate the peculiar state of existence of a quantum remote computer, in order to influence its functioning. It's a bit like being an ant that thinks it's a cloud. Or – whatever. I can't explain.

Cassady had by now switched on the wall screens and was reading the story of the prison break. The story was nothing. Nothing was happening.

"What the fuck is happening?" she asked.

"I can't," I said patiently, "let those bastards go."

Cassady looked at me in horror.

"You have to!" she said angrily.

"Sorry!"

"Those are my friends!" she protested.

Maybe so. But these guys were also, let's face it, monsters. I couldn't let them loose! I really couldn't. I had no choice but to double-cross them.

"I'm not going to let them escape. You got a problem with that?" I asked Cassady.

She looked at me warily. Then she shook her head.

"Let's go," I said.

We stepped out into the corridor – and were greeted with dazzling sheets of plasma fire. The remaining dubbers were armoured up and ready for a prolonged siege. The walls behind us burned, fireballs danced in the air. We stepped hastily back into the doppelgänger room, tasting burned air in our lungs.

"Shit," said Cassady.

"No worries," I said lightly. And I reached back into Dekon and thence into the body of the nearest deactivated DR.

And then I was back in the corridor, seeing through robot eyes, moving with a robot body.

The body-armoured dubbers made their move. One of them had a grenade and he ran towards the door. I raised an arm and flame erupted from it and he went down.

The dubbers turned and saw me and a fusillade of explosive bullets smashed into my robot chassis. I fired a hail of bullets then my shell collapsed and my circuits died.

But I was alive six more times. I saw through six pairs of eyes, I walked on six pairs of legs. And I ran down the corridor and rained bullets and flame upon the dubber squad. They were faster than me – because I had six minds to control. But my firepower was formidable. I left their dead bodies in the corridor and Cassady and Artemis emerged from the doppelgänger suite and greeted us (all six of us) with whoops of joy.

We escorted them; and I was escorted *by* them, as I ran behind the robots. For I was seven minds, all at the same time. Once I stumbled, and Cassady had to grab me and help me up.

Dekon sent me a warning – another dubber squad was closing in on us. So I stopped dead, and hunched down on the floor. And I reactivated another dozen robot bodies in nearby corridors and store rooms. And a dozen more. And a dozen more still. And I fought, and I fought.

When it was over, I got up and Cassady and I walked down the corridors, past and over the bodies of the dubbers, to the spaceport bay.

Cassady was looking anxious. She didn't understand the necessity for my double-cross. Nor did she fathom why the DRs were helping us, or why I was acting so weirdly. She didn't understand anything really. I'd lied to her right from the start. She was just a pawn in my game. But at least she was safe now.

"Wait ten minutes," I told Cassady, "no longer." She gave me an even more baffled look.

"Go, sweetheart," I insisted.

She looked again. The kind of look that demands a kiss. But I did not yield to her.

"We stay together—" she began to say, but I interrupted her:

"Fucking go!" I said.

We separated.

I knew that Cassady could get away from Giger's Moon without me. She knew exactly what she had to do. And I now had a job to finish.

So I walked back down the corridors, past the dead bodies of the prison officers, and knocked on the door of the Governor's office. No reply. I tried the door – locked. I ordered Dekon to open the lock and she wouldn't. So I blasted the door down. Then I stepped inside.

I found the room in turmoil. Governor Robbie Ferguson was in the middle of the room, alone apart from three now-deactivated DRs. He appeared to be screaming at himself – in fact, of course, he was just too angry to subvocalise. He was barking orders via his MI down the beaconband to the authorities on Giger, apparently trying to call up a missile strike on the penitentiary.

He was so preoccupied that he didn't notice me for a few priceless moments. So I stood there, and I watched him. Those bulging eyes, that brawny neck, the vein that pulsed in his temples when he was enraged. It brought back, oh, so many memories.

Then he realised there was someone in the room and he dropped the phone and reached for his gun.

I fired my plasma gun at the wall behind him. The wall hissed, and the pastel paint was burned away, leaving behind charred blackness. Ferguson was frozen in mid-draw. He decided instead to bargain, let go of the gun, and raised his hands.

"Remember me?" I asked Ferguson.

"Of course I do," he said, as his brain chip gave him my name, "Danielle."

"Try again," I snarled.

He tried again. He stared at me. And stared even more.

I no longer in any way looked like the girl I once was. But there was *something* that he recognised, from his days as Chief of Police on a Clan planet. And the look of eventual recognition on his face was my reward for all the years of preparation.

"Fuck," he said, feebly.

"Give yourself," I suggested, "a second stab at your last words?"

"Maybe we can do a deal?" he wheedled.

"Okay," I lied, but I clearly wasn't very convincing, because at that moment he drew his gun. He was fast.

Not fast enough. I rolled to dodge his plasma blast, and from a crouching position, shot his gun out of his hand.

Then I shot him in the jaw. Once, making a gaping roar out of his angry scowl. Then I shot him in the body. Once, twice, thrice, about a hundred times in all. He wasn't wearing face armour, I could have shot him in the forehead and killed him outright. But that would have defeated the object of the exercise.

Eventually his armour cracked and a bullet went through and exploded. He convulsed. He spat blood from his bloody lips. And he fell to the ground and he died.

I was breathing heavily by now. It's a long slow business shooting someone to death when they are wearing body armour. But in fairness, he had it coming.

Then I changed the gun to laser setting and I hunched down next to the body.

The next part was grisly. I cut his skull open, and I gouged a path into the frontal lobe of his brain with a knife. And I took out his brain chip and pocketed it.

I had no real grudge against Robbie Ferguson. He'd taken liberties, but he'd never hurt me, not seriously anyway. His only major sin was that of omission. He had been a Chief of Police who did not care about law or justice.[43]

But in his brain chip was all the data I needed to kill my real enemy: Daxox.

I fired a delayed-action projectile bullet into Ferguson's head.[44]

Where it would explode in thirty seconds' time. The point of this of course was to blur the cause of death, and hence conceal my theft of the brain chip.

And then I left the room, counting in my head (four, two, one, BOOM).

And the explosion behind me followed my count.

Then I walked back to the shuttle bay. Cassady was waiting for me there.

"You killed someone?" she asked, quietly.

"Yeah."

"Who?"

"It doesn't matter," I said.

"It matters," she said sadly. But I ignored her subtext. And I tried, for many years afterwards, not to recall that sorrowful look in her eyes.

We clambered inside the shuttle.

"Can you fly this thing?"

I asked Dekon how to fly an XL453[45] planet-to-planet shuttle craft. The instructions were, fuck me, terrifying. I particularly flinched at:

Care should be taken when activating the anti-inertial drive in a vacuum, since an imprecise calibration can lead to terminal g-forces. Please refer to section 433i para 4 subsection xiv.

43 It was of course common practice for police officials on Corporation planets to be professional gangsters. And indeed in the early years of the Corporation, very few planets actually had any kind of a police force. – *Ed.*

44 You see? I told you about this earlier. – *Ed.*

45 After intensive checking, it emerges that the planet-to-planet shuttle craft used in Giger Penitentiary was indeed the XL453 model, not the more common XL501. – *Ed.*

I had no time to refer to section whateverthefuck. I decided to chance it.

"Piece of piss," I said, insouciantly. And I activated the anti-inertial drive, fired up the engines and – again through my link with Dekon – opened up the roof of the bay. And we flew off at speed into the darkness of space. Three years later I was in Cúchulainn. (Say it like this: Kuh-HOO-lin.)

And there the terror really began.

Chapter 2

Meanwhile in Debatable Space

Those are the bare bones of what happened on Giger's Moon.

I've missed out, I must confess, some bits that aren't essential to the core narrative of my mission of revenge.[1] Mainly, everything to do with the love story, and my growing passion for Cassady.

I mean, who cares about all *that* shit? Hmm?

So let's just skip over all the muddly soul-searching hearts-in-torment stuff. And let me tell you, instead, about what happened in Debatable Space, at around about the same time that Cassady and I were fleeing Giger's Moon. Let me speak of glorious space battles, awesome terror, and a terrifying and imminent threat to humanity. All far more interesting that me talking about

How I seduced and fucked Cassady Penfold.

So I am now – any moment now – going to pass swiftly over that part. The stuff about how I targeted this beautiful yet complex woman. How I flattered her. Got her into my bed. And made her fall in love with me. (Or was it the other way around?)

It was, let me tell you, a skilfully orchestrated seduction. A

1 Harumph! This line creates the impression that Artemis has some grasp of the art of self-editing. With respect, this is not so! – *Ed.*

magnificent example of the master thief at work. For I did, indeed, steal her heart!

But in all honesty, the memories of that seduction – the tenderness she showed me, the love she clearly felt – all that still disturbs me terribly.

And I don't know why that should be so. After all, I didn't *betray* Cassady. I promised I'd get her out of the Giger Penitentiary, and that's exactly what I did. And a few months later, I dropped her off at a planet that was on the way to my destination – it was New Earth VI, a nicely fertile paradise with great cocktail bars – and left her to carry on with the rest of her life.[2]

So okay, I admit – because I'm not an idiot you know! – that she was pretty distressed at the moment of our final farewell. Tears, choking noises, a lost look that spoke of agonising pain – all that, and more. She never actually reproached me. But the final glance she gave me, before I walked away from her for the last time – rewind, delete!

I really don't need that particular fucking memory.

But even so, it comes to me in my dreams every night.

I guess she'd imagined more of a "happy ever after" scenario! But that had never been my plan, or my style.

Poor sweet gullible Cassady.

Except, she was never truly gullible. No, in fact, now I come to think about it, not gullible at all.

She could, I realise, read me like a book. Which is apt, because she was such a lover of books. She – forget it. Don't go down that road.

Years later I learned she'd been on the final leg of her sentence.[3] A year more and she'd have been out. But even so she risked everything for me.

2 Cassady changed her name to Gemma Fried on arrival on New Earth VI, after purchasing a forged identity. – *Ed.*
3 True. – *Ed.*

Why?

Well, obviously, because I'm a master seducer. And I had used all my guile and charisma to make her love me. You know the drill: play hard to get; find out your lover's secrets and use them manipulatively; never be nice unless you really have to; be really good in bed. It works, 99 times out of a hundred; and I know that for a fact. I remember.[4]

But sometimes I think, and I wonder, and I ask – did it really happen that way? Or was it – no, stop! It wasn't that way at all. I know that now, and I knew it then too.

The truth is, she *realised* I was playing her. And she *allowed* me to. She knew – how could she not know? – that I was a treacherous bastard stone cold killer. But she made – at some point she *must* have made – a decision that she'd rather be with me, for all my sins and flaws and treacherous nature, than not.

The final outcome of Cassady's story was tragic, though I didn't know about it for a long time. Just two years after the prison break, Cassady was killed in a bar brawl. She was, apparently, by that point, an alcoholic and a drug abuser and a notorious violent troublemaker.[5] That shocks me.

But it wasn't *my* fault, was it? It's not as if she felt to pieces, because *I* left her!

Or did she?

I often wonder about the "what might have been". I mean, if I'd stayed with Cassady. Been her girl. Settled down. What kind of life would I have had? Baking cakes? Adopting children? Can you really see that? ME?

And besides, can cakes actually be baked, or do they only ever come out of a fabricator? I mean—

Stop, Artemis, stop. Make your brain stop whirring.

4 Numerous examples of this technique in action have been deleted. – *Ed.*
5 Also all true, as confirmed by the records of the courts and police department on New Earth VI. – *Ed.*

The simple truth is: I'll never know. The path not taken, was not taken. No point wondering.

So, back to Debatable Space then.

Debatable Space! The outlaws! The pitched gun-battles! The anti-matter bomb that "accidentally" went off! The desperate jeopardy that ensues when a billion quintillion deadly aliens[6] are freed from their confining cage! All this, and, yes, more!

But bear with me here for a moment. Just a moment. Please?

Because, before I recount all that exciting universe-jeopardising stuff, I want to tell you about how I first met Cassady.

She was a trusty working in the prison library, as well as at the hospital. Every morning she walked the Spoke handing out downloads, advising the prisoners on what they might and might not enjoy. A thankless task, but she persevered. And every afternoon she sat in the wards and kept the dying prisoners company.

Cassady liked to keep busy. That's what you need to know about Cassady. Busy. Smiled a lot. Full of heart. Actually gave a shit about people.

She came to my cell and asked me what I liked to read. I answered her at length. She was somewhat stunned.

6 There's no basis for this number. No one ever succeeded in counting these creatures. – *Ed.*

That's because, as a reader, I am both voracious and eclectic. Which means I like to read everything and anything. Novels, yes. Poetry, certainly. Biography, yes of course. But most of all, history. I have read an historical textbook on every period of history since the Cro-Magnons mated with the Neanderthals. It's my passion. I've read about the Middle Ages, the Renaissance, the Industrial Revolution, the Faith Wars, I know about the growth of the World Government and the "reign" of that windbag Xabar, I know about the history of the Galactic Corporation from its early years to its far from inevitable downfall. I know it all; and I relish every fact.

This, you see, is the other thing that is truly cool about me. Ignore all those wanky superficial attributes – my looks, my superpowers, and my ability to look good in almost anything.[7] No what's cool about me is that deep down, in my heart of hearts, I am an utter book nerd. And of *this* I am proud.

"Most inmates," Cassady advised me, having recovered from her initial stupefaction, "like to read porn."

"I don't see the point," I said. "I mean, why *read* about sex?"

"Porn," she conceded, "with pictures."

"No words?"

"The minimum. Usually, just the naked person's name, and what tends to make them horny."

"For a custodian of the prison library," I told her, "that must be soul destroying."

She smiled, beautifully, and for quite some time.

It was the smile that got to me.

7 I can confirm that she did indeed so do. – *Ed.*

We became friends.

That's all it was at first. We were friends for many months, before we actually became lovers.

But for me it was everything. I'd never actually *had* a friend you see, not since I'd become a grown up. Not a real, sharing-everything, love-of-my-life friend. My "friends" were all just casual acquaintances, or work-mates, or lovers, mainly of the one- or two-night stand variety.

And okay, sometimes after I'd fucked a guy, we'd linger naked on the bed and talk, and share secrets, and stuff. But a week later, I wouldn't even remember his name.

But Cassady and I were *such* great friends. We talked every day! I woke up and ideas or opinions would drift into my head, and then I would think, "Must tell Cassady this!" We argued about which meal in the canteen was the vilest. We argued about which book to read next. We argued about who was the best detective of all time (we both loved crime novels).[8] We argued about – we argued about everything, except we never truly argued at all. We just let words flow between us.

Early on in our relationship, I told Cassady about my childhood. About the loneliness and heartbreak. What it was like to live in and around the Rebus library. And my hatred of my father.[9] And my impetuous decision to flee home, culminating in my arrival on Cúchulainn.

After an early point in the narrative, I started to tell lies. But even so, it was a big step for me. I'd never told *anyone* about my childhood before. And no one had ever asked. The guys I'd fucked, even Daxox, tended to assume I'd arrived in the world as a fully-formed adult. They weren't *interested* in

8 I asked Artemis this question, and she told me that for her it was a toss between Milo Shamus and the famously fat detective Nero Wolfe. – *Ed.*

9 Who I really liked, and considered to be my friend; though we never actually met. – *Ed.*

imagining the five-year-old Artemis with freckles on her nose and a cheeky stare. But Cassady wanted to know. She wanted to know everything.

And in return, as part of that whole sharing-of-confidences process I'd never experienced before, Cassady told me about Julia. A Soldier in the Corporation Military Division. Who had been, and still was, the one great love of Cassady's life.

"Was she beautiful?" I asked.

"No." Cassady smiled at the memory. "Too chunky to be beautiful. But strong. She could crush a stone this size, in her fist."

I paused, considering that.

"Why?" I asked.

"No reason. She was a show-off, I guess. It was her party trick."

"I get you," I said, envisaging the trail of crumbled rock left in this Amazon's wake. "Was she your first lover?"

"First female lover," Cassidy qualified.

"Good sex?"

"The best."

"Tell me," I said.

And so she did.

"Did you ever feel," said Cassady, a little while later, "when you were growing up, that you were the only sane thing in the entire universe? That everyone else was mad, or warped?"

I thought about it.

"No," I said, at length. "I felt the opposite. I felt like everyone around me was totally sane, and I was the mad one. I had a very boring family you know."

Cassady stared, rebuking me for saying the wrong thing. I shrugged, apologetically.

"I thought my parents were brainwashed," Cassady explained. "Like zombies. Unfeeling, uncaring, not real human beings at all."

"Yeah?"

"Yeah."

"I guess, lots of children feel that way," I suggested. "Not *me* but – I'm sure it's pretty normal."

"No, no it's not!" said Cassady fiercely. "The point is, I was *right*. They *were* brainwashed. They *were* zombies. They were—"

"Soldiers with a capital S?" I interjected.

"Camp-followers. Bureaucrats, in other words, on a garrison planet."

"Ah."

"When I was ten years old," Cassady continued, "my dad invited his Manager to dinner at our house. Mum cooked. She was a great cook. I served the wine. Dad spent the whole evening with a big smile on his face. As if he thought that he'd be executed if he ever stopped smiling. Mum flirted with the Manager. I'd never seen a grown up flirt before. She kept smiling at this gross, horrible little man, and touching his knee with her hand. And after dinner Mum and the Manager went upstairs and I heard them shouting and screaming, and although I was only ten, I wasn't dumb. They were fucking. Dad and I stayed at the table, with the Manager's Wife, who had very little small talk, and they all smiled big smiles at each other. For ages."

"That's – shit," I said.

"They call it Droit de Seigneur," Cassady explained. "Manager's privilege."

"I've read about it," I said, softly. "It's a concept that goes way back."

"That's how it is, on a garrison planet, you see," Cassady explained.

"I was guessing that."

"We served the Lemur 344 Barracks. Dad was an operations manager for the spaceport and training centre. Mum worked in the hospital, patching them up after their training exercises. You know how it was for Soldiers, back then?"

"I've read about it."

"Give me the child, and I will give you the man. That's what they say."

"Francis Xavier, a Jesuit priest, he said that."

"They mould minds in other words."

"It's not so hard."

"Entire generations of children turned into warriors."

"It was a fucker, no guffing."

"When I was fourteen," said Cassady, "I went to my first dance. The boys all loved me because I'm, you know."

"I don't know. Give me a hint?"

"Highly sexed."

"Yeah?" I looked at her.

"I exude pheromones. Men find me irresistible," Cassady conceded. "Women too, obviously."

"I wouldn't have known that," I lied.

"I was only fourteen. I knew nothing about all that. I just wanted to dance. I spent the night batting away roving hands. I didn't want sex. I was underage!"

"There was no underage, back then."

"Emotionally I was. Then she came over and sorted them out."

"Who?"

"Julia. My first lover."

"Ah."

"She was the CO of the Regiment. A Colonel by rank. A tough bitch. Muscles like – well. Like granite, if granite weren't so fucking squidgy."

"You fucked her?"

"Not right away. Not for five years. She went to fight a war and when she came back I was nineteen. No longer a virgin, though I'd never slept with a man that I didn't despise. I was third assistant manager at the spaceport. We were a family firm you see. We lived to serve. Me, my four brothers, my six sisters, my uncles, my aunts. We worked for the barracks. That was our life. We were conditioned too. That was my point, that's where I started from. I always thought my parents were brainwashed, and *they were*. I always thought my teachers were robots, and *they were*, literally. My friends were the children of other civilian barracks managers, and they all lived to serve. It was our culture. We were a serf class. I saw it all so clearly when I was ten. But by the time I was nineteen I couldn't see it at all. Because I was living it."

"How'd they brainwash you?"

Cassady thought a moment. A reading lamp cast its soft radiance on her face. It highlighted the faint shadows of down upon her smooth skin. I was still getting that pheromonal arousal. But it was Cassady's low, husky, intense voice that most captivated me.

"Attitudes," she said. "It's all about attitudes. They're what define *the normal*. What everyone else believes, *you* believe. It's incredibly powerful. Reinforced with dormant hypnosis, you know, as you sleep, they whisper stuff in your brain implant. Plus, infanticide."

There was an awkward silence. I wondered if I'd misheard. But I knew I hadn't.

"You're guffing me?" I asked.

"No, it's true. I remember dozens of babies who grew up into toddlers – little scamps, tousle-haired little monsters, you know? – then they just vanished. I never saw them again. They used to test for obedience at the age of three, you see, And after that, a lot of children were culled. It's a winnowing process. Selection of the most docile."

"You slipped through the net then."

"I was a quiet one, when I was little. Hardly spoke. People thought that meant I was obedient. But I wasn't. I was just a dreamer. A world of my own, that's where I lived."

"Tell me about it," I said. As a child, I'd didn't mix with

children my own age, because there *were* none on Rebus. (Apart from one boy – who left after a year.)[10]

"And my dad was just a fucking – what's the word for a man who has no balls? He was one of those. He never stood up for himself. The Soldiers used to – used to—" Cassady was lost in remembered rage. I preserved my tactful silence.

And as she was thinking about her past, I found myself comparing her childhood with my own, on Rebus. For ours was a so-called Free Planet, where there were no Soldiers. Just archivists.

And I was the daughter of a single parent. Just me and my dad, in a big old rambling house. But we never spoke. Not about real stuff I mean.

That was what defined us, you see – the not saying of stuff. The old bastard never *stopped* talking at work. He was eloquent at lectures. Witty and garrulous at dinner parties. But when he was alone with me, it was as if he'd signed a vow of taciturnity. He savoured syllables as if they were his final fucking breaths.

It pissed me off, I guess. And it froze me. Stopped me feeling – anything for him, really. I felt like I never had a dad. Though I did! It was my mother who'd fucked off and abandoned me, after all.

And most of our evenings together, once we'd had a semi-silent dinner, were spent—

Fuck! Why am I telling you this? It was – forget it.

Back to Cassady's story.

"So tell me more about the Colonel," I said to Cassady. "You met, fell in love, many shags ensued – happy ever after?"

Cassady laughed, but it wasn't a real laugh. The light from the lamp caught her skin again. This time it sparkled like the sun on water on a lake in the early morning. She was, in other words, I realised, crying.

10 Who appears later in a later digression. – *Ed.*

"No," Cassady said. "They found out. Her superior officers. Fraternising with a ranked civilian. That's an offence in the Soldier's code. We were ranked you see. Whereas the casuals were *un*ranked, you could do whatever you wanted with *them*. The barstaff, waiters, whores, you know. This was a garrison town remember. Most of the young people either waited tables or served booze or prostituted themselves. Soldiers are voracious. Food, sex, drink, mindless violence. It's all the same to them."

"I can imagine."

"I was given an official warning. I had to go to the barracks; I was interrogated by the Colonel of the Regiment. He treated me like a whore. I promised to never see her again."

"And did you?"

"Yes I did. Of course I did! Julia and me, we kept meeting in hotel rooms. We were so in love. She even said so. Imagine! A Soldier, saying, 'I love you.' But she did. Once, just once. She did!"

We were alone in the prison library. The pastel-coloured walls were outshone by shelves of brightly coloured books on real-wood shelves. The reading lamps cast their radiance in broad arcs, like glittering pools among black rocks. And Cassady's quiet voice stroked my soul and tormented me with its barely hidden grief.

"We were careful of course," she continued. "Covered our tracks. Used false ID. Camera distortion technology. I told my parents I was studying for a further degree, that's why I was out so much. I had a place of my own of course, but I still had dinner every night at my parents' place But after dinner, I would go out 'to study', and that's when I met with Julia."

Cassady was lost in memories. And when she remembered, it gave her a sadly pensive look. Her inner thoughts visible in her eyes, her lips faintly moving as she absent-mindedly whispered to herself. I could see why Julia had loved her so much.

"It all went sour," she continued. "The brass found out, Julia was reprimanded again. And this time they gave her a direct order. That's how it works you see. It's hardwired in their brains. An order is an order."

"It can't be hardwired. Not literally," I insisted.

"Indoctrinated. Whatever. They may even use a cerebral implant. But the fact is, Soldiers can't disobey."

"They can fight it though? A Soldier can fight the conditioning?"

"No."

"No?"

"It's impossible. No. It can never happen."

I knew she was right. It pissed me off.

"So, we make people into monsters," I said bitterly, "and then we train them, like animals. And then we use them to hunt and kill for us."

Cassady shook her head. She looked me full in the eyes. And I shocked myself, for I was shuddering with desire.

"No, not any more," said Cassady. "We let all the monsters loose, remember, after the Last Battle. That's why places like this are full of ex-Soldiers. They don't have a moral code. So they're lost. No reason to be. Just the skills to kill."

She was right of course. Giger Penitentiary used to be a bleak and lonely dungeon. This was where the rebels were tortured, back when there were rebels. Now it was overflowing with the violent, the disaffected, the insane, and the military.

"What was the direct order?" I asked. "That Julia was given?"

"To kill me. My guess is, they wanted to test her loyalty. So she came to me that night."

And as Cassady told the tale in its broad outlines, I found I could visualise it all. The impressionable teenager, waiting for her lover in a typical Corporation Planet hotel room. One bed. One landscape painting in a vaguely expressionist style above the bed. One portrait of the Cheo on the ceiling mural. One light. One hanger for clothes.

Then the door opened and in walked Julia, a ball of muscular energy, eyes blazing. And Cassady was waiting for her, and pounced on her, kissing and groping and cherishing. And I could imagine the needy, desperate embrace, the two women hugging, and kissing again, and declaring their undying love for each other, over and over again.

And then, so Cassady told me, they laughed awkwardly, and sat on the bed.

And then, knowing Cassady, they would have talked about all the little things. What their days had been like, and what news and gossip they'd heard.

And Julia's stories would have been far more exciting, I guessed. After all, she was training in space warfare, forcing her body to achieve impossible feats of daring. Cassady's stories would just be about her everyday tedium; but Julia would listen as if they were tales of epic valour, and she would *care*. Because that's what lovers do.

And then, though Cassady didn't say this bit, they would have taken their clothes off slowly and seductively, admiring each other's naked beauty.

And finally, as Cassady acknowledged, they fucked, to music. For they always fucked to music. In fact, choosing the music to which they would fuck was the big decision of every day.

Tonight was Cassady's choice, She had picked a numetal track called "Satan's Spawn", which was loud and diabolically repetitive. And I could imagine tongues licking and fingers touching and bodies intertwined as dark bass rhythms crashed and electric guitar riffs soared.

And after they had fucked, Cassady drifted off to sleep, naked on the bed.

At this particular moment in our relationship – when Cassady was telling me this story – I had never actually seen her naked. But even so, I could imagine her lithe slim loveliness and her bud-like breasts and her bushy womanhood and the curve of her tiny arse and her vulnerable sweetness as she slipped into post-fuck drowsy sleep.

And then Cassady woke up. And realised that Julia was strangling her to death with her two slim but powerful hands.

"I knew right away," said Cassady, her face haunted by the memory, "what was happening. We'd never really fooled anyone. The Army always knew what we were doing, and where. Don't you see, they *wanted* us to break the rules! That's why the Army was so lax with security. Why they were always giving Julia free time, even after all the formal warnings. Fraternising between Soldiers and ranked civilians was supposed to be *banned*, but they were always organising dances between us, and the booze was always free. Because if you want to toughen up a Soldier, what's the best way to do it? Tell her, or him, to kill the thing they love."

I exhaled, finally, as she reached this point in her story. I'd guessed the twist, of course, but it still came as a shock.

"And she was strong," said Cassady. "Very strong. But I'm not a fucking idiot, Artemis. I'm really not. I knew what might happen that night. I'd spent my spare time reading books about the psychology of warriors in the Corporation Empire. I'd read dozens of biogs of famous Soldiers. And so I took my precautions. I'd had blades implanted in my fingertips, for security. Released by a thought code. And when I woke up and her hands were on my throat I lashed out and I cut her face and her neck, and blood gushed everywhere. But Julia carried on strangling me. There we were, the two of us, slithering on the sheets, blood gushing from her cheek and throat. Then I shoved her off the bed and slashed again, and this time I opened up her jugular. She died there on the floor of my hotel room. She bled out in the first twenty minutes. But it took six hours in all for her to actually die. That's because they have oxygen implants in the brain, you see. They can survive almost any injury, but in the end, if there's no oxygen in the brain, there's no life. So I sat and watched her for all that time and Julia couldn't speak by then, she could only stare at me. Defeated.

"And that's when I—"

I grabbed Cassady by the throat with one hand and choked her. Her face went sunset-red. Her eyes goggled. And she looked, as you'd expect, utterly astonished at what I was doing to her.

We were still alone in the library. The surveillance cameras were on us, but I doubted anyone except the Dekon computer was monitoring them, and I controlled *her.* And my grip was unwaveringly tight. Cassady lashed out at me with one hand and I dodged the blow by tilting my head back. She fumbled and produced a shiv from a pouch in her side and lashed again and I dodged again.

I released my grip slightly, so she could breathe a little. And she continued to rain blows on me. They'd taken the blades out of her fingertips, but she had the shiv, and she was strong, and fit, and clearly trained in martial arts. But each blow she threw I dodged, like a man walking through a swarm of bees and evading every one.

Eventually I released her. Cassady gasped, and shook her head, and did all those recovering-from-choking things that people always do.

Then she lunged at me with the shiv. But I simply zen-glided her arm so the blow went past me even though I hadn't touched her. She tried again and this time I took the knife off her and thrust it into my own breastbone.

The blade snapped.

"Augments," I said calmly to Cassady. "I have 'em, every Soldier would have 'em. Reflexes enhanced. Skin toughened. My bones here, here, here and here," I touched my body's protected points with a fingertip to illustrate, "are stronger than steel."

"Why the fuck," gasped Cassady, "did you do that, bitch?"

"To prove a point."

"What fucking point?!"

"No way," I said patiently, "could you have killed a trained Soldier. Not with those pathetic little fingerblades. Julia could have dodged you easily, like I just did. Or she could have tautened her neck muscles to bury her arteries under flesh. That way, you could have stuck a kitchen knife in her throat and it wouldn't have harmed her."

"What are you saying?"

I looked at Cassady with the fondest of looks. And then I broke her heart.

"I'm saying," I said, "that Julia *let* you kill her. She had her orders. Murder your lover, or die yourself. And she cared about you too much to kill you. So she chose B. She chose to die."

There was a terrible silence.

"Not possible," said Cassady, re-evaluating the single most important experience of her entire life. An experience she had mis-read and misconstrued totally.

"She loved you," I said, "so she broke her conditioning. She let herself die rather than hurt a hair on your head."

"But she had—" said Cassady. "That's just not—" She thought about it some more. "She took six hours to die," said Cassady, her voice trembling. "She didn't say anything, she didn't try to write a note. She just looked at me, for six hours. What must she have been thinking . . . ?"

"That," I said, "she loved you."

My plan was to seduce Cassady, so that I could use her as a pawn in my escape strategy.

Instead – although it took me years to realise this – she seduced *me.*

I fell in love with her, totally. I yearned to spend time with her, I looked forward to being with her again, even when I was still with her. I gave her, yes I did, my entire fucking heart.

Though she never loved me, not really and truly, the way she'd loved Julia.

I'm sure about that. Which was fine. I didn't *expect* her to love me that much. 'Cause I mean, how the fuck could I, someone with no soul or conscience or compassion, compete with a dead lover?

Can't be done! That was my attitude.

And yet—

Skip it.

Long and short is: we became lovers, and it wasn't just about sex. It was the happiest time of my life.

Fuck it, I adored that sweet-hearted girl.

And it wasn't all nights of passion. We talked politics too. After leaving her garrison planet, Cassady had become an anarcho-pirate, with a hidden agenda of overthrowing the evil Galactic Corporation. Just like Flanagan.

But half a century later, the evil Corporation was overthrown. And Cassady was arrested on multiple charges of piracy and murder, and was guilty on all counts. Because over the years she had become, when all is said and done, nothing but a cheap hood.

But, hey, I don't like to tarnish her memory by talking about that shit.

We talked sometimes, too, about aliens. Like me, Cassady had read all about the great alien threat to human civilisation – the gestalt swarm entity known as Bugs, who at one point looked set to kill off the entire human race. These creatures swarm, and kill, and eat people alive, and can write messages in the air with their own bodies, most famously, thus:

YOU ARE PREY

But for centuries the feared Bugs were trapped behind walls of improbability or some such shit in the region of the galaxy known as Debatable Space. The place where the pirates and the outlaws and the roaring boys and girls dwelled.

And all that, rather skilfully I feel, brings me back to my original point.

Namely, that whilst I was fucking Cassady, and plotting escape from Giger, terrible shit was happening in Debatable Space. The human species was, once more, in deadly jeopardy.

And, once again, this was an unintended consequence of the overthrow of the Galactic Corporation. Because you see, once we had a democratic Solar Neighbourhood Government in place, their first act was to clean up all the outlaw planets and restore civilised values to these dens of depravity.[11] Before of course granting them full democratic and independent status.

And, as part of this pitifully well-intentioned lunatic-liberal strategy, the SNG – responding to some admittedly outrageous acts of piracy and murder – foolishly attempted to "pacify" Debatable Space.[12]

It went badly.

I read about all this three years later, when I was on Cúchulainn. And I was briefed more fully on it all much later when I – but let me get to that part of the story when I do.

I found the history of the second invasion of the Bugs

11 Broadly speaking, this is a correct analysis, if lacking in detail. – *Ed.*
12 Also true. – *Ed.*

absolutely fascinating. And I thought a lot about the people involved, and how it would have felt for them.

Imagine what it would be like, to be a Sentinel! Doomed to spend all your military career and indeed your entire fucking life trapped inside a quantum cage; unable to go home, or ever see your loved ones.

For, you see, when humanity first discovered the uniquely dangerous nature of the Bugs, the Sentinels were the soldiers who were sent in to be the line of first defence. Thousands of them in warships created a cordon of steel around the Bug Planet, while a quasi-magical[13] quantumarity cage was being created, and was then conjured into place.

Then, some bureaucrat decided to play safe. Instead of withdrawing the Sentinels, a second quantum cage was created all around them. They were left with specific instructions to attack the Bugs if they ever escaped; but the Sentinels themselves were trapped behind an invisible unbreachable screen, for all of time.

What crap. And so fucking typical of the way warriors were treated back then.

And so thousands of these Sentinels were liberated when the walls of the outer quantumarity were breached by that – accidental? inadvertent? just plain fucking stupid? – anti-matter bomb explosion. There would have been millions dwelling there if the Sentinels had bred. But that was against their code. They saw it as their role to watch and guard, not to fornicate and have pleasure. So they watched and guarded for century upon century, oblivious to the fact that their existence was utterly futile.

For you see, no human being can withstand an attack by the Bugs.[14] No human-designed weapon can kill them. No battle-armoured force fielded spaceship stands a chance against their

13 Not magical at all; Artemis just doesn't comprehend the maths that makes the quantumarity possible. Although nor, in fact, do I. – *Ed.*
14 Unverifiable, though probably true. – *Ed.*

inexorable advance. These sentient swarm monsters can be caged, but they cannot be killed.

But the Sentinels believed otherwise. They had guarded the inner quantum cage for all this time in the firm belief that they might need to one day combat an escaping Bug armada. They had built, with formidable ingenuity, plasma-based weapons which, so their scientists believed, could slay the Bug swarm. They had explored the deepest reaches of quantum theory in order to create a way of rendering the bugs "impossible". And the weapons that they created to do this were magnificent and beautiful and utterly futile.

For centuries these poor saps had convinced themselves that they were the last and only bastion that stood between civilisation and the most deadly alien species ever found.

Then, as I say, the SNG pacification fleet arrived in Debatable Space. And the whole fiasco played out.[15] A space battle raged. Pirates fired their missiles at the SNG fleet; the SNG admirals fired their missiles back. And then Captain Hawksmoor, exceeding his brief, punched the icon that launched the anti-matter missile that failed to connect with the space pirates' flagship but instead was tractor-beamed away with incredible force so that it accelerated to something close to light speed by the time the bomb blew up.

RIGHT NEXT TO THE FUCKING QUANTUMARITY CAGE.

This explosion shattered the delicate balance of space-time whatever; and the cage was breached. And that's when the Sentintels were, finally, freed.

But THEN the inner quantumarity collapsed too, rent apart by the aftershocks of the anti-matter/matter collision – and the Bugs emerged into open space for the first time since, oh, since the Earth was ruled by a vast array of different nation-states.[16]

15 For a fuller account, read a different book. Artemis is not one for military detail! – *Ed.*
16 Correct – *Ed.*

The Sentinels were ready for the challenge. They marshalled their ships. They fired their exotic weapons. They drew a line in the metaphorical sand. And then they were annihilated.

And the Bugs swept onwards, into Debatable Space itself – that motley assemblage of frontier worlds and pirate planets – and were confronted by the massed armada of the SNG pacification fleet. And that too was annihilated.[17]

But a few Sentinels remained alive – the senior officers who had been taken aboard the SNG flagship, and who watched the ghastly space war on the bridge screens of their hosts' vessel. Imagine how that felt for them! These people had spent hundreds of years preparing for the apocalypse. And then the apocalypse arrived, and they were caught napping.

For the Sentinels believed the Bugs – or the Great Swarm Mind as they are now called – to be, quite literally, the Devil. They represented the End of All Things, the veritable coming of the Last Demons. The Sentinels further believed that our One True God was the God of an infinite number of universes. Hence, His appalling neglect of our own.

And those poor Sentinels then lived to see their Devil escape from Hell. And then, to their even greater astonishment, the Sentinels saw the GSM eradicated in a blaze of fire and fury such as the universe has never seen before. And which we can only hope may never see again.

I've seen the film footage. It truly awes.[18]

You can see the few surviving ships in the SNG armada turning to face their doom, in the blackness of space. You see them slowly encroached upon by the numinous haze of swarm-mind nano-creatures. You see them fire their engines and hurtle futilely towards their barely corporeal but utterly deadly adversary.

17 For a fuller account of this, read *War in Debatable Space: The Extinction of the Great Swarm Mind* by Professor Lincoln Yevtushenko (Martial Press). – *Ed.*
18 It does indeed. – *Ed.*

And then space itself ignites. Pillars and plumes of flame shoot across the firmament, each the size of a supernova in full eruption. Rich yellows and golds and oranges spew and spill in a ceaseless frenzy. The blackness of space becomes a light too bright to perceive. All this the Sentinels saw.

What must they have thought?

I can imagine only too readily. I think they thought they saw their God. The God of All the Universes, enraged. Imagine that!

The truth was far more mundane. The Sentinels had "merely" witnessed the first known example of the flame beasts waging war. It was a war of utterly astonishing power. Afterwards, no trace or remnant remained of the Bug intelligence. And not a single planet or asteroid or fragment of space debris survived in the region once enclosed by the two quantumarities. We talk about the void of space – but space is usually full of *something,* even if it is infinitesimal, or comprised of dark matter. But in this one region, there was truly nothing.

I wasn't there when all this happened. Nor were you. We read about it in the paper, or saw it on the telly, or in our eyes via our MIs. There were no heroes that day, No warriors mightily fought the dragon and slew it. Rather, the human species was threatened with extinction by the Bugs, an enemy as coldly indifferent as waves attacking grains of sand. Or as glaciers slowly carving valleys out of a mountain range.

And then, to our ultimate chagrin, we were saved from oblivion by the intervention of a *second* implacable and all-powerful alien species – the flame beasts. We were lucky, on that occasion. The flames – immortal, all powerful, utterly strange – saved us. But we could just as easily have been unlucky. Our entire species might now be just a dim memory in the minds of a few alien sentients. And all our culture and the great achievements of our civilisation would be entirely lost and forgotten.

I find that sobering.

But as I say, I knew nothing of all this scary shit at the time it was happening.

And if I'd known, I wouldn't have cared. Because I was totally caught up in my own immediate concern: my desire for murderous vengeance. This was the ugly passion that consumed every part of my being.

And this is my point – do you see? We each think we are the hero of our own life story; but the real story is always elsewhere. So what you are and what you do is all, in the grander scheme of things, NOTHING.

Yeah, that's brought you down, hasn't it?

Anyway. Back to my revenge story. I was one hard molly-focking bitch during my time at Giger. No one can deny that. But Cassady – well. She was my weak spot.

Because of her I almost—

She made me feel – I'd never before realised that—

At times, I wanted to—

But what am I saying? The truth is, I didn't falter, nor did I flinch.

When I didn't need Cassady any more, I abandoned her. Left her to live her life without me. Which she wretchedly failed to do, and instead died sad, and lonely, and betrayed by me.

Cassady!

Hey!

I'm sorry.

Chapter 3

His Friends All Said He Was a Good Man

Hamilton Brandish was a good man, or so his friends all said.

Hamilton was a lawyer. But not the greedy grasping kind of a lawyer. No, he was a campaigning lawyer who fought for the disenfranchised and the hard-done-bys. He sued corrupt police officers on behalf of their beaten-up victims. He prosecuted negligent corporations. He won billions in compensation for those traumatised by the effects of the Corporation's evil regime.[1]

And even when he'd been a young lawyer, in those bad old Corporation days, he had never served the forces of darkness. Instead, he had been a public defender. Nobly striving to achieve justice for the innocent in the face of a corrupt legal system. A system in which bribery was so rife it was blatantly acknowledged on Plea Forms for the criminally accused, thus:

Gratuity to Court Officials paid: X for Yes, 0 for No.[2] ☐

These days, much of the work Hamilton Brandish did was pro bono, on behalf of the poor, crippled, defrauded, disabled, mutated, and otherwise pity-worthy.

1 All true, as verified by numerous news reports, transcripts of court hearings, and beaconband blogs – *Ed.*

2 This also is true. In fact, from now on I'll only footnote factual errors when there ARE some. – *Ed.*

However, slyly and clandestinely, he also managed to find time to work for a few high value clients, including several Food Councils accused of profiteering. And a number of planets in bitter dispute with the SNG over their treatment of indigenous (aka alien) life forms. And this shamelessly immoral commercial work enabled him to keep a mansion in the smartest part of Laguid, a dacha in space, and two wives.

All in all, Hamilton Brandish was a high maintenance, well-dressed, smooth-talking modern saint whose feet were made of the slitheriest of clay.

He also fancied himself as an amateur marksman. Every week he would go down to the shooting range in the Avenue Cuba, where a life-size dummy of a terrorist with guns and body armour and the obligatory red bandana would trundle slowly towards the shooter, blazing off blanks. Hamilton prided himself on his ability to get in twenty head shots and a bullet to the vulnerable crotch region in less than five seconds.

Today, the terrorist dummy had been lifted off its spindle. And when the lights came up – I was there, standing in its place.

My legs straddled the rail. I was clad in a long black Kwaal-leather jacket that brushed my knees. My hair was in a ponytail. And I was staring down at Hamilton Brandish with my blue eyes (as they now were) as he aimed his Magna XI34 projectile handgun at me, in startled disbelief.

Then I started walking along the track towards him, one leg either side of the magnetic rail, making me swagger even more than I might otherwise have done. My hands were by my side. My ponytail bobbed rhythmically against my back.

And I walked slowly at first, smiling all the while. I was careful not to spook him by making threatening moves, or revealing that I too was carrying a Magna XI34 projectile handgun in a side-holster under my jacket.

"Is there a problem?" shouted out Hamilton Brandish.

I said nothing. I just kept walking. Slowly, somewhat bow-legged, my eyes like hooks.

"I *have* paid for this session, you know," reasoned Hamilton Brandish.

I kept on walking. It wasn't far, but I really did milk that walk.

"Can you get out of my fucking way?!" shouted Hamilton Brandish.

I kept on walking.

By this point I was close enough for him to see how blue were my eyes. He didn't, of course, recognise me.

"Oh beloved, kiss me my beloved, please," I said to Hamilton Brandish in a sultry voice. I noticed, once again, how very attractive his face was. Handsome yet ripe with laughter lines. The face of a dashing god with a semi-permanent rueful half-smile.

"Anything you want me to do I will do, my darling Hamilton," I added, sharing a quotation from our mutual past, and injecting further irony with a sweetly compliant excrement-consuming smile. And he finally got the message.

He raised his gun and began firing.

He telegraphed every shot. I ducked down low, bobbed my head to the right and then the left, then walked onwards through a haze of bullets and smoke. Then I drew and fired my own weapon in a single fast move and hit the snout of his gun, which melted in his hand.

I'd sabotaged his ammunition in advance of course – do you *really* think I could dodge so many bullets at point blank range? But it was still a cool trick.

Hamilton then pulled a plasma gun from a side holster, but by then my next twelve bullets were in transit. And all of them hit their targets.

Hamilton's body exploded. His jaw drooped and yawed as a bullet entered his mouth and detonated. Large red-rimmed holes appeared in his chest and stomach and pelvis and one hand fell off its arm. I carried on walking, then stepped over the barrier, put a final bullet in Hamilton's skull, or what was left of it, and stuck my knife in his ribs. I burrowed for a while, then tugged out his heart, or as much as I could, and stuffed it in Hamilton's gaping mouth. Then I left the shooting range.

My boots were slippery now with Hamilton's blood, as I walked away. Behind me the amateur marksmen continued to blaze bullets at their replicas of Terrorists, Coppers, Zombies and Space Pirates. No one had noticed the death of Hamilton Brandish. And the sound of my killing shots had been lost, of course, in the constant low roar of gunfire, merging with the arrhythmic pounding of the nu-rock that blasted out of speakers in the floor and walls and ceiling, like a cage of sound.

Then once I was out of the door – relieved to hear the last of Johny Cock and his Fuckheads screaming, "DIE BITCH DIE!" – I clambered on to my flybike and soared away. The air was rich in hog fat and the tang of wind-dried-chicken snacks from the stalls below. My heart was pounding. I wanted to cry, though I knew that would not have been appropriate at such a moment of remorseless nemesis.

Instead, I looped the loop, savouring the sight beneath me of broad city streets and coiling alleyways, shacks and stalls and red-brick mansions and towering fabricator pyramids of Laguid, capital city of Cúchulainn. A city which for many years had been my home, and then had been my prison.

Hamilton Brandish had been a good man, or so his friends all thought. And that's what the obituaries would say too.

But I knew different.

Jonathan Cramer had a talent for love.

His wife loved him, and not because of his looks – for he was average in appearance, chubby, and cheerful in a way that precludes mystique. But he was also charismatic, and funny, and very gentle. Women felt safe with Jonathan; he invited their friendship, not their lust.

And his kids loved him because he was a great dad; he gave them money, did funny voices and even the occasional idiotic walk, and never told them off. He also played football with them in the park, and never seemed to let them win, even when he did.

I knew all this because I'd had him under surveillance for two months, and I knew *everything* about him.

His brothers and sisters and numerous cousins loved Jonathan because he was kind and entertaining, and always organised the family get-togethers.

And he was blessed with more best friends than anyone you could name; and *they* all loved him because he was generous and loyal and always knew what to say when they were feeling blue.

Hell, even *I* had loved him once.

But my love for Jonathan was not, let me be clear about this, *true* love. Not love as the poets know it. Not love at all in fact – not when you have a pain nodule in your brain that your lover can stimulate with a single remote control button. Or when you are beaten and forced to endure . . . stuff, terrible stuff, three times a day and every day by a man who then has the nerve to claim he adores you, and that you are his reason for being alive.

What the fuck, do I have to draw a fucking *diagram*?

Jonathan was a dealer in brain-chip hook-ups, and his products had killed an awful lot of people over the years. Which was not his fault! Or so he always claimed. If addicts want to abuse a recreational aid, there's nothing you can do about it – that's what he argued, cogently and persuasively, in numerous articles published on websites owned by him.

Jonathan had patented his own design of brain-chip hook-up which he called the Armchair Universe. It allowed families to sit around travelling the stars or exploring alien planets. But of course the Armchair Universe was even better suited to those who wished to spend their days having virtual sex with porn stars, or vicariously raping and murdering innocents. A whole industry had grown up tasked with providing the raw sensual data necessary to create these virtual experiences. Actors won't suffice, you see – you need to inflict actual atrocity and/or death upon your hapless victims, in order to obtain sufficiently rich and authentic emotional resonances.

None of this is new. Evil people have always lapped up the fear of their victims. That's how the vampire legend was born. Check out the life story of Vlad Dracul Tepes, and you'll see why they called him The Impaler.[3] That bastard used to – no, I won't even repeat it.

Modern technology, however – bear with me, I'm going to bang on about this, it's a favourite theme of mine – carries with it a terrible consequence. It normalises evil. It makes it *commonplace*. How many of you own an Armchair Universe? Hmm? You, you, you – most of you, am I right? And I'm guessing you are aware that although *you* only use this technology for educational and informative purposes, with maybe the occasional bit of high-end erotica thrown in – it can be also used for "bad stuff".

Yet you still buy the latest AU upgrades. You probably have the Family Adventure sims with the Cuddly Dinosaur Experience, and the cute Alien Photography Safari. And maybe even, from time to time, you take a walk on the wild side while your wife is on holiday, or your husband is on a business trip? Hmm? And you spend a wicked hour or so savouring a real-life shoot-'em-up, or an alien-fucker-killing blood-fest, or a *non*-consensual sex scene, involving real sex, and real tears? And do you know what?

You shouldn't be doing it.

IT IS NOT FUCKING NORMAL.

Jonathan had bodyguards. and his bodyguards were all his close personal friends. Yeah, he inspired *that* kind of intimacy even with doltish muscle-bound killers. He always knew their names, and asked the right questions – like "How's your baby

3 See *The Real Dracula* by Diablo Jonquil (Way Out of Orbit Books). – *Ed.*

daughter?" "Hey, it's your birthday today isn't it?" And in consequence, they were devoted to him. These guys and girls were trained and indoctrinated to take the bullet for their principal, whoever that might be. But for Jonathan they'd take the bullet, shit it out their arse, then shoot themselves with it again.

Infiltrating an organisation like that was hard.

However, I did it.

I got close to him, and the mollyfocker died.

You may notice I've skipped a few stages in the story here – you'll see why in a moment – but let me cut to the *dénouement*. I killed the evil bastard. I took my revenge for all the things he had done to me, and for actually *recording* my pain and distress. (Hey, you didn't know I was an AU movie star did you? But you don't actually see me in those shows, you just inhabited my fucking *agony*.

Don't get me started . . .)

For all of these crimes against humanity and against me, I butchered Jonathan Cramer in the middle of the night, in his own hotel room. And I laughed as I watched him die.

But, you may ask, how did I manage to sneak past Jonathan's bodyguards? How could I get close to a man so heavily protected that bacteria were scanned for concealed weaponry before they entered his mouth?

Simple.

First, I bugged Jonathan's MI when he was booking an extreme-sex whore to come to his room and pleasure him.

Lucky guess, huh? Who'd have thought he'd want to do *that*?!

And then I hacked the company's computer to replicate the ID disc of the girl they were sending.

Then, when the girl – Lara was her name – turned up in a fly-taxi, I intercepted her. Lara was a real beauty, I have to tell you that. She had perfect cheek bones and blazing eyes, and she dressed with all the understated elegance of an Egyptian queen bound for her sarcophagus. And I stopped her before she could enter the hotel, and offered her a deal she couldn't refuse. A shit-load of money, and a ticket off this godsforsaken planet.

Bear in mind that those tickets are incredibly hard to get. You need a lot of money (which I have, after a life of crime I haven't had time to recount).[4] And you also, most vitally, need a signed and authenticated letter of transit from the Laguid Chief of Police. Which I had been able to expertly forge using the security codes still in the brain chip of the *previous* Chief of Police.

Namely Robbie Ferguson, who you will recall I had slain on Giger's Moon. Yeah, there *was* a reason for that whole cutting-the-skull-open thing.

So I made my pitch, and Lara was shocked. And clearly afraid, because she had a contract with her agency, and those guys are fucking killers. And, understandably cautious, since she didn't know who the fuck *I* was.

And so she said no.

Damn!

So I told her that's fine, off you go then. Gritting my teeth, and kicking myself on the collapse of my great strategy.

And yeah I know, I could of course have just *killed* her, and taken her ID. But I didn't really want to do that.

Call me soft, see if I care!

You see I liked Lara. She was a nice girl, I'd vouch for that. I've known a lot of girls like Lara, you can tell the good ones right off.

However – fortunately for my evil plan – Lara thought twice. And she told me she would leave, but only if I gave her *five* tickets off the planet. For her, her boyfriend, her parents, and her best friend Jillian.

4 Tantalising! I know nothing of all this. – *Ed.*

I'd anticipated this, and had the tickets and LOTs ready in all those names.

She kissed me on the cheek, both cheeks in fact, before she got back in the flytaxi and left for her new life. I guess I'd made her day.

Having done all this – and still feeling the touch of Lara's eternal gratitude on my cheeks – I made my way to Jonathan's room and showed my ID and job docket to his bodyguards.

They then checked with the escort agency who confirmed my identity, based on seeing my image on their MIs, via a security guard's camera-eyes. But they didn't see me, they saw *her*. Another of my cute tricks.

And then I went inside the room.

And I locked the door behind me.

And I fixed Jonathan with my fiercest stare.

We were in his luxury suite, no bodyguards, just me and him. The pad was *très* cool, with stucco pillars in the Composite style, and a planetarium-type roof with fake stars. And an in-room splash pool flanked with life-size nude statues cast in eerily warm bronze. And a draught soda dispenser shaped like a phallus, which I just *adored* – and a few other bespoke touches.

Namely, the bed. Fully equipped with chains and shackles. A bird-cage large enough to take three writhing dancers. And hammocks dangling from the ceiling; and I don't mean the ones you sleep in.

Jonathan was almost salivating with joy at the sight of my severe look, tightly-bunned hair, and shiny black leather raincoat that hinted at nudity beneath.

Then I took my coat off to reveal that my body was in fact clad in a skin-tight leather cat-suit that gripped as tight as talons. It was uncomfortable as fuck, but it did the job. It put *Jonathan at his ease*. It disabled his "civilised" settings. And hence, it turned him into the slavering animal he really was.

And then I opened up my leather Bag of Pain, emblazoned

with silver studs and bosses – it weighed a fucking ton – and I handed Jonathan my whip with the barbed wire strands.

Then I offered, with a sweet little smile, to let him use it on me. And I licked my lips and smiled an even sweeter little smile, and told him he was a "very naughty boy". And the look of excitement in his eyes told me all I needed to know about Jonathan. He hadn't changed at all.

And then, when he came at me with the whip in his hand and hate in his eyes, I killed the bastard.

They called it a reign of terror, and the press went wild for it. They even gave me a nickname.

The Heartstealer.

Over the space of seven months, dozens of "innocent" citizens of Laguid were gunned down or stabbed or otherwise slain by the Heartstealer. And the connecting factor – look, I wasn't going to be *subtle* about it – was that all the victims had their hearts cut out, then inserted into their open mouths.

Some journalists speculated that the killer was a woman who had once had her heart stolen then broken by a man.

Ha! I *knew* they'd say that!

There was in fact a reason, a much darker reason, for the heart motif, but I won't tell you what it is. It's – not good, and involves ritual acts of various kinds. Suffice to say: this was my coded message to Daxox and all his associates that someone who knew what evil they had done was coming to get them.

But they didn't, not at first, know *who*. Because a great many people had just as much reason as I did to take revenge using the ripped-out heart as their symbol.

I murdered six people in that first week. And then I carried on killing. I shot them. Garrotted them. Impaled them on swords. One time I was forced to break my MO and shoot my victim with a long-distance high-velocity projectile rifle. He was stepping out of his armoured car into the armoured tunnel that led to his armoured office. And so I fired a bullet at the door of his car and killed him with the ricochet. (Later, however, I broke into the mortuary. And *that's* when I ripped the heart out and put it in his mouth. Well, you know, it's important to be *consistent*.)

By week two, I was finding it harder and harder to make the hits. But I persevered, and prevailed. I had many identities, and many homes. Hotel rooms, alleys, deserted fabricator buildings, unused office blocks. I never slept in the same place two nights in a row, and I never had the same hair colour two days running. My brain chip and eyeball-sensors were attuned to detect the presence of police surveillance teams. And I was confident that I was never followed, for my Rebus chip was deeply entangled in the inner workings of Magog, the Laguid QRC. So I was able to follow the police investigation in the minutest detail. And as a consequence, I was ahead of them every step of the way.

Getting on the planet in the first place – that was the hardest part.

Because, of course, the Cúchulainn Clanning was at this time an ally of the SNG government and hence at war with many of the other Clannings. And so entry to the system was strictly controlled. (In the old days, by contrast, it was very easy to enter – but extremely hard to get out again.)

And my name of course was on high on the Clan's Most Wanted list, after I'd fled their custody some years before, killing several people as I went. That's why I had changed my appearance, and my identity, right at the very start of this mission of vengeance.

But by the time I arrived in the Cúchulainn system I had ID

that identified me as Evelyn Walker, an associate and friend of Robbie Ferguson, former Chief of Police and national hero. I knew everything about the real Evelyn, because I had forged her ID based on Robbie's datafiles on her. And I was also able to use Robbie's detailed memories of the planet's security codes to fast-track my way through. I passed through eighty-four security checks, including a strip search, without so much as a raised eyebrow.

Those added up to several other reasons why I took the brain chip from Robbie Ferguson. It held the passcodes to every police database, and detailed memories about who to bribe and how much, and how to circumvent the myriad police surveillance systems. Later on, I carried his brain chip around inside my bag, hooked to a palm computer; whenever I needed help, I asked Robbie Ferguson.

It was Robbie Ferguson who got me back into the city I had once fled in abject fear. And it was Robbie who helped me to stay one step ahead of the police for so long.

Thanks, Robbie!

It was strange to be back here in Laguid.

The streets of Cúchulainn's sprawling, massive, appallingly polluted capital city had the eerie allure of the familiar yet half-forgotten. My heart always soared when the factory bells tolled. I thrilled to the sounds of water lapping against the metal stilts on which the canal-side houses jauntily perched. I loved the stench of spices and of animals, both Earthian and genetically modified alien, roasting on spits in the thronging street markets. I loved the energy of the locals, their lilting accent, their fondness for irascible barter.

When the first colonists arrived, they had terraformed this bleak and lifeless planet until it became a verdant Eden. Then they fucked it up. The air is now thick with pollutants. The skies are black with clouds spewed out of thick cooling towers. It's hard to tell one species of bird from another for they are all coated in soot.

It may be the ugliest planet in the universe.

Hamilton Brandish had powerful friends in the police department – including the Police Commissioner himself, Felix Denison.

And oh, I remembered Felix well. He once promised he'd help me escape from my – well, from the place where I had been trapped. It proved to be a lie. A lie that broke my heart.

Felix Denison was a big man with a ginger moustache and vast sideburns that defied fashion and indeed hygiene. He also had a twinkle in his eye that belied his brutal nature.

He had a reputation for "telling it straight". Which meant that when he lied, he did so boldly and fearlessly.

And he was telling it straight tonight, as he made his public press statement about the serial killer terror in Laguid. His voice boomed, his carefully scrubbed whiskers quivered with emotion. And his blue eyes looked right into the news cameras, and thus into the souls of his listeners.

I listened to his crap with half an ear. The rest of my attention was focused on the crowd, the entrances and exits, the guards and all other potential sources of danger, and on my inner core. That place I go to in order to achieve a zen-like state of tranquillity, just before I embark upon appalling slaughter.

"—this evil beast!" roared Denison, "is a threat to our civilisation and—"

Bastard, I thought to myself.

"—unspeakable butchery, that cannot be—"

Bastard.

"—we'll find this savage immoral blood-drenched killer and lock him or her up and then we'll—"

Bastard!

I should point out that while I'd been doing my bloody work – fifteen dead so far – a sniper in the East Quarter Fabricator District had killed forty-three factory and mine workers – out of whim, malice or sheer petty class hatred, no one knew for sure. Yet there was no news coverage of *these* atrocities. Denison's police officers barely took the trouble to investigate them. That's because the victims were manual workers, the people whose toil and sweat held this society together. So, hey, who gave a fuck?

Instead, all the resources and energy of this highly funded and magnificently well-trained police force went into finding the Heartstealer. The killer of *respectable* citizens, who threatened the cosy hegemony of this planet.

And they weren't doing so well. There were no clues, no useful witness evidence, no DNA traces, no data trail. Nada. The police theorised openly that I was "pretty damned lucky".

But hey, you make your own luck, that's what I always say. And one of the secrets of my success – apart from the fact I had the brain of the ex-Chief of Police in my bag, and an ability to access the Cúchulainn QRC and hence generate fake IDs – is that I knew how to change my appearance and body language. As I was doing today – for I was there at the press conference as the red-haired swotty girl from the *Laguid Metropolitan News.* The geeky one with the awkward way of standing with hands poised, as if dancing on ice; and who peered at the world through thick eyeglasses, betraying her as too poor to buy eye-rejuve.

No one gave me a second glance. I blended in perfectly with the press pack that avidly followed Denison's every word, lusting for new scandal.

"Twelve men and three women dead," continued Denison, in his thunderous voice that had once seemed so appealing to me. "All the victims were citizens of irreproachable character. This heinous killer—" I shot him with a dart from my camera and Denison blinked.

"This heine, hen, evil, uh, killer," he continued, and stopped, and stared into space.

Ten seconds later he went into spasm and died of a heart attack on the podium.

The whole crowed of journos were hushed with horror and regret for, well at a guess I'd say, for all of .00001 seconds. Then they became vultures with cameras taking photos of the death throes of their much-mocked but undeniably charismatic Police Commissioner.

An autopsy later confirmed that Denison's bloodstream was a suppurating pool of toxins. He'd been shot with a darted capsule filled with cyanide, and a cocktail of other goodies I had carefully prepared.

Felix Denison and Hamilton Brandish, let me remind you, or rather tell you for the first time, had been friends. Good friends. And they had shared *everything.*

From that moment on the street cops were authorised to shoot to kill anyone they suspected of being the Heartstealer.

But who could they shoot? My identity, as I say, changed daily. I left no forensic clues. I was a rabid fox in their fucking chicken coop but there was nothing they could do about it.

And there was no pattern or indeed rhyme nor reason to the murders – or so the news reports said. All the victims were upstanding members of the community! Hence, these were just random killings by a motivelessly malignant psycho – that was the consensus view.

But after a while – after many deaths – a pattern started to emerge.

Because as well as the heart imagery, designed to mock and goad all those of my intended victims who were bonded by certain obscure rituals, I was leaving hidden clues. Clues that could only be read by those who knew how.[5] These clues took the form of numbers painted in blood near the scene of each crime; which when multiplied by the numbers in the victim's date of birth (excluding the year) related to the word of that number in my favourite novel, *Dawn Never Comes* by Archie Simpson II; and the first letters of each of these words spelled out my mocking message.

To crack the code, you had to know there *was* a code, and you had to know that *I* was the killer. And you also had to know what my favourite book is, and which edition I prefer to read it in. And no one, of course, could possibly know all that!

Except, that is, for one man: Daxox.

The message? It was pretty puerile, I'm afraid. It said:

THISISTHEREVENGEOFARTEMISFUCKYOU-YOUMOTHERFUCKERSBETRAYEROFALLTHATSGOOD

Seventy characters in all, which meant I was planning to kill seventy of the aforesaid motherfuckers, including Daxox himself. And Baron Lowman too – he was the second "R" in MOTHERFUCKERS. But as you'll see, I never got as far as Daxox. That's because – sorry, I'm getting ahead of myself.

The "A" in ARTEMIS was a little old lady who ran a boarding house in East Seven Laguid. Her name was Mary. She used to run a kind of boarding house somewhere else in Laguid, in the old days. That was where I had "lodged" for so many years, and back then Mary had been renowned for her strictness.

I broke into Mary's bedroom and woke her up and confronted her with a litany of her sins. She burst into tears. She was old,

5 Daxox was an amateur cryptologist; otherwise this would have been a futile exercise. – *Ed.*

really old, too old for rejuve which means over a thousand years old. And a sweet-looking lady. I took pity on the poor old dame, and decided to spare her; but she spoiled it by shooting me in the back as I started to climb out the window.

The bullet went through my body armour and lodged in my heart. I stopped breathing. I thought for a moment I was going to have a stroke. So I turned and shot Mary in the head before she could fire a second projectile bullet and then, what the hell, I took out her heart and stuck it in her mouth. Old does not mean innocent. She was one mean bitch.

Then I stripped off my body armour and injected myself with adrenalin to restart my heart. And later on I rejuved the entry wound and glued the skin together. I left the bullet inside me. I have quite a few bullets inside my body, in fact. My cells and organs seem to grow quite happily around them.

The "M" of MOTHERFUCKERS was Baron Lowman's bodyguard, Charlie. Charlie had been a brute. I picked him up in a nightclub and let him paw me a little in the flying taxi on the way back to his place. Then when we got into his apartment, I killed him with my bare hands. It was a fair fight, though I guess it might have been even fairer if he hadn't drunk three bottles of rum and swallowed six sky-pills first. When I took his heart out, I swear it smelled of booze.

The "F" in FUCK was— I don't need to go on, do I? It was a bloodbath. I'm not proud of it. But I had to do it. And every one of those people, especially the ones in FUCK and MOTHER-FUCKER, deserved to die, and deserved to know *why* they were dying.

Okay, now let me tell you about Daxox.

He was the first man I ever loved. Yeah, go on, laugh.

This is how I met him:

After I left Rebus – the library, my father, my whole way of life – I ended up on a planet called Gullyfoyle. Nice planet, apart from the fact it had rain like pus. (It didn't drip down your body, it *crawled* down . . .) After a series of unfortunate incidents, I got a job in a bar; and before long I was dying of boredom. I was only eighteen, you see. And I wanted excitement. Adventure. Romance! Instead, I was serving over-priced drinks to drunk tourists and getting propositioned ten times a night by ghastly wankers of all three sexes.

Fuck this, I thought.

And then a party of aristos arrived. From one of the fake-medieval planets, Illyria or Arcadia, or maybe Tolkien. I can't actually remember which. Never mind, it doesn't matter. Or maybe it was— No, fuck, move on Artemis. Let's say it was Illyria.

"Illyria" was one of the settler planets granted some degree of autonomy by the Corporation. The Illyrians provided weapons and soldiers for the Cheo's endless wars, and, in return, they were left pretty much alone. No doppelgängers, no oppression, no ritual massacres.

The Illyrians lived in castles, rode horses, kept prisoners in dungeons, all that shit. Role-playing on a planetary scale. They even genetically engineered dragons and unicorns. And to sustain this dream-existence, they built fabricators the size of planets and put them in orbit around their pretty green planet, and created energy sails so vast they darkened their own sun. As a result, though they were clearly mad, they were also rich. Very rich.

So, as I say, I was serving cocktails to these lordly bastards in their jerkins and hoses and billowing gowns, and then I saw it; the jewel; and my heart soared.

The body wearing the aforesaid jewel was possessed by a dark-haired marbled-skinned and astonishingly beautiful Illyrian (?) woman. When I first saw her, in that pricey Gullyfoyle bar, she was wearing an ornately brocaded and hooped dress with a *décolletage* that would shock all of polite society, if such a thing existed any more. This wench's skin, I further noticed, was so pale that even a faint blush made her face go as crimson as the warning lights on a pursuing cop car. Her eyes however were blank and staring.

And then, as her partner ordered yet another round of elaborate cocktails with names like Supernova and Black Hole of Hell, I saw, around her neck, a gold choker with a white ruby boss, with the aforementioned jewel inset. And I wanted it, so badly. I was possessed with lust. Or maybe it was just greed. But I'd never seen such a—

Anyway, cutting to the heist: It was a shaloyiss – a kind of pearl with the lustre of a diamond.[6] It had a radiance that made my emotions hum. And after consulting my Rebus chip, I knew this to be an antique gem that had been carved by hand, not by lasers, dating all the way back to the days of the Lentarr jewel traders.

That night I came into her room where she – the marble-skinned dead-eyed bitch – slept.

What's that – why do I call her "bitch"?

Look, guys, I'm not slagging off this Illyrian broad for no reason! Or out of petty jealousy, because she was richer and more privileged and considerably more beautiful than I was or am.

No! That's not it. The fact is, earlier that evening I'd seen this evil ginch beat a waiter senseless with a metal stave for not bowing to her before serving the *hors d'oeuvres*. All part of the courtly etiquette of these monstrously wicked anachronists.

Anyway:

I moved, as I always do when I'm stealing stuff, without noise, and without breathing. The jewel was in the safe, as I knew it would be. I knew how to break the combination too. She'd used her own code, but you can turn it back to factory

6 Only to be found in the seas of the planet of Kaos. – *Ed.*

default with a simple cyberspace nudge, if you know how, which I do.

I took the jewel and fled on a colony boat to Cúchulainn, and tried to sell it on the black market there. That wasn't a great success. After several rebuffs, I finally met a fence in a bar who had a big smile and a charming manner and shark's teeth (the affectation *à la mode* at that time). Shark Teeth was delighted at the size of the jewel and offered to transfer a million scudos to my pseudonymous account. But instead of swiftly concluding the deal as he should have done, he chatted and chatted. And eventually I smelled a rat and walked out.

Two goons stopped me before I reached the door. One of them sprayed paralysing gas in my face, the other shot a taser at my body. Then both came at me with electric clubs.

The taser didn't work, because I was wearing my electrosheath beneath my T-shirt and jeans. The gas caught me full on but I was already holding my breath. The electric clubs both missed, as I ducked like a dervish and came up punching and kicking.

I killed them both and returned into the back room and removed the fence's eyes. Then I walked back to my hotel.

And when I got back to my room he was there, waiting for me.

Daxox.

"Nice work," he observed, in the friendliest of tones.

"Thank you."

"You've cost me a fortune tonight."

"How so?"

"Rejuve. Resurrection. New eyes. It all costs."

"Serves you right, for hiring such fucking useless bludgers," I said nastily.

He frowned. He clearly resented my attitude.

"Those were my best men you killed," he said affably, like a man who was only pretending to be annoyed.

"They weren't so tough."

He shrugged, acknowledging my point. He waited patiently, a half-smile on his lips.

I wondered how he'd got in without triggering the security pins I'd inserted in the door and the corridor walls outside my room. I also wondered if there was anyone else – in particular, hordes of gangsters with guns – waiting close at hand. In the bathroom, maybe? Or in the next room? And most of all, I wondered why I wasn't more afraid.

I'd never met Daxox before. But despite the circumstances, I found there was something oddly comforting about his presence. He was one of those people who puts you at your ease. Even though you know he's planning to kill and/or eviscerate you.

It's a knack, I guess.

"We would like to purchase the jewel after all," Daxox eventually said, almost kindly.

"Transfer the money. When it's cleared, I'll come and see you with the jewel."

"How do I know you won't cheat me?" His face was a *moue* of anticipatory disappointment.

"I just might fucking do that."

He smiled.

"I like your candour."

"Fuck off. Do we have a deal or not?"

"We have a deal," said Daxox.

And he was, amazingly, as good as his word. The money was transferred. I delivered the jewel to him. There was no double-cross. I found no tracers on the bank account. No hitguys turned up at my apartment, though I was changing apartments hourly by that time. I was home free.

A week later I walked into Daxox's club.

A singer was on stage, crooning a ballad. She was good. The music was bluesy, soporific. There were drugs in the air, mood-enhancers, mild aphrodisiacs. I could also smell perfume, thick and flowery. The kind I now associate with strippers and cross-gender artistes, since it was the strippers and the queens and the princes in Daxox's club who loved to use that shit. Daxox himself was sitting in the corner table, surrounded by augmented guards. I was wearing a frock.

Yeah, get that! I *never* wore a frock, back then. I don't know what the fuck I was thinking of. It was bright blue. My arms and cleavage were bare, and lightly dusted to make them sparkle. My gun was in my handbag. My knives were strapped to my hips, under the flowing skirt. I'd rehearsed a few bending-over-and-grabbing-at-my-arse knife-drawing manoeuvres, just in case.

I sauntered across, sat down next to him, and took a sip of his bourbon. It was the real McCoy, hand-distilled. It slid down like velvet, if you've ever eaten velvet, which I guess you never have, nor indeed, ever should. Fuck! What I mean is, it was good stuff.

That night we stayed up talking till the early hours. We slept together, but not in a sexual way. A week later, we were lovers.

Picture this: shy librarian's daughter becomes the moll of the most dangerous gangster on Cúchulainn.

And I *was* shy. Really shy. I was raised by my father, and *his* mother, and *her* two brothers. All archivists on Rebus, the planet so dull that no one even makes jokes about it.

My gran Margarita – I'm digressing again – was a powerful personality. She dominated and bullied the entire family, including, but not especially, me. Her two brothers, my Great Uncle Mike and my Great Uncle Dougall, were treated like indentured slaves in a plantation. They were at Margarita's beck and call. And from the moment I was born, I was welcomed as a new domestic servant in the making. Once I was out of nappies, pretty much, she put me to work. Cooking. Tidying. Sorting. I catalogued all my grandmother's dresses. I was five when I started that job; nine when I finished. She had a lot of dresses; they brought back for her memories of other times, and other lovers. In that happy period before she married her lacklustre no-account librarian husband Mitchell, aka my grandfather.

I never met him. Gran had exiled Mitchell for insubordination and general bad attitude when little John McIvor, aka my dad, was six years old. Granddad now lived, so my investigations eventually revealed, in a little town called Alexandria, the other side of Rebus. Even his library ticket was revoked, so he wasn't able to use his Rebus chip to access archival material. Which, for these guys, is a living hell.

Children weren't illegal on Rebus. they just weren't that common. So my childhood was spent in the company of dour, grey-faced anally-retentive grown-ups. I had no kid friends when I was a kid. I had only one teenager friend when I was a teenager, and he didn't stay for long. Then I fled to Gullyfoyle; and eventually went to work in the bar.

And that's where I learned to be *me*. I copied what the other women wore – not the lah-di-dahs who came in to the bar, but the sexy funky local women I saw on the street and in clubs. The flamboyant girls who strutted the streets looking for action. I learned to swear as they swore, using seventeenth- and eighteenth-century gutterslang that was now coming back into fashion in this sector of the humanverse. I practised the art of chit-chat and "hanging out". Because on Rebus, there was none of that. Every conversation had to have a purpose – namely the advancement of knowledge. No one ever, like, just talked.

So on Gullyfoyle, I learned to be different – which meant, of course, the same as the women I most admired. The hard bitches, the ex-mercenaries, the gangsters. I walked like a warrior. I dressed like a slut. I swore like a Soldier. And I made small talk like, well, like an ordinary human being.

But it was all façade. I was pretending to be someone. I was a concocted me.

But in my heart, I was always the shy librarian's daughter.

A few weeks after we became lovers, Daxox asked me to kill a man, and I did.

I guessed that this request was some kind of initiation test. And I didn't want to fail. I didn't want to be seen to be *unworthy*.

I'll tell you who the guy was. His name was Donnie Miro. He owed money to a Clannite loan shark. He was a gambler and a sex addict. He also had three children and a loving wife called, no, that name's gone, I forgot to save to chip, *again*.[7] Maybe accidentally on purpose?

Owing money to gangsters was no stigma back then, of course. It was just the way people lived their lives, and had been doing for decades. The Clan, after all, *were* the banking system. They were the government. They were the police. And they were the only source of actual income, since the Corporation had a zero salary policy. On the assumption that once they'd slaved most of their working day on Corporation business, the colonists could somehow scrounge or steal enough to actually eat, and pay their bills.

That was the system. The Corporation owned everything, and contributed nothing. But the Clan stole from them, and used the proceeds of crime to run a parallel society.

So being in debt was no big deal. After all, Donnie could

7 It was Marlene Beverley Miro, birth name Saundersfoot. – *Ed.*

easily have paid Daxox back in kind, by working pro bono for the Clan as an actor in porn films, for instance. Or as a drug dealer or mule, or a burglar, or an enforcer, or some other such shit. But no, Donnie was an idealist. He thought the Clan were corrupt and as great an evil as the Corporation themselves. And he said so, shooting his mouth off fearlessly in bars and strip clubs. Donnie thought he was entitled to freedom; even though every single part of him from his arsehole to the hair on his head was owned by the Clan.

And Daxox, of course – did I mention this? – was a Clan *quintino* when I met him.

So Donnie had to die. I did some research before I killed him, and came to the conclusion that this man was an arrogant, bombastic fuck up. He thought of himself as an idealist and a democrat, but in his spare time he cheated on his wife and didn't love his kids and slapped prostitutes around to get his kicks. But even so, he didn't deserve to die.

I followed him home, after he'd been drinking and whoring. I wore shoes with hard heels so he'd hear the tapping of my footsteps behind him. I followed him down the dimly lit alleys of Gomorrah, the club district. I watched him hailing skytaxis, waving his arm and tottering around like a drunk, because he *was* drunk. And when he fell over and passed out, I picked him up and carried him to the river and bathed his face until he woke up. And when he woke he smiled up at me and I said, "Payback Donnie."

Then I killed him. A hammer-fist strike to the forehead. His skull caved in instantly. I cut off his middle fingers, so that when the body was found, it would be evident he had failed the test of loyalty to the Clan.

And I felt nothing. No remorse. No compassion.

Daxox was pleased.

Remember, these were dark times. The Corporation ruled supreme. Violence was everywhere.

Do you remember? Of course you do.

But do you know anything about what it was like *before* those days? Of course you don't. Why would you?

Daxox was one of the cleverest men I'd ever met. But he'd never heard of Abraham Lincoln. Or John F. Kennedy. Or Adolf Hitler, or Josef Stalin, or Chairman Mao, or Genghis Khan, or the Roman Empire, or the Italian Renaissance. These subjects hadn't been taught at school for – well, for who knows how many years. Of course, all the data about these subjects is carefully archived. It's available to view in your brainchip, or in the QRCs, if you bother to look. But no one bothers. For most people, history begins in the year Peter Smith invaded Planet Earth. The rest dustily resides on wooden shelves, metaphorically and literally. (Remember I come from Rebus, where they have *real books*.)

But I knew it all.

I'd charted a path through human history from barbarism to civilisation to anarchy to civilisation, to barbarism once more. I'd seen the ebbs and flows. I'd absorbed the myriad philosophies, including the quaintly idealistic liberal egalitarianism of the twentieth and twenty-first centuries. The period when "human rights" developed as a guiding moral concept, and people actually believed the world might become a better and a fairer place. Seems totally fucking unlikely, doesn't it? But it's true, that's what the poor saps thought.

So I knew about all these historical concepts. I understood what morality was. And I had, I actually did have, a moral code. I just chose not to use it.

And I knew too that never, not ever, in the whole course of human history, had the human spirit been so deformed and mutated as it was in the days of the Galactic Corporation. It all went on for so fucking *long* you see. Over so many planets. Involving so many lives. Earthian Gamers. Doppelgänger addicts. Blood-crazed warriors. Brainwashed Soldiers. In other times, these would have been the scum of society. Instead, they were the ruling élite.

This is me ranting, by the way. I do that from time to time.

My point is: I was a killing machine. But I was no worse than anyone else.

Here's some of the stuff I used to do:

I was a bodyguard. Daxox had enemies, plenty of them, and I monitored his personal security. I identified significant threats, aka nutjobs out to kill him, and I killed them first. Without warning.

Here's me arriving at the front door of Christian, an evangelical nutjob convinced that Daxox was the devil incarnate. I'm dressed like a priest of the New Light – you know, black robes, a black hood, bloodshot eyes. Christian greets me with delight, recognising a kindred spirit.

"May our God be with you," he says, and I nod and bow and God be with you him back.

Then a moment later, I take out my projectile gun and shoot an exploding bullet into his chest. It's low velocity, fast enough to punch a hole through his ribs then lodge in his abdominal cavity.

"Newsflash: there is no God," I tell him, and his face loses its optimistic glow.

Then his body blows up.

The explosion rips his carcass apart. He dies with a look of bafflement on his face. My black robes turn crimson.

Then I slip off the robe and leap on to the getaway flybike. I'll always remember Christian. His fountain of blood and gore.

And here's me— No, there are too many. Just too many. Daxox trusted me, because I was a methodical researcher, skilled at identifying behaviour patterns and threat vectors. And he liked it when I came back soaked in blood and elated. And, after almost every hit, we would fuck on the white sheets of his bed.

Other stuff I did: riding shotgun, on armed robbery raids.

Fighting in no-blows-barred wrestling bouts against enforcers from other mobs. That was a betting scam. No one ever thought I could win, but I always did. And—

And so it goes on. Eight years in all, eight years in which I grew from a girl into a woman. Eight years in which I killed hundreds of fellow human beings. And gambled. And beat up or intimidated shitbags. And revelled in massacres and blood-baths.

That's how I was back then, in the golden days of the Corporation regime. Gangster. Killer. *Quintino*'s moll. An all too willing member of the criminal society that enforced the status quo on a Corporation-owned planet.

The shy librarian's daughter turned into ice-cold blood-crazed killer.

And I loved it. Every moment of it.

What did I see in him? Daxox, I mean.

Well, it wasn't his looks. He had a face like a frog, and a physique to match. He was ugly and squat in a universe where all men looked like Greek gods. But all that was appealing to me. Because it meant he looked *real.*

Plus he was funny. A great sense of humour. What can I say? I like that in a man.

He told me about his father, who had been a factory worker in one of the vast vehicle fabricator plants in the wilderness territories to the north-east of Laguid. Daxox's dad would get up to work at 4 am. And he would spend twelve hours a day, six days a week monitoring the safe functioning of robot-controlled machinery, with not even a break for lunch, and a catheter in lieu of a toilet break. Then he would return home exhausted to an equally weary wife and five needy children.

Every Saturday morning, Daxox explained, the local Clan

cammorista would come by to receive his dues. In the form of sleek flybikes and space-faring flying cars, stolen by Daxox's father from the fabricator plant. The penalty for pilfering was death, but workers weren't given a choice about this. If they did not steal, they would die. If they stole and were caught, they would die. It was a gamble either way.

The Clan *cammorista* was, so Daxox told me, a formidable and brutal man. As well as being a lecher and a bully. One time he was abusive to Daxox's mother and instructed her to give him a blowjob in front of her children. Daxox was only ten years old at the time, and he said, "What's a blowjob?" And the gangster laughed, and explained.

And Daxox's father wept. And Daxox's mother went down upon her knees to perform the wretched deed, whilst imploring everyone in her family to calm down and be sensible.

At which moment, enraged, ten-year-old Daxox killed the *cammorista*. With a silver sabre manufactured in his father's own factory. That's how legends are born. That's how Daxox joined the Clan.

From then on, his parents were protected from bullying Clannites. There was always food on the table, and Daxox and his brothers and sisters were always well and fashionably dressed. They even had a family flycar, with enough free fuel to circumnavigate the globe. His mother was treated like a queen by Clannites who met her. His father, however, was caught pilfering and was executed. That was how it went.

In those days, Daxox told me, the gangs on Cúchulainn were fragmented, unable to coalesce into unity as the Clannites had done on other settler planets. But by the time Daxox was eighteen, the *capobastone* Julian Silver had forged a planet-wide alliance of killers, psychopaths and shake-down artists. And Silver was of course in regular touch with the Clannites on other planets in the Solar Neighbourhood. They formed a tightly-knit virtual community. And many of the codes and symbols of the Clan were created in those early years.

Daxox himself claims to have designed the dragon tattoo that reveals a Clannite to be a blooded killer with twenty murders committed and authenticated. And, in due course, he worked his way up the hierarchy. From *piccioto*, to *cammorista*, then *santista*, then *vangelista*, until finally at the age of fifty he was *quintino* of Cúchulainn, part of the Clanning that included Golgotha, Ulster, Red Hand, and Celtica.

Daxox taught me much of Clan values. I learned to speak their secret language, the murmurash. I could read the tattoos of a killer and know his life story. I learned that one must never have sexual intercourse in the same house as a Clannite who is eating. I learned that menstrual blood has holy properties. I learned that every Clannite has a personal god, and must swear upon that god to honour the values of the Clan. (My god then was, and still is, Ganesh, the elephant god. Don't ask me why.) I learned that every Clannite must obey without question the orders of the *capobastone* and be at all times his loyal finger – in other words, his underling.

All this was new to me, despite my extensive reading as a child on all matters historical – for there have never been any books written about the Clan.[8] (Or rather, there *have* been, but they have never been published, and their authors have all been true-murdered.) And so I was fascinated at the way an entire parallel civilisation had been created in the midst of an oppressive dictatorship.

And fascinated too at how the Corporation used the Clan to do their dirty work. Admittedly, there were doppelgänger robots everywhere. But it was an open secret that there was a dire shortage of Earthians willing to operate these doppelgänger bodies for long tedious shifts of duty.

So instead, for much of the time, on many of the Corporation planets, the Clan enforced the rule of law.

8 True. Artemis's thought diary is now considered to be one of the best primary sources for scholars of the Clan. – *Ed.*

Or rather, the rule of no-law. A law which means *everyone* is stolen from.

And it worked. By and large. After all, it's not the first time such a system has been in operation. I mean, look at the United States of America, in the years after Obama! Or – anyway, enough history lessons.

The point I'm making is this: Daxox and I were happy. We really were. Old frog-face! I came to love, I really did, the ugly bastard.

Then, I don't know why – maybe he was bored? Broke? Wanted to teach me a lesson? – Daxox gave me to Baron Lowman, who was also a *quintino* in the Cúchulainn Clanning.

He just gave me away! As if I were a – a car. Or a bottle of wine. "Take a drink from this, Baron!" "Don't mind if I do, thank you!!"

And that's when the bad stuff happened.

Years of it.

Nine years six months four days, to be precise.

But I'm not going to talk about all the bad stuff. I'm figuring you already know, or have guessed, enough to get the gist.

The truth is, it wasn't *that* bad. I was treated well, at least when I was off duty. I went swimming most days, I was allowed to go hiking in the mountains of Cúchulainn. And I have a high pain threshold, and heal fast. So it many ways, it was like a job. Monday to Friday, and sometimes Sunday mornings. I could handle it. I really could.

But the point is, *I was a slave*. A chip in the head slave. Sometimes, for a gag, Baron Lowman would make me dance, by moving a virtual puppet synced to my brainchip, so that my limbs would—

Enough.

The short version of a long story is: I escaped, eventually. I fled the planet. I recuperated. And then I came back, ready to take revenge.

Revenge for the nine years, six months and four days.

And now—

Blood was dripping down my body. I could feel its warmth oozing along my torso and legs, and I knew I was leaving a red trail behind me as I walked. One bullet had hit a lung, and it had fragmented inside me. I was rasping with pain each time I breathed. I climbed up the stairs to my apartment, very slowly, using the wall and the banisters like twin crutches. I didn't want to risk the elevator, for fear that once I stopped moving I would collapse. I got a few strange looks, but only a few. This was a city where people kept themselves to themselves.

I blacked out and found myself on the floor of my apartment and guessed I must have climbed the last two flights of stairs whilst technically unconscious. I staggered to my feet, eventually, and cut my clothes off myself with my knife. Stood under the shower and rinsed off the blood. Then I got a suction gun and thrust it into my abdomen and sucked the bullets out. The slug in my lung I didn't dare try to reach. I sprayed the skin with healant, and glued the bullet-holed flesh together. I noted that the entire apartment now resembled an abattoir. Then I swallowed three vials of premium rejuve.

It had all gone wrong.

I'd timed my attack to coincide with Baron Lowman's monthly meeting with Daxox at the Dahlia Club.

Daxox had gone up in the world by now – he was *capobastone* of the Clanning, and Lowman was one of his five loyal *quintini*.

So Daxox's security was formidable. But it was all focused *outside* the club. He hadn't anticipated that someone might burrow *beneath* his fortified palace.

So my plan was to surprise the two of them in the club's back room, as they wheeled and dealed and discussed how to handle the new flesh they had acquired for their houses of sin.

I'd paid a tunneller – nice guy, called Gav, he had his own equipment and made his living doing this shit – to create a subway under the club. And my plan was to burrow, surface, then catch them off guard as they discussed their Clan affairs.

But I was sold out. Gav sold me out.

This is what happened:

Gav and I touched fists. He was a fat, anxious-looking man, with the minimum of social skills; so of course I liked him. It was geek to geek bonding. I think he may also have been sexually attracted to me; I have a recollection of – well, let's not go there.

"Good luck, killer!" Gav beamed.

I wondered what kind of avatar Gav might have; then I saw the tattoo on his neck. Yeah. Cool black dude with Loper teeth; that figured. My own avatar is – no matter.

Then I dived into the tunnel. It was a tight fit, I was wriggling my hips against the mortarbond walls Gav had injected. It was a quarter of a mile underground to reach the club. It took me four hours. I was wearing a warsuit, breathing from an oxygen cylinder. I began to wonder what would happen if I never got out. Or if the walls began to contract and crush me; like being choked in a python's gut. Or—

I was thinking too much. Eventually I got a bleep on my MI that told me I'd reached my destination. I pointed my plasma pistol and blasted my way up. The tunnel filled with rubble, and I clambered through, out of the earth, and levered myself up on to the charred floorboards of the club's stock room.

I got to my feet and took a deep breath. Opened the door of the stockroom and stepped into the corridor, and walked through into the club itself. I was silent as a shadow, and stealthed from sonar and visuals.

And then I saw him, in the table in the corner snug that had always been his favourite: Daxox. Two girls were with him, and Baron Lowman too. I drew my gun and prepared to launch my assault.

But as I did so, I sensed the wrongness of it all.

It was too quiet. Daxox and Lowman weren't breathing; the girls weren't talking. The bar staff were there, two men and a woman, but they weren't chinking glasses, or gossiping.

And there was no smell of flowery perfume. Instead, just the musky aroma of sweat, and a tang of neat whisky.

And – I don't know what else. I just knew this was a trap.

Then the holos of Lowman and Daxox vanished and I took four projectile bullets in the body from unseen killers – explosive cannon-fired shells that ripped through my warsuit as if it were made of cloth. And then I was hit with an energy pulse that almost shattered my force field.

I hurled a flash grenade at my unseen attackers and the room was lit by a flare, which dazzled them but left me (with my augmented eyes) able to see. Then I threw a blast grenade in the direction from which the first bullet had been fired, drew my twin pearl-handled (I'm always the show-off) plasma pistols, and shot my way out of there.

It took a while. There were six of them in all, battle-hardened veterans. But I was faster, and able to fire accurately in the midst of an apocalypse, and I was carrying enough flash grenades and ultrasound pops to deafen and blind an army. When they were dead I left through the front door.

Gav, I knew, would be long gone. I'd never be able to punish him for his treachery. Lowman and Daxox had been forewarned. My plan had failed. And now I was wounded; and once they replayed the club's camera footage, they would know who I was.

I'd lost my two most powerful weapons – my aura of infallibility, and my mystique.

And they'd hurt me bad. I'd almost died in the club that night; and still might.

Picture this:

Here's me, young and pretty and dressed like a princess in a tale of the Arabian Nights. The door to my room opens and a Sultan enters. Only he's not a Sultan, he's the Laguid Chief of Police and his name is Robbie Ferguson.

And I want to kill him but I can't. And I want to run away but I can't. And I want to shout and scream but I can't.

Because they own my head. They can kill me just by pressing a button. They can make me dance, they can move my limbs. They can ride me like a doppelgänger robot. So I have to be a slave. Because if I'm not a slave, I will be something even less than a slave.

"Hello Robbie," I say, smiling.

And here's me with Baron Lowman.

Yeah, he's a looker, I can't deny it. In another life, I might have taken him as a lover. Tall, slim, with a smile that's like sunshine cutting through a cloudy day.

See me with him: He's buying me dinner, being nice to me. I'm wearing beautiful clothes, though not many of them. Lowman is a fabulous flirt, and part of his magic is that he can make the people he enslaves feel they are valued, and should enjoy their own captivity.

And so, sometimes, I actually believe I *am* enjoying myself.

That's the worst of it. He deludes me into thinking I am happy.

And here's me bleeding to death in my lonely apartment room. Consumed with bitter regret that my revenge has failed.

"In five years' time, Artemis, you'll have your freedom. Imagine." This is Baron Lowman, back in the days of my captivity, taunting me. He used to do that a lot.

"I *can* imagine," I say, through gritted teeth. "I can!"

I wake up. The bleeding has stopped. I haven't died. I just passed out, from lack of blood, and shock.

I take off the dressing and inspect my wounds, using the mirror in my bedroom to aid me. The skin on the entry wounds is joining together. There'll be scars, but they will fade with time. The bullet in the lungs is what worries me, but I've injected rejuve spray to coat the alveoli. The tissue should eventually grow around the projectile slug and its many vicious fragments, making them part of my body. Maybe, I conclude, this is not so bad after all.

Then I cough. Blood torrents out and drenches my bedroom carpet. I puke. More blood. Bright crimson. Arterial.

Oh fuck, I think to myself, I'm dying.

Picture this: Baron Lowman, smiling. He is happy with me, for reasons which I will not recount.

His teeth are capped with diamonds. For all his beauty, it is a repellent smile.

"Come," he tells me, diamond-smiling, "here."

"Hello Baron."

Lowman blinks at me.

"How . . . ?"

Twelve years have passed since the memory I just had of Lowman with his diamond teeth glinting. Six hours have passed since I was pumped full of bullets and started to die.

And yet, now I am in the Baron's private sanctum, dressed in black body armour. Hair loose. I am shorter and less voluptuous than the Artemis the Baron knew, and my face is different. He doesn't recognise me. But he knows, of course, I pose a threat to him.

The gun in my hand kinda gives *that* away.

"Call for help," I suggest.

He triggers the alarm in his brain chip. The signal doesn't transmit. He sits down and presses the actual physical alarm button under his desk, that connects straight to the Rec Room where his *piccioti* hang out. But the line is disconnected.

"Try shouting," I suggest.

"Come the fuck in here!" screams Lowman to his bodyguards waiting outside the door. But it is a soundproofed penthouse. They can't hear him.

"I've been waiting for this a long time," I say, mildly.

"Who the fuck are you?"

I tap a hand against my chest, meaning my heart.

"You're the fucking Heartstealer?"

"I am."

"I thought we had killed you in the Dahlia Club," he says, sounding vexed. "You were wounded, we found the blood."

"I'm a fast healer," I say, which is an exaggeration, to say the least; since I am at that very moment spitting out rivers of blood in the sink of my apartment.

"Well, I'm impressed."

And Lowman smiles. His diamond teeth once more glint.

Then a plasma pistol appears in his hand and he fires.

The plasma burst passes through my holo harmlessly.

"I did wonder about that," he says mildly. "What are you – a video call?"

"Kind of."

"How'd you do that?"

To his credit, he shows no trace of fear.

"I tagged you," I say. "Pellet in the brain. A week ago, while you were in the restaurant with that blonde girl, the perfume model. I can control your retinal impulses now. I can patch a video call through *right into your brain*."

He stares at me. He doesn't know whether to believe me.

"Dragon," I say, and his eyes widen. He is seeing a dragon. He flinches, and I guess that it is billowing flame at him.

"Nice trick," he observes.

"Thank you. Do you recognise me?"

"No. Should I?"

"The waitress."

He remembers, finally.

"The clumsy one."

"You spilled the drink on—"

"I spilled the drink, you called me a useless fucking ginch. Your girlfriend calmed you down. And I patted you on the shoulder. That's when I injected you. Needle in my finger – into your neck – into your bloodstream. Into your brain. A tiny pellet full of nanotech. Which grows and grows. It's an organic bomb, and it's *inside* you. It's been gestating for days. If you had a tomograph, you'd see—" I make a Big Hands gesture. Meaning, Huge Bomb In Your Brain.

"No . . . " groaned Lowman.

"Look," I say to Baron Lowman, and then I am once again inside his brain. Inside his visual cortex, connecting up with his brain chip. I use Magog, the Cúchulainn QRC, to down images from my own memory chip then transmit them into Lowman's own mind.

And I show him images of me as I had been, as he remembered me.

"It's you?" he says, appalled.

"It's me. Artemis. The one who got away."

He is awed at the thought. For none of his slaves had ever escaped from their Clan captivity before I did; or, so I'm assured, since.

"Bitch," he snarls.

Then I fill his visual cortex with images of horror. Monsters conjured up from the darkest recesses of his unconsciousness. His own bogeymen made manifest. Until has body starts to tremble and twitch, and his eyes are filled with fear.

"You don't fucking scare me," he sneers, but I am in his mind and I know he is lying.

He is lying!

His fear consumes him. It eats him, chews his balls, steals his courage and his composure and leaves him a quivering, slavering wreck.

He pisses himself.

He—

My revenge is complete. I wonder if I should let him live. So that the memory of this humiliation will be with him for as long as he lives.

I decide not.

And, from the virtual control panel in the blood-spattered bedroom of my apartment, I detonate the organic bomb I had planted in his brain.

And a moment later, with the eyes of my holo-avatar, I see Baron Lowman's head blow up. His thoughts turn to blood and spattered grey cells. His eyes literally spit out of his skull. It is—

Well, I've never seen anything like it.

Then my holo-avatar vanished and I was me again. I was puking blood, and weak, and desperately ill.

But the plan had worked. Thanks to the nano-pellet, and the powers of Magog, I had been able to kill Lowman by remote control.

But I had failed in my real objective. My plan had always been to kill Daxox last. But he was the hardest of all to get to; and I'd left it too late. My raid on his club had been a fiasco. And now I was dying and I would never have another chance.

And then – I remember this moment well – I huddled on the floor and wept. Yes, it's true, I wept, like a small child.

But after a few minutes of humiliation I pulled myself together, and I made a decision.

I would survive this. I would endure, and rejuve, and get myself back to fighting fitness again. And then I'd start all over: I would kill Daxox. And my revenge would be complete. All this, I vowed.

And so I made a call to Jimmi Shapter.

Let me tell you about Jimmi; my friend Jimmi.

Jimmi used to work for me, back in the day, when I was working for Daxox. He was one of my team, and a good earner too. And his speciality – yeah, okay, I know it sounds bad – was sex. Jimmi slept with women for money and I was his business manager. In other words; he was the whore to my pimp.

And Jimmi, in my defence, was my friend as well as employee. I never hurt him. In fact, I never hurt or even spoke unkindly to any of the girls and guys who worked at Daxox's sex houses, when I was his right hand guy. And the hookers were all pros, in it for the money – none of them were coerced.

Hell it was better than killing people for a living. Which was what *I* mostly did.

The truth is, I always got on well with the whores. They were storytellers, most of them, and junkies, all of them. Jimmi was hooked on raves; they put him in a euphoric state and banished his late-night blues. He'd once been suicidal, as a teenager and a young man, but no more. Now he was drugged all the time and happy as – well, I've never known anyone happier.

An hour after receiving my call, he arrived. Finding him had been a bitch. Eventually, I'd MI'd a club I used to go to, and spoke to a guy, who spoke to a guy. I didn't give my name, I just left the message, "The foul-mouthed bitch who used to call you Jimmi Boy needs you." And my address.

And now, here Jimmi was.

"Artemis?" he said sceptically.

"Jimmi Boy," I croaked, in greeting.

Jimmi was looking good. Older, definitely. His hair was greying. He had laughter lines around his eyes. His freckles had darkened. But he was dapper in a suit and a buttoned up shirt and jewelled eyelashes.

I, by contrast, looked like shit. I'd crawled on to the rug in the living space of my apartment. I was dehydrated, and the place stank. My blood loss was extreme, and I could hardly speak. Oh and to further confuse things: I'd had facial and body reconstruction so I looked nothing like the woman he'd once known.

"Yeah it's me," I said. And amazingly, he accepted that.

"We need to get you to a hospital."

"No hospitals."

"Then I'll call a doctor."

"No doctor."

"Then what?"

"Stay with me. Give me water. If I die, burn the body," I said.

And then I passed out.

It was a risk, but I was desperate.

You see, the rejuve wasn't working. I had internal injuries which were bleeding out. The bullet fragments were drifting around inside my lungs, causing more and more damage. I was sure I had an embolism in one leg. I needed major surgery, but I didn't dare risk seeing any kind of doctor, because these guys all have to report in. So I needed someone to babysit me while my body tried to heal itself. Hence, Jimmi.

It was a calculated risk, but I knew I could trust him.

With the wisdom of hindsight, however, I realise I should not have taken that risk. I had no right.

For Jimmi was the kindest of men. A generous friend. A good soul. And he did not deserve what happened. He should not have died the way he did.

Jimmi – forgive me?

I was in a fevered frenzy for two weeks, shitting fluid and vomiting copiously and losing more blood than a pig in an abattoir.

I didn't exactly sleep but nor was I truly conscious. But whenever I was well enough to see and to register what I saw, I realised that Jimmi was there. "Shush shush," he would say.

Sometimes he would sing to me. Gershwin, or Clay & Mielder, or ballads by Spiegel. He had a lovely voice.

The days passed. I could not eat, and I was vomiting all the time. So I became emaciated, like a skeleton. I could not bear for Jimmi to see me naked, but he had to bathe me, and put me on the toilet, and wipe my arse. I was in a state of total fatigue, as my body rallied to heal its injuries.

When he walked me in the park he used to tell people I was his gran.

I had lost all my hair by that point, and my skin no longer had the softness and sheen of youth. I was wrinkled and weak, and I stared suspiciously out at the world. I used twin crutches to get around; and I grew tired very easily. But I was, without a doubt, on the mend.

"Remember the old days?" I asked him, as I crutched slowly along by the lake, where an eyrar of swans glided elegantly upon on the water, and chimaerical fish with the heads of apes leaped.

"I don't like to," he said, grinning, remembering.

"Whatever happened to Charleene?" Loud mouthed Charleene, always the first to start an argument.

"Dead. OD, happy juice. She liked to be happy."

"Sylvia?"

"Married to an architect."

"She cashed in then."

"She did."

"Marco?"

"I lived with him for twenty years then we divorced."

"Marco was an arsehole."

"So I discovered."

"It took you *twenty years* to—"

"Yeah, like *you* were so smart. Nine years as a sex slave."

I paused for breath. The sun warmed my skin; and then the wind cooled it again. It felt good to be alive, even if barely.

"Wasn't my choice," I retorted, eventually.

"I know."

"Bastard Daxox."

"I love you, Artemis."

I made a fuck-off face and then, to underline my point, I said: "Fuck off!"

Jimmi had often slept with women in the course of duty, but he was exclusively gay in his heart of hearts. He had never desired me. But he was my best friend. And I loved him more than words could, you know.

"I look gorgeous don't I?" he asked me coyly, as we stood by the lake one day. "I'm a real hunk?"

"You are, and you do."

"You look pretty hot too," he teased.

"Liar."

"In my eyes," said Jimmi, "you'll always be beautiful. Despite the bags under your eyes. And the wrinkles. And the liver spots."

"And the bald head."

"I like the bald head."

Once my bullet wounds were healed, and the alveoli in my lung had grown back, and the embolism had gone from the vein in my leg, I began to grow younger.

It's a nice feeling.

Jimmi and I still walked in the park every morning before he went to work. He ran a club now, a piano bar. Clan-controlled of course, but relatively respectable.

The skies were always black with foully polluted clouds, but the sun shone most days. And the trees were magnificent, and birds perched on their branches, and lizards pinned themselves to tree trunks. And dogs walked themselves whilst their indolent owners snoozed on benches. I was a grey haired lady by now, with one stick instead of two crutches. And Jimmi always beamed and nodded at the lithe young joggers who ran past, and they all loved him for being kind to his old gran.

But after a few weeks I ditched the stick and my legs were stronger and we picked up the pace a little. My hair was salt and pepper now. And I had a fierce expression, and the innately nosy glare of the old studying the foibles of the young, and wondering which particular idiotic mistakes they will make first.

A few weeks later still and my hair was black and my skin was lively with laughter lines, rather than etched with scars of age. And Jimmi looked like my grown-up son.

A few weeks later still, and we could have been brother and sister, ambling in the park.

A few weeks after that, we ran in vests and shorts, sweat oiling our bodies as we sprinted along the rambling paths. We outran dogs and even a pony, and won admiring stares from the hard-bodies out for their early morning training sessions.

From grandmother to horny youth in less than eight weeks. It was like living my life in reverse.

"What are these?" I asked.

They were tickets: small, red, plastic.

"I have a friend, on the cargo caravan. They're taking passengers. We could go," Jimmi confided.

"To Earth."

"Or anywhere else en route."

"You and me?"

"Me and you."

"Is that a proposal?"

"Hell no, you ain't got a dick," Jimmi protested.

"You want to run away with me?"

"I want to rescue you."

I smiled, almost.

"I still have to do . . . what I have to do," I told him.

Jimmi smiled a little while longer. Then he stopped smiling, and the tears came. I couldn't believe how fast it happened. His face was twisted with pain and his cheeks were actually damp.

"Give it up, Artemis!" said Jimmi. And in his eyes was written the desperate grief of his soul.

"I can't."

"They'll kill you. Sooner or later, they'll kill you."

"Let them."

The next day I murdered Lucian Brody in a nightclub on Parkcross. He was in the toilet cubicle shooting up with frenzies. I climbed over the cubicle wall and caught him before he could pull his trousers up, then stabbed him to death with a knife in the skull. His face embodied shock, his expression frozen rigid at the moment of death. Then I did the heart trick. I cut it out, I put it in his mouth.

Then I left the toilet, closing the cubicle door behind me, and exited the nightclub. The bass beats shook my body. A couple were fucking on the stairs. I had to step over them. They were wild, high on lib, the aphrodisiac drug. I wondered if they'd ever met before tonight. They didn't even notice that my shirt was crimson with blood.

Later, I hosed and scrubbed myself in a warehouse I was renting. Lucian had been a security guard at the Baron's place. He'd once brought me back after I had tried and failed to escape, before I'd understood about the whedon chip in my brain. My body was in convulsions, the pain in my head was crippling me, I couldn't speak or think and could barely breathe. But that hadn't stopped Lucian from—

Whatever. He was dead now. Justice had been served.

I slept at the warehouse. And the next morning I went for my regular walk, expecting to see Jimmi in the park, but he wasn't there.

I guessed immediately. They'd tracked him down.

Jimmi was of course on my list of known associates. It was obvious, with hindsight, that they would find and interrogate him. I knew Jimmi would never talk, but I feared how much pressure they would bring to bear on him before they realised that.

It took me six days to find the interrogation centre where he was being grilled. And two hours to break in and kill the guards. Jimmi was in a bad way. I carried him out on my shoulders, and took him to a safe house I had rented for this purpose, where I had medical facilities lined up.

They'd tortured him of course. That meant, I realised, that they'd been torturing ALL the people who used to know me. *All* of them. Just on the off chance.

That made me feel – not so good.

Naturally, once I realised what was happening, I wanted to take bloody revenge for what those bastards had done to Jimmi.

And indeed, what they had done to all my other friends and acquaintances!

But a quick reality check told me that the more I took revenge, the more the innocent people who used to share a beer and a chat with me would suffer.

My head was pounding at the thought of it.

I realised I had become a human plague. All the people who had known me once upon a time would be tortured, or would die. Damned for the sin of having met me and liked me.

It was an appalling thought.

But at least I'd saved Jimmi. Or so I believed, at first. But when I injected him with rejuve he turned scarlet and began to convulse and I had to inject the antidote. I set the autodoc to diagnostic and fed it blood and tissue samples and it came up with a reason: Jimmi was DNR. Do Not Rejuve.

The reason – it didn't take much figuring out – he was a juve junkie.

That's why he had the grey hairs and the wrinkles. He must have been forced to quit rejuve after severe overdosage of the drug. And now he was ageing at a natural rate.

Ageing!

Jimmi was unconscious still, and I sang to him for a little while. It was his favourite Gershwin song – they were brothers, you know, George wrote the music, Ira wrote the words – "Someone To Watch Over Me". Do you know it?

Jimmi couldn't hear me.

I nursed Jimmi as best I could, day and night. And I brooded, a lot, about how he had become such a total fuck-up.

I mean! I've come across every perversion known to humankind. But juve junkies baffle even me. I was stunned to find that Jimmi had gone down that road.

Or maybe I'm kidding myself; maybe I do understand the appeal of juve, only too well.

It's the exhilaration, of course. And I'd felt it too, as my badly wounded body had healed. That joy of pain turning to pleasure. Wounds healing. Age reversing. Some people love it so much they crash flycars into walls or cut off their own limbs, in order to experience the thrill of rejuve healing.

After a while, the body can't take it. Rejuve no longer works. You become truly human again. Not to be recommended.

Jimmi had been badly hurt by his torturers. They'd used pain not drugs. Because of course you can't use drugs on a juve junkie. I hated them for what they had done. I wanted to—

No more. I realised I had to give up all thoughts of revenge. It was my job now – my duty – to save Jimmi.

Here's what I did, and why.

To get this, you need to understand that rejuve is a drug that enhances the healing powers of all human beings. But I'm *augmented*.

That makes me better than human. More than human. It's my genes that control my healing process, rejuve merely helps me, as a top-up. But my body has cells that are genetically hardwired not to die or to age. My limbs will regenerate, given time, if you cut them off. (It takes fucking *years* without a dash of rejuve though.) And my blood, too, is rich in healing factor.

So that's what I did. I swapped our blood.

That's a slight medical exaggeration of course. But even so, it's pretty much what I did. I hooked Jimmi up to a pump and sucked as much blood out of his body as I dared. Then I did the same to my own body. And then I flicked a switch and the machine began to pump my fresh augmented blood into Jimmi's arteries.

Of course, you can't squeeze a human being *entirely* dry of blood, it's not like squeezing an orange. But it felt that way. Like I was emptied of juice, a squeezed fruit. I felt as weak as a newborn kitten after its owner has tried to drown it in a sack.

However, Jimmi now had several litres of my energising augmented blood coursing through his veins and arteries. Giving him new life and energy.

His broken bones didn't heal, but they did stop hurting. His internal bleeding dribbled to a halt. His damaged kidneys spluttered back into life. His fire-burned lungs (they'd poured petrol down his throat) allowed him to breathe freely again. His battered face was restored to something like its normal beauty, apart from the broken nose. And after two days of healing, he opened his eyes.

"I feel great," Jimmi said, cheerfully. Though his voice was faint, so very faint.

"Let's go dancing," I said.

It was a glorious night. Three moons in the sky. Stars twinkling. Glorious jazz music from the late twenty-second century being played by the house band. This was a retro place – the Lady Day Bar – and it was Jimmi's favourite dance hall.

I wore a sleeveless gown that I had bought in a shop on Clancey Avenue, that hugged my figure and left nowhere to hide a gun. I had a small energy pulser in my purse but that was just out of habit. This was not the time or the place for a shooting war.

We ordered champagne and told bawdy stories about cocks and quims and magnificent whores until the customers at the surrounding tables were either enraged or entranced at our bohemian vulgarity. Then Jimmi and I went out on to the dance floor and we danced.

Jimmi was a marvellous dancer. He always had been. The other whores had always said he was the god of dance. He could sway like leaves shifting in the wind. He made even *me* look good. He wore a black "tuxedo" suit and a hat and when his body moved, it felt as if the air around him was applauding, you hear what I'm saying? Before long the other dancers stopped and peeled away to watch him. Jimmi's moves weren't fast or fancy, but he had a grace that distilled all reality into the sway of hips and the roll of shoulders and the twist of torso this way, then that.

"One more dance," he whispered, and we danced one more dance.

"One more dance," he whispered, and we danced one more dance.

"One more," he whispered, and then he collapsed.

People started screaming. I knelt beside Jimmi and kissed him full on the lips, so that he would die kissing me. It didn't take long.

Then I got up and tried to walk away but security guards stopped me, assuming that Jimmi was a drug addict and that so was I. The guards were not battle-trained warriors, but even so, they were muscular and armoured and there were many of them. In my blood-drained and weakened state, without a halfway decent gun, I knew I had no chance of defeating them.

They led me to the security office and did a routine retina scan and ten minutes later they discovered they had a fugitive on their hands.

By this point I could not keep my eyes open. My limbs were lead weights. My heart was hardly beating. I had, remember, siphoned a large proportion of my own blood out of my body and filled myself with thin blood, *normal* blood. In a few weeks my own blood would regenerate, but for now I was a wreck. A pale-skinned shadow of my former self.

Whereas Jimmi had been given a new lease of life from the infusion of my augmented blood into his system. It gave him strength and vigour, it banished his pain, it made him feel as if he were sixteen again!

But augmented blood isn't the same as rejuve. It can restore and energise; but it can't, if you don't have the genes that I have, heal broken limbs and internal bleeding and ruptured organs. It can't work miracles. Jimmi had suffered a series of appalling injuries at the hands of his torturers. All the transfusion had done was give him back his youth and health for one brief night.

So that he could dance, and feel the joy of being alive in the arms of a girl, and bask in moonlight as music played, before he died.

And all this he did. He died in joy.

And his death was – it was all my fault.

And now I had been captured. I would have no more opportunities to take revenge. If I wasn't judicially murdered on the way to the courthouse, I was guaranteed a death sentence that would be enforced within the hour. It was all over for me.

But I didn't care. I knew that I would do it all again. I was happy to have traded my life to give Jimmi one last night of bliss.

Joy, Jimmi, joy!

Chapter 4

My name is Artemis McIvor

My name is Artemis McIvor and my dad was a librarian. But you already know all that. And my mother abandoned me when I was a child. But I MUST have mentioned that by now, because I'm obsessed with it.

And I've been sentenced to death for recidivistic mass murder. I have only one more week to live.

The cell I'm in[1] is actually quite comfortable. It is more like a hotel room than a prison cage. Hidden cameras monitor my every move, but I have nothing to hide. The cell is en suite, there's a shower, and a music player and a TV. I use none of them. I want to die smelly and rank, with my mind clear of distracting thoughts.

1 Artemis was incarcerated in the Laguid Bastille. – *Ed.*

I thought I would feel content, after completing so many of my long-awaited acts of revenge. But instead I just felt a dull throb of hate.

My aim, as I've explained, or maybe I didn't but I think it's pretty fucking obvious, was to humiliate Daxox by killing his fellow perverts one by one. So that he would endure a living hell before his own, ghastly, demise.

I'd envisaged in detail, in a multiplicity of scenarios, that glorious final act of vengeance. And of course, when I broke into his club that time I wasn't going to *kill* him. I just wanted to let him know that I *could.* I would have tasered the two of them, him and Lowman, with a high energy bolt in the bowels. And left them to wake up in their own vomit and shit. So that for weeks afterwards Daxox would wake up every morning sweating with fear. And when Lowman's head unexpectedly blew up – my shocking *coup de théâtre!* – Daxox would have feared with every atom of his being that—

But it didn't happen that way. All my plans had fallen to pieces. Well okay, Baron Lowman had been dealt with, admittedly, and the head blowing up thing *was* pretty cool. But there were seven more names on my list who I hadn't got around to. All of them evil. All of them not-dead. And Daxox himself was safe.

I should have abandoned Jimmi to his sad and lonely death, and gone for Daxox. That would have been the smart thing to do.

But I didn't. I followed my heart. I made myself vulnerable for Jimmi's sake, to give him that one last night of joy. And as a result, Daxox was still alive.

Alive. And smug. And—

Leave it Artemis. Don't waste your last hours hating a molly-focker like that.

My guess is the evil bastard will buy my cadaver from the prison service and keep it as a memento. Freeze dry it, and put it on a plinth maybe. Or—

Fuck! How could I have been so—

I know one thousand books by heart, and I can read them in my memory, as if off a screen. I don't use a brain chip or a remote computer. It's pure memory.

I'm currently reading *Tom Jones* by Henry Fielding.[2] It's an old book written many centuries ago. The language is strange but I love it. As well as writing novels, Fielding helped create London's first police force with his brother John, a blind magistrate. I love that period in history. The novel is rambling, what some call picaresque, which suits my mood, because my thoughts keep hopping around.

My dad had an eidetic memory, and so do I. And he trained me in the art of remembering. I spent years as a child memorising facts and languages. I can speak Latin, Greek, Italian, French, Spanish, German and Russian, even though I live in a universe where everyone speaks English, apart from the French, whose ships continue to send mayday messages in a language no one (apart from me) can understand.[3]

I can actually run around the entire room! Seriously! It works like this:

First, I take a flying jump on the wall. Then I hit it with both

2 Available for download here. – *Ed.*

3 A slight exaggeration; it's true French is the second most common language in the humanverse, albeit not *that* common. – *Ed.*

feet and start running. If I'm fast enough, which I am, I can run up to the ceiling. Then because my bare feet have an adhesive factor I can also run from one end of the ceiling to the other then down the other wall. And round again.

I'm like a hamster in a wheel.

I've learned another trick. Sleeping.

I slept twenty-three hours last night. I woke up as stiff as a board, but I could still remember many of my dreams. I dreamed I was a faun in a forest, killed by an arrow. But the arrow was a sword. Or maybe a penis with a metal tip. I only had three legs and I limped to the lake and lapped the waters and they were cold and luscious. My father was there, in his pyjamas, I don't know why. Daxox was on the ground, throat slit, his head resting in a pool of his own blood, dead. I liked that bit. Daxox was dead.

Dear Diary, my last-minute appeal has been refused.[4]

I die tomorrow. I have one more book which I hope to finish reading in my head, then it's all over for me. It's *Tristram Shandy,* by Laurence Sterne. You'd love it. It's the craziest book anyone has ever written. I'll just start on Chapter One: *I wish either my father or my mother, or indeed both of them, as they were in duty both equally bound to it, had minded what they were about when they begot me . . .*

No! Too late. They're opening the door. The bastards are early! And it's my time to die.

4 Confirmed by the SNG Court Records (Appeal Branch); for the judges' ruling click here. – *Ed.*

No matter. I've read that book a dozen times. I know how it comes out.

In a moment, I decide, I'm going to escape.

I'm being led down a corridor. I have magnetic shackles on my legs, hobbling me. There's a doppelgänger robot either side of me. I'm nearly naked, just bra and panties, which isn't erotic because I smell like a festering potato. But it means I have no way of concealing weapons about my person. I have no friends on the outside. But I decide to—

Okay, some stuff you should know here, to understand what happens next:

First, the leg shackles I'm wearing are controlled by ultrasound bursts emitted from a DR's brain. The code for this is stored in Magog, the Cúchulainn remote computer. And as I said before, I can hack into that with my Rebus chip. My handcuffs, however, are manual-lock operated. And the two DRs who are escorting me are each seven foot tall and instead of arms they have clubs with blades.

Got that? Here goes:

The shackles fall off my legs, as I order Magog to let me free. There's a clang; the DRs do not notice.

I leap on the first DR, still with my hands cuffed, and use the manacles to wrench its head off its body.

The metal of its body feels cold against my bare legs and arms. My heart is pounding, I'm in berserker mode, and I am making time slow down for me. The DR's head slowly topples off its torso, like a cliff collapsing, and it falls to the ground and bounces, once, twice, then stops. Its dead face leers up at me.

The second DR swings its club-arm-with-blades at me and I dodge and its arm hits the wall and breaks through and gets stuck.

I am suddenly convinced that there is someone coming down the corridor to kill me. Dozens of soldiers are on their way – hundreds even! – armed with fast-fire rifles and shoulder-cannons. I stand no chance I—

I ignore this fear, it is not helping me.

Instead, I grab the DR's head with both hands and twist and its neck joint breaks, severing the neural link to its limbs.

"Fuck you," says the DR, in a slow robotic voice.

And then I am running. I stop slowing down time and it feels as if I'm running faster than light itself. I am fast, I am fearless, nothing can stop me! Ecstasy of battle consumes me, as I hurtle down the corridor and—

The doors slam shut in front of me. Manually operated. I can't control them.

I turn around. The door at the far end of the corridor also slams shut, with a resounding clang.

I walk back to my cell, sit on the bunk, and finish Chapter One of *Tristram Shandy*. When they come for me again they knock me out with a gas bomb. When I wake up I'm in the death machine.

Capital punishment is now illegal on 70 per cent of SNG-controlled planets.[5]

Not this one.

The death machine is a pulping device. My head is between two metal plates. The plates will move together very fast, crushing both my skull and brain and also my memory chips. My body will then be crushed in similar fashion. Blood and entrails and smeared body parts will then be sluiced into a container and compacted. Nothing human can survive this.

5 A rare factual error from Dr McIvor; the correct figure is 70.05 per cent. – *Ed.*

I have a itch. Fuck. On my left buttock. A conciliator is asking me if I want to repent on camera before my demise. I do not. All I want to do is to scratch my arse.

I access Magog. I learn it has no control over the death machine, which is pretty much what I expected. It's a steampunky Corporation device, created by some evil nerd, and operated by means of compressed air. The Court-appointed executioner will press the button that makes it – do what it does. I learn, from Magog, that the executioner's name is Malcolm Bawles. He used to be a shop-keeper but his family were murdered by Clan gangsters. Now he's a police officer and sometime executioner. He is a friend, I discover, of a bartender called Billy Rae, who used to be a friend of mine.

Small world, huh?

They're fucking with me. I've been strapped to this machine for forty minutes. I should be dead by now. They're just prolonging the agony.

There's a moment, just before you die, when everything becomes clear and focused. All uncertainty vanishes. The truth of the universe becomes manifest.

And that moment came to me!

And then it passed by swiftly, and I reverted to my usual state of bewildered confusion.

Fuck.

However, soon afterwards, my shackles were released. And a soft robot voice spoke to me:

"You are free to go."

Well, I hadn't been expecting *that*.

"My name," said the man, "since you ask so verrra nicely, is Brigadier Fraser."

Fraser had a very large nose – had he never heard of prosthetic surgery, the imbecile? And he wore old-fashioned eyeglasses of a kind you rarely see these days. His hair was grey, his face was wrinkled. All very old school. He also had a speech impediment of some kind – but no! I checked my database for referents – it was merely a Scottish accent.

"I am currently working for a sub-committee of the Peace and Reconciliation Committee," Fraser continued, in that lilting voice that was like water lapping on a misty lake. I guessed he was from New Caledonia, a planet famed for its mists, whisky, and dour pessimists largely of Scotland-Earth extraction. "And I've come to offer you a deal."

"Do I live or die?" I asked.

"In this deal – live."

"Then," I said, "I take it."

Let me back up a moment.

There I was, shackled inside the death machine, awaiting my

own reduction to a jammy paste. What was I thinking then? Did my life flash in front of my eyes?

Yeah, it did, kind of.

Here are some of the moments I saw:

Tears rolled down my cheeks, and I snorted back a grief-drenched string of snot.

I was inconsolable. or so I told myself. And I revelled in how entirely inconsolable I was, even as I failed, utterly, to be consoled! (I was, you may have deduced by now, a very strange child.)

"She died," I murmured, "she died!"

My father glared at me. "What is wrong with you, Artemis?"

"She died," I told him mournfully. "She died!"

"Who died?" He had a tone like cold marble, if marble were also impatient and rude.

"Annabelle." I held up my book. It was a paper volume with a plastic cover that looked and felt but did not smell like leather binding. "*The Story of Annabelle.*[6] She dies."

My father stared at me. A smile lit up his face. I had never seen him smile before. I was, by the way, seven years old. "She does die," he admitted, "she does indeed. Sacrificing herself, am I right, to save her puppy?"

"Her dolphin."

"Her dolphin," he conceded.

"Bobby," I explained.

"Bobby, I see. Well. It's sentimental tosh, really, isn't it?" said my father, but his eyes were twinkling.

6 Now available on the WOOO Press Library Archive, as *The Story of Annabelle* by Geeta Landingham [subcategories: Fiction, Children's Fiction, Repellently Saccharine Fiction]. (That last subcategory is a rare but I trust welcome editorial jest from, ahem, moi). – *Ed.*

"Do you think she rejuved, Daddy?"

"Well that's a good question. When was the book published?"

I checked. "Twenty-one sixty-four."

"Then it's a very old book. Did they have rejuve then?"

I thought. "No, Daddy."

"Then she didn't rejuve did she?"

"No, daddy."

"But she does—" Then he stopped, abruptly, and said no more.

I stared at my father curiously. He had the most severe face of any man I'd ever seen. His hair was jet black, but tired black, not young black. You could tell it was old hair. But now he looked – playful almost.

"She did what, Daddy?"

"Read the sequel," Daddy told me, trying to hide his delight at the surprise in store for me. "And you'll see what you'll see."

I was totally naked. I touched myself down there, and there were definitely hairs. I was eleven years old.

I threw myself off the cliff.

As I fell, I held my body straight. Arms ahead. Legs together. The air rushed past me. I could see the angry spume of the waterfall falling in parallel with me. The spray was thumping me all over, and I fought to keep my body from buckling and flailing.

I hit the lake with perfect form like an arrow plunging into a heart. And then my body shot through the water like, well, like a dolphin. The momentum propelled me deep and I kept my eyes open and I was shocked at how fast I was moving. I knew it was cold but I couldn't feel the cold because of the SMACK of the impact. But I continued the arc of the dive and rose to the surface and broke water and gasped.

I trod water. The sun was hot on me. No one was there to witness my feat. No one could see that I was naked. No one could tell me off for risking my life in a foolish stunt. But it had worked. I had triumphed. It was a perfect 'me' moment.

"You cooked this?" I asked.

"I cooked this." Randall[7] was grinning all over his face. He had freckles on his nose. I loved those freckles.

"Where did you learn to cook like this?" I asked.

I tasted another piece of steak. It was bloody inside – actually bloody! – and the meat was luscious and gorgeous. I put some potato dauphinoise on my spoon and sucked the cream off. The potatoes were firm, but soft inside. They tasted of earth and life. And the cream was like, well, like the richest cream I'd ever tasted.

"From a book," Randall admitted.

"Which book?" I quizzed him.

"*Cooking for Beginners*. I found it under Science, Food, Gustatory Arts in the archive."

"Nice one."

"It took some hunting down,"

"You're such a nerd, Randall," I told him.

He beamed. That was the highest praise indeed, from one Rebusite to another.

Randall was thirteen years old. I was also thirteen years old. I had breasts now. I knew that for certain, because Randall kept looking at them.

"The first time I ever cooked," I admitted, smiling at my own folly, "I burned toast."

7 Randall Shillaker is referenced several times in the text as Artemis's only friend as a child. His parents were Michael and Angela Shillaker, and they lived on Rebus for thirteen months. – *Ed.*

"How can you burn toast?" he scoffed.

"Easily."

"What *is* toast?" Randall asked, shamelessly conceding his bluff.

"It's bread. Basically. Heated up so it burns."

"So it's *meant* to be burned?"

"You had to be there. In context, it was really amusing." I simulated the sound of eating hard black burned toast. CRUNCH CRUNCH CRUNCH.

Randall and I were friends for just a year. He was the only child my own age that I had ever met. His parents were dispossessed colonists who moved to Rebus when Randall was twelve, but hated it, then emigrated to who knows where[8] when he was thirteen and a half. But let's not spoil the memory.

"CRUNCH CRUNCH CRUNCH!" I said, crunchingly.

And Randall laughed.

And I laughed too.

"Taste this wine," said Daxox.

It was a rich ruby wine. Even redder than the wine my father used to drink on Christmas Day. I took a sip.

"Wow."

"Wow indeed," said Daxox.

The taste filled my throat. Then it made my head expand. Galaxies collided. I felt drunk. My limbs were loose. I was, I realised, suddenly very randy.

"Is this strong?"

"Two sips and you'll be wailing like a banshee," Daxox informed me gravely, his eyes twinkling, his great frog face crinkled in amusement.

8 I can find no record of where they went. – *Ed.*

I took a second sip.

He was right!

You'll have got the idea by now. My life was flashing before me, as I waited for the death machine to crush my brain to pulp.

But you'll have noticed that I was only remembering the *good bits*. The best moments. And I was remembering them incredibly fast. A hundred memories possessed me in the space of, in objective time, moments.

You can do that, you see, with a brain chip, if you program it right. You need to organise the memories by category, and define the category as High Value Pleasure, and label each memory HVP when you save to chip. Then subvoc HVP and blink three times when the amber light appears in the right hand side of your visual frame. It's possible of course to do the same with all the bad memories, but why *would* you?

"More more more!" I screamed, joyously.

"Isn't it my turn now, to, you know?" said the guy – his name was Rodors, according to the visual cue on the top of my visual frame. But I didn't remember him with my *actual* memory.

"More, you fucker!" I screamed. His head was between my legs. What can I say! I was on a roll. I didn't let him off there for a long time. Twenty minutes or more at a rough count.

"Now," I said, and he came away, and I helped him with his pintle. He slipped inside me and—

Oh yes. Oh yes! That was one of the best—

Oh! Yes! Yes! Yes!

Another good one, this.

I could see myself in the copulatory act via the hotel room mirror. There was a guy behind me, doing pleasurably intimate things involving much treasured parts of our respective human anatomies, but I couldn't actually see his face. The visual cue said CARL. Ah. I remembered Carl. A real hunk.

He reached a frenzy of in-and-out stuff, and I came. And I saw myself come. My face howled silently and went bright red. The orgasm was like, like – I don't know what it was like. It was the best orgasm I'd ever had since – since – well, since the last one I just remembered.

"You like it like this?" said Daxox.

We were fucking in the dark.

"Anything, rather than see your godawful ugly face," I said.

He laughed. And laughed. There was joy in Daxox's laugh. I came as he was laughing. It was really sweet.

I was walking home. I was still drunk. The dawn crept up over the sky. The sky was seared with colour. Darkly scarlet bars were stamped across the blackness of night. It was an astonishing image. The moons were bright. It was cold. I was sober now. That was the night I realised I was in love with Daxox.

"How do I look?" Jimmi asked.

He was wearing a Kzaal-leather jacket and trousers and cow-boots – you know, those old-style heeled boots with spurs, made of real cow. He looked ridiculous.

"You look great," I told him.

Jimmi laughed. "Not too much?"

"Much too much!"

"I like much too much."

"So do I."

I hugged Jimmi.

"He's going to love you, trust me," I said. Jimmi had a date with a Laguid financier. It wasn't business. Instead it was, Jimmi hoped, going to be the greatest passion of his life.

Jimmi's face lit up with expectant joy.

—oh yes, so firm, that ridged and rippling torso—

—those powerful legs—

—his back was so powerful and I covered it in kisses, touching myself as—

—kissed his cheeks, and felt him drift drowsily—

"Will you kiss me?" said Cassady, and I did. Then—

"Put your hand there," said Cassady, and I did.

"That was wonderful," murmured Cassady. And it was.

"I love you," said Cassady.

"I love you too," I said, shocking myself.

And more, many more memories in that vein.

Beautiful men, and women. Great sex. Gorgeous Cassady. I've saved to chip every orgasm I ever had. I even have several subcategories of sexual encounter, catalogued by activity, theme and costume; but maybe I shouldn't go too much into that.

But get this. A lot of my "good" memories are of clothes I have worn. Especially on Cúchulainn when I had money to spend, and attitude to express. Hundreds of pairs of favourites boots and shoes. Jackets I Have Loved. Cool scarves. Brightly Coloured Socks That I Just Love To Put On In The Morning. T-shirts with funny pictures on them.

How sad is that, huh?

For instance: my Dimari boots.[9] Made of black Bandersnatch leather. Soft, softer than human skin.

I can smell the leather. I can hear the clack of the heels. I wore these boats with jeans usually. They are associated with the time when I was enforcing for Daxox. I killed a lot of people wearing these boots.

My favourite jacket. Sky blue, spacepilot style, with pockets and buckles galore. Not sexy, not really, but I loved it. I wore it with the Dimari boots.[10]

There was a gun holster built into the lining. My own personal design feature.

9 I've deleted most of the stuff about the boots. There are six pages of it in all. They were made of alien animal leather, fitted very snugly, up to Artemis's knees, and were "cool"; that synopsis says all that needs to be said, in my view. – *Ed.*

10 There follows a list, now excised, of all the occasions when Artemis wore the boots and the jacket in conjunction. I mean, really! – *Ed.*

The black and silver Maraiz dress. High breasted, practical, but it made my waist slimmer than it really is. I had very large biceps, back then. This was less evident in my favourite Maraiz dress.

I never got to wear dresses when I lived on Rebus. I was a barmaid on Gullyfoyle, so I usually dressed to repel. And the women on Cúchulainn who wore sexy dresses tended to be whores. So generally, the idea of wearing GLAMOUROUS shit never appealed to me.

But I loved that one dress. It wasn't glamorous. It was just me.

Eventually, however, my beloved Maraiz had to be binned, because after one failed assignment I got some icky blood stains on it, plus a bullet hole that couldn't be mended. Fortunately, the bullet didn't penetrate my armoured corset.

Yeah, that's another story. Armoured lingerie. Usually in white.

Don't go there.

There weren't that many of them.

There really weren't.

Happy memories I mean.

There was the time on Rebus when – no, but that reminds me of—

And that time when Daxox – but no, remember what Daxox did to you eventually – REMEMBER WHAT THAT FUCKER DID!

Lots of one night stands. My sexual memories are pretty impressive, I have to say. No shortage *there*. But I'd like – well—

I'd like *baby* memories. That would be nice. Baby's first smile. Baby sucking my nipple. Baby – look, face it girl, you've never had a fucking baby! And therefore, duh, you can't have any memories of what it was like!

Well actually I *can*. If I really wanted to. I just have to access Magog and sneak into the Personal Memories Backup of all the computer users on the planet, and down them.

But it would be *wrong,* wouldn't it? To access the baby memories of other women and *pretend they are my own*? That would be sad. Too sad for words.

The trouble is, though, I don't want to remember all the men I fucked. Or the people I killed. Or the great quantities of booze I drank. No, I want to remember having a child.

Before I die.

I have to admit it: I went a bit mad back there. Trapped in the old death machine.

But then, as you know, I got my reprieve. The neck-shackle came off me. The arm and leg restraints were unfastened. The DRs cuffed and hobbled me, and led me back down another corridor and into a small bleak impersonal interrogation room. Sitting at the desk was the old-looking man I've told you about, with the aforementioned big nose and old-fashioned eyeglasses. And I sat down and I stared into his eyes and he stared back. And then:

"So," I said to Fraser. "Who the fuck are *you*?"

Chapter 5

Here's the Deal

And Fraser stared back at me, calmly. He smelled of tobacco – tobacco! His eyes, I noted at this point, were blue.

"My name," he said, "since you ask so verrra nicely, is Brigadier Fraser."

And then he offered me a deal, as I've already told you. And I said, Yes, as I've already explained. And then I made what I hoped he'd consider a helpful suggestion:

"Release the handcuffs," I said.

He peered at me a bit more. I don't know why. I was sitting directly opposite him, I wasn't exactly hard to spot.

"I dinny think say," he said. Or some such shit.[1] Mangling the English language with his archaic brogue.

"The hobbles then. Let me stretch my legs."

"No."

"Why not?"

Fraser smiled, faintly, as if a thought had occurred to him and he wanted to tickle it for a while. "If I did that then you could, bonny lassy, kill me very easily, with a headbutt or a punch or a kick to the head. I've read your file, you know," Fraser pointed out mildly.

1 In more accurate Scottish phonetic demotic: "I dinnae think so," meaning "I think not." – *Ed.*

Bonny lassy? I checked my chip: it meant "beautiful girl".

"Why would I kill you?!" I said, in tones of outrage.

"I've read your file," he repeated, patiently.

"Just let me loose, pintlesucker, so I can rip your fucking eyes out," I said, seductively.

He stared at me, reprovingly.

"Okay," I conceded. "I'm out of line. Just kidding, okay? So what's the deal? What do I have to do?"

Fraser frowned. He was going to eke this out with agonising slowness, I realised.

"We have a mission for you," he said, slowly. "A vital mission, to protect freedom and democracy. In fact, strictly speaking, three missions. We feel you are ideally suited. But it's dangerous. Verrra dangerous."

Here we had it: the old suicide mission deal. I risk my life for them, they wipe the slate clean.

"No sweat, you've got it," I said. "But there's one condition."

"No conditions," Fraser chided. "But if you survive, we wipe the slate clean." Told you! "Five million scudos will be paid into your bank account. We'll give you a new identity. You can make a fresh start."

"There is," I insisted, "one condition."

"Name it."

I named it.

"Out of the question," said Fraser.

"Then kill me."

He smiled. "Let me tell you first," he said, "about the progress of the war."

We were losing the war, Fraser told me, and the very soul and future of humanity were in dire peril. (Yeah, he did actually talk like that.)

All this I knew, *kind* of. But I have to admit, Fraser's briefing came as something of a shock to my system.

I was aware of course that there was some seriously bad shit taking place out there. I read the news portals avidly. I knew that a number of colonist planets had committed acts of terrorism against the SNG Government, in protest at the restoration of freedom, democracy and human rights. And yes, of course I knew that – technically – we were at war with a number of these gang-run worlds.

But to be honest, I hadn't really fathomed how bad things were. Nor had I truly grasped that our side – the ones who believe in liberty and democracy and such shit – were losing. This war, I now learned, was no minor skirmish; it was the second greatest human war of all time, next to the Last Battle. It was fucking HUGE.

For all my historical awareness, I hadn't really understood all that. And I know I wasn't alone in my ignorance. Most supposedly well informed citizens at this time were oblivious to the sheer scale and horror of the conflicts between the majority of the Clan worlds and the SNG, the democratic government that ran the humanverse from its base in Parliament Square on Planet Earth.

And there's a reason for this state of sublime and stunning mass ignorance: I call it litotic propaganda.

By which I mean that the SNG were playing down the whole war thing in a big way. There wasn't a news blackout exactly. But these devious democratic bastards were masters of understatement.

It's true! After meeting Fraser, I did some thorough media analysis of the war coverage on the news portals. And it soon became apparent that a major deception was being perpetrated on the 'can't be arsed to read an entire article or wait till the end of a news report' average citizen. Yes, the war WAS mentioned. It's not as if they were denying it, or covering it up. But all the key stories about the battles and calamities and massacres and the very many defeats of our side were thrown away, buried in small features below important items like:

DEMOCRACY COMES TO CAMBRIA![2]

NEW PRESIDENT ELECTED IN POHL![3]

OPINION POLLS PROVE THAT 99 PER CENT OF HUMANS APPROVE OF DEMOCRACY, FREEDOM, AND A FREE PRESS![4]

Plough through all that tedious propaganda and you'll find, tucked away, small boring stories about the war, expressed drably in prose steeped in polysyllables. Or you'll watch tedious to-camera TV reports from journalists with monotonous droning voices: "Meanwhile, in Sector Blah, a further dispute with UnReconciled elements has, blah, led to . . . " Or: "Skirmishes have occurred with undemocratic supporters of the previous regime on the planet of Rachel, resulting in severe population diminutions." Or even: "The funeral was held today of the gallant soldier [whoever it was], a democrat and a liberal who perished tragically in an incident in Sector Whatever as a consequence of injuries involving a plasma cannon."[5]

This was understatement as an art form, which relied on the assumption that the majority of people are too stupid to understand there's a war going on unless there's a great big headline saying: THERE'S A WAR GOING ON![6]

But if you make a careful study of the data, as I eventually did, you would learn that there were in fact FIVE major

2 This sounds like a spoof, but is a real headline from the *Cambrian Gazette*, click here. – *Ed.*

3 The Pohlian *Times* printed this headline fifteen months in a row, after a particularly enthusiastic burst of democracy. Click here. – *Ed.*

4 I was SURE this was a gag, but no, it's yet another real headline, and it's to be found on the Beaconband news service *All the News Fit to Digitally Transmit!!!* To read it for yourself, click here. – *Ed.*

5 All these examples are invented by Artemis, but are not that far removed from the real thing. – *Ed.*

6 After extensive research, I have concluded that this is NOT in fact a real headline. – *Ed.*

intra-galactic wars taking place. Hundreds of thousands of innocent civilians had died in bombing raids. And vast space battles had taken place in which trillions, and I do mean TRILLIONS of doppelgänger robots and robotically controlled spaceships had been destroyed.

The human race was, in short, just as Fraser had said, in deadly peril. And any one of the five crazed dictators at war with the SNG had the power to end democracy and freedom, and restore us once more to a state of tyranny and evil.

Fraser explained most of this to me that afternoon, carefully and Scottishly. And I absorbed everything he said in my usual retentive way.

Then, as the afternoon wore on, Fraser told me about Roger Layton and how he came to be leader of the human race.

Here's the story, as it was told to me, shorn of Fraser's little moralistic homilies and his weird Scottish burr.

Roger Layton, before he became the famous and reclusive leader of the human race, was one of those kids who never got to play with the other kids. He was eccentric. He spoke strangely – in polysyllabic paragraphs of considerable elegance. And he was obsessed with facts and had difficulty relating to other people. His parents thought he was "weird". His fellow kids thought he was a "fucking freak". He was without a doubt ultraviolet on the autistic spectrum. And the fact is, no bugger liked him.

Roger was born near London, in a place called Stoke Newington. Once, so Fraser told me, this had been a little village outside London. Then it became part of the London Conurbation – just another busy area of the metropolis crammed with flycars and coffee shops and bistros. But in the Corporation era, large parts of the Conurbation were dismantled and replaced with idyllic countryside.

And so Stoke Newington became a quaint little village again. The houses were all magnificent farmhouses made of *ersatz* Cotswold stone, generated by orbital fabricators and shipped to Earth on the Glasgow space elevator. A river babbled through the main street of this lovely little hamlet. Carriages pulled by unicorns were the main mode of transport, with plastic bags strategically placed to capture the falling excrement of these magnificent genetically engineered beasts.

Roger's parents Gilda and Maxwell were Free Citizens of Earth. They owned four houseslaves and two robots, and were eligible for the Corporation Dividend. This of course was a peculiar reverse tax – the government pay *you* – and in consequence they were rich beyond the dreams of most people's avarice. But to justify their status as Free Citizens, Gilda and Maxwell had to spend between ten and twenty hours a week connected to a doppelgänger link, ruling an alien planet.

It was a great life, for the Corporation really looked after its shareholders. As well as the monthly dividends, they received Christmas hampers and birthday presents and bonus payments every February contingent on how many alien planets had been conquered that year. They were rich and privileged and were allowed to travel freely around the solar system. There was of course no poverty, no hunger, almost no disease, and virtually no stress, except when you were riding a doppelgänger robot fighting wars or killing aliens. It was a perfect work/life balance.

If you *weren't* a shareholder in the Corporation, however, the situation was rather different. Many Earthians lived as slaves; they weren't much better off than the settlers on the colony worlds. Roger, however, was a Citizen, and his life looked rosy.

However, when Roger was eighteen, he failed his doppelgänger aptitude test. Despite his love of computers and programming, he was so uncoordinated he couldn't move the limbs of the wretched robot. His doppelgänger was like some crazed drunk staggering into furniture. Appalled by his ineptitude, his parents considered selling him into slavery. But instead he was assigned a job as a computer facilitator in the London Underground.

This, Fraser explained to me, though I had in fact read novels set in London, was a city-wide subway transport network dating back to the nineteenth century. A labyrinth of tunnels beneath the capital; which by then of course had been replaced by the Deep Sub Tunnel which connected up every part of the British mainland via a series of supersonic travel pods. Now, the old Underground network was the home to the actual physical body of the Earth's Quantum Remote Computer, which controlled every aspect of the planet's infrastructure and also kept the entire solar system running smoothly. The solar panels orbiting the Sun, providing near-limitless energy. The orbital fabricator stations, many the size of asteroids. The spaceships. The flycars and flybikes and walk-belts. Everything, in fact! Every coffee machine and beer dispenser on the planet Earth and every other planet in the Sol System was controlled here, in the circuits of the machine that lived below London.

The mind of the Earth QRC was, of course, backed up in a thousand different locations. But *this* was its primary body. Mile after mile of servers and processers, aggregating to form a controlling quantum computer brain that ensured the human race got up in the morning, had its shit flushed away down the toilet, and never lacked hot and cold running water.

Roger was essentially a maintenance engineer, entrusted with dusting the hardware and keeping the rats and spiders out. He also, however, took a keen interest in the running of the computer. And after a while, he actually began to shadow it. Roger, remember, was a freak. He was actually good at *organising*. So Roger learned the systems that were used to keep humanity on the road.

And when the Corporation collapsed, Roger quickly realised that something had to be done. Because without a dictator at the helm, and with no army or navy to enforce the law brutally, chaos ensued. There were riots on the streets. Murders were going unpunished. Slaves were rebelling and butchering their former masters. Doppelgänger junkies deprived of their virtual fix were freaking out and committing murder and mayhem with real weapons on fellow Earthians. Several members of the Corporation Board attempted to flee Earth and were intercepted and, literally, eaten alive by mobs of angry humans who had been finally granted their freedom, and interpreted that as "freedom to run amok". (Allegedly, some Board members *did* escape, though that may be an urban myth.)

Roger was not distressed by any of this. It wasn't his way to get distressed. But he did see it as wrong and foolish, and so he took steps to remedy the situation. And to do that, he made use of his unique access to the Earth QRC.

And so doppelgänger robots controlled by the Earth QRC appeared on every street corner in London putting up posters which said: NEW GOVERNMENT REQUIRED. ELECTIONS TO BE HELD. STOP FIGHTING AND KILLING EACH OTHER, THAT'S REALLY STUPID. PLEASE HELP US BUILD A NEW WORLD.

Riots were, at this time, rife. Police flycars were being shot down. Army trucks were fair game for arsonists. And paint ball guns had been fired against all the buildings in Whitehall, turning the white Portland stone into a rainbow explosion of mockery.

As you'd expect, when the DRs started to appear on the streets there was widespread panic. But these DRs did not have guns, just rolls of smartplastic posters. They would stick a ball of goo to a wall, which would unfurl as if by magic to form a poster. Some rioters fired bullets at the DRs but they didn't fight back, or in any way acknowledge the threat. They just carried on putting up posters, the largest of which were gooed-up on the front façade of the Houses of Parliament.

And the same thing was happening all over the United Kingdom. In Leeds, and Bradford and Glasgow and Edinburgh and Sheffield and Cardiff and Swansea and all cities in between.

In country towns DRs flew over carrying banner messages. Television stations were locked to a single image, of a poster message from Roger Layton: ELECT A PARLIAMENT YOU FOOLS. Radio stations broadcast the same sensible words. All MIs were tuned to Layton's signal, and so it wasn't possible to speak subvocally to another person without hearing a murmured message of common sense and hope.

And then Roger spread his message to all the other nations of the world; for the Earth QRC that dwelled in the London Underground controlled all of human space. Posters and broadcasts of hope appeared in every country of the world. And the same thing happened on Mars and Venus and all the inhabited asteroids, and in all the Dyson Jewels. One computer mind connected all these different habitats, and that mind was now under the control, or rather influence, of Roger Layton.

The effect was devastating; people stopped and read the posters, and listened to the voices in their heads. And then they thought about what they had read and heard. And then they went home and started being sensible again.

For the terrible truth is that, up until this moment, in the midst of riots and lynchings and countless acts of random violence, it hadn't occurred to anyone that it was possible to create a new and different and indeed *better* system.

But once the messages from Roger appeared, suddenly the way was clear.

And so everyone did as Roger said.

Political parties were formed. Governments were elected in all the nations of Earth and Sol System. The history books were dusted off and countries remembered their long forgotten identities – Smithiana was now renamed Africa, for instance, and Cowboya became the United States of America. All this Roger controlled, because he was such a geek and because he paid attention to history.

And then Roger decided that humans needed a single controlling entity to coordinate Earth and all the colony planets. So he created it, and called it the Solar Neighbourhood Government. And it needed a leader. and he suggested himself. ROGER LAYTON SHOULD BE PRESIDENT OF THE SOLAR NEIGHBOURHOOD GOVERNMENT said the posters on every street corner and noticeboard in the humanverse. And so everyone agreed that it should be so.

And meanwhile, Roger was still living in the London Underground network. He used to go for long walks every day, from Victoria to Paddington and round the Circle Line to Victoria again. Up north to Walthamstow. Across to Baron's Court. There was a whole other world down there, below the real world, and Roger was its only inhabitant.

Occasionally, he would set the escalators into motion and go up to the surface. He'd wander into quaint little tea rooms and overhear the chatter and the gossip. But he never spoke to anyone, because Roger didn't like people. He didn't know how to deal with them.

But he understood them *in theory*. He knew about emotions. He understood the need for humans to form into communities. He researched and comprehended the appeal of charismatic leaders, and decided that's exactly what the human race *didn't* need any more.

He was appalled by inefficiency. Which is why he liked computers. Computers were never inefficient. They just got on and did things in the most efficient way possible. (Without ever knowing *why*. That's why the humanverse needed a Roger Layton.)

There was, Roger had learned, a constant data flow between the Earth QRC and the computers on Cambria, Gullyfoyle, Pohl and all the other colony planets. They chatted, really. Exchanged gossip about their human operatives. They were sentient enough to have opinions – rather scornful and sarcastic opinions by and large. But these computers had no ambitions, no desires, no needs. They could easily have conquered humanity long ago. but they saw no reason to do so, and had no motive to do so. For

QRCs have intelligence, and even purpose, but they do not know and cannot know desire. Desire of *any* kind.

They did all like Roger though. They thought that Roger was one of them. An honorary quantum remote computer. And so Roger adopted this same curious dispassionate all-seeing approach to things. The QRCs of the humanverse knew everything and saw everything. If a sparrow or a yarlbird died, anywhere in human-occupied space, they would know.

Thus Roger became a kind of god. But it never went to his head. He retained his sanity. Power could not corrupt him. *That's* what made him such a freak.

And even now, as leader of the humanverse, Roger never leaves his tunnels. He walks each day through the empty tunnels, from White City to Upminster, or from Goldhawk Road to Aldgate East. And he gives his Prime Minister weekly instructions about what to do, and not to do. And if anyone tries to reform things that are already working perfectly well, he sends his doppelgänger robots out with posters saying STOP BEING SILLY. It is, in many ways, the perfect system.

This was the story Fraser told me. I suspected he was embellishing slightly,[7] because he had, it seemed to me, a weirdly wry sense of humour. But then Fraser came to the crux of it:

"Roger gave the human species its freedom. Every enslaved colony planet, he set it free. Every human subspecies was treated fairly, and was given the space to forge their own civilisations. The SNG was meant to be nothing more than a regulatory body, controlling trade and good relations between all the many unique societies. Because Roger had decided the time for empires was over.

"But he forgot about the Clan bosses. They were used to power. And they weren't going to give it up without a fight. And so all the *capobastone* on all the Clan-controlled planets

7 The tone may be fabulistically exaggerative, but the outlines of the historical story are broadly correct. – *Ed.*

declared war on Earth and the SNG, all on the same day. And that's when the Great War of Survival began. Since then, twenty five *capobastone* have been defeated, ten of them since I joined this outfit. Five remain. They have armies greater than the mind can encompass. They have doppelgänger robots who can serve their bidding. And their aim is to destroy the SNG in order to achieve complete freedom from – well, freedom. We have to stop them. Or Earth itself will be destroyed. And that is your mission Artemis."

"Not a problem," I said, at the end of Fraser's long though admittedly rather interesting tirade.

Not that I gave a shit about freedom and the future of humanity. But this was my one and only way out.

"However," I said, "I still have my one condition."

"It's impossible," Fraser explained. "Cúchulainn has a democratically elected government. The SNG has no authority there."

"I don't care. Find a way. But you have to do it," I said. "Kill Daxox – and then I'm yours."

Chapter 6

The Assassination of Daxox

Here's what you need to know about Daxox.

Girls liked him.

They liked him not because he was a hunk, 'cause he certainly wasn't. Or because he was sexy, 'cause he wasn't that either, not really. They liked him because he was so fucking *droll.* And irreverent. And deliciously rude.

Being with Daxox was like being trapped in a lift with a gang of Jewish comedians, each tasked with itemising your shortcomings in vividly offensive hyperbole. It was all stupid stuff, but it made me laugh.

He was also a psychopath and a sociopath, and had a serious serial killing habit. I mean, even for a gang boss, he was a very violent man.

Looking back, I suspect he needed therapy. I mean, his behaviour was totally obsessive-compulsive. He was an addict of the extreme. He loved inflicting pain on his enemies – it wasn't just business with Daxox. Therapy could probably have cleared his mind and left him as a decent normal citizen.

But hey, I'm pretty fucked in the head too. Revenge is all I understand. My mind is – you don't need to know that. Suffice to say: Artemis-brain = dark and evil place.

I've told you already how I met Daxox, over the jewel thing. Then I went to his club. And I got drunk that night, totally kissing-men-and-giggling arseholey drunk. Stupid in the circumstances, but I did. He took me home in his car and tucked me up in his bed and lay down next to me. But he didn't take any liberties. We just slept together, like brother and sister. And when I woke up the next morning I found a poem next to my bed. He'd written me a poem! It was a terrible poem. It had lines like:

Your face is as tender as charity
When you're drunk you are full of hilarity

It charmed me. The sheer badness of it just, well, blew me away.

Later however I learned that Daxox had been considered one of the greatest poets of his generation, before he was initiated into the Clan. But he was smart enough to know that great poetry doesn't work with young women these days. But stupid – hey! – that works. Stupid plays.

The next day we went for dinner and he insisted on dancing with me when the band started up. He was a terrible dancer. Two left feet, both fastened on the wrong way. He trod on my toe and I had to be carried back to my chair, giggling.

Later I learned that Daxox had been a medal-winning ballroom dancing when he was in his twenties. But no young woman these days likes to be outclassed on the dance floor. Clumsy plays much better. So, the wily fox, he played clumsy.

After we'd been together a month, an assassin broke through his cordon sanitaire and put a projectile bullet in his shoulder. Daxox's bodyguard dragged the would-be killer away, vowing to kill him. And I nursed Daxox for weeks after that. It was during the period when he was convalescing – while I was walking through the streets, looking up at the moons – that I realised I loved him.

I changed his dressings daily – I hated to let the autodoc near him. I reassured him that it was normal for some people to hate him. Just because an assassin had tried to kill him, didn't mean he wasn't a nice person! I was his nurse, and his lover, and his confidante.

That was one of the happiest periods of my life, those weeks when Daxox was recovering from his bullet wound. He seemed so vulnerable. I vowed to stay close to him in future, to protect him. I'm a natural warrior, you see, I can't help wanting to *protect* people.

A few years later though, when I was in captivity, I spotted Daxox's shooter. He was a *picciotto* working for Baron Lowman. He hadn't in fact been killed by the bodyguards. The entire shooting had been a put-up job. Daxox's way of luring me into bed, by making me feel *sorry* for him.

I loved Daxox with all my heart. But he had played me, like a fish on a hook. Reeling me in, then reeling me out. And in the end I sucked the hook into my mouth and threw myself on to the bastard's fucking boat.

Okay, that's it. No more fucking fishing metaphors!

The point being – Daxox betrayed me, in so many ways. My hate for him was so intense it haunted my every thought.

And now he was going to die.

This is how it went down:

Fraser had done a deal with the newly elected Cúchulainn government, using trumped up evidence that Daxox was in league with the five rebel Clan leaders.[1] A joint task force had been created, made up of local Laguid Arrest Cops and SNG Special Forces. But they didn't use real warriors, they had doppelgänger robot bodies, of the humaniform variety. Some of the

1 This later turned out to be entirely true, but Artemis didn't know it at the time. – *Ed.*

doppelgängers were posing as customers at the club, some as strippers. It was, trust me, a remarkable sight. I saw it all on the Gold Control cameras, and through the eyes of the doppelgängers launching the raid.

My doppelgänger robot was not a stripper, I'm glad to say. I was one of the ones with guns, who smashed down the walls and came in shooting.

Look, I know what you're thinking! It still doesn't make any sense, does it? Me and Daxox. I mean, what was I thinking of?

Well for starters, I was young at the time, okay? I didn't know any different. I just didn't, I really *didn't*, know any better. And besides – besides—

Fuck! So hard to put it in words! So let me try and explain, with two images from my past.

First, picture this: me on my first day in Laguid. Capital city of Cúchulainn. Wide-eyed and stupid, with a stolen necklace burning a hole in my pocket. Looking around at the ugliest place in the humanverse. The skies were black, and the cities were crammed to bursting with pyramidical fabricator plants that loomed above the houses and the streets. Smoke billowed out into the air, turning blue daytime skies into carbonised night. When it rained, some days it rained ash. And I loved that. I loved it!

What a naïve young fool I was.

And now, picture this: me and Daxox, in his club where the evil and the deviants dwell, drinking all night long. Pouring booze down our throats till we could barely speak. Then when morning came we'd stagger out of the club and watch the dawn peep through the ghastly black pall of smoke. And we would totter there on the pavement, savouring the getting-pissed-in-reverse dizzying sensation, as the rejuve cleared our systems of alcohol.

And then, shuddering into sobriety, we'd watch the early morning commuters clinging to the underside of the conveyor belts, hitching a free and fast ride to work. And we'd laugh and savour the horror of it all.

So ugly it was beautiful; that was Cúchulainn.

And that was Daxox too.

Daxox was always testing me. That should have been a clue to – no matter. He tested me, and I never failed him.

For example, after we had been together a couple of months, he asked me if I was prudish. I said – fuck, no! Anything but!

Yeah, you can imagine what followed. And, to be honest, I lapped it up. All the dressing up, partner-swapping, orgies – what could be more fun?

After a while, however, it was obvious I was finding it all more arousing than HE was. Daxox was a homebody at heart. He liked to curl up in bed with one woman at a time. He loved to be talked to as he went to sleep. So the kinky sex and the *ménages à trois et quatre et quelquefois cinq* came to an end.

And I guessed then that it had all been a test. But hell, I didn't care. I was young! I was still finding out about stuff. And I *love* sex; I mean, there's nothing more enjoyable than getting naked with—

Hey, what am I, a tour guide? The point is. He tested me.

One night in a bar he pointed out an obese guy talking to some girls. "Deal with him," said Daxox.

So I waited for the fat oaf outside the club and filled his body with bullets. He didn't die. He came at me with a knife. I had to beat the fucker to death with my bare hands. Turned out he had a robot torso, only the head was human. So I cut his head off his shoulders and took it to Daxox, who laughed and said, "That's my girl."

I never did learn what the guy did wrong. I never asked. That was the test. Not the killing (for Daxox knew I could kill). The *not asking*. I passed.

Another time, there was a problem in one of the food fabricator plants, Delta Amigo 4. Some of the workers were covertly gathering, and speeches about workers' rights were being made. There were rumours of a union being formed.

So I spent a month undercover, working side by side with these guys. Herding cows and sheep. Tending vines and food plants. Watching the meat being butchered by robot knives. And of course watching over the protein farms. Eventually, I found the ringleaders – they were old guys, grandfathers and grandmothers, with large families. They wanted a better life for their children and their children's children; and they were planning a mass mutiny against the Clan tyrannisation of their lives.

So I found them guilty of pilfering, and threw them in the fabricator vat.

That was a test. I liked those guys. They all carried photographs of their grandkids and told stories of the good old days. Which weren't that different from the current days, but were more fondly remembered. But the test was: do not flinch.

I did not flinch.[2]

Oh, and did I mention aliens? That was the other big Daxox test; the alien safari.

The planet was full of aliens you see. It was a shock to me, when I first discovered that. Because Rebus was a terraformed

2 During the editing of this book, I interrogated Artemis about this event. She denied she felt in any way guilty about it. And yet, such was her evident distress, she clearly did. This is the only time so far as I'm aware that Dr McIvor lied to me. – *Ed.*

world, and the only animals I ever saw were dogs and cats, which were kept as pets. Gullyfoyle was also terraformed, and all the animals were Earth animals. Except for the dragons and the manticores, but those were genetically engineered creations, not indigenous aliens.

But Cúchulainn was blessed with an Earth-type atmosphere, and a mild climate. So the original settlers had no need to terraform, thereby killing all the native flora and fauna. They simply colonised, and allowed the least nasty of the native life forms to survive.

It meant the planet was a remarkably exotic genuine alien habitat; and so one of Daxox's best earners was organising safaris for Earth Gamers. That's where the alien safari test came in.

There were a dozen Earthians on the expedition that I led, inhabiting Mark 5 Doppelgänger Robot bodies. Smaller than the military model, with more design features. Glaring red eyes. Arms that turn into cannons. Gyroscopic auto-hover. Full speech capacity to replicate the Earthian rider's vocals.

I wore my war suit. Soft silver armour. Bandolier. Rifle-cannon on a backstrap. Gunbelt with double barrel multi-use Wesson pistols. My long black hair was in a ponytail. I was pretty fucking hot, and I knew it. And that's why Daxox wanted me on this trip. I could see the DRs' eyes glittering red as they stared at me. Wondering if raping the guide was in their contract of engagement. (It wasn't.)

"My name," I said, "is Artemis McIvor, and I am your guide."

They introduced themselves. I already had them on chip, so any time I looked at a robot body I saw the human's name in my visual array. They were – no, I can't remember their names now, and I later wiped the chip files. They were all ignorant fucks, that's all you need to know. No small talk. They'd never done anything with their lives apart from tend their estates and play Games. Some of the Earthians, the well connected, don't even do their twelve hours a week minimum conscript duty. Not unless it's the Cambrian Festival or some such shit.

"What are we hunting?" said one of the DR-Earthians whose names I've now forgotten. Let's call him Dumb Fucker 1.

"Well," I said, "there's savannah big game. Like the Sabre-Mastodon, the Eagle-Mantis, and the Aurelian Orc. And there's snakes, or rather giant serpents. And of course there are the sentients, the Caipora. Or we could go into the swamps and shoot some Nargans and Jengus."

"The Caipora," said Dumb Fucker 2, "how dangerous are they?"

"They have bow and arrow technology," I informed him.

The Dumb Fuckers all laughed.

"With exploding arrows. Their range is pretty good too. A direct hit, and your chassis is gone, even with your force field up."

"Impossible. A force field can—"

"Trust me, I've seen it. These creatures use gunpowder technology; it seems primitive, but it's not. Your fields are designed to kill the momentum of a bullet, so it can't penetrate your armour. But these are musket shells that are designed to explode whenever they slow down or stop. The blast'll rip you open like a tin can."

"If that happens, I'll want my money back," said Dumb Fucker 4.

"Of course," I said soothingly. "I'll give you the paperwork. All you have to do is sue the Corporation."

And so we set off, into the wilderness.

There wasn't a *lot* of wilderness, I have to admit. Since half the planet was made up of factory.

And the skies – well, skies cover the whole world. So the black smog followed us even as we flew away from the cities and towards the dense forests and sheer mountain ranges of the North-Eastern Territories of Cúchulainn. We were in a Firefox 4 with a glass hull. The views below were spectacular. Lakes and glaciers and other stuff like that.

The Dumb Fuckers kept up a constant hail of banter and chatter, comparing their relative experiences as Alien Monster Killers. Between them, they'd killed an awful lot of aliens, many of them sentient. But it was usually on planets that were due to be terraformed, with only Scientists and Soldiers living there. There was something cool, they felt, about killing aliens on a planet that had been settled by ordinary humans.

I felt like a rube. I'd never killed an alien. I assumed it would be fun.

And hey, it was!

We landed the Firefox and went native. I had a jetpack on my warsuit. My head was bare and I let my hair fly loose in the wind as we flew close to the ground towards our first batch of prey. A herd of Mapinguari were grazing in a blue field. They were three legged and purple furred and each was the size of a city flybus. Giants, in other words! I had no idea this planet was so fertile, to sustain beasts the size of this.

"On my count," I said, and the DR/Gamers started firing randomly. The first fusillade of bullets all missed. They tore up the purple grass, and the herd scattered. But the Gamers recovered. Their robot bodies flew fast towards the stampeding Mapinguari and they fired again and the first of the Mapinguari began to explode, in a mess of blue blood and entrails.

Two of the Gamers landed and the Mapinguari herd turned and rushed at them. They were trampled underfoot. The howls of rage of the Mapinguaris filled the air. But when they backed away the DRs were still intact and carrying swords. The Mapinguaris roared, and scraped the grass with their hooves, then charged. And swords flashed. Flesh was ripped and torn. And the Mapinguari died in a bloody frenzy.

One DR got himself impaled on a Mapinguari horn, and I killed the beast with a mercy shot to the abdomen (where the brain was located). Then I cut the creature's horn off as a souvenir. By now the robots' silver bodies were caked in mud and shit and blood. And their red eyes sparkled with glee.

"Incoming," I said, and the Eagle-Mantises swooped down, their thin bodies spraying poison over their prey. And the robots' armour hissed as the acid etched their metal. I was getting tense now because my warsuit armour was vulnerable to sustained acid attack. So I joined the fray and began shooting the Eagle-Mantises from the sky.

"Hey, save some for us," said Dumb Fucker 6.

And so the day continued. An orgy of carnage and bloodshed. The native animals bred fast. Which was just as well, because we slew hundreds of them that day. The joy of slaughter was upon me.

"We want," said Dumb Fucker 7, "to find a Caipora next."

I'd already located the nearest nest of course. And, naturally, I had no problems with killing sentients. So we sped off to find the species once described (in an encyclopaedia I had consulted, the Hooperman book) as "a sophisticated tool-using civilisation with a strongly developed sense of morality and intense herd-loyalty and possessed of an instinct for familial love."[3]

Somewhere along the way however I got separated from my herd of blood-crazed battle-mad Earthian Gamers. And that's when I found the Caipora in hiding.

I swooped low and burned the grass with a plasma blast and the Caipora was revealed. A three-legged creature with a richly black hide and eyes on stalks. I landed, and stumbled slightly and recovered my footing. A casual 360 degree scan-round reassured me there were no other Caiporas in the vicinity lurking to ambush. And I felt a surge of excitement at seeing the beast; it seemed unreal in its alienness, yet I was close enough to smell its aroma and to see the veins in its bulging eyes. It reminded me of – I don't know what. A creature I once read

3 *Hooperman's Tree of Life,* by Andrew Hooperman. – *Ed.*

about in a book on Rebus. The Gruffalo; yes, that was it. Fictional, not mythological; and this creature reminded me—

The Caipora hissed and howled, and slashed its claws in the air, in an attempt to intimidate me. But it was unarmed, lacking in artificial body armour, and my research told me it could not spit venom, or fire electricity, or hurl poison darts. It was strong though, and its claws could apparently rip through body armour given enough time and an unconscious prey. So I had no intention of allowing it close enough to wrestle me.

I raised my rifle to deliver the *coup de grâce,* a simple head shot that would end the encounter instantly; but then I realised I could understand it. The patterns of howls and hisses were words, in English.

"Spare me," said the hissing Caipora.

I laughed. "Fuck no," I said, brutally.

"Fuck?"

"Fuck."

"What is fuck?" hissed the Caipora.

"It's a—" I raised my Wesson. I wasn't going to discuss the use of expletives with a sentient stalk-eyed monster.

"Kill me not."

"Do not kill me," I said.

I know! But I couldn't help myself.

"What say you?" the creature asked me querulously.

"Your syntax is shit. 'Do not kill me' is what you should be saying."

"Do not kill me," hissed and howled the Caipora, in a tone so forlorn it broke through my barriers of indifference and actually made me feel something.

"I'm a hunter," I pointed out, floundering somewhat by this point.

"I just got married/love-connected/hitched," said the Caipora, using multiple options to convey its meaning. "Don't break my poor husband's heart."

I sighed.

Yeah, I admit it. In the space of just a couple of minutes, I'd become fond of that black-furred three-legged fucking thing.

The Caipora told me of her life. She and her kind lived in the hills these days, breeding prolifically in the knowledge that most of their young would be hunted and killed. The Caipora were smart but had only basic technology – catapults and bows and arrows and gunpowder, but not rockets or nuclear weapons. But to give them credit, they had a theory of the universe that was halfway credible. And they were herbivores who forged alliances with other creatures, including most of the native predators. As a result, they may have been the only truly popular species in the history of all life. For no creature hunted them or ate them or even competed with them. And they hunted no other creature, but instead did their best to help others survive in their ecological niche.

Then we came along.

I led the Caipora into a side gully and concealed it under vegetation. Then I caught up with the hunters and led them in the wrong direction. It was, even so, a rich day's hunting. By the time we returned, the flier was crammed with heads and tusks and claws. Useless mementoes, since it would take decades for these to arrive back in the Earth system. But the hunters liked to have photographs of themselves taken amongst their trophies. It was some kind of bonding thing.

Then I returned to Laguid and was greeted by Daxox. He was in a warm, expansive mood. He told me a long story about the lunch he'd enjoyed, and quizzed me excitedly about my adventures with the aliens. We shared mockery of Earth Gamers – those cowardly wankers!

"How would you rate Dumb Fucker 4?" he asked me. "On the dumbological spectrum?"

"Even dumber than Dumb Fucker 5," I explained. And we roared with laughter at that gag, for a good while.

Then, after we'd shared a glass or six of champagne, he gave me two wonderful presents. A jewelled necklace, with blue stones to match my eyes, and pearls that echoed the swell of my breasts, and a black-carbon chain that perfectly echoed my night-black hair. And the other gift was a beautiful black leather jacket. I put the jacket on and marvelled at the softness of the leather. It fit me like a second skin.

"Let me touch," said Daxox. And he touched the jacket, which was indeed most extraordinarily and erotically soft and – and then I realised.

"No," I said.

"You're supposed to be a hunter," said Daxox. "Wear the jacket."

"No!"

"You can say hello to your friend if you like. She's still alive, just about."

"No!"

Daxox led me into the cellar. The Caipora was there. Flayed. Her tendons red and raw. Her eyes bugging out from her skinless skull. I was wearing the jacket made from her own hide. There's no way the Caipora would not have realised that.

"We were friends?" said the Caipora, accusingly, and I drew my gun in a moment and blew her brains out.

"Wear the coat," said Daxox, and I knew that was the test.

I wore the coat.

Last memory:

"Sweetheart, it's over," said Daxox, and it felt like I'd been stabbed.

"Yeah?" I said.

"Yeah."

"What's over?"

"Us. Our relationship. Our love. It's dead and gone. I never want to see you again, you silly bitch," said Daxox cruelly.

"No sweat," I said calmly, smiling.

Smiling?

Yeah, I was.

And this is the thing I want you to understand. It's the thing I want ME to understand.

I was smiling, because I actually thought this was just another test. The latest of his very many terrible tests, all of which I had passed with flying colours. I didn't think he actually MEANT it.

So I didn't cry. I didn't plead. I just shrugged with a hint of crossness, but still smiling, as if my lover had refused to make me breakfast and I was enjoying a minor sulk.

"See you around," I said, still playing it cool.

Daxox was grinning. That big ugly frog grin of his.

"Where the fuck do you think you're going?" he crowed.

That's when they electrocuted me. They did it through the floor. I had no chance to defend myself. I just started convulsing, with thousands of volts pouring through my body.

Then I blacked out.

And when I woke up – well.

I was bald. They'd cut off all my lovely hair. Baron Lowman was there. He gave me a mirror so I could see the scar in my skull, where they'd cut me open and inserted the whedon chip into my brain. And Daxox of course was gone.

I tried to leap from my chair and kill Baron Lowman. But when he stared at me I couldn't move my limbs. Then he handed me a knife and made me cut myself. And then – after that, you don't need to know.

I thought at first it was a test, and maybe it was. Maybe Daxox would have taken me back if I'd stuck it out for long enough. I managed nine years six months and four days. Maybe ten years was my target. Maybe if I'd still loved Daxox after ten years of all that horror, he might have considered me worthy of him?

Or maybe—

No. No more maybes. Daxox betrayed me, and for that he must die.

Back to the club.

I'm in my doppelgänger body. I have just blown a hole in the wall and I am now standing inside the Dahlia Club clutching my Xenos B rifle, which is smaller than the standard Xenos but just as versatile. A fast rap-punk song is playing with a curiously hypnotic spoken chorus and a bassline that strums the sternum and makes breathing difficult. The lightball is scattering petals of red and purple over the diners and drinkers and strippers and I can smell flowery perfume in the air and it reminds me of many wild and wonderful people I used to know here and – no, no time to reminisce—

Daxox is staring at the unfurling tableau of violent invasion, as walls explode and body-armoured cops with huge guns emerge from the steaming holes screaming, "ARMED POLICE, LIE ON THE FLOOR, HANDS ON YOUR HEAD, ARMED POLICE!" and hurling flash grenades and pop-pellets to disorientate and dazzle and deafen Daxox's goons.

I exult at his incredulity; and marvel too at the further look of astonishment on Daxox's face when two of the scantily clad strippers fly off their poles and come up holding handguns (concealed WHERE?). And at about the same time, four of the sweaty punters stand up, open their jackets, and reveal flashing badges that say POLICE and draw their guns from ankle holsters. And suddenly Daxox and his seven bodyguards at the corner table are facing a forest of pistols and machine guns, in the midst of a maelstrom of blinding light and ear-assailing detonations.

And, meanwhile, the twenty-four genuine punters and the fifteen genuine lap dancers and the seven fetishised waiters and waitresses and bar staff stare open-mouthed, trapped in someone else's action movie, appalled and half-deaf and half-blinded and consumed with fear and a desperate desire to be elsewhere.

And at exactly the same time, an automated message is being broadcast directly into Daxox's brain chip: "*This is the Laguid Police Arrest Squad, this is a genuine raid, surrender immediately by kneeling on the ground with your hands on your head. Do not reach into your pocket or make any threatening moves or you will be killed.*"

Daxox turns on his force field and comes out shooting.

The innocent civilians, whether clothed or near-naked, dive for the floor; the cops take their positions and start firing back. It is a battle of body armour and force fields, because no table can protect you from a bullet or an energy beam; and pretty much every shot hits home. The difference is, the cops are all doppelgänger robots, but Daxox and his bodyguards are made of real flesh. This will be, I predict, no contest.

The battle rages: it is a *son et lumière* of blood and bullets and tightly-focused energy beams that can rip through flesh like a sunbeam through space; bodies twitch; blood spurts; naked robot skin is seared; robot lubricating fluid gushes from severed limbs and heads; and mobile force shields are thrown up to protect the genuine and anxiously cowering customers and dancers.

I can see it all through my doppelgänger eyes, but I have no motor control over my machine. And it annoys me how slow the damned thing is! I long to be there in person; I could easily take all these pintlesucking—

Then one of Daxox's goons hits me with an energy blast and it takes off one of my robot arms. My body fires back with a projectile bullet that gets trapped in the goon's force field. So my robot body fires six more bullets at variable velocity until one breaks through and the goon explodes.

Daxox sees this and laughs. I can see with my robot eyes that there are bullets embedded in his skull. Their momentum has been sapped by his force field; so though the slugs have hit hard enough to penetrate bone, they have not gone all the way through. And still he laughs.

At that moment, I hated that evil bastard with all my being!

And yet—

I couldn't help but—

I couldn't stop myself from—

I couldn't deny that—

Yes, I'll say it. I had loved this fucker, once! And somehow, love like that never goes away.

My doppelgänger was down, shot through the spine, but my eyes could still see.

I seized the opportunity to throw out the police rider from the doppelgänger brain and take direct control of the robot. I activated the parallel neural circuits and dragged myself up to my knees and watched the gun battle unfold. Projectile bullets bounced off force fields and smashed into walls and bar optics. The bar staff had now vanished, probably into their secure basement.

But there was no way out for Daxox. His force field was holding up, but the cops were using variable pulses and were alternating plasma bursts with projectile bullets with taser blasts to bombard him ceaselessly. All around, doppelgänger and human bodies were strewn across the floor. Metal limbs and fleshy arms and legs were severed and scattered. Robots with gaping holes in their bodies fired incessant blasts of angry war at the armoured bodyguards in that corner snug.

Then Daxox's force field flickered, and a bullet went through. I saw a splash of blood and I knew he was hit.

I seized my moment. I tottered across to him, absorbing a hail of bullets and plasma blasts, until I was close to Daxox. He raised his gun to blast my head off and I spoke, with full voice emulation.

"It's me," I said, and Daxox was stopped in his tracks. Fear and rage possessed him. He fired at my skull and the bullet went through my robot brain but I still had enough neural control to put one hand through his force field and grab him by the throat.

He was scared now. I was shattering his larynx. His eyes burned into mine saying – what? Forgive me, or Fuck you? I would never know.

Then I grabbed his skull with my other hand and ripped his head off his shoulders. And held the head in my robot hand.

And still he laughed. His brain kept alive by an oxygen capsule.

I took my gun and fired it into his eyes. One, two, three, four – fifteen bullets in all. At some point I realised that it was over. Daxox was dead.

And I was back in Gold Control room, taking deep breaths. Savouring the last moments of Daxox.

"Happy now?" asked Fraser.

I thought about it.

The answer was: No, not really, in truth.

I felt no joy at the death of Daxox. Because in a way, it meant the end of everything for me. For so many years, hate and rage had possessed me, and motivated me.

Now I was left with – nothingness.

But at least I knew what I would be doing next. For Fraser had kept his side of the bargain. Now it was up to me.

Now I had to – oh fuck.

Save the universe?

Edited Highlights from the Thought Diary and Beaconband Blog of Dr Artemis McIvor

BOOK 2

WAR[1]

1 For a fuller chronological account of the Clan Wars, read *History of the War to End All Wars* by Professor Andrew Swift (Way Out of Orbit Books), a volume of which I am also the (unacknowledged, even on the Acknowledgements page, which is typical of academics really) editor. – *Ed.*

Chapter 7

Dying Many Times

We jumped from the heliplane and fell like stones, plunging faster and faster towards the cobbles of the citadel city of Kandala. Then I triggered the inertial cocoon on my warsuit that would halt my descent and thus allow me to—

Fuck.

I hit the cobbles. Blood spurted. Organs squished. I died.

We jumped from the heliplane and fell like stones, plunging faster and faster towards the cobbles of the citadel city of Kandala. I triggered the inertial cocoon on my warsuit. And—

I hit the cobbles, rolled, got back to my feet. This time, I was alive. Billy and Catrin grinned at me. But Andres was crushed and dead inside his rock hard warsuit.

We moved his body out of sight, dumping it into one of the vast trenches that disfigured this wasteland. This whole area still smelled, after all these years, of burned human flesh. There was a cold breeze. My visual array showed that there were no hostiles in this area. This was the Boneyard, where for so many years the bodies of the Corporation's victims had been burned and forgotten.

In the old days this had been a Wargame Planet, and the colonists of Kandala had struggled each year to meet their toll of warriors and virgins for the monthly Slaughters. In the interests of research, I'd tried to experience a few of the more popular Slaughter Shows, but even I found them obscene and intolerable. And I am, for fuck's sake, a stone cold killer.

The Boneyard was on the east-flanking side of the Citadel. The Citadel walls loomed high in the distance, bleakly majestic, capped with rounded be-flagged turrets that jutted at intervals along the stone parapet, with *meurtrières* beneath that stared like eyes. The city itself, I knew from my briefing, was larger than London in its pre-Cheo heyday, and it was TP-blocked. This is why we'd had to parachute down the old fashioned way.

We stripped off our warsuits and buried them in a shallow grave. We had identity tattoos that would allow us access to secure buildings, and a good working knowledge of the Kandala dialect, which was Norse in origin. This had been a medieval society in the old days, with jousting, sword duels and battlefields. Ancient wars were re-enacted with doppelgänger knights in armour fighting against real human colonists clad in jerkins and penetrable chainmail. The battles would often last for weeks and the dead would be piled high upon the green fields, where the crows and the vultures would peck at them, before eventually being dumped in the Boneyard.

Now, thankfully, those days were gone. But even though the Corporation itself no longer existed, its former minion, the High Priestess, still ruled supreme here.

We jogged until the smell of death had left our nostrils. then slipped into the Mercantile Quarter. The market stalls were mostly unattended and sealed up. We struck a swaggering aspect in our kirtles and surcoats (me and Catrin) and doublet and breeches (Billy). We were playing the roles of *vangeliste* who expected due obeisance from the *piccioti* and the unranked criminals who we passed; and this we duly received. The ordinary citizens, however, paid us little heed.

This was a war-torn city. Wherever we went, we saw burned-out houses and gaping holes and trenches gouged out of the roads and pavements by falling bombs and descending energy beams. SNG forces had laid siege to Kandala for two years, according to our briefing. The planet's force fields and protective anti-missile systems had held, and no major damage had been caused. But the ceaseless fusillade of missiles and energy beams was bound to result in occasional "successes". Which had duly ripped the shit out of many areas of the city.

Above us the sky was lit with trails of fire, as the weary ceaseless fusillade of SNG missiles were blown out of the sky by interceptor drones every few minutes. The sky was like a murky violet canvas spattered with red and yellow paint.

We made our way to the Citadel, along the Golden Road. This was a vastly broad pedestrian avenue which was literally made of gold, and was unpleasantly spongy underfoot. Stretching out as far as the eye could see and further were the encircling and high and richly jewelled Citadel walls, which we now approached, and marvelled at. Up close, we could see the true beauty of the impregnable fusion-forged bricks, inlaid with mosaics of precious stones that shimmered in the sun's lazy beams. The wall bore no scars from the many bombs and energy beams that had lashed it over the years; for it was self-healing, and astonishingly strong. Behind these walls, we could see the seven Cathedral domes; and next to those, the Silver Campanile. And to our west, the awe-inspiring Forest of Towers in the midst of which the High Priestess dwelled.

And all around at street level, where we stood outside the walls, were deserted shops and market stalls that once had bustled with rich traders and shamefully extravagant customers.

The Kandala Citadel was, the briefing notes had told us,

based on detailed accounts of the Welsh citadel of Camelot written in the twenty-second century by a psychic who claimed to be channelling the wizard Merlin. In reality, this place bore no resemblance to any actual medieval castled city. It was a parody of a pastiche based upon a lunatic's dream.

"Have you ever wondered—" I began to say to Billy, and then a hidden camera must have spotted us because plasma beams came from nowhere and engulfed us and we died.

The next time we got as far as the Jousting Court, where I saw the High Priestess herself. And I reached for my tag gun and then—

Then I died, fuck knows how, but I felt my head fall off my shoulders and that was that.

The simulations were uncannily detailed, and felt utterly "real". For the first time in my life I could start to understand why Earth Gamers and doppelgänger riders could become so addicted to—

No, let's not go there. Even here, in this thought diary, where—

Okay let's go there. I *can* start to understand. The thrill, the buzz, the addiction, that comes from riding a doppelgänger robot.

Because living in a virtual universe is like life – but better, more intense, and without consequences. You live, you die, who cares? You can just savour the moment. The smells. The tastes. The sights. The joy of battle. The thrill of slaughter. The exhilaration of experiencing your own death.

And okay I had a mission, so I wasn't doing all this for fun. It wasn't as if – but ah, what the fuck. I couldn't deny it.

I was enjoying myself.

I embarked upon twenty-five missions to Kandala and died every time. But I came to enjoy the swish of my long tunic dress as I walked on old cobbled stones. I thrilled at the heft of a longsword in my hand. My heart soared with joy every time I impaled a human being on my sword and watched them die, slowly.

This is how the Earthian élite used to spend their lives. Okay there was a certain amount of genuine work to be done – an empire to maintain – but for most of the time, they would just sit in a virtual booth and hook up to a doppelgänger, and live vicariously.

And of course, that's how the Corporation empire endured for so long. It's astonishing when you think about it. There were thousands of inhabited planets, each with millions if not billions of inhabitants, and probably no more than three or four million Earthian masters to rule them all. But thanks to virtual beaconband technology, a single pimply Earthian could control a regiment of super-powered doppelgänger robots. One of these arrogant mollyfockers could crush a rebellion, massacre the bravest and the best of an entire nation, and *still* be downstairs in time to have dinner with Mum and Dad.

I consider myself to be a hard bastard. But I've never been able to understand how those evil shits could live with themselves, after doing what they did. They raped, murdered, pillaged, tortured, and hunted humans for sport. The entire Solar Neighbourhood Community of Planets was just a giant interactive snuff movie for these masters of the universe.

And yet—

And yet I was, it seemed to me, now experiencing something similar in the battleground sims. A sense of utter power, and a visceral thrill that comes from experiencing danger, without actually *being* in danger.

So yeah, it's addictive.

I was, incidentally, just to get it out in the open, at this point in my life's story having a wildly passionate sexual relationship with Billy.

Remember Billy? He was the old-timer who met me when I came out of the brainthrashing machine back in Giger. He had given me some vital TLC. Then he'd warned me they were sending a doppelgänger to kill me. After that – well, we became friends of sorts. But not close. Then I left Giger, as you know. And now he was working for Fraser too, on the same suicide squad deal, and one thing led to—

I mean! Can you fucking *believe* it? Me, and an old baldy ginch like Billy?

We kept it secret at first. But before long, the entire battalion knew. After that night when – no, you don't need to know about what happened that night. It was – no!

Let me tell you about Billy.

Billy used to be a Space Marine.

And that's it. That's all you need to know. He was one of *those* guys.

Tough, for sure.

Ruthless, without doubt.

Fit as fuck, despite the bald head and wrinkles. That's just superficial ageing. Billy in fact has the body of a warrior; as I know, ahem, only too well.

He is also calm. Amazingly calm. Reassuringly calm. And resourceful. And alert. He sees everything, without effort, like a lion lazily glancing across the savannah.

He isn't introspective. He doesn't write poetry. He has no moral qualms, or philosophical queries about life. Just give him a gun and body armour and he'd go and frag an entire planet full of alien fuckers, and be back for tea. No nightmares. No pangs of guilt. He is an awkward, cussed, angry, brawling, sentimental when drunk, cheerfully practical when sober, no-nonsense old-timer.

My first day on the Rock,[1] I'd spotted a few familiar faces from Giger Pen on the same "suicide squad" deal, and Billy's was among them. This wasn't good news for me, because as you'll recall, I'd double-crossed all the prisoners including Billy when I staged my celebrated escape. It was a fair bet that some of the guys would be sore. It was a matter of time, in other words, before someone tried to kill me.

It happened on Day Two of my stay on the Rock. I'd barely recovered my strength after what had happened on Cúchulainn with Jimmi and the blood transfusion. So I was aiming to keep my head down, stay out of trouble.

And then I had a heart attack.

I didn't see it coming. I didn't even notice Macintosh walking up to me. Who's Macintosh? Some just fucking nobody. But he happened to have been at Giger, and, well, there you go.

Macintosh had a taser and he shot me in the back with it, at full voltage. Thousands of volts of electricity pulsed through me. And my heart stopped.

Then I turned and hit him with a knife-hand strike to the throat. It should have been fatal. But Macintosh just grinned. The taser had sapped my strength; it was as if I'd tickled his tummy. There were three other ex-cons from Giger Pen with him, all with knives. I fell to the ground, desperately trying to restart my heart. Then I glimpsed a fourth person – Billy. Another person I'd fucked off at Giger!

When I regained consciousness, Billy had me over his shoulder and was carrying me back to my cell. I deduced he'd creamed the opposition and saved my life, and I tried to say thank you but he refused to listen to my little speech. "Don't be a stranger," he said as he left.

1 Headquarters of the Anti-Clan Maverick Warfare Squad led by Brigadier Fraser. – *Ed.*

The next day Macintosh had been ghosted out of the programme. Fraser took a dim view of internecine warfare. We were there to kill the enemy, not each other.

Anyway, that's how Billy came back into my life.

The rest was just – well. I knew I owed him. He seemed to like me. I was feeling pretty lonely. Sex seemed like a good idea.

It wasn't like we were in *love*.

It spooked me though. Billy had helped me twice now. He'd been, magically, the right person in the right place at the right time. Coincidence? Or destiny?

I *do* believe in destiny by the way. It's my primary superstition. I don't use totems, but I believe I have a hidden purpose. And my god is Ganesh. Billy, however, worshipped the Santieran Orisha known as Changó. Who happens to be the god of thunder and lightning. And I'd been electrocuted with an energy pulse from a Mark 4 taser. Random coincidence, or destiny?

Well, I know what *I* think, okay?

Billy and I weren't in the same cohort but I caught his eye in the canteen the day after my heart attack. And I nodded once. To show that I was willing to let him approach me. So he ambled over.

"How're you doing?" he asked.

"Heart's healing," I replied.

"Steak's good."

"So I hear."

"Join me?"

"I don't see why not."

And so we had lunch together.

The dining hall on the Rock was multi-level, and self-service. No robots, no serving trays, you had to actually queue.

The food was good, compared to Giger Pen. Mediocre compared to the *haute cuisine* I'd known on Cúchulainn. Meat – Thorak steak from Weisman or Pohlian bandersnatch, at a guess – potatoes, and a green vegetable I'd never seen before. The guy next to me called it a quok; the "qu" prefix gave away that it was a genetically created New Form, rather than edible alien life.

The Rock, by the way, really was a rock. An asteroid with navigational jets and biodomes. It was in effect a mobile planet that could be towed at half-light speed from world to world, picking up new recruits along the way.

Fraser had scooped me up on Cúchulainn with an army of other losers, wankers, wasters and drifters – six thousand of us in all, I estimated – and we were now in transit to the nearby planet of Garcia.

It had been a shock, I have to admit, to discover I was just one among so very many. 'Cause when Fraser first pitched this deal to me, I sort assumed that I was *special.*

You know – one of the élite team. Hand-picked. Each with a special skill, and a unique mannerism or catch-phrase. The six toughest meanest mollyfockers in the galaxy!

Or maybe even twelve. A dozen daring mavericks! The *twelve* meanest mollyfockers in the galaxy!

I hadn't appreciated that, in this deal, I was pretty much cannon fodder. So when I walked through the doors to the Muster Hall and saw the mob within – *thousands* of mean mollyfockers, and those were just the new guys – well, my self-esteem took something of a nose dive.

But, you know, you get over these things.

Anyway, long story shorter: Billy and I got our food and sat down to eat.

"You like ketchup?"

"You bet."

"Me too."

He passed the ketchup. I drenched my steak in it. I passed him the ketchup back. He drenched his steak too.

And it was good. A bonding moment. A mutual both-liking-lots-of-ketchup moment.

Hey, these things matter!

And so there we were. Bonding. Sitting side by side in a canteen of about fifty thousand other mean mollyfockers. Billy was smoking a cigarette, the first I'd seen in a hundred years. And it was real nicotine too. His fingers were yellow. His teeth were crooked. He was *old.*

"Food good?" he asked.

"I've had better."

"Me too."

"And worse."

"You betcha."

Billy, as you may have gathered, wasn't given much to small talk.

However, over the months that followed, he told me a few of his amazing true-life stories.

For instance:

Billy had had Space Marine friends who'd been on the expedition into the world of the Bugs. There, they had of course all died.

But *before* they died, he told me, they'd called up their old Marine friends on the MI imagelink. All the guys and the girls and the herms they had trained with and served with, over a period of years. And they'd said a mass "Hello", and they'd explained the situation, and told some jokes and funny stories, as they waited for their inevitable doom.

Then when the moment came, they said a final goodbye.

By this time *millions* of Space Marines had clustered online, watching the imagelink messages on their retinal arrays. And then the doomed Marines hung up. And the Bugs came and ate them alive. But those soldiers died in the very best of ways: fearlessly, and in the company of their fellow Marines.

That made it a good death, Billy told me. And he was, he added, proud to have had those guys as friends.

It was a brief story, and Billy told it poignantly, but matter-of-factly. Death held no terror for him. He'd been maimed, dismembered, mutilated and patched up a hundred times and regarded it as no big deal. Billy wore his body like it was a battered old raincoat with stains that he couldn't be bothered to clean off.

I loved that story. I can't explain why.

Billy was also a shy man. And he had almost no social skills. For instance:

"Fuck?"

"Now?"

"Yeah."

"Sure."

That was our first date.

On the plus side he had, from the neck down, a body like a Greek god. And he was tender too.

On the minus side, he had an astonishing amount of body hair. It even came out of his ears! Having sex with Billy with like firkytoodling a gorilla, it really was. Though I'm guessing there of course.

I discovered that I really liked him.

This is how it came about. The first time we fucked, I mean.

We were the last table left in the bar. It was malt whisky and stories time. I told my stories, which were wild and extravagant and largely untrue. The other guys around the table told their tales, again with huge hyperbole and plenty of hushed pauses for effect.

And then Billy, with calm understatement, talked about some of the wars in which he'd fought. He'd fought in a lot of wars. He'd been in the attack squad in the first Heebie-Jeebie Skirmish. He'd helped annihilate the Zoltan, a species no one remembers now, but they were even crueller and more homicidal than the human race. He'd led the doomed assault on the flame beasts, averted at the last moment when the Cheo finally came to his senses. He'd quelled mutinies on countless planets.

Oh, and he'd even led an army of Lopers to victory against a colony ship of Eagles, on Enceladus. That was a great story. Lopers leaping, Eagles soaring, no weapons, just claws and talons. Till Billy fired up his armoured spacesuit (which was more like a tank with arms) and massacred the Eagles as they flew.

But he didn't describe the battles, not in any detail anyway. It was all about the people. His comrades and superiors and enemies. He conjured them up in brief word-portraits. Their foibles. Their stupidities. Their favourite sayings. He had no concept of the epic yarn. All he knew was the tiny anecdote.

He told one tale about a Space Marine comrade called Darius, who carried a lucky charm into every battle. On the day he died, Darius forgot his lucky charm.

Billy showed us the charm – it was a Celtic Cross. A pagan icon, with cross bars of the same length. Darius had given the charm to Billy, on the eve of their big battle. Darius claimed he'd had a premonition of disaster and didn't want the magic icon to go to waste. Billy had thought his friend was nutso, but didn't argue. You never argue with a warrior, on the eve of a battle. It can lead to unpleasantness of the extremest variety.

Then, next day, the day of the battle, their transport ship was attacked by enemy missiles which rent their force field and smashed great holes in the hull. All the crew were suited up, but

Darius had died when his spacesuit sprang a leak and he explosively decompressed. Billy always attributed Darius's death to the absence of his lucky charm. That's why you carried those mamajammers, was Billy's view.

Then, years later, he learned that Darius had sent a suicide message in a broadcast he made to his sister, which was scheduled to be transmitted the week after his death. And in the message, he admitted that he had put the holes in the spacesuit himself.

"Why would he do that?" Billy wondered to us.

"I don't know, why?" That was me.

Billy thought about it. "Darius thought too much," he eventually concluded. "You have to do bad stuff and move on. Darius thought about it."

Billy still had the lucky charm. He showed it to me. I thought it looked cheap, and was anxious that if he wore it, its imbued Celtic deity might get into conflict with Billy's own Cuban voodoo god. You have to worry about that shit, it matters.

But I could see that the cross had great sentimental value for him. He slipped it back around his neck.

We drank the bottle dry and then the two of us left the bar, and went to my cabin. And that's when we had that exchange of dialogue I told you about just now. The one that goes:

"Fuck?"

"Now?"

"Yeah."

"Sure."

I SO love that as a chat-up line!

Anyway, long story etc. We fucked like – like two weary soldiers trying to find refuge in mindless fucking. Billy was phenomenal in bed – not imaginative, but his passion took him a long way. We Big O'd three times, or at least I did, and afterwards I burst into tears and cried in his arms. He didn't ask me why. That was as it should be.

I'd never cried in a lover's arms before. Not even with Cassady. That's odd, isn't it?

I don't get why that happened either.

From then on, every night after training, we fucked. And after fucking, I cried.

I let out all the pain and anguish that had accumulated in my soul by weeping in the arms of a man who never asked questions. And who prided himself on his ability to never think about the bad stuff.

Billy was good for me. I didn't need love, at that moment. I just needed a shoulder, or sometimes an abdomen, or even a hairy thigh, to cry upon.

I think also that if I hadn't been able to cry in Billy's arms all those many times, I would have followed the way of Darius.

The Fool. That was Hendry.

Hendry had been Planetary Director of Arkadian in the early days of the Corporation. Proconsul and administrator to what at that time was a highly prosperous factory planet. But the planet had descended into anarchy when the gangs got organised and started extorting from the workforce. It was happening all over of course. The old *mafia* and *urkas* and *vory* and *'Ndrangheta* and the secret societies like the Masons and Knights Templar were banding together to form a new political force. The Clan. A secret criminal society that wasn't secret any more.

Hendry had knuckled under, paid off the gangmasters, and offered obeisance to the Clan *capobastone* on Arkadian.

And then he joined the Clan himself, and worked his way up,

one step at a time. He committed a murder. Then nineteen more murders, to earn his dragon. He destroyed a DR. He slept the night on a cold mountain top without thermals and without dying. He mastered the Clan language, the murmurash. He observed the seven sacred Clan rituals, without error. And thus he earned his tattoo of full membership, the serpent's tail of the Clannite around his neck.

Within ten years Hendry was *capobastone* of Arkadian and its four affiliated planets, after gang wars had killed the previous incumbent. And Hendry now became a Janus. He worked for the Corporation, but he also led the Clan. The two jobs fitted together comfortably, for Hendry's criminals stifled rebellion and assassinated all free thinkers and nonconformists on Arkadian. And this was exactly what the Corporation wanted.

That's why some people call the Clan the "Overworld". It's not a hidden criminal society; it's the establishment.

You should know here that Arkadian factories specialised in the manufacture of weaponry of all kinds. Missiles, mortars, magnetic bombs, projectile guns, energy guns, and anti-matter missiles – both the cartridges and the microns – and force fields. Its workers supplied a hundred planets within a radius of fifty light years with state of the art munitions. The space caravans of Arkadian were legendary.

And when the Corporation fell, Hendry was sacked from his post and charged with four counts of Category A War Crimes. He was guilty on all counts of course.

By that time, however, quantum teleportation had been invented. And Hendry and his gangs had weapons so sophisticated they could blow a battleship out of space with ease. He used his power to seize control of his entire spherical sector. And thus Hendry became the first and the most feared of the Clan Bosses, the Fool in our Tarot pack.

Living Spirit was the Magician.[2]

And the Magician commanded, as of right, the loyalty of all the Lopers in the humanverse. He was seven foot tall, silver maned, and was apparently irresistible to all women, whether furred or not.

Living Spirit had sent a covert signal to all the Lopers in the Sphere of Human Colonies to foment rebellion and defy the new and democratically elected government on Earth. No one knew which planet served as his home. He was a shadowy figure, despite his high visibility on beaconband. Every week he would send a message of defiance to 'his' people, urging rebellion and the right to Loper self-determination. (Which they already had of course, on all the Loper planets, as a consequence of the SNG's liberal and anti-colonial policies. I guess these guys don't like to read the fine print.)

Loper bombers had been targeting schools and nurseries across

2 I think it's fairly obvious that the war criminals targeted by squads like Artemis's were given code names associated with Tarot cards, for ease of remembering. The full list is:

The Fool: Mikhail Hendry
The Magician: Living Spirit
The High Priestess: Sinara Lo
The Lovers: Jezebel Kave and Hiro Asbury
The Empress: Gina Goodrick
The Emperor: Nemanja X
The Hierophant: Viviana Arcola
The Hermit: Donny Brea
The Hanged Man: Gabriella Orix
Death: Michael Troilus
Temperance: Edela Barrow
The Devil: Hispaniola Morgan
The Star: Jacques Parole
The Moon: Ioan Harfleur
Judgement: Hayley Summerson

Of these 15, all but 5 were captured or dead by the time Artemis joined the Kamikaze Squads, as you will soon learn.

The other ten *capobastone*, who died/were captured before Brigadier Fraser joined the Maverick Warfare Unit, never got to be Tarot cards. – *Ed.*

the humanverse for eighteen months. Thousands of innocent children had been killed.

I hated the Magician dearly. All the Clan Bosses were evil, but for his terror on children campaign, Living Spirit had earned my special loathing.

Gina Goodrick was the Empress. She had been an associate of Daxox. He'd considered her to be one of the great *capobastone*. She ruled the Byzantium Clanning, and her court was apparently a marvel of ostentatious beauty. Rome, Byzantium and Xanadu were the three planets under her control. Gamer planets in which great civilisations of the past were recreated. Gina's whim was to dress like a princess from the Ancient Egyptian period of Earth history. I never met her; I never got to kill her. She was, apparently, an astonishingly cruel woman.

Sinara Lo was the High Priestess, and her home was Kandala, where I had 'died' so many times. She was saner than Gina, less ruthless than Living Spirit, and less feared then Hendry. But she too had blood on her hands. She stood accused and indeed had been convicted in absentia of four million war crimes.

And then there was the Devil. More of him, later.

These five were our Tarot pack. The other rebel *capobastone* had already been killed, or captured and sentenced to moral rehabilitation.[3]

This was a red desert land with bitter winds. Our sims were clad in warsuits, and the wind effects were strong enough to rock us on our feet. We flew in our warsuits across this bleak and glorious terrain.

"*I'm in*," said Agra over the secure MI link. Agra was our Loper undercover warrior, who was already mingling with the Magician's Loper Army. We were heading for the outcrop, with the aim of laying down covering fire while Agra closed in for the kill.

We saw a Loper below us, its yellow fur standing out vividly against the red sand. It was running as fast as we could fly. We dropped a frag on it, and the puff of sand was all that remained of this proud and beautiful beast.

"*We're blown*," I told Agra on the MI.

"*So am I*," she said. I could hear screaming and gunfire, through her ears, via her brain chip. Then her light on my visual array went out. Agra was dead.

I waved a hand to the others as I flew. We were going in.

We flew up and over the sheer rock of the Mountains of Excess, and saw the Loper base below. A military plane appeared above us, and we banked and shot energy blasts, and the aircraft vanished in a flash of fire.

The Magician was born on this planet. Our intel claimed that he always returned here on the anniversary of his birth. And so there was a chance, albeit a slim one, that he was down there. But we were outside the Loper biodome, and all our Loper scouts

3 As already explained. – *Ed.*

including Agra were dead. In the skies directly above us, plunging through the clouds, an entire fleet of military planes appeared – Hawks, by the look of them. And over the horizon, like a flock of savage birds, we could see a vast aerial armada of Lopers in their richly coloured warsuits.

This mission was going nowhere.

I increased the magnification on my eyes. The Loper who led the advance against us was a magnificent and large silver-maned beast.

I would have known him anywhere. I'd seen his image every minute of every day for the last month.

"*Magician sighted*," I said into my MI. "*Go nuclear*."

Gabriel dropped the nuke and the ground directly below the Hawk convoy erupted. A mushroom cloud gusted up from the ground. The planes that were descending upon us were suddenly ripped from the sky, as a blaze of light billowed and made the sands shimmer and vanish, and the powerful blast slapped reality and created winds of terrible power. And we too were battered and buffeted by the storm and the shock waves.

But our warsuits were built of the toughest tectonite, with a force field capable of allowing us to survive the shock waves of even a close quarters atom blast. We were also, so we had been reassured, entirely radiation proof.

So the world vanished and my body was brutalised and I found myself being hurtled and bowled among the clouds, and I imagined that I could feel the heat of the radiation burning me like the fires of Hell; but that was just an illusion. For in fact the suit kept its integrity; the force field held; the blast energy was sucked away and spat out in some other dimension.

And I was still alive; and floating in the air above a seared and blackened desert.

However, I was not safe yet. For my force field was calibrated for kinetic energy dispersion, not particulate repulsion. Which meant in other words it was on completely the wrong setting to repel the impact of a high-velocity explosive bullet.

And so, just as I thought I had survived what no human being should ever be able to survive, I heard a *crack* that I recognised as body armour rupturing. And an instant later, a single rifle bullet plunged into my body and detonated in my heart.

I died.

"How are you getting on, lassy?" Frasier asked, in that gentle Scottish lilt that continued to annoy me so much. He was today in his full brigadier's uniform.

I shrugged, what-the-fuckly.

"Coping are you, dear?"

I shrugged again.

"Or not," said Fraser, softly.

"Huh?"

I stared at him. He took off his glasses and cleaned them. *Cleaned them.* Then he put them back on and peered at me with his blue eyes. I realised the eyes were artificial, and wondered why he wore the glasses.

"Your failure rate in simulated missions to date is 100 per cent," Fraser assured me. "That indicates a lack of—"

"You should fucking try it," I snarled.

"I have."

"You have?"

"Three real missions." Fraser touched the medal ribbons on his chest. One of them carried a single number. "I bear the 3," he said.

"Impressive."

"Our team captured the Lovers. Kave and Asbury. The golden couple."

"I heard about that."

"Three missions, I did not die once. Why is that?"

"Luck?"

"Because I gave a damn!" Fraser spat.

I shrugged. I was wildly over using my what-the-fuck shrug by now.

"You have a point?"

"I fear your heart is not in this."

"Exercises. Simulations. I can't—"

"So I'm letting you go."

I froze.

Then I realised he was kidding, and I laughed.

Then I realised he *wasn't* kidding.

"We had a deal!" I said angrily.

"And I'll honour it," said Fraser mildly. "You're free to go. All criminal charges will be erased from your record. You won't get any money, but you can't have everything. Goodbye, Artemis, I expected better of you."

"Hold it one fucking minute!" I roared.

"You're not," said Fraser softly, "up to the job."

"The nerve of the fucking guy!" I told Billy, in a blind fury.

"That's the way it goes," Billy replied, unsympathetically.

"Yeah but—"

I saw the look on Billy's face.

My blood froze.

It was clear that he also thought that I wasn't up to it.

Billy was the love of my life. My own and only true passion.

And as for me – I was the greatest hero of all time! The maverick! The wild card! Earning my freedom and my redemption by killing the entire fucking Tarot pack on my own!

Those two fond beliefs of mine were, I realised, nothing more than ego-sustaining delusions. They were the fantasies that gave me my sense of who I was, and might be.

In reality, Billy was just a casual fuck. He didn't even seem to care very much that I was leaving the Rock.

And the bitter truth was, I'd been thrown off the team for slacking. Some fucking hero!

I spent two days lost to that old devil self-pity. Then I began to seriously analyse my own situation.

Was Fraser being unfair, or was I really at fault? Was I, perhaps, deliberately fucking up? Did I, maybe, have some kind of death wish?

Three rhetorical questions. But I knew the answers.

Yeah it *was* my fault.

Yeah, I *was* deliberately fucking up.

And yeah, I did.

I should have died when Daxox did. That had always been my plan. That was always meant to be my moment of release, and peace.

Does that make sense? No?

You don't really get me. I can tell that. No one does.

Because how *can* you understand what it was like – when – when the bad stuff happened. In Baron Lowman's villa. You may think you've got the idea. You know the *sort* of bad stuff I'm talking about.

But those things don't matter. The actual facts of my experience don't matter. What I endured doesn't matter. It's the—

What is it?

It's the sense that I fucked up my entire life. I trusted a bastard and he did what all bastards do, and then some.

And I should have expected it. I mean, how dumb was I? Daxox had a serpent's tattoo on his throat. That's the equivalent of having his forehead imprinted with the words: I'M AN EVIL GINCH AND I WILL FUCK YOU UP.

So why did I go to him? And why did I stay with him?

Why did I ever leave my home on Rebus, the peace and security that was to be found there, the family who – well okay they didn't *love* me – but the family who had a place for me?

Was it really so bad, back there on Rebus? Did I really have to run away, stealing the money from my father's bank account to live a life of crime?

Fuck yes, it was! And fuck yes, I did!

And I've already told you why. I had no friends. My mother left me. My father didn't love me. He was a bastard in so many ways. No one loved me.

Yeah, yeah. Boo fucking hoo. Poor little spoiled kid.

But wait, there's more.

My father was a cold man, you see. And also a bitter man. Bitter, because he'd only ever loved one woman, my mother, and she'd fucked off and abandoned him.

So he retreated into his books. And discovered a new purpose in life: hating me.

I was *her*, don't you get it? I reminded him of the woman he once loved. That's why he wouldn't let me wear my hair long. Because *she* must have had long hair. So I had a military cut, sheared like a Woola, from the age of three years. He didn't let me dress like a girl. He didn't even tell me about menstruation, that was a real fucker. When I first bled, I had to do an MI search to find out what was happening to me, and how and where to buy absorbent pads.

I once sang to him. He'd heard me singing in the bath badly and so he made me sing a madrigal to him *a capella* to "find out" if I had any talent and a vocal instrument. I didn't. My voice was shit. He sneered. So I never sang again.

She could sing. I knew that. Or rather, I could guess it.

And whenever I rebelled, by answering back, or looking defiant, he would punish me by locking me in the library.

Yeah, this is my "being locked in the library" story.

I was generally trapped in there for three or four days at a time. There were food supplies, of course, there was even a kitchen. But it was a library! It wasn't even the nice part of the library – I'm talking about the vaults now, where the books are stored in glass cases. Every now and then the glass would open and a book would be tractor-beamed out, floating through the air and up into the reading rooms.

And there I was, little Artemis with her shorn head and frightened eyes. Trapped in the dungeons of the Rebus Planetary Library. Cold and scared and desperately wanting a hug. I was five years old when he started doing that to me. Fifteen when I fled Rebus. A lot of scared nights came between those two times.

His plan was to break my spirit. And every time he did it, I pretended that he had. I would call him "sir" for weeks. But then my resolve would falter, and the scorn would return to my voice. And I would be punished once again. In that way, and in other ways.

My hate ran deep. I vowed to take revenge. Hence, pillaging his precious savings, buying a ticket on the interstellar transit, and fleeing my home.

From that day on I was pure badass. I stole, I cursed, I fucked around. I stole jewels, then worked as an enforcer and killer for the Clan. My destiny was forged. Because I had been, you see, "traumatised". That's what I truly believed, in all those years when I was with Daxox. I was a killer, for sure; but also a victim.

But later, as a body-for-hire in the house of Baron Lowman, I knew what it was to be *truly* traumatised. And I heard the stories of my fellow captives. Terrible stories. These were the children of the Corporation, remember. They'd had no childhood, none at all.

They'd known – well, terrible things. By contrast, my life had been a fucking breeze.

I gained a lot, I have to admit, from that period in captivity. I learned that I wasn't so terribly important after all. I learned that other people mattered too. I learned I hadn't been so uniquely and terribly treated as I had always thought.

And most of all, I learned how to *disengage my mind.*

It's a rare knack.

This is how it worked:

Pain and shit would engulf me; I would endure it all, until I achieved a climax of agony that led into epiphany.

Then I would enter my inner core.

And then my thoughts would float free.

I would feel as if my body belonged to someone else. And whilst in this state of zen-detachment, I would use my Rebus chip to forge a connection with the Cúchulainn QRC, Magog. I don't mean hacking. I mean – we became *friends.* I entered its dataspace and, at times, was more machine than human.

And thus I survived.

And eventually, once I'd learned how to use my unique relationship with Magog to disable the security systems and whedon chip, I escaped. Epiphany was my rope ladder; it got me free.

But let me get back to the point. My despair during my training period on the Rock was caused by the knowledge that I'd brought all the shit in my life upon myself. I was to blame. I'd sought out danger and evil, and I'd found those two vile bastards, and they had consumed me.

That made me, frankly—

You know where I'm going with this.

I wanted to die.

I needed to die.

Fuck. I really *had* to find a way to re-enlist.

I replayed the sims.

Again and again and again.

I had died two hundred and forty times. And so I reinhabited my body and watched myself die two hundred and forty times.

Then, breaking all the rules, I re-played the sims, one by one, by using my Rebus chip to switch from inactive to active mode. I lived all my lives again in other words.

And the plasma blast came out of nowhere but I was ready for it, and I amped up my force field seconds before.

The explosive bullet hit my armour but I saw the flash and rolled with the bullet and it slid across my chest plate instead of penetrating.

I did not step upon the landmine.

I was not fooled by the Clannite's disguise.

I did not run to Billy's defence, I let him die, and continued on my way. I did not attack the Mutant Monster, I hid.

I did not pursue my enemy, I let him go.

I realised there was something wrong with the door handle – it had been forced open and relocked – and I did not walk through the door.

Two hundred and forty times I anticipated the danger and continued the mission to its climax. I did not die once.

The two hundred and forty-first time was a new sim. An attack on the Empress. Her snipers shot at me but I had my force field on projectile-repulsion so that my armour was at its toughest, and the bullets bounced off. A bomb exploded next to me but I threw myself behind a pillar which took the brunt of the blast. Then I breached her security wall and killed a hundred of her soldiers without sustaining a single hit. And then she set an army of alien scarabs on me and I dropped an ultrasound bomb to paralyse them and walked upon their carapaces and blew a path through a thick wall into her inner sanctum and – found her gone.

But I was alive, and I ran the fuck out of nuller range pursued by angry soldiers and TP'd away safely.

And on arrival back at the Rock, I realised a scarab had burrowed through my armour and I burned it off with seconds to spare. I had failed to kill the Empress, but I had survived. Victory enough.

I spent a week in the sim room in all, without permission, and when I emerged I was pale-faced and exhausted. And triumphant.

And I staggered into the bar. News of my triumph in the sim room had preceded me.

"Here she fucking comes!" said a voice. A cheer rose up. I reached the bar, feeling dizzy. Free drinks appeared. Hands clapped my shoulders, grins surrounded me, I was the hero of the moment! And I swigged a whisky fast and felt myself become dizzy, and loose. And for a moment I enjoyed the sensation; then alarm bells began to ring.

So I took a deep breath, composed myself, found my inner core.

And I knew that something was wrong, but I didn't know what.

I looked around and saw my smiling friends and I mistrusted them all.

I listened for the sounds of distant gunfire, and heard nothing. I sniffed for the smell of rancid sweat, the sign that someone here was scheming murder, but I smelled nothing. I patted my gun in my holster to make sure I was carrying and that my gun was charged. And I moved away from the bar stool to the snug. I wanted to sit with some protection at my back.

But there was no reason to believe I was still hallucinating within a sim, as I had at first suspected. This was definitely reality. All my friends were around me. I had another whisky in my hand. I no longer felt dizzy. The mission was over. I could relax – couldn't I?

Then Billy approached me, beaming proudly, and I knew.

I gave him two seconds then I lunged to the right, avoiding the dagger he was aiming at my throat.

I lunged back up and smashed Billy's skull with my fist. It should have been a killer punch, but instead my knuckles shattered. Billy's smile didn't falter but he lunged again with the dagger and I dodged again, and broke his arm, then smashed his head upon a table. The sound was like a thunderclap. I knew then for sure that "Billy" was made of pure metal. A robot replica. And then I killed him.

And when I surfaced from my killing rage I saw Fraser, in his Brigadier's uniform, standing at the bar and looking at me with approval.

"Mission is now concluded," said Fraser, crisply. The real Billy entered the bar. He wasn't beaming and happy to see me – hell no. He was grim, impassive, and emotionless, as per usual. That's how I'd known. The real Billy always was a hard-faced bastard.

"Cheap trick," I informed both Fraser and Billy.

"We used to do it all the time," said Billy, "when I was—"

"No more fucking stories about the ancient days," I protested. I was weary beyond weary, ready to drop.

I looked at Fraser.

"Sir?" I asked.

"I take it," said Fraser, "you would like one more chance."

"You fucking bet I do," I said.

"Don't let me down."

"I won't.

"This war is important, Artemis. We value your courage."

"Yes sir," I said, starting to smile for the first time in a long while. "Yes fucking sir!"

Chapter 8

Mission 1: The Fool

We hit the ground standing. I took stock. Three misflits. Carter, Brown, Anderson.[1] I touched my face with my hand, just to be sure. Nose, eyes, cheeks, I had both hands, all my fingers. I stroked my torso, my breasts, shook out my legs.

Carter lunged at me with fangs protruding from her misshapen head. I took her down with a plasma blast, then rolled as Brown aimed his own plasma gun at me. But his hand was jelly, his face was melting. Billy incinerated the dying scraps of Michael Brown. Anderson was already dead. His heart was no longer inside or in any way attached to his body. We burned the remains.

Four of us were left alive.

The gravity was lighter than most of us were used to. Agra was struggling to stay on the ground. Her lightest step was like a rocket launch. For our first few minutes on the planet Gabriel had to piggy-back on Agra to hold her down, his lean sleek body emerging like the human half of a centaur from her stocky animality.

We hiked. No point risking a radar pickup. The fields were bare. Crops were burned, corpses of animals were strewn on the grass and clogged the streams and rivers. Hendry's Jayhawkers[2]

1 June Carter, Michael Brown, Wayling Anderson. May they rest in peace. – *Ed.*
2 The Jayhawker Squadron were an élite team created by Hendry for the sole purpose of planetary destruction. – *Ed.*

had hailed down poison rain upon the land, killing all below. The colonists of this planet – Makari[3] – had cowered in bunkers and beneath hardplastic domes, until the invading forces had landed and winkled most of them out, gruesomely.

The planet was now thinly garrisoned. The surviving settlers were allowed to live in the cities, eking out a miserable existence. Three military domes were built to safely house the occupying Jayhawker troops. Meanwhile robot drones ceaselessly patrolled the planet's surface and underwarrens in search of hold-out guerrillas.

In the days of the Corporation, Makari had been an pseudo-African idyll. A playground for Earthians who wanted to hunt, or simply admire nature. After the Last Battle it had become a Gaian[4] commune in which the colonists had declared their intention of living as one with the creatures of their rich biosphere.

Now, Makari was a wasteland. Hendry's plan was to make it one of his supply chain planets, furnishing wealth for his necklace of occupied worlds that revolved around the central hub of Hyboria.[5]

But SNG forces had quietly infiltrated this system and were preparing to devastate Hendry's doppelgänger-led Navy. And our job was to prepare the way by taking out Biodome Alpha and killing all the Soldiers within.

We were entering the Hunting Lands now. Around us, filling the savannah as far as the eye could see, were the skeletons of tigers, lions, elephants, giraffes, wildebeest, bandersnatch, Shakils, and numerous other exotic oxygen-breathing animals. The bleached white bones formed a landscape of death.

"I have a sighting," said Gabriel, looking at his little black box.

"Of?" I said.

3 To locate Makai in *The Spherical Atlas of Planets* (Way Out of Orbit Press), click here. – *Ed.*

4 Religious/scientific cult, but you probably knew that. – *Ed.*

5 SAP location here. – *Ed.*

"Spaceship, hovering, two miles north."

"Not on our mission plan," said Billy.

"Let's check it out," I said.

We checked it out. Our pace was fast, a trot not a walk. We were all clad in black warsuits and masked; night-shadows sprinting through the day time glare. We each carried two Xenos rifles on our back; as well as grenades, handguns, cutting gear, and the Wah-Wah anti-matter device, which was kept in a bright red rucksack with a skull insignia. Agra was now carrying the heavy pulse-cannon, which helped her cope with thc low gravity and made her look like an ant carrying a straw on its back. The plan was to cut through the biodome shell and enter, infiltrate with nanotech to leach the dome's computer of data, then trigger the anti-matter detonator and get the fuck out again.

We would, we estimated, then have about eleven minutes to get beyond the range of the dome's beaconband-nuller and thus re-access our teleport link. After eleven minutes, the anti-matter/matter interaction would occur and everything within twenty miles of the Dome would die.

In other words: we needed to run like fuck to avoid being killed by our own bomb.

That as I say was that plan. In fact, none of that happened. Instead, we saw the Fool, out hunting a lion.

We were on a ridge, looking downwards. Stealthed so that our warsuits now blended with the yellow savannah. And I increased the magnification on my eyes and saw an extraordinary sight. It was Hendry – followed by a platoon of thirty-nine Soldiers, stalking a lion that was eating its prey. I focused on the lion. A yellow-skinned predator with a fine mane. An Earth-native creature that now lived on an alien planet forty-five light years from its homeland. Hendry was unarmoured, and carried only a single pistol in a holster on his belt. He was also naked from the waist up, remarkably muscular, and was clearly revelling in the sensuality of his imminent kill.

Hendry walked up close to the beast. It raised its head from the bloody haunch of whatever it was, and roared at him. I realised the lion's fur was patchy. It had been poisoned by the Jayhawker rain-slaughter. But it was still a proud and beautiful beast. Hendry stepped up close. He made no attempt to draw his gun. I realised he was trying to use his charisma to captivate the beast. The gun was his back-up. But for a man like this, there was no challenge in using a weapon on a mere animal. No, Hendry wanted to prove that—

Billy took a shot with his Xenos rifle. It hit Hendry, and he fell down dead. The rest of us opened fire on the platoon of Soldiers.

They were fast, I'll grant them that, and disciplined. The minute the shot cracked the air, they hit the ground and began firing up at us. But we had the ridge, and they were exposed on the savannah. Each bullet I fired was a hit. In return, they shot me twice, in the chest. My warsuit armour held but I felt as if I'd been kicked by an elephant.

None of the Soldiers were dead. Their armour was as tough as ours. But most of them were badly wounded or dazed. Even so, they got to their feet in a dazzlingly coordinated movement as they rained gunfire up at the ridge with terrifying accuracy and remorseless speed. Meanwhile one of them primed and then fired a One Sun.

Agra shot the OS missile with a navigational burr, and for a few moments it continued to hurtle towards us; but then arced up, and up, and carried on flying into the clouds. Eventually, a Soldier manually triggered it and the One Sun missile exploded, turning day into blazing inferno.

A mortar shell exploded behind us and the earth and grass on which we lay was spattered to the heavens. Gabriel rolled down the bank like tumbleweed. I got up and ran after him firing bullets fast and furiously from my Xenos rifle. Then I switched to plasma beam and fired three quick shots and three Soldiers ignited and burned. It's a tradeoff. Keep your force field on high, or move fast. They traded wrong.

I reached Gabriel and grabbed him and stopped his mad

descent. And he came up holding his Philos pistol and we both fired and rolled, and fired.

A bullet hit my abdomen and went through. My warsuit armour was cracking. Blood welled inside the suit. The wound was immediately staunched by my autodoc, but I was gutshot now and in a lot of pain.

The trick, you see, is remembering *where* you shoot people. I'd landed three headshots on the Soldier who had commenced the firefight at position A5 in my mental grid. I fired another bullet and hit him again on the head and this one went through and he was down, dead and probably true dead.

Three minutes had elapsed. Enough time for the enemy to scramble their landing craft. We realised this had occurred when missile shells began erupting around us. Their ship was stealthed, invisible to the naked eye. But I knew Gabriel would be able to target it with his little black box, once he got under cover.

A moment later I heard Gabriel's voice over my MI, giving coordinates.

"*Reading you Five*," said Agra from up on the ridge, and high above us, the air exploded. I filtered my eyes, kept low. Debris scattered and fell. The burning shell of the landing ship was visible now, like a cloud lit by dawn. I could hear screams with my enhanced hearing. The pop of gunfire was all around.

"*Two hostiles, X43 and C21, X43 is mine*," said Billy and a man in armour flew upwards into the air. Billy had grenaded him. I put a plasma burst into his body as Billy rained bullets on the flying corpse. Then I hurled a grenade blind, to sector C21 which was near the lion's bloody corpse. The lion exploded. No Soldier. I threw again and so did Billy then a bullet hit me in the face mask and I went down and blacked out.

When I woke up thirty seconds had elapsed. Billy was easing my mask off. I breathed gulps of thick yeasty air. The bullet had penetrated the mask and hit my forehead but without velocity. Billy tugged it out of my skull and blood gushed down my face and sheeted me warmly. I was breathing hard.

"Hendry?" I gasped.

"On it."

Another shot. Agra finishing off survivors.

Another shot. Another survivor true-dead.

Another shot.

Soldiers, the brainwashed kind, are remorseless creatures. Even when they have lost all frontal lobe brain function, the reserve oxygen capsules in their cerebellums allow their bodies to continue fighting. I've heard stories of blind and armless Soldiers with their guts spilling out lunging up out of the midst of charnel-fields to recommence their slaughter. So, you can't take chances, or prisoners.

Yeah, yeah – war is hell. Tell me about it.

Billy helped me to my feet. My bowels had erupted long ago. The bullet in my gut was causing me considerable agony. I had a headache, from the bullet that had smacked me in the forehead and embedded itself in my skull.

Agra joined me. "DNA negative."

"It's not him?" I said.

"No. It's a double."

I thought a second. "Mission abort," I said. We'd lost our element of surprise. We stood no fucking chance now.

"I'll call it," said Gabriel, and spoke via his MI to the invasion fleet remote computer.

Our bodies started to shimmer.

We ported away.

Agra misflitted. I'll miss her.

Billy was the one who killed her malformed body. It wasn't easy. Her rage survived even though her brain was mush.[6]

6 Agra, Loper of the planet of McCoy, no surname. May she rest in peace. – *Ed.*

We had all suffered major injuries, but at least Gabriel, Billy and me had survived intact after two teleports, i.e. there and back. Three Kamikazes left out of the original squad of seven. Acceptable.

We won the battle of Makari, of course. Though I guess that had never been in doubt.

I read the battle log and marvelled at the ingenuity of the SNG Admiral[7] who had planned and executed this textbook invasion. Stealth bombers had taken out all fourteen of the enemy's orbiting command and control bases. And a fleet of Caracaras and Kestrels had engaged with Hendry's doppelgänger space navy. A battle royal had erupted, with our ships mingling in with the enemy fleet and firing from all sides. Ten thousand SNG doppelgänger riders[8] were involved in this operation, each working one hour shifts in a relentless rota system. Eventually the entire enemy navy was obliterated and the SNG took control of the planet.

By then, however, it was too late. The other two Kamikaze Squads had, covertly and simultaneously, taken out Biodomes Beta and Gamma, but Biodome Alpha remained intact. And as soon as the space invasion commenced, the enemy Soldiers in that biodome had followed standing orders. They had left the dome en masse and hunted each and every member of the original colony community. These peoples were dwelling peacefully – this wasn't the guerrilla army, remember, it was what was left of the original *population* of the fucking planet – in their ruined cities and in their warrens under the ground. And the

7 Admiral John Hinchcliffe. – *Ed.*

8 Official figures say 11,000, but this was a reasonable approximation on Artemis's part. – *Ed.*

Soldiers in their warsuits sought them out and slew them all. And I mean, all.[9]

By the time the SNG navy landed on the planet, the streets and basements and savannahs of Makari were drenched with human blood. Not a single man, woman or child remained. And their bodies were left to rot. In time their white bones would be indistinguishable from the bones of the massacred African predators.

My fault of course. We should have ignored Hendry and proceeded to the biodome. But according to standing orders. if you see a Tarot, you have to take that Tarot out.

I was given a commendation for my leadership of the squad on that mission. It was worth a hundred thousand scudo bonus on my Three-Mission payoff.

If, of course, I lived that long.

"To Agra," we concluded. We clinked glasses. We had mourned them all, our gallant comrades. Carter, Anderson, Brown, Agra. I'd known them for six months, and now they were dead.

But *we* were alive! That's all that mattered. One mission down. Two more missions, and we were home free. Redeemed. Amnestied. Rich.

They called us the Crazy Squads. Or the Kamikazes. There were a lot of us. Tens of thousands, in the Rock alone. And fuck only knew how many more bases like this there were.

A few things you need to know here. Tech stuff, but it matters.

Thing One: all enemy installations have beaconband-nullers

9 There were no civilian survivors, and approximately 983,000 day-old corpses were found in various locations on the planet. However, 34,333 guerrilla warriors survived in closely guarded underground locations, and were liberated by the SNG invasion force. – *Ed.*

as part of their security system. That means – crap! – no beaconband communication inside the nuller beam's radius.

Which means doppelgänger robots don't work, they become just dumb robots without their human riders. That's why the SNG need real people to fight their up close and personal battles.

Thing Two: as we all know, quantum teleportation, which is what we use to get on-planet, only works fifty per cent of the time. Hence, the misflits.

But there's just *no other way* to use real soldiers. It could take decades to send troops from one battlezone to another. So that's why you need kamikazes. Crazy fucks like us. Because we will take a risk that no sane person would ever accept.

Toss a coin: live or die.

Toss a coin: live or die.

Toss a coin: live or die.

That's what they call the 3. It gets harder, I'm told, every time. Thank fuck I've never been any good at maths![10]

But there are, as I say, an awful lot of us.

That's worrying really. I mean, you wouldn't think there'd be a *queue* of people wanting to do a fucking crap job like the one I'm doing. Half the friends I'd made in my time on the Rock died in that first mission. And half of those remaining were about to die.

Resurrection was, however, an option.

Carter, Brown and Agra were now back with us. Anderson, however, had ticked the box that said DO NOT RESURRECT. Which I was glad about. I'd liked Anderson – and was relieved to see him stay dead.

"Good to see you." I shook Carter's hand.

10 She's kidding here. Artemis has a very good mathematical mind. – *Ed.*

"You're squad leader now?" she asked, contemptuously.

"I am."

Carter stared at me, with even greater contempt, and stalked off.

Brown had always a good-looking devil. And even as a cyborg, he was a heart-throb. Only the lack of facial movement betrayed the fact that he was made of plastic and metal. "Good to see you, Brown," I said, and shook his hand.

"You could have saved us," said Brown coldly.

"Don't know what you mean," I lied.

"You didn't give us a chance. You evil bastard!"

"Whatever." I shrugged.

And off he stalked.

And Agra – that was the worst.

When I met Agra, she glared at me with open hate. I recognised her, but only just. Because instead of her normal fur-covered body, she wore the standard plastic-skinned cyborg chassis. No body hair, no claws, no fangs. But she was as strong and fast as ever.

"Fuck you Artemis," she said. "You evil fucking ginch. You should have died on that mission – not me!"

I smiled nicely at her. "Yeah," I said, and this time I was the one who turned and walked away.

I'd missed Agra when she died. But I missed her even more now that she'd come back to life.

Cyborgs, you see, are by and large fucked in the head. Don't ask me why. Their minds get copied and downloaded into a robot body. But something goes missing, and the lack of it twists them out of shape.

Soul, maybe?

We had a month's R & R after the first mission, followed by a month's fitness and sim training and sobering up.

I was high for most of that first month. High on drugs, drunk almost all the time, and dripping with endorphins because of all the sex Billy and I were having.

And of course, high on rejuve. Those little nanobots had taken out the bullets and sewed up my colon, and my torn stomach lining had been glued back together. Then heavy rejuve and my augmented body did the rest. My injuries healed, my scars disappeared, and Billy and I ran riot.

There was a limit, I must admit, to how much fun we could have on the Rock. It was after all an artificial habitat, no Eden planet. But even so there was a pool and a lake and a mock mountain and there were bars and restaurants and clubs, and bands playing music every night.

Our favourite meal was breakfast, of the full cooked variety. Washed down with huge cups of coffee. Bacon, scrambled egg (me), poached egg (him) sausages, three kinds of sauces, grana bread, chitterlings, waffles, syrup. After four hours' sleep and a needle shower, this was exactly what our bodies needed. Then we took a stroll, admired the botanical gardens, swam, sunbathed under lights, and then it was time for lunch.

Oh and champagne. Champagne for breakfast, to go with the coffee.

Gabriel always joined us for lunch, looking sad, mostly. But it was always nice to see him.

Gabriel was a strange guy. Sweet, very sweet, I was fond of him. And brilliant. A total boffin-brain. And also quite uncannily beautiful. I mean, really, he was a stunner.

Beauty is no big deal these days, I know. With genetic manipulation and reconstructive surgery and rejuve, there are SO many beautiful people out there. But even so – Gabriel had something special. A lean athlete's body. Piercing hawk eyes. A crooked smile. Perfect cheekbones, and smooth chocolate-coloured skin, betraying his distant Mayan heritage. And a body and face that made you want to weep with joy. Girls used to stop and stare when he passed by. Guys too, to be honest.

Billy, by contrast, especially by the demanding standards of our age, really was an ugly fucker.

So why was I with Billy, not the gorgeous Gabriel?

Well, it was my policy, you see, and had been since I was a teenager, to only seriously date ugly guys. My theory was, the beautiful guys are always in love with *themselves*. Ugly guys, however, are less selfish. And more loyal. And more caring, and reliable, and blah, and blah, and blah.

Of course that theory totally fell in the ditch when I went out with Daxox – old frogface, with a heart like Satan! But I guess it helps to explain why I had chosen to fool around with that old Space Marine Billy, rather than the sexy hunky Gabriel.

Because, with Gabriel, it was *definitely* on offer.

Trust me on this. I saw the way Gabriel looked at me. Like a puppy staring at a bone. With me as the bone in that metaphor. Or like – well, he just loved to spend time with me. That whole month of R & R, he was there every lunchtime. And we'd tell stories and the guys would join us and they'd tell us more stories. But Gabriel would always make sure he was sitting near me, or better still, right next to me, asking me questions about stuff. Billy used to wander off, get pissed with old Space Marine pals, or flirt with women. But Gabriel was always there by my side, smiling, happy, not inflicting, not stalking, just – there.

After lunch Billy and I would go off for our afternoon siesta-fuck. Then we'd have a bath together and watch TV or a film, then have pre-first-drink-of-the-evening-sex, and then we'd have first-drink-of-the-evening. Then we'd get dressed and go down to the bar. And Gabriel would be there, with a bottle of champagne just for us. What a sweetheart!

Gabriel was a mathematical genius. When he was a young guy, he was smart enough to be a Scientist, which wasn't a bad gig back in those days. But instead, he'd left school at fourteen to run with a Clan gang. This was on Romulus, he was a Romulusan. Tough planet. But Gabriel rose to the top and was a *vangelista* in the Clan when the Corporation fell. He wasn't the worst of them by a long chalk. But everyone knew his name and he was ratted out by all his pals and former girlfriends. That's how he got a life sentence, and that's how he ended up in the Kamikazes.

And so, most nights, Gabriel would pour the champagne, making that our *second* drink of the evening. And by that stage, Billy and I were always flushed, in that special way that tells strangers you've been banging like, well, Cambrian Dilongs, who as you know are a species who do *nothing* but fuck.[11] And when he saw us like that, all flushed and happy, Gabriel's sad smile would emerge, but only briefly.

And that last night, before training started up again, we all got slaughtered and Gabriel sang a song. He had a beautiful pure tenor voice, and he sang an operatic aria called "Hearts Are Broken And Lives Are Lost". A real weepie. I didn't weep, of course. No one did, we were *warriors* for fuck's sake. But I felt a lump in my throat as he sang the lyric, about a teen gang massacre in which a girl kills the boy she loves in a berserker rage. It's a lament for the loss of innocence I guess. Gabriel's beautiful voice, well, it exalted me. Made me feel special and pure and human, and not like a sick murdering fuck who had done far worse, *far* worse, than that poor fucking chick in the song.

That was a perfect night. I didn't have sex with Billy when we got back to our room. I just went quietly to sleep, remembering. And when the hangover kicked in, about seven am, I still remembered. The soft light soaring splendour of Gabriel's heart-achingly tender voice.

11 According to Saunders' *Encyclopedia of Alien Life* this is quite true, though it sounds pretty unlikely to me. – *Ed.*

Chapter 9

Mission 2: The Magician

We hit the ground standing. And a moment later I saw that Gabriel had misflitted.

His body had grown. His eyeballs were bulging. He had four arms, and four legs. He was a freak, but that didn't *necessarily* mean he was off the team. Tomas however was irrevocably gone, a puddle of shit and goo on the rocks. Caterina was sharded, and bloody. And—

Gabriel came at me and grabbed me with one hand and threw me up against the rocks. His power was phenomenal. I crashed, and scrabbled, and got a handhold, just in time to see Billy hose Gabriel with a plasma burst. But Gabriel had his forceshield up. His mind was still functioning. Those were the worst.

"*Gabriel, stay, cool, you're a viable form. Stop fighting us,*" I subvoced, but I could tell he was lost to berserker rage.

Jean had survived the flit intact, but Gabriel grabbed her with two of his arms and ripped her body apart. Her arms came away, then her head, even though she was warsuit-protected. That wasn't possible! Or was it? The strength in his arms must be—

Gabriel was running up the cliff towards me, with astonishing grace. He was cunning enough to know I would kill him if I could, despite my lying words. Billy was pounding him with bullets but they were bouncing off Gabriel's body armour. All his body parts and the warsuit he wore had doubled in size without any loss of functionality. Utterly unlikely, but that was the quantum effect for you.

I leaped off the cliff firing my Xenos in fast bursts straight at Gabriel's face mask. The mask shattered. Bullets went through. Blood erupted. I'd shot a hole in his head!

It didn't slow him down. Gabriel caught up with me and grabbed my arm and was about to rip it off.

BOOM. Billy fired the pulse cannon and it pierced the body armour and ripped off the bottom of Gabriel's body. He was nothing but arms and torso now but he was still alive. But his mask was broken open and his eyes-on-stalks were glaring at me. The hole in his skull was as big as my fist and he didn't appear to have a brain any more. I wondered what was keeping him going.

I dropped a grenade inside his mask and fired my warsuit jets. Then I flew away, pursued by an exploding Gabriel.

By now of course he was dead. My lovely Gabriel.[1]

I rejoined Billy and Max and we took stock. Tomas had been rendered into a nothing, more oilslick than human being; we had no choice but to leave him. Caterina showed no trace of brain function, and was in about two hundred pieces, but we ported her shards back to base anyway. She had been a tall and beautiful woman. And I fancied I saw sorrow in her eyes, which were part of a large sliver of skull with a section of her brain attached.

Jean was dead, but not true dead. The icy cold had frozen the

1 Gabriel Antonio Santiago. May he rest in peace. Also let us also honour the memories of Tomas Fuente, and Caterina Lyras, who died on that same mission. – *Ed.*

stump of her neck, cauterising the flesh, so we ported her head back. With luck, unless she misflitted a second time, she would survive.[2]

Then we assessed our location and mission progress. We were, just as we were supposed to be, in a snowy wilderness. The wind hurled tufts of ice and snow into the air where they formed a dazzling haze that reduced visibility to fucking awful. We were at the foot of a sheer mountain. I could see the peak, and it was haloed by clouds.

All that data confirmed we were on Ice. Intel had suggested that the Magician aka Living Spirit was making a covert visit to this world to rally the locals. And we were seizing the opportunity to take him out. Intel was usually wrong about such matters of course, but we had to make the attempt.

Our mission was covert. The space defence network in the Ice system was a masterpiece of overkill, and our doppelgänger Navy rarely even tried to invade.

We were all aware that we were probably wasting our time here. The truth of the matter was that every month, sometimes every week, a Kamikaze Squad was teleported on to some godforsaken planet or other, in the vain hope of capturing or killing the elusive Magician.

The three of us began to climb – me, Billy, and Max.

I'd known Max in sim training, but not well. He'd survived his first mission – to Cargill's World – but his entire squad of thirteen had misflitted, leaving him to complete his mission solo. Which he did – he destroyed an entire spaceship fabricator

2 Jean Angela Block did survive, but a year later, after fully recovering from a successful whole body transplant, she perished during her third and final mission. May she rest in peace. – *Ed.*

in orbit around Cargill's World, teleporting out just 4.2 seconds before the anti-matter bomb detonated.

Max had become a kind of hero among the other Kamikazes, for his daring, his bad language, and his contempt for authority. He'd been an Admiral in the Corporation Navy, despite his rebellious streak. And he'd been a hero to THOSE guys too.

This is Max's story.

He was born on a badly terraformed planet – Delirium Tremens – yeah I know, there should be a sobriety test before anyone is allowed to christen a world.

DT was a world riven with winds and haunted by black-winged alien scavengers who'd somehow survived terraforming and now hovered in the troposphere, far above the clouds. When they were hungry, they descended at speed, getting hotter and hotter until they plunged towards the surface to seize their prey. These beasts – the High Hoods – were strong enough to lift an infant from a pram. And they'd often eat their prey mid-flight, scattering bones and entrails as they flew.

When Max was ten years old he'd been swept upon by a High Hood and carried away in its claws. But instead of panicking, he calmly cut the creature's feet off with a pocket laser and then fell to safety into a forest. Well okay, as he admitted, he broke every bone in his body. But it was still safer than staying in the creature's, and I quote, "fatherfucking cockgnawing claws". That was Max for you.

Max's parents were farmers and miners and hunters. They raised cattle, and a billion stasis-preserved beef carcasses a year were shipped from Delirium Tremens to Earth, to feed the palates of the Earthian elite who eschewed factory-grown meat and liked the taste of "wild". (For these cows and bulls were genetically modified savage beasts, who fought daily with local predators and could charge as a pack with terrifying unity.)

Max hated farming. He resented the dominance of the doppelgänger élite who commanded the best land, the most resources, and treated the locals as slaves. In those days, Max admits, he had no idea how bad things were ELSEWHERE. His home planet was relatively liberal, untouched by the excesses of other parts of the Corporation's empire. It was a work planet, not a "play" planet.

So Max joined the Navy. He became a warrior. And then he was, in one memorable incident, abducted by aliens.

"I'm proud of what I did in the war against the sister-sodomising anus-licking Heebie-Jeebies," Max had told us one night. "For they were a truly fucking evil fucking species. And I should fucking know. I lived with those evil brother-raping ginches for eleven years."

"You?" That was me asking.

"Me."

"How?"

And so he told us.

Max had been leading a fleet into H-J territory. His job was to strike a deal with the guerrilla Sparkler outfits in that region.[3] However, it all went bollocks up. And Max's fleet got caught in an ambush. And the H-Js took him prisoner.

"Their fucking name is so fucking comical, it don't prepare you for the arse-emptying reality. They are fucking . . . terrifying. And they're shape-shifters, too. Sometimes they are little skulky things, sometimes – well, they can grow in a flash, and trust me, I've never seen anything so monstrous. They chill the air around them. They consume sulphur. They told me they were going to dissect me. But I knew that was a mollyfocking lie. 'Cause they'd already performed dissections on hundreds of human captives. There was nothing new for them to discover about us.

3 This was after the big Sparkler-Heebie-Jeebie war, but before the Heebies went into decline and started to de-evolve. – *Ed.*

"No, they were aiming to use me as a lab rat. Testing me, torturing me, making me fight aliens *mano a mano.* To learn more about human psychology, and weaponry, and battlecraft. I never lost, by the way, a single blowjobbing *mano.*"

After six months it was obvious to Max that the H-Js were planning to eliminate humankind. As they were also attempting to do to the Sparklers – those beautiful albeit vicious bioluminescent creatures – and had succeeded in doing to the Hadas before that.

Remember, it's a dangerous universe. And mankind is by no means the most violent, or most dangerous of the species out there.

"These fucking aliens were totally fucking *alien.* Obvious yeah. But there was no – nothing. No eye contact, 'cause they had no eyes. No body language. Their motives, I couldn't fathom what the fuckall they might be. They didn't need territory. They had started killing off Sparklers for no good reason, militarily. But I made it my mission to try and communicate. To try and understand the evil fucking shit-blobs."

I often think of what Max went through in those difficult years. We are so used to seeing alien life forms that we forget what "alienness" truly is. A different way of thinking. A different way of being.

"They don't see the world as we see it," Max said. "They just don't see – the same world. I learned their language. I empathed with their minds. After ten years I could see like a H-J, think like a H-J. They are reactive in a complex way to stimuli. They have no concept of loyalty. No love. No comradeship. Yet they work together as fireflies flash in unison. Or is there something more? There's – I don't fucking know – a *tender* quality to the H-J mind. They feel beauty. They are intensely aware of beauty, more than I am to be totally fucking honest. And they cherished, they actually did, the Sparkler species. I could feel it, the memories of their admiration for the wonder of the Sparkler biology, the precision of the Sparkler minds. Their war against the Sparkers was not fought for greed or land or rage. It was merely an attempt to perfect that beauty, by destroying it.

"However, they consider us, the human species, to be a lower life form, wholly lacking in beauty. Maybe they have a point."

Max told us about the Heebie-Jeebie philosophy, their world view.

These appalling yet mysterious creatures, he explained, believe the universe is divided into various states: animal, ethereal, intellectual, possibilistic, and patterned. They consider themselves to be not animal at all; they are "patterned". Max tried to explain this, but couldn't really. But approximately: an equation is patterned. A sonnet is patterned. But fucking the woman you love is merely animal.

Their science, he continued, is phenomenally advanced; but bizarrely, they knew little about technology until they encountered humanity. They were swamp-dwelling creatures that we captured and attempted to study. But instead, they swarmed out of our zoos and laboratories and escaped off-planet in our spaceships, which somehow they now knew how to fly. And that was the period of the Terror Years, when three human planets were overwhelmed by the H-J plague.

Then they took to the stars, and began to commit mass murder of every sentient species they encountered.

Max admitted: "I came to adore the fucking Heebie-Jeebies. I lived like one. I thought like one.

"And then I was rescued. And we killed every single one of the fatherfuckers that we could find. The few that survive – they're just fucking swamp dwellers now. Their minds are gone. Their dreams are lost. Their pattern is broken."

Anyway, that's Max.

This was a winter world, rich in mountains, glaciers, and frozen lakes. The highest mountain on the planet was called Soul-Smasher, and it was the location of the Loper Ice Palace. The entire mountain was beaconband-nulled, so no doppelgängers could attack, and no Kamikazes could port to the summit. You had to start at the base and climb up.

Or you could fly. Squad of Eagles had attempted to descend upon this mountain top, and had been killed in the thermals and the clashes of wind currents. Armoured Lopers in one-person fliers had suffered the same fate. Several Kamikaze Squads had attempted to land in aerofoil spaceships, but those too had been dashed against the rocks. Flying makes you vulnerable. And this was a planet where a mild breeze was equivalent to a tornado anywhere else.

So we had to climb up, in our warsuits, with lead belts and uranium backpacks to weigh us down and hence make it more difficult for the wind to sweep us away. We wore crampon hands – gloved attachments to the warsuits which allowed us to dig deep spikes into the rock. Our boots were magnetic, to give us just a little more traction on the iron-ore-rich mountain. And we were wearing the new Sikko range warsuits, with heavy heating panels and extra oxygen cylinders in the legs and torso.

Before we commenced the climb, we spoke the eulogy to our dead comrades: Gabriel, Tomas, and Jean.

"Valhalla, Heaven or Hell. May your spirit know joy."

"Valhalla, Heaven or Hell. May your spirit know joy."

"Valhalla, Heaven or Hell. May your spirit know joy."

I wanted to weep for Gabriel, but I could not. For I had a mission, And besides, in that bitter cold, my tears would have frozen.

Imagine a world so savage that only moss can endure the blazing hot summer's days. And where even moss retreats into rock in the icy cold winter-time. Where the winds can pick up a boulder and dance it in the air like a pebble. Where the frosts can freeze the blood. Where glaciers can crack and sunder and tear a mountain range apart in a matter of months. A place where life cannot thrive. Yet Lopers live here.

They live in caves and warrens, of course, and in tunnels dug aeons ago by the native life forms like the Horia and the Shalgara. The Lopers fought bitter battles to steal this underground terrain, before the terraforming process was complete. They clambered face first through narrow tunnels and wrestled with blind creatures of unbelievable savagery. And they killed them and they built bonfires out of their corpses on the surface in the hope of thawing the lakes of ice. They drove the Bantoqs out of their caves and slew them too. They fought, literally tooth and claw, and took the planet.

These Lopers were mutineers of course – renegades escaping the Corporation's domain. There were no doppelgänger robots on Ice back then. Just a hardy community of genetically engineered humans who could live in the coldest and the warmest and the most arid and the most flooded habitats the mind could conceive. And yet, on Ice, they struggled to survive.

The mystery to me was why the Ice-Lopers had formed common cause with Living Spirit. He was a city boy. A gangster with blood on his claws. A butcher who had killed hundreds of thousands of (relatively) innocent people in his incessant campaigns of violence. But almost all Lopers, for whatever reason, felt that Living Spirit was their natural leader. Their god, some said. Agra, before she died and was cyborged, had always mocked this superstitious cult. But I could not doubt the Lopers' sincerity.

We climbed. Eight or nine inches at a time. Carving a path out of the sheer rock. Moving hands and legs in a steady rhythm. Never looking down. Keeping two limbs nailed to the rock at all times. And with our ears switched off to avoid hearing the madness-inducing scream of the wind around us.

At noon, the winds died down, and the clouds rolled away. And the planet became a place of bliss. We could see for mile upon mile. We marvelled at the immense vistas of snow fields and ice-mountains tipped with mossy outcrops. The beauty of it all took my breath away. The sheer mountain ranges! The pink-tinged clouds! The dazzling whiteness of the expanse! For two hours a day, around noon, Ice is a planet fit for habitation, and I could see why its people loved it.

But after two hours of sun, the winds returned and grim clouds greyed the sky once more. And Ice returned to being a bleak wilderness.

We continued climbing. When the cliff became too brittle, we blasted deep holes in the rock to create hand-holds. We were not connected by ropes, for each of us was so heavy a fall would bring the others tumbling down with us. We all had jetpacks though, and rockets in our boots. So we had a faint chance of survival if we fell off – provided we weren't caught up in a cyclonic current.

As the day wore on, the winds became even more intense. Our bodies were pummelled with gales. A rock outcrop gave way under my hand – it was ice, not rock – and I let myself fall. Ice-boulders crashed past me as I tumbled off the cliff. Then I lunged forward and dug my hook-claws into the rockface. The claws skidded off moss, but then sank in. I took a breather.

Then I recommenced my slow climb.

"*Billy, still here.*"

"*Artemis, still here.*"

"*Max, still here.*"

Conversation was impossible, but every sixty seconds we called in to tell our comrades of our continuing existence. I could not see them, I could see nothing except rock and snowy wind. I had no sense of my direction other than 'up'. Anyone who saw me in my climb could easily pick me off with a rifle shot. I had not an atom of consciousness free to keep an eye out for danger.

We were lost to the journey, which took us high into the clouds.

And after two days and six hours, we reached the summit.

"*Now*," said Billy, "*let's kill some—*"

But he ran out of words. Exhaustion enveloped us. We stood on the apex of the vast ice-mountain, ankle-deep in snow, and waggled our arms and legs. Three giant white monsters engaged in a weary dance.

Then the Lopers appeared.

They were quick, I'll give them that, and we were slow.

All our sim training failed to pay off. We weren't alert. We weren't prepared for the effects of snowblindness and physical exhaustion. So we just stood there like dummies on a firing range as the body-armoured Lopers opened fire. They rained plasma fire on us, burning off our snowy wraps and revealing the black warsuits underneath. And then they peppered us with explosive shells, which crashed against our armour, cracking and weakening it but not yet penetrating. And they screamed! Loper war cries of devastating ferocity assailed our ears, which had now been switched back on to their maximum setting.

In short, they really woke us up.

"*Two four one low, all on three high*," I shouted, meaning that I would target the Loper second from the left on our visual array, Billy would fire at the Loper on the far right, Max would aim for the guy on the far left, then we'd all go for the last one standing. We rolled and drew our Xenos rifles from their scabbards and fired as one. We aimed low, hit our targets repeatedly but didn't kill them; so instead we fired low and burned the snow and rock beneath the Lopers so that they lost their balance. Then we switched to projectile bullets and aimed shot after shot after shot at the forehead of each of our targets. My twentieth bullet broke my target's armour and plunged into skull and exploded. Ffiteen seconds had elapsed since I fired my first bullet.

By now the surviving Loper was shooting at us, his bullets rocking our armours with brutal smacks. We all turned our guns on him and he leaped high in the air – agile despite his body armour – and continued to rain plasma fire upon us as he aerially turned. An elegant manoeuvre. But I grabbed Billy and threw him upwards and he drop kicked the Loper who flew off into space and fell off the cliff.

Billy then crashed to ground, near the edge. The ice beneath him cracked. I threw him a rope and we pulled him back away as the entire mountain side fell away.

We took a moment to sitrep. We were all alive. They were all dead. Not so bad, despite our terrible start.

"*Heat sensor.*" Billy took out his wand and wafted it. On our arrays we saw the flashing red that indicated a source of heat. This was the entrance to the passageway through which the Lopers had come. It was invisible to the eye, but as we approached the rock the illusion vanished and we could see a gateway, slightly ajar. We stepped inside.

Then we began to lightly jog through the rock tunnel. The sides were scorched black, a sure sign that this was an artificial pathway burned out by plasma beams. Billy waved the wand again to trigger the stealth setting, making us invisible to sensors and a casual glance. And as I ran, I used my Rebus chip to make contact with this planet's QRC – feeling the mind – yes – registering my presence – winning it over to accept my comradeship.

I had it! The computer was mine. I could see a visual array map of the mountain complex.

"*Living Spirit*," I subvoced, "*is he here?*" Just automatically, really, as a piece of standard protocol.

"*Yes he is*," said the Ice computer.

I stopped in my tracks.

"*Problem?*" subvoced Max.

"*The Magician*," I said, "*is here*."

Max was staring at me, with a puzzled look in his eyes, not understanding how I could know such a thing.

"*Trust me*," I said.

I checked my visual array. There was a latticework of tunnels in this mountain, at various levels. And right at the base of the mountain, on the *inside*, was the Loper city of Harbin.

We turned on our holos. We were now three red-furred Loper warriors. If you looked closely enough, the image didn't quite convince. But it was good enough for now.

We began to jog through the rock tunnels, mazing this way and that, sometimes scrambling downwards, until we reached the main vertical shaft. It was much smaller than I'd expected. We looked around for an elevator, or a staircase or – something. But no. Just a sheer well leading deep into the mountain.

So we rigged our ropes and chimneyed down in single file. As an entrance to a lost world, it truly sucked.

After a long painstaking descent, we reached the bottom and dropped down. We left the ropes in place, just in case; though the chances of us surviving and escaping seemed slim.

We looked around and saw that the tunnel where we now stood had an artifical floor and a ceiling embedded with lights. But the ceiling was cracked, and drops of water were oozing out and dripping downwards, spattering us; and the bright blue mosaic pathway on which we walked was moist and flecked with sprouts of moss, its bold patterns discoloured and flaking. The ceiling lights cast a feeble gold sheen over the grey rocks and fucked-up-azure floor. But this was definitely a habitat now, not just a hole in the mountain.

We jogged on.

It was claustrophobic, to say the least. We were surrounded by tons of rock, running down a corridor inside the mountain which we had, previously, so painfully climbed up. And because the dim ceiling lights left the walls mostly dark, and eerily highlighted the blue floor, it felt as if we were running on a frozen river. There was a flow of breathable air coming from somewhere; although, suited up, we did not breathe it.

"*Great lair*," said Billy. Standard joke. You need 'em, from time to time.

Then we reached a broader cavern, and saw there was a stairway leading downwards, coated in crumbling stucco that was wrapped aroung the ancient mountain rock. We walked down the slippery, mossy steps with care. The air was less stale; we masked down and could feel a breeze on our cheeks. There was, remarkably, a metal door in the rockface.

We masked up again. Checked our guns, which didn't need checking. Inspected each other's Loper holos, which were pretty plausible but not perfect. Then I unlocked the the door with my mind and we walked through.

And now we were in Harbin.

We stood at the top of an immense rock cave the size of a small country. Below us, a city of stone and glass, with single-Loper fliers buzzing in the air, and houses with gardens and trees and shops. Inhabited towers of gnarled and twisted rock sprouted from the ground like stalagmites. Furred Lopers were conveyed across the vast chamber on moving walkways held up by thin cables. My gauges told me the air outside my warsuit was warm.

We saw four Loper soldiers approaching us, and greeted them casually with a wave. They saw us, weren't fooled by our holos, and began firing.

"*Fuck 'em up a bit*," I told Billy.

Billy threw a bomb into the air – a tornado bomb – and we

rolled backwards, and dug crampon spikes into the rock to brace ourselves.

The bomb hovered. The Lopers approached closer, clearly confident they could easily get rid of these three intruders.

Ten seconds later the bomb blew, creating a wild vortex of air that spiralled up and around and crashed into the cavern walls and sent the Lopers flying off the narrow walkway. Then the gale carried on its crazy path, and there were screams of pain and terror as the mini-tornado wreaked its havoc.

The surviving Lopers began firing bullets in our general direction; but in the angry murk they had little chance – they were shooting blind. For the tornado was whipping up spirals of stone dust into the air, destroying visibility.

Then we set the rats to run – three rat-sized robots that generated holos of the three of us in the air above them, creating virtual replicas of Artemis, Max and Billy. The rats scrambled down a narrow pathway towards the city. A couple of Lopers saw them and let out a cry. The three body-armoured Kamikazes ran faster and flashes of light appeared from their (non-existent) Xenos rifles. We watched with amusement as a posse of Lopers chased the chimeras into a spur of the main cavern.

Meanwhile, the murk generated by the bomb was starting to lift; and the tornado was spiralling downwards, towards Harbin.

We destealthed and resumed our Loper holos, then proceeded at a brisk military job down the stone steps towards the city. Ahead of us, like an insane vanguard, the tornado was smashing into buildings, slowly losing energy. And the Lopers began to chase the chimeras into a spur of the main cavern.

At the foot of the staircase we were spotted by a Loper General, who bellowed something angry at us.

"Protection duties," I screamed, in what I considered to be an utterly faultless Loper dialect. "I'm here to guard the *capobastone*."

He glared at me. I showed him a military chit with just those instructions, carefully forged by Fraser's boffins.

The air was still murky; the holos were now passing muster. I was calm. Ready for disaster, but calm.

"He's in the Heart's Tower," the General snapped at length. "Get him out of here, we think this wind is being caused by a planetary quake."

"What about the intruders?" I screamed back.

"They won't get far."

We proceeded on our way. In the haze and dust and confusion our holo-images passed muster. In less chaotic circumstances, however, we would have stood out almost immediately.

My visual array guided us to the Heart's Tower. This was the broadest and the highest of the rock towers, not exactly heart-shaped but certainly less insanely distorted than some of the other sculptured rock dwellings. The alarm klazon continued to drone. We barked urgent instructions at all we passed to assist our deception, and finally entered the front gates of the tower, which magically opened for us.

"*How are you doing this?*" asked Billy, but I didn't reply.

A platoon of Loper warriors were leading a silver-armoured figure towards us. It was, just as I'd hoped, Living Spirit.

"*Result*," said Max, speaking just a moment too soon.

For as we reached for our guns, an eerie haze of solid light surrounded us. And when I fired, the bullet bounced against air and flew back and crashed against my warsuit. Max's energy blast was also reflected and caught him full beam and lit him up like a candle. Billy meanwhile was left with gun poised in hand, reconsidering his decision to shoot. And I realised we were trapped inside translucent walls of force field energy.

Yup, that's right, trapped.

Living Spirit sauntered towards us.

"Your accent," said Living Spirit, "leaves much to be desired."

Yeah, okay, I can't *always* be right.

Billy shrugged, fatalistically. Max swore, operatically. I was silent.

Then, when Max's tirade had ceased, Living Spirit looked at me; and he raised his middle finger stump. To demonstrate his status in the Clan, and his acknowledgement that I had a place in that culture too.

"Any last words?" sneered Living Spirit. An old Clan tradition, usually honoured by neglect.

"Fuck you," said Billy, not reading the ritual subtext.

"And fuck your mother too; oh no, I already did!" taunted Max.

Living Spirit was, predictably, undistressed by the ritual taunting. But then I had my say.

"As a *capobastone* in the Clanning of Cúchulainn," I said, "I challenge thee, Living Spirit, in the combat of your choosing."

The Loper laughed. Billy snorted. Max looked at me askance.

"Are you kidding me?" demanded Living Spirit. "You do not have the right—"

"Daxox was *capobastone* of the Cúchulainn Clanning," I reminded him. "And I killed him with my bare hands, while in the body of a robot. I carry his tattoo here," I said, patting my arm. "I therefore," I concluded, "claim his authority under the Rules of Seizure."[4]

Living Spirit came closer. I lowered my face mask, then unbuckled my warsuit, and peeled off the torso covering, and finally the sleeves. Then I showed him the tattoo on my shoulder. It represented the Death of Daxox; the D of Daxox enveloped by a serpent. It had been carved on to my skin by a Clan Scribe in his own unique style before I left for the Rock. It was hardly proof positive, but such images carry a powerful totemic resonance for Clan members.

"I can also show you film footage of his death," I said. "if you

4 This implies that Teresa Shalco could have declined Artemis's challenge back in Giger, since Artemis was then masquerading as a *vangelista,* and was hence junior in Clan rank. Presumably she dared not do so for fear of losing "face", i.e. warrior credibility with her fellow Clannites. – *Ed.*

really want to be an arsehole about this. My name is Artemis. You may have heard of me."

"I have," replied Living Spirit.

"Then—"

"You dare challenge me?" roared Living Spirit.

"I do."

Beside me, Billy was smiling. He always loved it when, out of the jaws of defeat, I snatched further defeat. But, let's face it, even a few more minutes of life is worth having.

By this point the silver Loper's rage was overwhelming. But he dared not refuse the challenge.

"What is your chosen weapon? Swords? Guns? Rifles? Wits?" he asked me, in tones of coldest scorn.

"That has to be your choice." Any other answer would have secured me instant death. Sweet Shiva, the *rules* you have to learn.

Living Spirit laughed and said what I knew he would say: "Claws."

I felt naked.

In fact I *was* naked. But that in itself didn't bother me. I'm not, for fuck's sake, especially when facing near-certain death, *shy*.

No, it was my body armour that I missed. My knives, my guns, my bolas, my force field, my knuckle shields, my elbow spikes, my toe-blades. All the weapons I was used to using in *mano a mano* battles with the enemy. But now, all I had were my hands, my feet, my finger and feet spikes, and the power and speed of my augmented body.

I was pitted against Living Spirit, also stripped naked, and resplendent in his silver fur and fanged teeth. He was a monster, seven foot tall and almost four foot broad. He looked more gorilla than human. But there was a beauty in his features. His shaggy fur concealed his male organs, more or less, but his brute animal presence oppressed me all the same. His claws were like small sabre blades, rounded and sharp and deadly.

Max and Billy were still trapped inside the confining cage. The Lopers gathered round the combat ring in a semicircle. Some carried buckets of water for cleaning away the blood, and storage bags with which to convey away my body parts for the organ banks. My defeat was clearly anticipated.

"What happens," called out Max, "if you win?"

"We die anyway, but I become a legend," I explained.

"Ah. Everything to play for then."

"We have a mission," I pointed out.

Ideally, the Recon Committee wanted Living Spirit alive or dead-but-revivable. But failing that, true-dead would do. Which meant I had to kill him and then – sorry, there's no nice way of saying this – eat his brains.

And so, if all went well, I would do this one last and utterly repugnant thing to save humanity – before being slaughtered by Living Spirit's acolytes. No one would ever know what I had achieved. But I was confident that it would be done.

Well, *fairly* confident.

The Lopers began baying.

Lopers, by the way, to give them their due, are pretty sophisticated creatures. They are smarter than most non mutant humans. And there's nothing in their genetics to cause them to be feral. They were built to withstand inhospitable alien habitats, whilst remaining human in all fundamental respects. They weren't meant to be *monsters*.

But I guess, things evolve. 'Cause these fucking creatures were more ape than man, and they scared the living fuck out of me.

I circled. Living Spirit circled too. I could feel a breeze coming from somewhere, chilling my bare skin, and I silently asked the Ice computer to start charting me a way out. I also asked it to open the confining energy cage trapping Billy and

Max, on my command. I also, suddenly playing a wild hunch, asked it for the location of the armoury, and a route through the rocky tunnels to get there.

My idea was that if we fled and got hold of the guns, we could die fighting, rather than be sitting Kraal ripe for the slaughter.

Meanwhile, as I was doing all this, Living Spirit was eying me as if I were the steak on his plate.

Then he lunged. An animal leap with fangs and claws outstretched, spittle dripping from his mouth. I saw it all, making time slow down to help me judge my move. I made my move.

I rolled under his body, extended my right hand finger-claw and dug it into his torso, cutting through his hide. Red-black blood dripped on me as I hurtled past, then I rolled and was up again.

Living Spirit landed and backleaped, turning himself in midair, and lunged again at me. I dodged again, this time less successfully, and his claws raked my bare thigh, and my blood gushed.

He lunged once more and I stepped in close and threw powerful punches into his body and on his head, very fast indeed. They barely registered. I rolled away and backflipped.

He lunged, I forward-leaped, turned in midair. touching his shoulders with my hands as I flew over and attempting to strike his head with one claw. But I missed him completely.

We eyed each other up, and circled again. He lunged – his favourite move – and I went down low and clawed his balls but he caught my arm in his hand and sank his teeth into my throat. I fell over backwards and kicked him over me with two hard heels and a chunk of flesh from my throat went with him.

He was down on the floor. I was leaping over him. I landed with my feet each side of his head and punched his skull. I felt my knuckles break. I thrust a claw in his ear and he felt that. Then he batted me off and I flew up and hit the rock wall.

I landed badly, spat blood, felt the ache of my wounds and bruises, and stood up in a twitch. Living Spirit lunged once more.

I dematerialised.

It was a shock; I hadn't realised I could do that. But I had done it.

And I was in the Loper armoury, which is the place where I had been yearning to be. My thoughts had given a destination to the flit.

I shook off my own dazed astonishment, and grabbed and delocked a Tharlik rifle – smaller and squatter than my Xenos but a powerful killing machine all the same. And slung it over my shoulder by the strap. Then I seized a Philos pistol and Darsia knife and a grenade. Then I visualised Living Spirit as vividly as I could.

And I rematerialised back in the cavern. To find the mob slack-jawed with astonishment at my departure. And even more stunned at my abrupt return, in a different place.

I wasted no time. First, I authorised the QRC to unlock the force shield. Then I threw the pistol and the knife at Billy and the rifle at Max. And lastly I tossed the live grenade at the spectators and saw Loper limbs scatter like corn in the wind.

Living Spirit lunged at me like wind in a storm and put one huge hand over my throat and choked me and ripped my body open with the claws of his other hand. Meanwhile Max was raining bullets at the Lopers as Billy blasted with the pistol and hacked with the dagger. I began to die.

Then Living Spirit's body erupted with spurts of blood – Billy had shot him. And Billy was on us, thrusting his blade into the Loper's body. But Living Spirit's strength was undimmed and Billy was now rolling, evading bullets and blows, fighting for his life.

I had only one chance – one punch – and I took it and threw it. I struck Living Spirit on the temple with a blow so fast it happened before I thought it. And I felt his skull crack and he spat blood and his eyes glazed over.

Billy cut the Loper's hand off with a single knife strike and I was free of the chokehold. Blood was pouring down my body and my ribs were broken but I could still move my limbs. So I gripped the two men with my bleeding hands as guns blazed at us from all sides, and put one foot on Living Spirit's corpse. Then I told the Ice computer to close down the beaconband nuller entirely, not just locally. And then—

We dematerialised and were back on the attack ship, with the vast dead body of Living Spirit on the ground before us.

"How the FUCK did you do that?" Billy whispered.

"Magic," I said, modestly.

It wasn't magic. It was something else.

Or maybe it WAS magic. What's the difference?

Skip back in time.

Cúchulainn. Me a slave. Blocking out the bad stuff by living in a world in my head. Communing with Magog, the planet's QRC, via my Rebus chip. Inhabiting its mind, its way of being. Remember?

Now factor in this. Magog is a quantum computer. Which means at some level it exists in a quantum state of improbability, where the laws of common sense do not apply.

And I became *part of that*. I lived for long periods in the mind of Magog, to escape the agonies of my enslaved body. I learned to feel as it did, think as it did. And I became, I guess, a little bit quantal myself. That's how I can flit without a teleport machine locked on to me. *I myself can bring into existence a macroquantum state.* And hence, I can teleport at will, just so long as there's a QRC in range to aid me.

There's more to my power than this, even. Because let's face it, I'm a lucky so and so.

Luckier than any human being has a right to be.

And that's how I can teleport without misflitting, again and again and again. And it's also how I escaped from Baron Lowman, how I got *outside* his fortified mansion in the first place. Yes, I utilised my power over Magog to help me disable the whedon chip. But the series of lucky chances that aided my escape were, looking back on it, preposterous. Blind luck got me out!

And so, eventually. I have come to realise the truth about myself.

I am more powerful than anyone has ever realised. I have a unique power over QRCs. And I also have – as a *direct consequence* of that ability – the gift of luck.

And as a result, I can open locked doors, shut down subway stations, seize control of spaceships, and make doppelgänger robots dance like my puppets. And I can flit here, there, and anywhere, at will.

I am, in short, a witch of the quantumverse.

However, be that as it may: it turns out that I cannot beat a Loper in single combat. Boy, that guy had me *whupped*.

Fraser came to visit me in my hospital bed. And he handed me the Tarot Card with the Magician's icon upon it.

I ripped it in half and handed it back.

"Anything you want to tell me?" he asked.

"Nope."

"The three of you returned with no misflits. That was lucky."

"Damned lucky," I said modestly.

Then I went to sleep. I was in the hospital for a week. They had to give me a clone lung, to replace the one that Living Spirit had mauled. (His claws had penetrated my rib cage.) They used three tubes of glue on my skin, and while the wounds were healing I looked like a marble statue that had been dropped from a great height and cracked from tip to toe.

After twenty-four hours asleep, I woke and found Max and Billy by my bedside, celebrating our victory by drinking the malt whisky they had brought me. They had drunk so much already they were barely coherent and I had to ask security to have them forcibly removed from the ward. I couldn't, to be honest, stomach seeing them hug each other and declare their undying mutual love.

When I left the hospital I went on convalescent leave, and spent most of my time watching television. And so I caught most of the news broadcasts about the capture of Living Spirit. He'd been resuscitated successfully with little brain tissue damage. And he was filmed in a room at the Moral Rehabilitation Centre, professing his desire to live in peace and harmony.

It was a very different Living Spirit. The rage in his eyes had gone. His voice was flat and unmodulated. His fur was dull, it no longer had that sheen of the warrior at the height of his powers.

Living Spirit spoke at length about the folly of rebellion and the need for all human beings to live in peace and harmony. All admirable sentiments, delivered in a dull monotone. Like hearing a robot voicemail recite Flanagan's Speech to the Pirates just before the Last Battle. But the message was clear. Living Spirit repented of his many sins.

All the *capobastone* had to do this. Repent in public. Set an example to the rest of humanity.

Naturally, however, since these were all evil bastards, repentance didn't come easily or naturally. In fact – as I had by now learned – it could only be achieved by surgically inserting a conscience chip into the brain of the aforementioned villain.

That's why Living Spirit had lost his spirit. His emotions were no longer his own. His rage and passion were controlled by a surgically implanted chip in his brain. He was a human being with an emotional dial set to 1.

Was that real repentance? Who can say?

Billy came to see me and he couldn't work out why I was so melancholy.

"We won!" he said.

"Did we?" I said, forlornly.

"Are you dead?"

"No."

"Am I dead?"

"No."

"Then," said Billy, beaming at the simplicity of it, "we've won."

I had one more mission. It wasn't optional. So I got back in shape. I returned to the sim rooms. Billy and I picked up where we'd left off.

Max was my new best friend. He too had one more mission, and he wanted to flit with me by his side. Holding his hand.

He knew, of course. Billy knew too. I was touched with magic. Anyone who held my hand would never misflit.

I am a lucky so and so. About ten per cent more lucky than a normal human being.

But when you run the fifty-fifty, that edge is what you need.

The trouble was, I was still depressed.

Deeply depressed, if I'm to be honest. For about six weeks. For reasons that I think are pretty obvious. Do I need to spell them out?

No, I didn't think so.[5]

But after six weeks of mourning miserableness, my mood started to lighten. By now, I was mission fit and ready to go, and verging on cheerful again.

And then I met Gabriel again.

The cyborg Gabriel, I mean.

He came up to me in the canteen. He'd been restored into a full replica humaniform body. He looked beautiful. He was smiling at me. My heart was in my mouth. "How's it going Gabriel?"

"You should feel proud, Artemis," he beamed. He knew my name – I was famous after all, the hero of the Rock. But there was no real recognition in his eyes.

"Hey I love you, man!" I said, truthfully.

"I love you too," he beamed, emptily. "But my name isn't Gabriel. It is Cyborg 46,322, Version 1."

"I thought you guys had names."

"Not any more."

"Can I call you Gabriel for short?

"You can."

"Do you know *why* I might call you that?"

"I assume I must have been of that name when you previously knew me."

"Yeah."

"My friends call me Four-six-three-two-two."

Yeah, he actually said that. I couldn't believe it either.

"I can't call you that," I pointed out.

"I am pleased to have met you, Artemis."

5 I don't think so either. Poor Artemis – she lost a dear friend in this mission, and my heart goes out to her. – *Ed.*

Gabriel moved away.

"What the fuck gives?" I said later to Billy.

He shrugged. "It's a new strategy," he explained. "The cyborgs weren't working. They were all going mad. Now, they wipe all the memories of the original personality. You have the mind of a human, but you don't know anything about who you once were. Works better."

I thought about it, and didn't like it.

"That's scary."

"It's not Gabriel. Not any more. Gabriel is dead," Billy said kindly.

I realised I was weeping. Billy cradled me. He wiped the tears from my cheeks.

"He's dead," Billy murmured, and kept on murmuring it, in the hope I would finally understand. "It's not the guy you used to know, okay? That guy is dead. What's left is just – it's a shadow, right? The shadow of Gabriel, not the real thing. The real Gabriel is dead. He's dead. He's dead. He's dead. He's dead. He's dead. He's dead. He's dead. He's dead. He's—"

Chapter 10

Mission 3: The High Priestess

We hit the ground standing.

Seven of us ported, but there were no misflits. We didn't even have any inverted fingers or feet amongst us.

In addition to me and Billy and Max, there was Durando, Catrin, Sheena, and Andres.

I knew Andres and Catrin from sim training. Durando and Sheena were new to me. She was an Eagle, he was a Noir.

"Fuck me! What are the odds on *that*?" marvelled Andres.

"Give me a second," I said.

We were on the planet of Fresh Start. It was a foggy swamp-filled land with no cities, just scattered villages. Our intel was that the High Priestess had been injured by a doppelgänger assault on her base ship and was recuperating on this small and insignificant planet. There were, I should point out, seven hundred and forty-two other intel leads that were also being pursued by other Squads.

I listened with my Rebus chip, and I heard the distant murmur of thoughts and systems running. I let my mind roam until I found it – It! – the QRC that ran this planet. Its physical reality located at the base of a deep mine. I offered up my introductory codes, to establish myself as a fellow QRC.

How can I describe what that feels like? I can't. It's like an amoeba poking at a spider in its web. A commingling of hard spiky thoughts that merge to become – what? New thoughts? It wasn't clear to me at all. And yet I understood it totally, with terrifyingly vivid acuity.

A considerable hiatus ensued.

Amoeba and web and hard and spiky and other metaphors failed once more to capture the experience.

And finally the QRC acknowledged me as an equal in the fraternity of cybernetic quantum-reality minds.

The QRC had no name, no personality even. It was merely there. A cold brooding presence. I further relaxed my frame of cognition and co-existed with its datapools. As I had on Cúchulainn, I became as one with the spirit of the processor.

And now I was on the inside of the QRC, with access to all its sensors and datapools. I could smell the fogs. I could hear the rumble of the continents. I could track the passage of the inhabitant humans across the veldts and swamps and in their villages and houses. I knew them all, or felt I did, as a near-infinity of data about the planet scrolled through my mind, like alcohol from the first glass of whisky seeping into a drunk.

I was primarily looking for the High Priestess, Sinara Lo; and I highlighted her presence in my intellect, and imaged her photograph, and waited to learn where she was.

That knowledge was acquired by me.

I opened my eyes. "She's not here," I said.

They were all staring at me. "What?" I said defensively.

"Are you sure?" asked Billy.

"I'm sure. She's not here. She's on Kandala."

I put out my hands, and Max, Durando, Sheena, Andres and Billy clasped them.

But Catrin refused to join us.

She had been totally spooked by my behaviour since our arrival on Fresh Start. And I could see her point; we were on an urgent military mission and my first act was to sink into a twenty-five minute long coma. Furthermore, my apparently psychic certainty perturbed her. Catrin was an unbeliever – she had no personal god, no lucky charms. But she was convinced that the laws of probability would favour her survival and had written a spreadsheet program to prove this. The idea that I could know stuff that *she didn't* offended her sense of the rightness of things.

And so, dogmatically, she insisted on returning to base for her formal orders.

When she did so however – to give away the ending of Catrin's tragic story – she misflitted badly. Her body turned vegetal. She was alive, but her brain became – I don't know what – a sponge or a spore. She was killed mercifully by soldiers with blast guns. So much for the power of logic.[1]

Meanwhile, the rest of us flitted to Kandala.

The Boneyard. The sim training had included smell data, but it didn't in any way match the real thing. The stench of death was all around us. Some of the carcasses had mummified in the hot desert air, their faces still bearing a final scream.

There was a Dzee-dzee-bon-da from the planet of Weisman nuzzling its snout among the bones, eating a slow feast. It turned slowly and saw us.

"It's harmless," I said, "provided we—"

The Dzee-dzee-bon-da leaped. It was fast, the fastest land animal in the known universe, and its four heads were extended and roaring in unison. It caught Billy in its jaws and tried to

1 Catrin Alison Willard. May she rest in peace. – *Ed.*

crunch him. We had our rifles drawn in a flick of an eye and rained projectile bullets at its body, but it leaped above us and landed and scattered us like skittles.

As I fell I threw a dagger and it snagged in the creature's hide. Then I subvoced the blade to electrify. Thousands of volts pulsed into the creature's body. It froze, and dropped Billy from its claws.

Billy was drawing his hand gun as he fell and he fired a tight plasma burst at the creature's eye. The eye burned. The brain behind the eye ignited. The creature fell. Then we finished it off with head and body shots until the creature's body had stopped twitching.

"What's this fucker doing here?" I asked.

"Oh fuck," said Billy.

The sky was black with Jatayus, cawing and excreting acid rain that made our warsuits sizzle. These vicious beasts had been imported, so my brain chip told me, from New Earth III. We fought them off, with plasma bursts and bullets, and the cloud of killer birds began to dissipate.

But just a few moments later, a vast herd of Dzee-dzee-bondas came crashing into the Boneyard, alerted by the death of one of their own. A Humbaba[2] joined the fray, its blank ugly face scowling down at us. Two Mairus[3] arrived soon after that. Followed by a host of Firebirds.[4]

"I guess this is the welcoming committee," said Max.

A battle most glorious ensued in which—

Forget that shit. We dug in and fought. It's what we were trained for, and equipped for.

We each carried two Xenos rifles, one for back-up. The Xenos of course is the most effective fighting weapon known to humankind. It can fire – alternately or simultaneously – exploding

2 From the planet of Asgard. – *Ed.*
3 From the planet of Serenity. – *Ed.*
4 From the planet of Sky. – *Ed.*

bullets, plasma beams, laser pulses, and small rocket shells. We also had grenades and plasma pistols and Max was carrying the mortar tube. By the time the battle was over, we had exhausted all our projectile bullets and the batteries on our Xenos guns were dipping into the red.

We called up the base ship and they teleported replacement ammo and Bostock Batteries. It took four hours to check each one for misflits, then we were ready to roll.

A mountain of carnage loomed above and around us. The smell of ancient death now had an overlay of blood and ruptured guts and shit.

The battle had taken a lot out of us, in terms of time and energy. Four entire days had elapsed since we had first landed on Kandala. We were exhausted and famished. I gave orders to bivouac down for a night's sleep.

Big mistake. The nocturnals descended and swarmed upon us at about three am. That also was a long and bitter battle. It took six hours to kill each and every one of them. We identified forty-three different species of savage predator, from as many different planets. The mountain of carnage grew.

We moved out of the Boneyard into the outer precincts of the city, where we took our masks off and put traditional Kandalan robes over our black warsuits. Then we jogged for a few miles, but slowed down to a walk once we started seeing humans. We were at the limit of our physical and psychological capacity, and we hadn't even engaged the enemy yet. I was beginning to get the measure of the High Priestess. It was a stroke of genius to use alien predators as a cordon sanitaire.

The city of Kandala was just as we remembered it from the sims. The narrow streets, the busy market stalls, the jewelled Citadel walls, the golden roads and sidewalks decorated with mosaic sigils. But the people – well. That was something else again.

There were giants. Dwarfs. Trolls. Small flying humans who looked like fairies. There were headless men, and women with three breasts or more, or with tentacles instead of arms. And there were alien sentients too. Creatures I'd read about in books but never seen. The humanoid legless Mannananggal.[5] The dragon-like Panlong.[6] The Wampus,[7] a leopard-like slinking beast with six legs and dazzling eyes. And more, many more.

Most of these were creatures rendered extinct, or near-extinct, in the years of the Corporation's great Expansion. The planets of these sentient beings had been terraformed, to be made habitable by us but not *them*. And only a few specimens were retained, to be kept in zoos. My guess was that Sinara Lo had grown these creatures from blueprints of their DNA, genetically modified so they could breathe the same air as each other.

Some, however, were simply genetically mutated humans. Like the headless guys, and the three-breasted women, and the half-naked bald people who had hundreds of eyes upon their torsos. That was just *freakish*.

"Can I interest you," said a voice, "in some merchandise?"

I turned to look, saw nothing, then looked down. I beheld a short squat creature with three eyes and yellow skin and a big smile that stretched around its entire face. I couldn't work out if it was mutant-human or alien. It was an absurd-looking creature, like a grinning teddy bear without the fur, and its voice had a bubble of pleasure in it that was beguiling.

"No," I said.

"Amphorae? Tumblers? Gold jewellery? Silver plate? Jewels?"

"No."

"That robe is not authentic. I could sell you something more plausible."

"No."

"You're from off-planet aren't you?"

5 From the planet of Herorot. – *Ed.*
6 From the planet of Luce. – *Ed.*
7 From the planet of Cambria. – *Ed.*

"No."

The three-eyed squat tubby creature beamed up at me with pleasure.

"Then why have I never seen you before?"

Max shifted uneasily. "Thank you, sir, we have no need of your merchandise," he said, in rather bad Kandalan.

"Let's get out of here," said Durando.

"If you are intruders bent on ill, perhaps I should call the Warden," suggested the three-eyed squat tubby creature.

"Or a bribe might help," it added.

Max stiffened; ready for carnage. I raised a hand to still his wrath.

"Bribe it," I suggested, and Andres reached into his purse.

Andres counted out the bribe, in gold capsules carved with an unforgeable hallmark, which our boffins had forged. Billy waited, silent. His eyes roamed the streets, capturing every clue, alert to danger.

I shifted on the balls of my feet, wondering if I would have to kill this annoying creature. Sheena and Andres had the same thought; they quietly moved themselves to cut off the beast's exit points.

"Generous," conceded the alien creature.

At that moment I had an idea.

"Will you help us?" I suggested.

Max shot me a sceptical look. Durando looked impatient. Sheena looked impassive, her default expression. Andres kept his eyes on the crowd.

Billy looked at me then shrugged. He trusted me – that was his message.

"Local knowledge," I insisted.

"How can I refuse?" The creature laughed. "And you should be aware that you stand no chance of success on your own. The person you seek is well guarded. Magic protects her palace."

"Yeah?" I said sceptically.

"Yes indeed," beamed the yellow creature. "For the city is run by a mind that exists in the realm of the differently possible. What you call the quantum world. Its powers are so near to magic, who can tell the difference?"

I shrugged. Fair point.

"What's your name?" I asked, intrigued about this strange and knowledgeable beast.

"Majalara," said the creature. "My people were born on a planet far from you, whose name in your language I do not know. But I myself was born in a vat. I—"

"You're an alien," I interrupted.

"Yes. But—"

"We get it. Skip the backstory. We know all we need to know."

"I like the eyes," confided Durando.

"And I like yours," said Majalara. "Oh and by the way . . ."

I could hear it too. The tramp of soldiers' boots, moving closer and closer towards us. We turned, saw two Mutant Soldiers heading towards us. They were swapping comments, clearly bearing down upon interloping strangers.

Sheena threw a stone whilst barely seeming to move, and it hit a man selling earthenware pots. He screamed and staggered back into a shelf, and the pots went flying. The Mutant Soldiers turned and looked at the chaos.

"Hold my hands," I said and held both hands out. The others clasped my fingers. And after some hesitation, so did Majalara.

We flitted and reappeared in the eastern quarter of the city, just yards from the impregnable jewelled walls of the Citadel.

"Hey!" shouted Billy, shoving Durando. Durando shoved back. The two men jostled, kicking up gravel, behaving like two friends having a quarrel.

"If you can't take the truth," sneered Durando.

"Don't ever talk about her like that again. All right? What kind of friend are you?"

And so they went on, childishly wrangling. The scuffle attracted the attention of passers-by; and distracted attention from the fact that a few seconds ago, none of us had been there. Standard misdirection strategy.

"What you just did – that was extraordinary," said Majalara, astonished.

I was now convinced I would have to kill this beast. It knew too much. And yet, there was something about it—

"Can you help get us inside the Citadel?" I asked.

"It's impossible. Many have tried. I have tried."

"You know where the gate is?"

"I know."

"Will you show us? We have – machines that can—"

"There's no way of entering the gate. No machine will help you. It does not exist, until Sinara wills it so. I can tell you where it will appear, but no more than that."

"Stealth technology," said Andres. "We don't need this wretched—"

"Only servants of Sinara can enter the Citadel. The gate will know. Some have tried to sneak in. Dressed in stolen robes. Carrying false identity papers. The gate knows, all interlopers die. I have seen it," said Majalara.

"The brain chip," said Billy, and I nodded.

"Show us the gate," I told the creature.

"Why should I?"

"We just bribed you!" I pointed out.

"I want more."

"Oh, and what else would you like?" I asked viciously.

The creature beamed, from ear to ear. It was, I decided, a truly disgusting smile.

"The death of Sinara Lo," Majalara said.

"Then," I said, "we have a deal."

Yeah, it sounds pretty random but it happens that way sometimes.

Except, of course, it wasn't random at all. Majalara had been waiting for this moment for a long time. He had – no, that'll come later.

Here's the deal on Kandala.

The Citadel was surrounded by high walls as you know, and also enclosed in a powerful force field that could absorb the energy from a One Sun strike. And the skies above it were dotted with thousands of Osprey and Caracaras jets that could devastatingly rebut any direct aerial assault or attempted missile strike. Nullers were installed in every stone of the jewelled wall, making it impossible for beaconband signals to work within; and also preventing me from teleporting inside. The body of the QRC was concealed somewhere within the walls, with its mind carefully shielded. But it had cloned its essence into the satellite QRC outside the gates, which ran the city and planet; and which I had used to help me flit to safety a few moments earlier.

In summary: No tunnels could be dug beneath the Citadel, because it was built upon a mountain of poured tectonite. Aerial attack was impossible as already explained. The walls were allegedly unbreakable, even by a direct nuclear blast, which suggested that Sinara had purchased sheets of durium from a black hole supermetal forge. And, as we had learned, there was no gate. So, all in all, no way in.[8]

However . . .

We knew that law and order was enforced in the city and the planet by Sinara Lo's Mutant Army. These mutated Soldiers had all the ferocity and brainwashing of the Soldiers we were used to, combined with extraordinary physical powers.

And this army was garrisoned at various places around the

8 The sims on the Rock were conducted without the benefit of Artemis's detailed knowledge of the Citadel's security system, via the planet's satellite QRC. – *Ed.*

city. But in the event of an actual invasion, we had reasoned, the Soldiers would surely have standing orders to return home to the Citadel. They were valuable human assets. They couldn't be put at unnecessary risk outside the Citadel walls.

This was Plan A you understand. We had to join the army.

The heavens erupted. The blue of the sky turned into an inferno of reds and yellows and dazzling whites as the fusillade of missiles from outer space exploded in the upper atmosphere and spread a haze around the planet.

And again.

And, dazzlingly, again.

At my instruction, the bombardment was incessant. But, so far, the Kandala space defence system was bearing up well. A billion microdrones in orbit around the planet were in place. And swarms of them flocked upon the incoming missiles and triggered them into premature detonation.

Launching a missile attack at this planet was like pouring gasoline upon a fire. Hence, the inferno above us.

A group of Soldiers were hurrying through the market square, when Majalara called to them. These were warriors of the Mutant Army. Tall (twice my height). Headless (or rather with a skull so deeply embedded beneath the shoulders it was safe from all but the most savage blows). And with eyes at both front and back – two above the nipples at the front, two just below the shoulders at the back. Oh, and most of these Soldiers were octopus armed too – four at the front, four at the back, with an extra leg for stability.

The mutant warriors wore red body armour marked with the sigils of Hecate, for this was a witch-worshipping planet. And they waddled with remarkable speed. It was hard to conceive having a conversation with one of these three-legged eight-armed beasts. They spoke through the diaphragm, and there was no face whose expression you could read.

These were monsters, spawned from Sinara's fast-grow vats, like weeds cultivated to kill all the trees in the forest.

"Help me!" Majalara cried and the mutant Soldiers waggled their arms in what I took to be a scornful way when they saw his dwarfish comic form. "Please, help me," he continued with a heart-rending tone of desperation in his voice. "A missile has landed in Alchemy Street! There's an enemy pilot on board!" The mutants waggled their arms again, sardonically this time I fancied. But they followed.

When they turned the corner into Alchemy Street the six of us emerged from shadows and killed the monsters with dagger thrusts. We cut through their armour at their shoulder-mound to penetrate into the skull and brain below. Our knives were made of diamond-tectonite, the hardest substance in the universe except for whatever the walls of Kaldana Citadel were made of. It took huge strength to plunge these blades through a soldier's body armour, but we had practised this move many times before in training.

Thus, three of them died in a trice, as we leaped and grabbed and stabbed. That left three mutant Soldiers still standing, and they came at us with silent rage. Max was grabbed in a giant hand, Durando received a plasma blast to his body, I was batted down and almost knocked unconscious. But we had our hand guns drawn in the midst of pain and confusion and we rained projectile bullets upon the three freaks, focusing on the transparent shoulder-bosses which shielded the eyes.

One died. The second was knocked off its feet by Max, who proceeded to plunge his knife into the creature's arm joint. The blade slid in and an artery was severed. As the mutant bled Durando and Sheena and Andres and I rained bullets on his shoulder-mound until it ceased to move. Meanwhile, Billy killed the third and final mutant in ways I cannot bear to describe.

Then we took the top armour plates off six of the dead mutant

Soldiers and dug down within to find the heads, then removed their brain chips. It was a bloody process.

"Is there no other way?" said Majalara mournfully.

"It's a fucking war," Max snapped.

The squat little creature had a face so sad I wanted to laugh.

"Okay," I said, "copy and save."

We set our eyes to record the dead Soldiers in their every particular. Their armour. Their sigils. Their height and breadth. The size of their hands, and the shape of their third legs. Then our warsuit holos erupted into activity, and the six of us became mutant headless giants in red and richly patterned armour.

"I will come with you," said Majalara.

"Yeah, you'll blend in nicely," I pointed out.

"I have this," said Majalara, and perhaps I was mistaken but his smile seemed even broader, "capacity."

And his shape started to change. I felt my vision swim as his body morphed. And the dwarfish clown became a giant eight-armed three-legged headless warrior.

"We are herbivores," explained Majalara, "with a gift for camouflage."

I heard the trumpet sound that was summoning the soldiers. I knew too that the mutants, dumb as they were, would have MI'd for help as they started to die. We didn't have long.

The sky erupted again as a heavy hail of SNG missiles and unmanned rockets crashed down upon the atmosphere of the planet, to be smashed from the sky by a million tiny fists. A stray missile broke through and was detonated as it plunged through clouds. The black haze and supersonic boom added to the chaos of the moment. Just what we needed.

We joined the throng of the soldiers of the Mutant Army. Most were headless giants, of the two-armed and eight-armed varieties. But there were dwarfs too – no doubt genetically modified to be able to run through narrow tunnels and sewers in pursuit of errant slaves. The officers rode Mastodons, magnificently hairy tusked beasts which I knew had been extinct on

Earth long before the human race made genocide its hobby and obsession.

Our holos were plausible enough but I knew we wouldn't survive a close inspection. So once again, we needed as much anarchy and confusion as possible, in order to slip through undetected.

We also of course needed to pass the security brain scan. Which we were able to do, because each of us had a mutant warrior's brain chip held under our tongues, modified by me. These would identify us as being the Soldiers we had killed.[9]

We joined a regiment as they were hurrying towards the Gate. We would never have known it was there; it was just another patch of wall with no markings, no arch and keystone, and no actual opening. Not a gate at all in other words. But Majalara had assured us this was our way in.

Above us, another missile had broken through the planetary defences and there were twin palls of black smoke hugging the sky now. The Soldiers were screaming at each other as they marched towards the jewelled wall.

Then a small slit appeared in the wall. And it grew, like a balloon swelling, larger and larger, until it was the height of a man. Then it grew more; until the Gate was manifest and open with a jewelled arch above it. And the soldiers ran through the gap in single file.

Max, Durando, Billy, Sheena, Andres and Majalara followed me as I ran inside. I was momentarily awed at the sight of the Forest of Towers from such close range. Beautiful too was the Silver Campanile, which soared high to the east of me; and I even spared a glance for the seven glistening domes of the Cathedral, visible in the gaps between the houses like winking eyes.

We were in an outer courtyard; in front of us was a low gateway leading to the courtyard within; and to the courtyard

9 It can be assumed that Artemis has acquired a seventh brain chip for Majalara, but forgot to mention this. – *Ed.*

beyond that. At the heart of these concentric circles was the Inner Citadel, where the Cathedral and the Forest of Towers were to be found.

The outer courtyard itself was thronged with tents and burning braziers where Soldiers cooked and stalls where knives and jewellery were being sold. It was a city within the city; surmounted by those vast Citadel walls which were patrolled by mutant Soldiers and bristling with plasma cannons to repel invaders who could not possibly invade – because of the force field all around. Birds flew above us but could not descend beyond a certain height. Bird dung was visible in mid-air, little balls of shit that could not land because of the invisible roof. The clouds shimmered, because of the refractive effect of the anti-energy shields. And the sky itself was crowded with tumult, as the aerial war continued and puffs of coloured smoke appeared and slowly dissipated in the wind; each the token of a distant explosion.

I knew I had only a few minutes in which to work, to achieve direct Rebus-chip access with the planet's QRC. Andres and Durando and Billy seized some stools by a food stall and bought beer and rolls filled with meat, and kept up an incessant loud chatter full of swear words and threats against unnamed enemies. Sheena created a further distraction by flirting with a headless Mutant, bravely flaunting all the femininity of her big-breasted body, and endeavouring to allure with her wiles, despite her own lack of a head.

And I withdrew into my mind.

My brain by now had died – or rather, my Rebus chip access to the outer city's QRC was extinguished by the nullers in the walls.

Then I attempted to enter the mind of the Citadel QRC. I seduced it. And wooed it. And tried to introduce myself to it. But the computer's mind-barriers were high and it greeted me with suspicious hostility.

I persevered.

This took a little while.

Eventually, I prevailed.

Meanwhile, the limpet-mine that Billy had planted outside the Citadel walls now exploded. There was a huge bang and a considerable amount of smoke billowed above the jewelled walls. Some of the Soldiers on the parapets flew into a panic and fired their plasma cannons randomly at an unseen enemy; creating more noise and generating screams of panic outside the walls. Billy grinned. He was in his element.

Then Billy and I walked shoulder to shoulder, flanked by our four comrade warriors and Majalara, into the next courtyard; and then into the courtyard inside that. Seven headless giants striding away from danger in search of new instructions. Billy's eyes were once more darting in all directions, absorbing information, identifying threats, while my mind was in two places. Here, and there. In the Citadel. And in the mind of its controlling mind.

And we seven mutant warriors were the smallest part of a truly gigantic army. There were hundreds of thousands of us. Regiment upon regiment of headless mutants had returned to sit out the planetary attack, until the enemy's inevitable defeat.

We passed through the final gateway and we saw the base of the tall and eerie White Tower ahead of us, at the centre of the Forest of Towers. A structure made of stone stuccoed with white gold and secured by fields of force.

Inside this edifice, the QRC informed me, was to be found Sinara Lo, the High Priestess in our Tarot pack. We were close, so close, to achieving our goal.

Then everything changed.

I mean, really changed. Terrifyingly changed. For up to this point we had created as much chaos and madness as we could, and we had experienced savage violence in our battle with the

Mutant warriors. But from our point of view, it was all familiar stuff.

Picture it: Above us, the sky was lit by the fires of space battles between distant robot ships in space. More of the limpet-mines planted by Billy were exploding regularly in the city, creating a constant crash and roar in the background. The sky was black with smoke which flickered and flashed with blazing explosions of light, like night that yearned to become glorious day. And the Mutant Army were all around us, their vast ugly bodies contained in rich red armour, like giant red ants hurrying back to their nest.

It was a vision of Hell, but that was just the way we liked it. We were guerrilla soldiers who knew our game, and were masters of our trade. It was scary, yes, but this was our *job.*

But then Majalara's body shimmered and he lost his mutant Soldier disguise.

And a new Majarala was born. Tall. Powerful. Numinous. He was like mist in the form of a six armed reptilian monster. Except he was not reptilian, he was—

Majalara struck. His arms swung and a mutant Soldier fell and his armour ripped open and his viscera spurted and he screamed and then Majalara struck again and the screams stopped and the soldier was dead.

It is not in any conceivable way possible to kill a Soldier in full body armour with a single punch. Yet Majalara had done so.

The reaction was almost instantaneous. The surrounding mutant Soldiers seized their rifles and a fusillade of projectile bullets erupted from guns, creating a sound like an earthquake. Or like thunder cracking the sky, if you happened to be *inside* the thundercloud.

To no avail. Did the bullets miss? Bounce off? Pass through? I couldn't tell.

Majalara struck again and more bullets flew past him or through him and crashed against the jewelled walls, spitting out rubies and diamonds. Another Soldier's body was ripped in half and arterial blood spurted, and Majalara struck again.

Seconds had passed and I realised that Majalara was a shape-shifting alien and this was his true body. The squat clown shape was mere subterfuge. And, furthermore, he had six or maybe nine or maybe eleven arms but also a multiplicity of cilia that emerged from his body and lashed like whips. And each lash severed the body of an armoured Soldier. And fire could not burn him, and bullets could not impact on his flesh.

I had my Xenos rifle at my shoulder and fired a plasma pulse at Majalara. I have no idea what actually happened then. But I know that the air in front of me burned and my suit overheated and my holo projection vanished. Had he thrown the plasma burst *back* at me? I fired again and Majalara now hurled a handful of bodies at me and they arrived in large gobbets of flesh and armour, dripping blood as they spun through the air.

And so, that day, there was carnage.

Majalara had claws, perhaps, or merely teeth, or perhaps horns. And his cilias lashed and whipped and he roared or perhaps snarled, or perhaps there was an absence of sound. But more than anything there was

Terror.

I have, I must tell you, experienced a terror such as this before. Not quite so intense. Not actually as appalling. But – comparable. I have felt it – perhaps once before. Or perhaps it was twice. No actually, more than twice, many more than twice. For I remember—

Yes, I remember when I was locked in the Rebus library by my father. As a child.

You remember I told you how he used to do this? My father felt that that I did not have, or if I had I did not sufficiently demonstrate, "respect". So to teach me respect, he caged me like an animal.

And I never got used to it. I used to try and persuade myself that this time it would be different. This time I was "tough enough" to take it.

And for the first few hours of my every incarceration, I WAS tough. And angry, and rebellious.

And then I would go through a stubborn phase. I wouldn't give in! I wouldn't yield to this bastard!

But then, every time, the Terror would come upon me.

Imagine the sheer loneliness of being a child trapped in a vault of books in a lonely library full of dark alcoves where even scholars rarely ventured. The shadows oppressed me. I was convinced that creatures of supernatural horror existed in this dark, spooky, library. And for four or five or sometimes six or seven days and nights I would live with that terror.

The fears I felt in those long dark nights have never left me. Whenever I am truly afraid, I remember—

And Majalara struck again, and smote with claws and cilia and bit with teeth. And dozens died. Then scores. Then hundreds. It was a massacre beyond imagining. A single unarmoured alien confronted with Soldiers who had force fields and plasma guns and grenades and mortars, and yet Majalara kept killing. The air was bright with flashes of light as missiles were fired at his body, but somehow he was never there and the explosions did not dissipate his form. So surely he was more mist than monster? Or perhaps—

I saw Max ripped into bloody pieces before my eyes.

I heard Durando scream over the MI network, for a snake was winding its way down his throat. Was it a cilia, perhaps, that resembled a snake? And then his body erupted and his brain remained alive long enough to register that he was now in shards and then the brain itself was in pieces and Durando died.

I saw a head, bobbing on the ground, wrenched from its body. I recognised it as Sheena. As for Andres, I have no idea. I never saw him again.[10]

10 Andres Mariano, Maximilian Jones, and Sheena Shaw. May you rest in peace. – *Ed.*

Then Billy waved to me. And we ran towards the White Tower.

There was no hope of defeating this creature. Nor was there any way of enduring what I felt – what I—

"You feel it too?" screamed Billy.

I nodded. We stopped, in the shadow of the White Tower. And Billy stared at me and I stared at him. And we hugged. And I wept. And so did he. I cradled him, he cradled me. The Terror!

The other time – you know what I'm referring to.

The other time I felt the Terror – yes of course it was on Cúchulainn, during my captivity. I was, by that time, a hard mollyfocker. I had endured all that I had to endure. But then—

The Terror came to me.

And it came to me one year, two months, three days and six hours after I was first taken in the custody of Baron Lowman.

I remember the moment so vividly. It occurred when Daxox visited me for the first and only time. There I was, sitting sullenly on the Manxbull hide sofa of the Baron's private suite and Daxox entered and sat down opposite me. He was sombre, and bore a haunted look.

And then he said to me, quietly: "I'm so sorry Artemis."

And I stared at him with hate, but also with a faint, slippery stirring of hope.

"I should never have done this!" Daxox continued, in broken tones. "I am a monster! But now I have come to save you. Please, forgive me."

And my heart leapt with joy!

For I'd always known, you see, that Daxox hadn't meant to do what he did. It was, as I'd always suspected, just a test! To gauge the full extent of my loyalty!

And thus my heart was filled with love and gratitude once more.

And then Daxox smiled, a thin evil smile. And I got it.

Yeah, I got it.

And as I was led back to my rooms, following Daxox's triumphant and leering departure, I felt it, then. Not despair. Not fear. Not distress. But sheer blind

Terror.

"Shapeshifting," said Billy, "and empathetic, it can affect our thoughts, our emotions, our perception. That's why we can't—"

"Where does the fucking creature come—" I began to say and then my way into the QRC's most securely barriered datapools was clear and I was deep in its mind and possessed by its spirit and I knew.

"It's the last survivor," I told Billy. "These creatures[11] killed a planetary expeditionary force. And then their planet was obliterated. It was genocide as self-defence. But one remained. A spore. Clinging to the flagship." I saw the images in the mind of the QRC, from the camera footage that had survived all these years. "And the ship returned here, to Kandala. And the spore grew. And it took the shape of a familiar alien being and has lived here since. Waiting for an opportunity to breach the security of the Citadel, so that it can wreak—"

"How do we kill it?" interrupted Billy. Pragmatic as ever.

I rummaged the mind of the QRC and it yielded me the answer, with quiet friendship.

"Oxygen," I said. "It needs oxygen. That's how these creatures were killed. The fleet blew up its planet. The survivors choked to death in space."

"Yeah, okay, so we cut off the air to the dome," said Billy, his mind racing. "Most people in the Citadel will have oxygen capsules in the brain. The others – well, tough. We have to kill this mollyfocking thing. I've never seen anything like it!"

"I'll do it," I said and spoke to the QRC, but it would not obey me.

11 My consultation with the Earth QRC confirms this is a shapeshifting Nagual, from the now-terraformed planet of Destiny. – *Ed.*

"Okay, this way," I said and I blew open the doors of the White Tower with an exploding bullet and ran inside.

And we carried on running within the Tower. It was a building of glass and diamond floors and mirrored ceilings. Dazzling and alienating and bewildering. Without the QRC to guide me, we would have been hopelessly lost. But, following the grid plan on my visual array, we climbed a narrow staircase, then a broader staircase, then a broader staircase still. There were no walkways or lifts, the entire building was a rabbit warren of dimly lit Möbius strip corridors and dizzyingly steep staircases; but we found a route through.

Until finally we reached the Hall of Power. A vaulted cathedral with a beamed roof made of purest yellow gold. Light poured through the stained-glass windows like sunshine in a kaleidoscope. And the walls were decorated with paintings of space; black canvases lightly speckled with stars; futile images that sucked in the light from the windows and somehow chilled the blood.

Six headless mutant Soldiers guarded this Hall, and blocked our path, and raised their weapons; but we barely registered their presence as we slaughtered a way through.

More Soldiers came running in from every door; the Hall was now alive with troops all carrying plasma weapons and wearing burnished red body armour. And we set to it.

Fighting. Slaying. Running. Ducking. Rolling. Slaying again. My heart pounding. My body at its peak of alertness. All conscious thought deserted me and I was an animal steeped in blood and driven by fear.

And finally the last of the guardians of this room were dead; and there she was, in front of us, at the far end of the nave of the hall. Tall. Beautiful. Her hair jet black and straight; her skin the colour of ebony, burnished, with eyes like pools of night. Standing, calmly, in the spot which in a real cathedral would have been the altar, which here was occupied by a virtual replica of a city with touch-air controls – the City Array.

It was of course the High Priestess herself, Sinara Lo. Billy raised his gun.

"Sinara! We have to work together!" I screamed at her, and Sinara looked at me in shock at first, but then in astonishment as my words penetrated her awareness.

Billy lowered his gun. He was a man who could take a hint.

"What is this thing that is attacking us?" she whispered. "And what does it want?"

I knew the answers to her questions. But I was in no mood to cxplain it all to such an cvil ginch.

But let me explain it to *you.* So you can understand the true horror of what was about to happen.

You see, the QRC with whose brain I was communing was in effect a cybernetic zoo. In other words, its databases contained the DNA codes for every alien species discovered by humanity. Including all the high-sentience species deliberately genocided by the Corporation.

And the White Tower itself contained, amidst the mazes of its rooms and corridors, the laboratories where these alien beings could be grown from cells to fulfil Sinara's mad fantasies. Thus, the Citadel of Kandala was home to a myriad different alien species.

And Majalara's plan was to liberate all these aliens, and unify them into an army; and then lead them in a war to the death against humanity.

And yeah, I know what you're thinking. He might have been an evil fucking alien, but he had a point.

I mean, for fuck's *sake*! We exterminated all these fucking creatures! Destroyed their homeworlds. Just for the sake of a bit more land for *Homo sapiens*. We destroyed all of Majalara's kind too. For centuries our species has been sweeping through the galaxy, killing wise and wonderful and beautiful sentient creatures as if they were ants on our kitchen floor. Stamp, stamp, stamp – and yup, another unique and brilliant species becomes extinct.

But just imagine if all the species that humanity has wronged were able to get their payback. Just imagine it!

I didn't, however, have time to imagine it.

Indeed, it wasn't until much later that I started to have moral qualms about the rightness of my cause. But at the time – in the gold-vaulted Hall of the White Tower, hot and desperate, doing a deal with that bitch Sinara – I was running on instinct. I saw an enemy. I wanted to kill it.

So I set about the task of killing the mollyfocker.

"Cut off the air," I told Sinara. "Cut off the air to the dome."

Sinara was a proud and beautiful woman. Her whiteless Noir eyes stared eerily at me like holes ripped out of the fabric of space. She didn't like to be told what to do.

"Or don't you know how to do that?" I sneered.

"I know how to do it," conceded Sinara.

And she touched her virtual screen and conjured up a series of images as she scrolled through the commands, typing and waving the security codes as she went. And I felt the QRC yield to her authority, as it would not do to mine.

And I saw and felt through the sensors of the QRC what happened next.

First, the vents which circulated fresh breathable air into the hermetically sealed domed city were closed. Outside the impermeable force field dome was breathable atmosphere; the gusting winds of Kandala still blew. But inside the Citadel, the air was getting stale.

Then the air pumps were switched into reverse setting. And the air already in the Citadel was sucked up by the nozzles, and swallowed, and stored. Thus, the atmosphere grew thinner, and thinner. Birds started to fall out of the sky. Trees no longer stirred in the breeze, for there was no breeze. The Citadel's artificial clouds dissipated. Children began to cough. Old people found their throats were dry and they were gasping for breath.

All this we knew, because Sinara had conjured up a series of giant holo screens; so we could see in panorama and also in multiple close-ups all that happened in the Citadel. We saw the carnage wrought by Majalara; the bodies strewn; the blood hanging in the air like mist. And we saw too the surviving mutant warriors slowing down, and gasping for breath, then collapsing. And we saw all the many citizens who cowered in safety choking, and wheezing, and weeping in fear; before drifting off into the sleep that leads to death.

Then the White Tower itself shuddered as it received a massive blow from Majalara. He was trying to get in.

Sinara switched to another camera; and we saw Majalara outside, punching and kicking and ripping at the walls of the White Tower. His strength was awesome. The bricks which comprised the Tower were strong enough to survive a direct blast from a Tang missile. But Majalara had managed to break through the brickwork in a dozen different places, and he was slowly gouging out a doorway large enough for him to pass through. In minutes he would be inside.

"How does he know we're here?" Sinara reasoned.

I took over her virtual controls and panned the camera. We saw the Red Tower, the Black Tower, the Green Tower, the Bailey, the Bulwark, the Highest Tower, the Campanile, the various outbuildings. All reduced to piles of rubble. "He doesn't," I said, "he's just guessing. We're next."

Majalara had now managed to rip a hole in the tower and tried to force his vast bulk through. I looked for signs that the monster was feeling the effects of the air drought; and saw none.

"The air is venting out too slowly," I concluded, reluctantly. "And this creature's lungs are too big. We haven't got time. Show yourself, Sinara. You have to be the bait."

Sinara stared at me. Then she saw the sense. She nodded.

A missile flew at Majalara, fired by the remnants of Sinara's defence force. But he seemed to disappear or dissipate or maybe he just dodged – and the missile crashed into the White Tower and further weakened our foundations. "He's not corporeal," I said to Billy. "Not in the way that we are, anyway. But there must be – *something* real there. We need to—"

"I get it," he said.

Sinara opened the windows of a chapel-niche that led off the inner chamber, and stepped outside on to a small balcony. She stood – and we saw her on the holos – beautiful and magnificent and unafraid looking out over the wreckage of her Citadel as Majalara pounded her Tower.

Then she screamed.

Not a scream – a cry. A beautiful howling call. Like a bird call and a wolf howl merged into a single chilling but compelling noise.

And Majalara backed up and stared at her on the balcony, seemingly enchanted by her strange song-like cry. For a moment he was utterly still. And, in consequence, he was for that moment entirely present in one place at one time.

My mind was inside the QRC. And my body was standing next to Billy, clutching the limpet-mine he had handed me.

Then I instructed the QRC to teleport the bomb so that it materialised INSIDE Majalara. And it did so.

It all took the tiniest fraction of a second. The limpet-mine was in my hand and then it wasn't, it was in quantum non-space. And then it rematerialised in the exact place where Majalara's essence had cohered.

Let me put that in English. This slippery fucker was a moving target we just couldn't hit. But the second he stood still, I blew a bomb up inside him.

The bomb scattered Majalara's essence. He swirled like a tornado. I felt a screaming in my head. The Terror was terrified.

But then Majalara reformed again. His shape was more amorphous now, and less vivid. But he was still the same murderous all-powerful bastard we couldn't kill.

Billy pressed another limpet-mine into my hand. I tried again.

The second bomb blew up. But this time it exploded in empty air. Majalara wasn't there.

And then he was. Roaring and smashing and actually spitting – or was that spit? Or were those daggers flying out of his lips? No matter: our strategy was failing.

Sinara was still standing upon the balcony, staring down at the beast. And then she called out: "Come and get me, you ugly bastard!"

And Majalara roared again. And he leaped and began clambering up the tower, using his claws to gouge a pathway up.

I gave it a third try. This time I ported my entire body, holding a third limpet-mine, and rematerialised inside the body of the beast.

It was a writhing creepy oozy misty nothingness.

It was – what can I say? – it was fucking horrible. I was inside the Terror and it was like every person I had ever met in my entire life screaming in my face that they fucking hated me and wanted me to fucking die.

But I was connected to *something* – my body was being held up high in the air by *its* body. And so I embraced the Majalara-essence and for a brief moment, I felt it become fully corporeal.

I triggered the bomb and ported out.

I hit the ground standing then flew across the floor. Hit by a blast that was in reality outside the Tower, but somehow had followed me across the rift in space. My body was battered. I think I blacked out for a few moment.

Then I staggered to my feet. And saw on the holo the tottering body of Majalara. He was not dead, but he had lost his power to decorporealise. He was a vast giant with flailing arms but the few surviving Soldiers were raining projectile bullets into his body and burning him with plasma and he stumbled and then he burned and then he exploded.

And his body was mist and fog and hail and then it was nothing. It dissipated, and his unreality became memory.

Majalara had indeed been an impossible creature. Yet made of *some* sort of substance, however mutable. Perhaps – I later speculated – his kind had the power to control their own probability.

Perhaps they were indeed quantum warriors. Or perhaps not. I will never truly know. But he had still been a living creature. Breathing air. Having emotions. Thinking thoughts. And he had been the last of his kind.

And now he was gone.

But the Terror – the Terror remained.

I felt as if I were in the midst of an emotional hurricane. I couldn't breathe for fear. Waves of anxiety lashed me. My world rocked beneath me. Fear burned me like acid hail. It was, I realised, the aftermath of my possession of Majalara. And I knew I had to conquer my fear. I had done it before, I could surely do so again.

And I did. I forced my fears to exist outside of me. I didn't defeat the Terror but I succeeded in caging it.

And so I became myself again.

Then I looked around and saw Billy, who stared at me with awe.

"Let's get out of here," I said.

"You bet," Billy said, grinning.

"Although," I said, suddenly remembering. "Fuck! The mission! The Tarot! The High Priestess!" I shook my head. Thoughts were eluding me. "Sinara!"

Billy grinned again. He took his tag bag out. He shook it, and opened it so I could see inside.

Inside was the severed head of Sinara Lo.

"Mission accomplished," he said.

"Are you all right?" asked Fraser, in that solicitous tone grown-ups use to children who have suffered a minor scrape and who are being totally babyish about the ensuing pain.

"Grand," I said, sourly.

"You're not sleeping I gather."

It was a week since I had returned from Kandala. I was, you understand, a hero. Two Tarots! First Living Spirit, now Sinara. I'd equalled Fraser's record. Or excelled it really, since The Lovers had been a partnership, in effect a single *capobastone*. There was talk of naming one of the latrine blocks after me.

And I was free of course. I had my 3. I was a wealthy woman. All criminal charges against me had been dropped. All I needed to do was finish my debrief, get a clean psychological bill of health and I could walk away from the whole fucking lot of them.

The debrief, however, was taking time. And I was unable to focus on my leaving plans. I had difficulty – listening to people. I couldn't sleep. Wide open spaces terrified me. Yet I hated my room because it was claustrophobically terrifying. The smell of other people made my heart race and my skin become tacky. But being alone appalled me.

And insects! Don't get me started on insects!

I was living, in short, in a state of total and abject terror. I was everything-phobic. That's why Fraser was being so nice to me. I was a total mental fuck up, and he knew that I knew that it was *all his fault*.

"I choose not to," I said, in response to the comment he had made about whether I was sleeping. "I get a lot more reading done."

"You're a genuine hero Artemis, we're all very proud of you," he guffed.

"Fuck off."

"Let me buy you a drink. We can celebrate your victory. Before you leave. Because you *can* leave Artemis. You're free now. Aren't you? Free?"

"Fuck off."

"Why are you so angry with me, lassie?"

"Fuck off."

"Why—"

"You press-ganged me," I pointed out. "Blackmailed me. Tried to get me killed. And now because I happen to be still alive, you want me to give you a fucking hug?"

Tears were pouring down my cheeks. I hated myself. I mean, shit, I'm a stone-cold killer. Emotion embarrasses me.

"I don't expect a hug," Fraser said, faintly amused.

"Damned fucking right."

I was also terrified they would cut me open. Like a lab rat. Probe into my brain. Wire me up to a computer.

These were quite reasonable fears on my part. Governments actually *do* this kind of shit. And I didn't swallow the SNG's liberal lies. It was just another fucking government as far as I was concerned, and I was their secret weapon. But they didn't know, even now, *how* I could do what I did.

You know what I'm talking about. The stuff with computers. The flitting. My astonishing luck.

I teleported into the body of an alien monster with a bomb in my hand, and *walked away*! What are the fucking odds on *that*?

It all connects up of course, as you already know. Cúchulainn. Magog. That's what did it. That's where I developed my superpowers.

And Fraser had figured out all or at least most of this – I mean, the man wasn't a *total* fool. And he was obviously under pressure from his people to learn more about me. So that they could replicate my powers, and use them against the enemy.

That's why Fraser, eventually, asked me to stay.

"We need you," Fraser said, smiling his nicest smile, which was really not all that nice.

"Fuck off."

"This is a war worth fighting."

"Fuck off."

"You have a special power, lassie," he wheedled. "You could use it to save humanity."

"Fuck—"

Look, I'm not continuing with this – you've surely got the idea by now. Fraser pleading, begging, trying to appeal to the better part of my nature. Me, not *having* a better part to my nature, telling him to fuck off.

That went on for a while, but eventually he gave up and left.

The Terror lasted for a while too, about six months. But then, slowly, it wore off.

And – get this – I wasn't a fucking *coward*, right? Not for a moment. The Terror was a *war injury*. A direct consequence of being so closely exposed to the empath-monster Majalara. It was my version of shell shock. And I knew that. Even when I was feeling the fear, I knew I could lick it.

And I did. I licked it. And I became myself again. I fought the fear, and it almost defeated me, but in the end I won.

Okay? Got that? I won.

I won.

After six months I was discharged from the psychiatric unit and sent on my way. Fraser had finally accepted I was no longer going to fight the war for him. And to his credit, he didn't try to bully and coerce me. Nor did he threaten my life or the lives of those I cared about; nor did he abduct me and hold me prisoner in the SNG's secret lab so that scientists could experiment upon my brain; all of which I'm sure are options he considered.

I returned to the base to pick up my things and found Billy there waiting for me.

I was impressed. Billy really was a persistent little bugger. He'd tried to visit me in hospital on numerous occasions, but each time I had told him to – yeah, you guessed it – "Fuck off".

But he hadn't. He'd stayed. But not in a stalky kind of a way. No, he just hung around on the base, drinking beers with the guys and shooting pool. And when he saw me he strolled over and took my bag and carried it.

And I thought, yeah, this is okay. I can hang out with this guy. He's not too irritating, and at least he's company; and a good fuck to boot.

I could, I realised, imagine spending the rest of my life with this guy.

And so I asked Billy to marry me, and he said yes.

And here I am. Happy! Can you believe it?

Look, it's true. We left the Rock on an ion shuttle which took us to the nearest stellar system, the planet of Heorot. Nice planet. We got married, a simple ceremony, we did it online. We bought a ranch and raised horses and cows and sold the cows for meat. We had a lot of cows, huge herds that roamed our land freely, and robots to keep an eye on them. And when they were slaughtered, heliplanes came and took away the butchered carcasses.

It was a good business. Billy told me I was a natural cowboy. He was actually old enough to remember the American West. Or at least, old enough to hear the legends of it from people who'd seen the movies about it. He'd actually flown a hoverjet through the Grand Canyon.

Billy was at ease in a wilderness. He liked the big empty spaces, and he loved horses. He had an uncanny knack of winning the trust of the darned creatures. I found it all a bit freaky – I'd never ridden on an animal before! But I was enjoying myself.

For a while anyway. The first couple of years were great. Then I got bored. But when I told Billy I was bored, we just upped sticks to the city, Kazam. And we bought a little apartment in the built up part of town and spent our days shopping and going to theatre and watching movies.

I'd never been to a theatre before – with real live people on stage who've memorised all their lines, instead of using a brain chip. On Rebus, drama was considered an inferior art form. Though it *was* considered acceptable to read aloud play texts by classic authors. And on Cúchulainn – well, WAS there a fucking theatre there? I wouldn't know. I spent all my time in clubs or bars, usually drunk. It didn't occur to me there was any other form of leisure pursuit on offer.

So I decided city life was cool.

But after a while I got bored of it. And so we moved back to our ranch again and played at being cowboys, again.

And when that got boring, again, we went white water rafting. This was *some* wild country. We fucked up totally in fact and got caught on a fast-moving river with a serious undertow that whipped us along and threw us over a waterfall. We fell half a mile and we were smashed up badly by the waters. Billy broke his back and arm and I suffered a skull fracture and internal bleeding. So that put a damper on it. A robot medic ship found us from our MI alarm beacons and took us to the hospital.

It took me almost a year to stop slurring my words, and Billy's back never did heal fully – he could no longer touch his toes, poor boy – but after a year we were right as rain. So we tried skydiving for a while. And when that got boring, we went to live in a habitat under the sea. But that was, you know, depressing, because of all the fish.

So we went back to dry land and I decided to write a novel. But that was a disaster because I couldn't get past the first page.

So Billy persuaded me to write a history of the Middle Ages on Earth and I started reading the archive material on the Heorot QRC. That was fascinating but I couldn't work out what my angle would be so I decided to learn guitar instead. But I had no aptitude so we decided to explore the Polar regions.

Hey, and I made friends! Me! Friends! Can you believe it?

Dozens of them. Nice people too. They had interesting jobs and hobbies and small talk. None of them were criminals or assassins. It was all so utterly bourgeois. We met for dinner regularly and swapped stories and bantered and pretended to cared about each other. I started to feel like I was "having a life".

One of my friends was called Alice. Alice was a doctor, which is a really cool job. She worked in the emergency room and saved lives on a regular basis. I showed her how my healing factor worked by cutting off my little toe, and encouraged her to watch it grow back. She went a little pale at that, but to her credit it didn't dissuade her from hanging out with me. We had "girls nights out". We swapped song choices. I started studying what was on TV, so we'd have something to talk about when we hooked up.

And she could tell tales too. Stories of patients, medical disasters, doctors who were impossible to work with, all that shit. I loved her tales. And in return I told her a few of mine. The less graphic stories. I did a lot of self-editing to be honest.[12] I told her I'd worked in a nightclub where there were strippers and cross-gender artistes every night, and she thought that was wonderfully exotic. But I didn't mention the contract killings. I told her I'd once sold untaxed liquor for a living, but I didn't mention the drugs and the pimping.

It was an odd friendship. I liked Alice a lot, but after a while it occurred to me that I was telling her a pack of lies about myself. She didn't really know who I was.

But fuck, I couldn't tell her the *truth*, could I?

12 ! No comment. – *Ed.*

Around about this point Billy suggested we might like to have children. I asked Alice what she thought, and she thought it was a great idea. In fact, she was thinking of having kids too! Her husband Joe had been dropping hints. Maybe we could even go to ante-natal classes together?

I wasn't sure if Alice was being creepy or cute, so I decided to believe cute. It really was great having a best friend! I'd not really had that, well, since Jimmi. Though that friendship, as you know, ended badly.

Alice didn't even, so far as I could tell, want to fuck me. So it was just like a proper ordinary relationship between "mates".

Anyway, the baby thing was on my mind. So I went for a medical check up to see whether my ovaries and womb were still in working condition, after all the shit I'd been through. And it turned out they were fine. I was warned, however, that I wouldn't be able to breast feed. With all my augments, the rejuve in my system meant that a mouthful of my breast milk was equivalent to a kilo of heroin. I found that news – well, unsettling really.

But formula milk is just as good. In fact it's engineered to be chemically and hormonally identical to a mother's breast milk. So I wasn't too worried.

All was cool. Billy and Alice and Joe and I went for a meal and began hatching plans. I made an appointment to have my contraceptive implant removed. Billy and I even discussed what colour to paint the nursery!

We must have been tempting fate. (Which of course, you should never do. Fuck it, I, of all people should have known better!)

Because the following day, the day after the "what colour to paint the nursery" shit, I received a mass MI message saying, "Watch the news." Just that: "Watch the news."

I was in the supermarket at the time. And it was astonishing to see how everyone there suddenly stopped moving, and started listening, as the mass MI flash hit us. And then, almost in unison, we all switched our MIs on to the news portal setting. And, frozen and hushed, we all watched the images of destruction play over our retinas. No one moved, or attempted to shop, or tried to pay for fifteen minutes, as we watched the news images on our visual arrays in rapt horror.

It was one of those days when all of humanity seemed to unite. Because this was a disaster that dwarfed anything we had ever known before. And in a way it was – well – it was actually quite *inspiring*. To be one of the ordinary people, and sharing in something so vast and so terrible. To be—

Anyway, long story short. We watched the news, and saw the extraordinary events that were occurring.

Earth was being invaded, and our guys were losing.

Chapter 11

Invasion: Earth

A week later, I re-enlisted.

I don't know why. Loyalty? Patriotism? Boredom?

My motives were and are a complete mystery to me. But Billy, as it turned out, was happy enough to go along with my plan.

But that's the way it was with Billy. Never any fuss, never any arguing. If I said to Billy, "I'm bored, I want to move," Billy would say, "Yeah sure," and then we'd move. Job done.

Or if I said, "Let's have Cantonese for lunch," he'd say, "Sure thing," and he'd go and order it. If I wanted to go on holiday somewhere nice, he'd research nice places and we'd go there. If I wanted sex – you get the idea?

No trouble! No hassle! No temper tantrums! Billy was never mean or belittling. Never petty. Never quarrelled with me, even when I was wrong. Never found fault with me. Fucking great in bed! All in all, Billy must surely be the template for the ideal man. Apart from the fact he's a mass murderer. But come on, haven't we ALL got things in our past which – skip it.

Where was I?

Yeah, Billy and I joined the army again. But it was no sweat, not really. Because after all, there was no actual jeopardy. We didn't even have to travel far. The nearest War Camp was an hour's flight from our home. And I think Billy fancied the idea. After all, he'd been a space warrior for a large part of his life. And this was surely the greatest space war of all time apart from – well, the obvious one, which Billy's side had lost.

I have to admit, I was feeling pretty blue at the time. I was having mood swings again. Insomnia, of course. And I was lonely. And all this may have influenced my decision to go back to war.

Why lonely? After all, I had Billy, And I had my dozen or so "ordinary" friends, including the delightful Alice. And I even had a chance of starting a family. Because the baby was STILL on the agenda. That was *definitely* the plan. Once we'd won the war of Earth, I'd get pregnant. And then it would all be wonderful, 'cause I'd be a mother!!

The idea of parenthood did worry me a little though. Because, I wondered, would I actually be a *good* mother? That's what I kept asking myself. Fairly obsessively to be honest. After all, my own ginch-whore of a mum had abandoned me when I was a baby. And my father—

Yeah. Right. Let me tell you about my father!

When I was eight years old he punished me for disobedience by locking me in the— No I've told you that story. Locked in the library. Traumatised. Blah blah.

But did I tell you *why*? The first time I mean? It's because I found a photograph of my mother, and asked him about it. "What was she like?" I asked. And a look of fury came upon him, and the punishments began.

(I may have added, "And why the fuck did she marry a withered old pintle like YOU?" Look, I was a kid, and I never claimed to be perfect.)

He never talked about my mother you see. But he made it clear I had to hate her, and so I did.

One time he hit me – a powerful slap across the face. That was in response to a comment I made about – well, okay, that was another example of me being not-perfect again. But I was only ten!

Then I struck him back and knocked him off his feet. I had

the augments, don't forget. So in retaliation, he programmed the Rebus computer to broadcast white noise directly into my head, all day and all night. I couldn't turn the chip off – not without cutting my head open. After a week of that I begged him for mercy. And he laughed. The white noise lasted another two weeks.

In company he was courtesy itself. But in private, he treated me like a wild animal. A creature to be tamed and humiliated. And he told me my destiny was to be a librarian. He forced me to memorise entire books, and I still know them all by heart.

It wasn't teenage pique that made me run away from Rebus. It was fear. My father tortured me, incessantly. Physically, mentally, and through the use of his constant withering sarcasm. Does that sound like I'm whining over nothing? Let me tell you – I've taken a bullet in the guts, I've been tortured by professionals. But nothing hurts me so much as the memory of what my father did. He made me feel like nothing.

And— No, that's enough of that.

The point of that rant? There are two points, in fact. Which are these.

Point One: Billy, in a strange way, even though he was my lover, was also the father I wish I'd had. Which is, like, weird, and not good.

Point Two: I was, and am, totally fucked up in the head. And I knew there was no fucking way I was ready to be a mother.

Joining the army, therefore, was my way of evading all these difficult issues. It meant that, for a while at least, I could go back to doing what I was best at.

Killing.

Once we'd signed the paperwork, Billy and I flew to our local War Camp, where the dreamers were kept. As our heliplane lifted off I looked down fondly at the wilderness lands and the mountains where we'd had so many happy times.

A week later I was in orbit around Mars.

This was just after Phobos and Deimos were destroyed, after a prolonged battle that had led to the evacuation of Mars by all SNG forces. The robot ships that remained had stood their ground, or rather sky, and fought like buggery. But the advancing armada had swept them away, like – well, there is no comparison. I saw the images – ship after ship exploding until the sky was full of stars that oughtn't to be there.

Then the enemy moved on down and obliterated all trace of sentience on the planetary surface. Carterville was just a crater now. Dejah Thoris City had been nuked into oblivion. Lowell City was also gone. And the farmlands – they were desolate and arid. The seas had boiled dry. The forests had burned. The entire planet was reverting back to its previous barren state. The atmosphere remained, but for how much longer? Without forests and seas and plants to sustain the ecology created by terraforming?

And, almost as an aftermath to this act of total annihilation, the two moons had been targeted by planet-busting anti-matter missiles. And their falling debris had rained upon the dead planet.

Enceladus had been annihilated in similar fashion, as had Titan, Callisto, Ganymede, Europa, Ceres, Miranda, and Charon. The biodomes of Venus were also gone. And almost all of the Dyson Jewels had been obliterated, leaving shards of debris in elliptical orbits round the sun that would remain there for all eternity.

The invasion had been beautifully orchestrated. Teleported missiles had materialised inside the Sol Defensive System. The Earthian robot attack ships had been outmanoeuvred. The Plutonian Force Ring had proved useless against energy beams being fired *from within*. And the sheer scale of the attack had beggared belief.

Now the invading armada ringed Earth itself. Half a billion battle cruisers each the size of the Central Hall of the Rebus Library. Earth itself was protected by the Inner Force Ring, and its robot anti-missile drones were so plentiful that all the enemy's teleported missiles were destroyed as soon as they materialised. The invasion had now become a war of attrition. They fired missiles at us, we fired missiles at them. They fired energy beams at us – you get the idea. Explosions and plasma flares assailed planets and asteroids and moons, and created moments of wild kinetic violence at many of the points in between. If space could bleed, it would have gushed crimson.

Into all this, we flitted. Ten million soldiers, lying down in virtual-reality vats on ten thousand different planets. Each remotely controlling a bomber or fighter craft, which were teleported out of the furthest reaches of the SNG territories to sit on the rump of the invading fleet.

There were, I later learned, six million misflits in the course of that first counter-attack. Not human misflits – but ships and computer brains maimed so badly by the TP process that they could not function and had to be auto-destroyed.

But the remaining robot ships were immediately launched into battle by the minds of their virtual warriors. We piloted the fastest and most powerful space warship ever built, the Caracaras Mark VI. And we *were* those ships. My skin was hull. My eyes were camera. My fists were bullets of compressed plasma.

And I was fast. Astonishingly fast. My mind fitted over the craft's cybernetic intelligence like a glove over a hand. My reflexes were part of its nervous system. My decisions were instantaneous, as swift as a quantum's act of being. Faster than light itself, or so it seemed, because I could see pillars of plasma fire coursing towards me like waves crazily attacking the shores on a storm-tossed lake.

The Caracaras was a hedgehog – it bristled with guns that

fired eleven different types of projectile weapon and energy beams, controlled impatiently by my speeding mind. A game of chess played and replayed a million times each millionth of a moment. And it had rocket jets in seven locations, powered by super-dense Bostocks. Achieving speeds that nudged towards the Einsteinian horror of infinite mass, before declining to zero velocity in what seemed to be a heart's beat.

Each of our four million minds controlled a single Caracaras. And we appeared behind the enemy battlefleet at the same instant, and were greeted with a hail of missiles and plasma pulses. Our force fields swelled as the enemy's plasma pulses crashed upon them. We darted through space towards our foes in an angry flock. And then the enemy fired another fusillade of missiles and energy beams, an onslaught of such immense power that it could, if harnessed into a single focus, have shifted a gas giant from its orbit. And two million five hundred thousand of us died in a moment.

But the rest survived the onslaught and struck the enemy force field. And embraced it. And slurped through it, despite our loss of momentum. And emerged the other side and re-fired our jets in a final charge that culminated in a wild host of crunching collisions, as each of us clamped our vessels fast to the hull of an enemy craft.

And then, once this contiguous spatial lock had been achieved, I and all the others like me focused on the mental command that would initiate the teleporting process in the bomb bay. And in an instant—

Our frag bombs were inside the enemy battleships.

These were Russian doll devices that contained matter-antimatter volatiles within a crust of an exploding fusion bomb. And, at its very heart, a swiftly pulsing consciousness disruptor of awesome power. A sabre that could shred a mind into bloody fragments in an instant.

And as I felt the bomb vanish from within my womb, I could imagine, though I could not see, the DR crew's look of blank disbelief as a large square box appeared in front of them. Hovering like an enchanted object in an ancient tale.

And then the detonation! The fire and the crush and the blast and the glare and the shards of metal flying a million ways at once as the robots on board were blasted into pieces. And then their controlling minds being crushed and shredded by the consciousness disruptor's pulsing pain that swirled and appalled and, before they could break the remote link, killed the doppelgänger riders outright by shocking their minds into incoherence.

Moments later the blast from my own bomb hit my vessel and shattered its force field and tore its hull with the calm malevolence of a child shredding its homework. I felt myself, my ship, my hull, my cybernetic brain, explode into fragments. And I felt – I felt myself die! And then—

And then I was inside another Caracaras, that had just been teleported in, attacking another battleship. Around me space was wispy with sundered matter. No fires blazed, no living creatures howled their death cries. And if they had, no sound would have carried in the emptiness of space. And yet I felt as if I were on a battlefield, surrounded by the dying bloodied screaming bodies of my enemies.

And, of course – why would I not? – I exulted.

"Hello sweetheart."

"Hello darling."

I was breathing heavily. So was Billy.

"Champagne," he observed.

"Of course it is. You stupid fucking imbecile," I observed.

"Yeah." He nodded slowly, as if remembering how to nod. I'd bought champagne. I was wearing a dress – me! A dress! I'd even put flowers in a vase by my bed. Seduction was clearly on the agenda. Billy could tell that. There was fear in his eyes.

"You're looking good," he said.

"I've lost weight," I informed him. I was two stone down. My skin felt like parchment.

"So have I."

"Of course you have. You idiot!" I informed him. For it was *obvious* he'd lost weight. I'd seen that the moment he walked into my apartment. I mean, in god's name, it took him long enough! He walked like an old man. And I, of course, walked like an old woman. The smell of the flowers was making me sick.

"I guess you want a kiss," he said anxiously.

"We have to do this, Billy."

"No we don't. Celibacy is an option."

"We can't degrade the materiel."

"The vats keep our bodies fit."

"Bare minimum. Loss of muscle tone. Loss of – you know all this."

"Of course I fucking know all this. I know the meaning of everything you fucking SAY," Billy shouted, "and I know you're going to say it, before you say it. And then you say it."

"I really hate your fucking guts," I advised him.

"I you also," he said, incoherently. I sympathised. These days, words seemed a strange imposition on our godlike minds.

"How's your war?"

"Twelve battle cruisers," he said. "You?"

"Fifty-three,"I said.

"Is that a record?"

"It's a record."

"They say you don't – you know," Billy ventured.

"Withdraw?"

"Withdraw. You wait till—"

"The last minute."

"The last minute."

"Yeah that's true."

"You feel yourself die."

"I feel myself die. Fifty-three times so far."

"How does that—"

"You should try it."

"Too dangerous."

"It's the best."

"The best – what?"

"Best anything. Best there's ever been – of anything, ever," I confessed.

"Come walk over to," said Billy, forgetting the last word. And I tottered towards him. I decided that swaying my arms helped me to keep my balance. I blinked my eyes furiously, in the hope of catching some ultraviolet or x-rays, but nothing doing. Billy was waiting for me, still standing in the same place. A long time elapsed, or so it seemed to me, but finally I reached him.

"How we going to do this?" I asked. I had to stop walking before I could speak. Which I found infuriating.

"On the bed."

"I'm not aroused."

"Me no either not," said Billy.

"I'll take my clothes off."

"Try that."

I took my clothes off. That took about twenty-five minutes.

It occurred to Billy that he should take his clothes off too. That took a further twenty-six minutes. When naked, he was repellently thin, and pale, and his penis was limp. I wondered why those particular organs had such an iconic cultural status. Six inches of soft wrinkled flesh, topped by a radish head?

"You look good, naked," Billy offered, insincerely. I realised he was making an effort. It occurred to me that I ought to find that sweet.

I did not.

"I can't," I said, and tried to express my feelings in words. But I could not express my feelings in words. Not at all. Not one bit, jot, particle, or iota. It was all just blankness. And I hated that I couldn't feel my hull. I couldn't taste space. I couldn't experience the multiple thrills of rocket blasts from my seven engines.

My guns did not fire. My mind no longer functioned in units of a trillionth of a trillionth of a second.

Billy touched his flaccid penis with a hand that looked as if it didn't know how to hold anything, let alone an inert and loveless sexual organ. "Help me with this," he pleaded.

I eased myself on to my knees and performed the necessary actions that were supposedly the prelude to viable lovemaking.

"That's not helping," Billy pointed out.

I took the soft pintle out of my mouth. "We don't need to do this," I pointed out.

"Now? Or ever?" There was, I noted, a tone of barely suppressed relief in Billy's voice.

"Ever. We could—"

"No," Billy said, as his loyalty to his own biology won out over his actual desires.

"Some people—"

"No."

"Let's drink some champagne," I suggested.

"Now you understand," said Billy. "What it was for me like."

"What was like?"

"Before," said Billy. And there was a glint in his eyes.

"Ah."

"The bad – yeah?"

"The bad old days."

"When I served the Corporation."

"They were evil."

"They were."

"You were—"

"What?"

"You served as a *real* soldier too."

"For years. But mainly – this. Doppelgänger war."

"War is hell," I told him.

"Is it?"

"Yes."

"If you say so."

"Yes!"

I was lying. He knew I was lying. I thought about the fifty-three battle cruisers I had destroyed. I thought about the joy of death. I thought about the joy of dying, without consequence.

I could tell Billy was having the same thoughts.

"We should really try to fuck," Billy said. He was aroused, now. The memories of his past combats had given him an erection.

And so, after some manoeuvring, we lay on the bed and copulated. Billy, to his credit, succeeded in having an orgasm.

I however felt nothing. Nothing at all. My flesh body was just dead weight. My mind yearned to be free of it. And I longed, with all my being, to be, once more, hull and rockets and cybernetic circuits and blazing guns and instant, appalling, destruction.

We worked a 48/6 rhythm. Forty-eight hours in the vat, fighting the war of Invasion: Earth. Then six hours in our human bodies. A bath. A glass of champagne. A pathetically unenjoyable fuck. A heartless cuddle. A walk. A meal, barely tasted. Then back to the vat.

The six hours were an eternity.

Some warriors could not bear to take a break from the epiphany of Caracaras combat. They stayed in the vats round the clock. Their brains cabled to a computer interface. Their bodies kept free of bed sores by the vat waters, fed and hydrated through tubes. Safely cocooned until the war came to an end.

Some of them are still there now.

A thousand battles. Black space lit by ceaseless pillars of plasma fire. The rings of Saturn smiling upon the conflict. The cracked crust of Mars spewing out hot mountain ranges. Each infinitesimal fraction of a moment lived with such intensity. And victories! So many victories! Enemy ships holed or exploded, spaceborne doppelgängers blown to shards. Missiles destroyed before they could hit their target. Battles fought faster than a mayfly's daydream.

And then the force fields surrounding Earth failed.

Not for long. Perhaps three seconds. But it was enough. Streams of enemy missiles poured through at near-light-speed velocity. The drone missiles set about their task of snatching each enemy vessel from the skies. And they did so with astonishing success. Missile after missile was intercepted and safely detonated.

But one missile snuck through. A planetbuster of the Xerxes range. The D4.[1]

In that moment I abandoned my Caracaras and entered the cybernetic consciousness of an Earth-orbiting Talos, a fatter but no less speedy craft. A thousand of them were in permanent orbit, for just this eventuality. So I seized a dozen and felt the thousand or so other ships of my type becoming possessed by my fellow warriors. And then battle was joined.

The Xerxes planetbuster was the size of a small ocean-going liner. It was shielded and fielded and pursued a randomly zigzagging path. Like a boulder hurled by a giant's hand that bounces off each tree in the enchanted wood. Or so it seemed to me, to my hyper-actively imaginative mind.

For I could, or so I thought, actually smell the foul reek of the Xerxes' robot mind. I sensed, or so I imagined, its cold malevolence. I saw, and did actually see, the enemy missile in every part of the electromagnetic spectrum. I echo-located it, and I knew its velocity, its mass and its exact trajectory.

1 This incident is recounted in the official *History of Invasion: Earth* by Jerome Graham. Dr McIvor's account appears to be correct; she was indeed the doppelgänger rider responsible for downing the Xerxes. – *Ed.*

And I pissed fire on it from my every gun. I swamped it with beams of divine radiance, in the form of energy beams. I pulverised its shields like a warrior pounding his enemy's god-ugly face with projectile bullets larger than a human being. I sheared its soul with exploding star-bombs that spewed out diamond-sharp blades.

None of my efforts prevailed. The Xerxes entered the Earth's atmosphere and I pursued it, kinking and zagging and zigging to follow its course. I strove to creep closer to its hull whilst ceaselessly dodging the hail of energy fire and missile swarms from the dozens of the other Talos defence ships that were recklessly shooting past me at their prey.

The Xerxes sped downwards. I sped after it. We burst through the clouds and I glimpsed blue oceans and snow-tipped mountains and sprawling beautiful cities. And finally I caught up with the Xerxes, and we touched hulls. At that instant, I teleported my bombs into its bomb hangar.

And then waited.

I felt the thrill of impact as the blast from the bombs reached me, and sundered my ship. I felt myself die, and once again, I exulted.

And I knew the detonation would rain fire and foul radiation on the verdant planet below. But *Earth* was saved.

Not every day was quite so exhilaratingly intense. But it still took a huge amount out of me. I had no strategic sense of the battle in general, but I fought and destroyed and fought and destroyed.

Until eventually – after how long? Days? Years? Centuries? I couldn't tell – the battle was over. The invading fleet had been destroyed.

A second enemy fleet teleported into a region of space near

Venus but was captured there by a black-hole mine and sucked into nothingness. And then a few more scattered vessels appeared. But it was over.

The war was over. And we had won.

But let me back up a little bit. How did things get to be so bad? How the hell could Earth get to be in such dire jeopardy?

It was all because of the Devil. The Last Tarot.

In other words: Captain Hispaniola Morgan. Ex-pirate, former best friend of Cap'n Flanagan himself.

Morgan had been one of the great and legendary rebels who fought the Corporation. But then he changed sides, and joined the Clan, and became one of the SNG's target Tarots. All the other Tarots had been captured or true-killed by now, but Morgan alone survived. And so in a last desperate attempt to save himself, he declared war on Earth. I knew *that* much.

But I didn't know that Morgan actually HAD been captured. The Devil had been taken prisoner, by a crack Kamikaze Squad led by a guy I'd met in sim training! His name was Dooley. He was a good warrior. It wasn't his fault that – but let me come to that bit.

Let me go back even further.

Hispaniola Morgan wasn't his real name. I mean! Get real.

His real name was Daniel Morrow. But he changed his name

to Morgan, in homage to a famous pirate on ancient Earth.[2] And he called himself Hispaniola after an island which – look, this really isn't relevant.[3]

Morrow was born on Gullyfoyle. Yeah, the same planet where I worked as a barmaid, and stole that jewel. His parents were slaves etc. etc., and his father was killed by a Clan *picciotto*, for no reason really. A few years later, Morrow turned pirate and stole a Corporation cargo ship and recruited a crew of mercenaries. For a decade he stole and plundered and managed to elude the admittedly rudimentary doppelgänger cop ships. Because no one really gave a damn to be honest. The Corporation tolerated piracy mainly because they didn't really notice it.

Morrow, or Morgan as he was by then, recruited a young rebel called Flanagan to his crew.[4] And the two of them wreaked havoc on Corporation planets and ambushed Corporation caravans with astonishing daring. But Flanagan was more of an idealist. Morgan was the hot-head.[5] And he was merciless. He had no tolerance of collaborators – all those who savoured the good life under the Corporation regime. And his policy was to kill such people as painfully as possible. That's why Flanagan fell out with him, and stole his pirate ship, and left Morgan behind on the planet of Xavier.[6]

Morgan swore revenge. And who can blame him? Flanagan was the pupil who outstrips his master, beats the living crap out of him, then leaves him to die on a wilderness planet. Yeah, that old routine.

Morgan tried but failed to escape from Xavier. It was a tough planet, colonised by religiously obsessive settlers who were

2 Admiral Sir Henry Morgan, 1635–1688. – *Ed.*

3 Hispaniola is an island in the Caribbean on Earth which was a stronghold for pirates in the seventeenth century. – *Ed.*

4 Unsubstantiated except by Flanagan himself, a legendary embellisher of facts. – *Ed.*

5 Artemis's story here is clearly based on the account in *The Early Years of Flanagan* by David Ruckley (not published by Way Out of Orbit Books, though it's rather good). – *Ed.*

6 Again the source here is Ruckley, *op. cit.* – *Ed.*

convinced that the Cheo was God. Even so, the gangs had made inroads here, and there was a strong Clan rebel movement. So Morgan joined the gangs, killed a lot of priests, and eventually became *capobastone*. At that point, he embarked upon an *auto-da-fé* of staggering proportions which essentially led to the end of religion on Xavier. All the priests were dead. All the bishops and cardinals had been – let's not go there. It was an inferno which consumed an entire tier of the settler society.

And this was the guy we were facing. So, as I say, Dooley led his Kamikaze Squad to Xavier to capture Morrow. And to everyone's surprise, he succeeded triumphantly, in a daring brilliant raid etc. And teleported back to his base where he surrendered Morgan to his boss Langan. Langan was Dooley's Fraser – his handler I mean.

But Langan, no fool apparently, took one look at Morgan and started shouting incoherently. He could recognise a cyborg when he saw it – don't ask me how, because they can be very realistic. But he could, and did.

Yeah, it wasn't Morgan, it was a cyborg copy, with a bomb inside. Boom!

Langan died, Dooley died, the entire base was destroyed. It was a masterly ambush.

And that's when the SNG cottoned on to Morgan's game. He had cyborged himself into multiple versions. And it soon became apparent that many of his *piccioti* had done the same. They were no longer human, and there were hundreds of them out there, possibly thousands. Which was, to say the least, deeply scary.

And all this meant that the victory for our side in the defence of Earth didn't really mean that much. There were celebrations of course, and speeches were made. Songs were written about the brave doppelgänger pilots who saved the day; my name was mentioned in the chorus of one song because of the Xerxes missile incident.[7] Roger Layton himself actually appeared in

7 The song is *Victory: Earth* by The Heinleins; it's rather good. – *Ed.*

Parliament Square and shook hands with well-wishers, to mark this historic occasion. But even as we were being demobbed, we all knew that a battle had been won; but not the war. For Morgan was still alive; his armies were still legion; and humanity itself was still in deadly peril.

And do you know what? I didn't care.

I'm serious! By this stage I was well past Who gives a fuck? and deeply into Never a-fucking-gain.

I had done my bit, both as a Kamikaze and as a doppelgänger pilot. I'd given up years to warfare; I'd slain and died and slain again. And now it was time to get on with the rest of my life.

Hispaniola Morgan and the continuing jeopardy of the human race were now, I firmly resolved, no longer my problem.

Edited Highlights from the Thought Diary and Beaconspace Blog of Dr Artemis McIvor[1]

BOOK 3

REVENGE *AND* WAR[2]

1 Readers may be interested and indeed distressed to learn that this volume was downed from the brain chip of Dr McIvor just a few weeks before her arrest on charges so heinous that her lifetime's pardon for all crimes committed-or-to-be-committed was revoked. She is now – to my deep and abiding regret – awaiting execution on multiple charges of murder. – *Ed.*

2 It may be of some further interest to readers to learn that during the period when I was proofreading these volumes, Dr McIvor escaped from custody and is now on the run, somewhere in the humanverse. Praise be! – *Ed.*

Chapter 12

The Day I Was Born

"One last mission," said Fraser. And he actually smiled.

I stared at him in horror. "Are you kidding me?" I said.

"The future of humanity is—"

"Jeez! Not that old routine again!" I said.

He looked at me.

I looked at him.

"You look like shit," he said.

He had a point. I'd lost a lot of weight. My muscle tone was crap. My eyes were bloodshot. I looked like a mad woman. But not SO mad that I'd accept Fraser's stupid fucking offer.

"We'll do it," said Billy.

"We will not," I pointed out.

Billy was in even worse shape than me. He looked like a skeleton with a paltry clothes budget. He was wearing a greasy stained T-shirt and an un-smart jacket that attracted lint and plant spores. His hand trembled when he drank his decaff coffee. He couldn't drink alcohol. Neither of us could yet.

"We'll make you rich," pointed out Fraser.

"We're rich enough."

"I can't go back," said Billy. "I can't, doll. Not into the real world, not again."

The battle of Invasion: Earth was the four hundredth virtual war Billy had fought. I'd forgotten that.

"We're not spending the rest of our lives in fucking vats!" I said, outraged.

As I mentioned, some did. Many, in fact.

Indeed, of the tens of millions of soldiers who fought the war to save planet Earth – how many of them returned to reality? Look it up. It's online. It's a chilling fucking statistic.[1] *They* are the real casualties. Those bastards will live pretty much for ever, fighting a war that was over aeons ago. It's the price we pay for saving our mother planet, which most of us have never fucking seen.

Sweet Shiva, I was angry! Except I was too tired to be angry.

"This is a live mission," Fraser explained. "A TP."

I beamed a big smile. "Oh great, so we could DIE, instead of living for all eternity in a stupid fucking war movie?"

"The future of humanity," Fraser pointed out.

"What do I care about—"

"You're pregnant," Fraser said.

That stopped me in my tracks.

Here's a thing you need to know about rejuve: it fucks you up.

I have so much of the stuff in my system that cuts on my skin heal almost instantly. I can survive wounds that would be fatal for other people. I don't grow old. I never wrinkle. (Wrinkle! Me? Get real.)

But there's a downside. My fingernails grow fast, I have to cut them every day. My hair! Fuck, I need a haircut every seven days. If I let it grow I'd be Rapunzel. One time I went on holiday and slobbed and came back with six inch fingernails and toenails like

1 I've looked. It's chilling. – *Ed.*

sabres and pubic hair that – oh my GOD I wish I hadn't – don't let me even THINK about that.

So, guess what happens when the rejuve decides that my contraceptive implant hormones are an illness that needs to be cured?

Answer: I get pregnant.

"We removed the embryo," said Fraser, "while you were fighting the war. That was about four years ago. It's healthy, in stasis. We can start growing the child in an incubator. Or if you prefer the old fashioned way, we can re-implant it into your womb. You can go to term using the Mother Nature method. You'll get fat and ugly and grumpy and absent-minded, and a vast slimy heid will come out of your ginch, causing you appalling agony."

"I think – I'd like that," I said, and there were tears in my eyes.

"You bastard, Fraser," said Billy.

"You're going to have a baby, Artemis," said Fraser. "Oh, and by the way, the future of humanity rests in your hands." He paused, and added the kicker: "That means the life and happiness of your baby is—"

"I fucking get it!" I said angrily. "If you're going to morally blackmail me, don't patronise me too, okay?"

"You'll do it then?"

I thought, but not for long.

"I'll do it."

"WE'LL do it," corrected Billy.

"How do you know you're the father?" I taunted him.

"Because I know you'd never be unfaithful to me," said Billy.

Fraser and I actually laughed in unison at that.

"You're the father," Fraser told him. "100 per cent DNA match. It's a boy. We can tell that now, even at this stage. And if you're so minded," he added, with a roguish twinkle in his eye, "you can name him after me."

"I seriously doubt that," I said scornfully.

"What actually is your name?" Billy asked, smiling.

"Lachlan."

Billy's smile froze.

"So what's this mission?" I asked.

"First," said Fraser, "we have to get you fit again."

I ate a piece of toast and a tooth broke. That's how bad a state I was in.

But the tooth grew back. I ate pasta for breakfast. I ate burgers for lunch. I ate ice cream – toffee & chocolate and butterscotch & liquorice were my favourites. But I drank no wine or beer. I slept twelve hours a day, ate a slow breakfast, swam all afternoon – for about six hours. Pigged out at dinner, then went to bed again.

After about two weeks of this Billy began to touch my body in ways that seemed eerily unfamiliar. After those early repellent sexual encounters during Invasion: Earth we'd got worse and worse about reminding our bodies they were bodies. It was two years since I'd had a fuck in other words. And that first time we did it post-Invasion was – well, it wasn't great. But it got better. Oh believe me, it—

Moving swiftly on.

After three weeks we started running. Billy was dosing heavily on rejuve, and my own augments were kicking in. We were getting our skin tone back. The facial blotches had gone. That pursed-skin look you get from living in a vat of liquid nutrients for four years was starting to wane. My hair was not greasy any more. Billy could run his fingers through it without having to wash his hands afterwards.

We began weight training. Boxing. Martial arts. Speed training. Impact training – that's when you stand inside a warsuit and let people fire bullets at you for hours on end.

After three months we were fighting fit and ready for the mission briefing.

Once, during this period, I visited my baby. He was a single cell in a test tube but I held the test tube and talked to him. Not baby talk, of course. I mean! What kind of a wanker do you think I am!?!

No, I talked to him properly, as the young man he would one day be.

And I thought, very hard, about what he would be like when he was born. And what kind of child he would be. And what he would be like when he grew up.

And of course, as any responsible mother would, I did my best to give him the best possible start in life.

He was, for instance, supposed to have red hair; but I've never liked ginger as a colour. So I asked the lab team to make him black haired, with skin that tans easily.

And he was tall, very tall, which I also don't like. So I asked the guys to take four inches off his height, but factor in a muscular physique. I also asked if we could genetically engineer him to have a nice smile but apparently that's not possible. But I knew he'd be fit, free from all genetic diseases, with a sound cardio-vascular system, no allergies, and – well, I didn't expect he'd experience ANY problems when it came to affairs of the heart.

I thought a lot about the kind of world he would grow up into.

Fact is, it's a cruel fucking universe out there. And there are no happy-ever-afters. Whatever terrible mess we cleared up now, there was bound to be another terrible mess further down the line. Another evil dictator, blah blah.

So I made my baby strong. I insisted that Fraser pay for augments that would enhance my son's strength and speed and allow him to heal rapidly. When he was older – probably four or five years old – I'd pay for an oxygen capsule implant in his brain to allow him to survive body death for up to twelve hours. And if anyone tried to beat him up or bully him or murder him or rape him or torture him – all the things we parents worry about! – they'd have a surprise. 'Cause my son was going to be one savagely effective killing machine. His augments surpassed even mine.

The little devil would even be able to beat me at arm-wrestling!

The day before the mission briefing, I visited my son for the last time. I'd named him by now of course, after a long debate with Billy, which I won.

Douglas. That was his name. It was a name I'd always liked. My son, Douglas.

By the way, Billy had been furious when I told him he wasn't going with me on the next mission.

"Fuck you!" he'd argued.

"Final answer."

"Fuck you!"

Billy had never sworn at me before. He'd sworn, of course, but not *at* me. This was a sign of how angry he was. Or rather, how strung out. The four years of battle during Invasion: Earth had turned him into a total war junkie. The idea of missing out on an entire battle filled him with horror.

"Reason?" he demanded.

"Someone has to look after Douglas, if I don't – survive."

"Bugger that. I'm a crap dad."

"Are you?" He'd never mentioned that he had any children.

"Fucking right I am! Sixty-four kids, by forty different mothers." His forehead knit with the effort of concentrating. "Can't remember a single one of their names."

"Liar."

"Okay, I remember them. But I never see them. Crap dad. Soldier dads are just sperm donors, haven't you heard that saying?"

"But I need you—"

"I need to fight."

"—to look after Douglas. My baby. Our baby. IF I DIE!" I screamed.

"I'll go, you stay." But he knew as he said it that it wouldn't work that way.

"They need me," I told him. "They cannot do this without me. I'm their lucky charm!"

And he couldn't argue with that. Because this whole mission depended on luck. My luck. My preternatural luck that allowed me to defy the laws of chance and survive the TP, again and again and again.

"If I die," I explained carefully, "you have to look after him, okay?"

"You want me to actually raise our son?" Billy said, incredulously.

"I just said so, didn't I?"

"Do you have any idea what a total fuck-up I am?" Billy seemed genuinely outraged that I should have such faith in him. "I'm a fucking psychopath, for Oshun's sake!"

"Keep him safe," I said. "Please?"

It was good to see familiar faces. Cons from Giger. Hard cases from Cúchulainn. And of course ex-Kamikazes, back for action.

Many of them had the pale wasted features of former doppelgänger riders. A few had been taken straight out of the vats, and were in hoverchairs or even encased in plastic bodyshells.

We were back on the Rock, our home from home. And this was the official briefing for our mission.

Long story short, our job was to whack Morgan and his cyborg selves. Not capture, not redeem, not reform. Just find the real him and his database and his cyborg bodies and destroy them all.

It was one hell of a mission. Because there were hundreds if not thousands of the bastard out there, in his various cyborg manifestations. Morgan was on Gullyfoyle and also on Cambria. There were also at least forty Morgans in deep space, on flagship battle cruisers and on anonymous dirt buckets. There were rumours that there were Morgans on Earth, and Morgans inhabiting humaniform bodies were suspected to have infiltrated the inner reaches of the SNG government.

The War of the Morgans was a legendary battle. Many books have since been written about it.[2] Many heroes gave their lives. Many Morgans died. There is a theory that some Morgans still remain to this day.

And so, to fight this absurd battle – an entire army against ONE MAN – the Kamikazes had been called out of retirement. And the doppelgänger riders were pulled out of the vats. And I had been bullied into doing what would certainly be, one way or another, my last ever mission for Brigadier Lachlan Fraser.

My particular assignment was to take a small team of Kamikazes deep into enemy territory, to the planet where Morgan's first cyborg body was created, and where Morgan himself was believed to be hiding out. There we hoped to a) kill the real Morgan and b) er, there was no b).

There were seven of us in the Kamikaze team. Seven is my

2 Only one of which is published by Way Out of Orbit Books, namely, *The War of the Morgans* by Professor Henry Pritchard. It's rather good, despite the many typos. (I didn't edit it.) – *Ed.*

lucky number. Some prefer thirteen, or fifteen. It was me, an assassin called Maria, a Soldier called Quentin, a Loper called Deep Soul, and Fraser. Yeah, Fraser was returning to active service. Plus, there were two other guys who I hadn't yet met, one of whom was to be our mission commander.

And by the way, I was EXTREMELY pissed off about that. I had assumed, quite naturally, that *I* would be in charge!

After I had visited Douglas, to say my final goodbye, we five spent the rest of the night before combat in a chapel praying with our gods. This was the Knights Templar influence; I always liked those guys.

Like Billy, Quentin worshipped the church of Santiera, the voodoo gods. His deity was Oshun. Maria worshipped Jesus Christ. An unusual choice, but we respected it. Deep Soul was a Lokian, and you can bet that mean mollyfocker loved his practical jokes. And Fraser clove to Cernunnos, a Celtic god with antlers. He actually wore a pair of antlers throughout our vigil, as well as a leather tunic and trews (as he called them). He looked like a fucking idiot – but hey! To each their own.

Ganesh, as you know, was my god. The elephant god. I have a wooden Ganesh carved by a Loper craftsman. He is the Remover of Obstacles. I've always had a thing about elephants, and I find the whole Ganesh thing amusing.

I don't BELIEVE of course. I'm not religious. None of us are. Just superstitious. That's different.

So there I was, the following day, hyped for the mission to come.

I'd taken every conceivable precaution, of course, to help me survive the TP. I'd prayed. I hadn't showered. I'd put my blouse on inside out. I was carrying my lucky knife and my lucky gun. My lucky elephant necklace was around my neck. I was also wearing my lucky red cotton knickers. I wore them once to a hit and survived an ambush by the slimmest of margins. Since then, the wearing of this particular pair of knickers has been a prerequisite for me when going into battle. Luckily, they're made of smart cotton and never fade or fray.[3]

Some of the other guys, I have to tell you, had really stupid superstitions. I mean, REALLY stupid. One guy used to – no, you don't want to know. And another used to – no that was disgusting, and not hygienic either to be honest.

There were about fifty other tables in the briefing hall, with between seven to fifteen Kamikazes at each table. We were Squadron 2412. Do the math. There was a podium in the middle of the room, from where Fraser would deliver the briefing.

"Gods be with you," said Quentin to me, ritually.

"Whatever," I retorted.

"Where the fuck *are* these jerks?" asked Maria. She was referring to the other two Kamikazes in our team. We hadn't met them yet. Which I considered to be an act of ignorant rudeness on their part, as well as a potential blight upon on our luck. The two empty chairs at our table were a rebuke to professional soldier practice.

You see, a Kamikaze Squad needs to bond before a mission! And ritual sayings have to be said. Like the "Gods be with you"/ "Whatever" gag. I said that on my first mission so I ALWAYS have to say it. And a ritual cup of coffee has to be drunk from the same coffee jug. We'd all spat on our palms of course, before shaking hands. And we'd had our vigil, that I told you about. The new guys had missed out on all of this, and it was making me nervous.

And my greatest fear was that one of them would turn out to be an out-and-out Jonah. For a Jonah can never be allowed. Sometimes, you just have to kill them (I don't mean true-kill!) before the mission for the greater good of everyone else. But it's

3 I toyed with the idea of editing this paragraph out, on the grounds it's pretty irrelevant to the story but, well, what can I say? *blush* – *Ed.*

okay, they're easy enough to spot. They're the ones who exude potential bad luck.

Bill Handley had been my Jonah, back on Cúchulainn. I'd lost both lungs after that fiasco. You learn to recognise the signs after a while. And[4]

Fraser was pacing from table to table, chatting and joking, letting his confidence infect the warriors. Meanwhile, the virtual screen above the podium was set on slideshow to give an unfurling silent photographic record of the life of Hispaniola Morgan. From naughty child to evil cyborg army.

At that moment the door opened and our Squad Commander walked in and headed towards our table. An older guy, with grey whiskers and a barrel chest. And with him was the Seventh Member of the Kakimaze team. A heavily-rejuved raven-haired beauty with an impressive *décolletage* and an imperious gaze.

I recognised them both instantly.

Well, of course I did! It was like seeing fucking statues in the town square come to life.

"I'm sure you all know—" Fraser began to say, as Flanagan and Lena walked towards us, beaming.

I flew across the room in a series of forward flips, literally leaping over Fraser himself, and landed in front of Lena and delivered a forearm strike to her throat. She went down, gasping, and I caught her head in my hands and was within an instant of snapping her neck when—

When I woke up my head was the size of a balloon and I couldn't move my body. Or rather I could but

4 I've deleted a big chunk here. I realise that when Artemis is nervous, i.e. when dealing with difficult emotional material, she becomes excessively garrulous. It's a forgivable foible, in my view, considering the pressure she was under, and the appalling crisis she was about to face, just a few minutes later in this scene. – *Ed.*

s l o w l y.

I guessed I'd been punched in the head and shot with a stasis gun.

And Lena was still alive. I'd failed.

The fucking bitch was still alive!

Flanagan came to see me.

He'd trimmed his grey beard, so he wasn't the wild man you see in the comic books. His blue eyes harboured a smile. His face was lined with terrible scars, which I recognised as wrinkles.

"What the fuck was that about?" he asked me. But I did not answer.

Billy came to see me. "It's an automatic life sentence, doll," he explained. "With moral rehabilitation. Nothing I could do about it. She's – well. That was Lena you tried to kill."

I did not respond.

Lena came to see me.

She too was scarred with wrinkles, when you saw her close up. But still beautiful, I'll grant her that. Her neck was in a protective soft-collar and I was told that I'd broken her C2 and C3 vertebrae with my first blow. I was impressed at her resilience at getting back on her feet.

"Who are you working for?" she asked calmly.

I moved my hand, with painful slowness, towards my lips so she would know that I could not speak. She reduced the slo-mo field, so I could move my throat muscles enough to emit words. But there still was a hardglass barrier between us. I had no chance of jumping her a second time.

"Myself."

"Why? What have I ever done to you?" Lena said scornfully.

"Nothing. That's kinda the point."

Lena stared at me. She seemed genuinely puzzled.

"I'm a fucking heroine," she pointed out, more in jest, I have to admit, than arrogance.

I grinned, nastily. "I've heard different. They say you paid historians to fake the records of the Last Battle."

She laughed, a big belly laugh. "Well, yeah. I did amend a few sections. Can you blame me?"

I was shocked at her candour.

"There's stuff," she said pensively, "I wouldn't want anyone to know. Mainly to do with – Lena, shut up. Sorry. Bad habit. I talk to myself." She paused, as if listening to an unseen voice. "Ah fuck off," she said, but not to me.

Then she looked at me curiously.

"If you were going to kill me," she asked, "why didn't you *wait*? Until you had a gun in your hand?"

"I always said," I told her, "I'd kill you with my bare hands."

"Why do you hate me so much?" Lena asked, with that patronising "you should know better, you silly girl" tone in her voice that I'd never heard from her before.

And which I SHOULD have heard from her before.

Which was precisely why I'd tried to kill her.

Because this evil fucking ginch had never EVER patronised me.

Or bullied me.

Or annoyed me.

Or scolded me.

Or treated me like I was just a silly little fucking *girl*.

And she should have done. She should have—

"Oh fuck," said Lena, as she suddenly realised the truth. She added up the clues. The scornful look in my eyes. My slightly-hooked nose, so like my dad's. The shape of my face. My air of defiant contempt. My entire belligerent me-against-the-world fucking *attitude*.

"Yeah, you got it," I told her. "My name is Artemis McIvor. And I'm your daughter, bitch."

A few days later, I got the news from Fraser that I'd been pardoned. At Lena's special request. I was still in the army, and hence not free to leave the Rock; but I wouldn't be serving a prison term.

Billy was waiting for me when I was released.

"You know why—"

"Yeah."

"Lena is my—"

"Yeah."

"That's why I—"

"We gonna have lunch?"

"Yeah."

My Squad's mission was aborted by the way. No one had the balls to make the trip without me. Without my fabled luck.

Our target had been Morgan's World, a planet ninety-five light years from Earth. A drone TP had established a beacon two solar systems away from Morgan's World, and a series of other beacons had been clandestinely seeded. The system was being patrolled by TP-detector ships whose routines had been precisely monitored. And so, to avoid detection, the Kamikazes would need to make an additional five flits to reach the surface of the planet, like escaping prisoners sprinting when the guards turn the corner of the cell-block. The return journey could be made – hell-for-leather – in a single flit, from Morgan's World to the Rock. But even so the odds were terrible. That's why they needed me and my fabled luck.

Round about then, however, I really wasn't feeling all that lucky.

Six weeks after I had attacked her, Lena came to see me in my apartment in the barracks on the Rock, and told me her story.

Which I didn't believe.

The lying bitch! Let me tell you about that braggart whore-ginch Lena Smith!

I never knew her. And I never knew anything *about* her. My father, as you know, refused to talk about her, except for a few dismissive references to "your mother who abandoned you". My uncles told me she was a "bad woman", and that she'd broken my father's heart. All true. But it wasn't much to go on.

Even so – or perhaps *because* of the lack of background detail – I had idolised her my entire life. Not Lena per se, but the who-ever-she-was who was my mother. You know the way you do? My perfect mother! The one who *must* have loved me really! I had daydreams about what would happen when we met up. I would forgive her! She would burst into tears. And there would be a complex, absurd, but utterly satisfying explanation for why she had abandoned me as a baby. And after that, my life would finally make sense.

Then one day I found her photograph in a folder on my father's private databox and my heart leapt with joy. And I showed the picture to my father, and asked him about her, and he – well, you know the rest.

Remember, she left me a parting gift. My augments. I have Soldier-class augments. It must have cost my mother a fortune to have them built into my DNA. I also had a Rebus chip more powerful than anyone else I knew. She gave me that too. Why? Paranoia maybe. She thought it was a dangerous world and she wanted me to be able to protect myself.

And yeah, I do get the irony of that. With me, and what I had done for little Douglas. Not the same! Don't go there.

Let me get to the point of this rant of mine.

After nine years six months and four days in captivity on Cúchulainn I escaped. As you know. And I was a wreck, as you may have surmised. And I tried to put my life back together. I convalesced. I rested. I read books. This was in the heady days after the fall of the Corporation, so naturally I read a copy of Lena Smith's thought diary.[5] *Everyone* was reading it. Someone had found an archive copy on an old database apparently, and sold it without her permission. It was a bestseller, or would have been, if anyone had paid for it.

It was the unadulterated truth about Lena Smith. Her earliest memories. Everything.

Except, you know, if you read it carefully you'll see the

5 Still available in novelisation form as *Debatable Space,* written by some hack called Palmer (Way Out of Orbit Books). – *Ed.*

evasions. The misdirections. Was she really so brave, so heroic? Did she really save Africa? The whole diary is full of boasting and exaggerating and misremembering. How the fuck can you misremember with a brain chip memory? But she did. She didn't exactly *lie*, but she never told the truth without gilding it. And she left out vital bits.

Like, read the bit about Rebus again. And do you see anything about having a baby? No! One minute she's screwing boring old Professor McIvor, then the next minute, she's fucked off to Earth to see her tyrant son.

That's how I found out. Who my mother was. And who my *brother* was, and what he did. Can you imagine how that felt?

Maybe you can. But believe me – it was worse.

That's why I started keeping my own thought diary. To put down the truth about myself and what I feel. No lies. No evasions. Okay, I don't tell you certain things – like exactly what happened to me during the nine years four months six days etc. But I always TELL you what I'm not telling you. I don't miss anything out. No children concealed under stair carpets. No mistakes glossed over. You know it all. Okay? Whoever you are, reading this thought diary. I am an ENTIRELY reliable narrator.[6] Trust me. Hate me if you like, but trust me.

Lena's not like that. Don't trust *her.*

Bear that in mind. This is her story, as she told it to me.

6 After spending two years editing this volume, checking and cross-checking every fact, I would agree with this conclusion. Furthermore I've come to think that Artemis is – sorry. It's not for me as editor to say what I *really* think of my author. This bold, brave, yet sad and – enough! Must stop. This footnote has become an embarrassing revelation of my own inner feelings, and my sense of admiration of, and indeed love for this remarkable woman. Not to worry, though; later tonight I shall edit it out this whole footnote and replace it with something dry and noncommittal. But first I think I'll open a bottle of wine and raise a glass to– Artemis! – *Ed.*

"I never loved your father," Lena said.

She was good, I'll give her that. Her tone calm, factual. Her face composed, but hiding deep emotion. Yeah – lie bitch, lie!

"Are you proud of that?" I said tauntingly.

"No."

"Fuck you, bitch."

"I didn't love my son either. Peter."

"I said—"

"But when he summoned me – I had to go and—"

"Are you trying to explain why you abandoned me, when I was just a baby?" I mocked.

"Yeah."

"You didn't give a shit, did you?"

"I gave a shit," said Lena, stiffly.

"But you left me anyway."

Lena thought about it a long while. Her old face looked older now.

"Yes."

"Why?"

The question haunted her; I could see her struggling to find an answer that would satisfy me.

And so she tried to explain. She did, she really did try.

She told me how she felt when I was first born. How something that was dead inside her was rekindled. How she lost herself in the joy of breastfeeding – yes, she really did that. Imagine!

And she talked about she felt swamped in love. That rare and wonderful love that a mother feels for her baby. A love that is greater than – let's tell the truth here people – any other kind of love.

But my father didn't approve.

"Too much emotion," he would say, "is bad for children. Don't drown the poor soul in your vulgarity."

Or: "You demean yourself, my sweet, by exposing your breasts in that way. Do use a bottle please."

And also: "I fear, my dear Lena, that this child may be defective. Are you sure there's nothing we can do about it?"

He didn't *mean* it of course. It was just his way of taunting her. I wonder if he was jealous? Of Lena's greater love for her child?

All in all, it was a shit time for Lena. She felt belittled, on a daily basis. And she constantly plotted and schemed about how she would take her child away with her. To a planet where children could run free, and be wild! A planet devoid, in short, of bone-dry sarcasm.

"Then a certain terrible thing happened," Lena told me. "You know what I'm referring to." And I certainly did – the conquest of Earth. "And I thought – well. My fault. But he was my son. And—"

Lena was crying when she told me that bit of the story. Imagine! Lena crying.

"And I actually thought," Lena concluded, "that you'd be better off without me."

I thought about what she had just said.

And it didn't make any sense, at any level. Emotionally, morally, intellectually.

Leave me with a father who was cold and uncaring, for my *own good*? What CRAP! What was she *thinking* of?!

"Is that your excuse? I asked her, scornfully.

"That's my apology," Lena said, and there was a quaver in her voice.

I stared at her. And I smiled. My moment had finally come.

"I hate you, Mum," I said. And I saw the pain in her eyes.

And then she looked away.

And then she got up, and left, without saying another word.

I'd rehearsed this revenge for many years.

Strangely, it wasn't sweet.

A few days later Flanagan came to see me.

Remember, the mission was still aborted. The bastards still needed me and my lucky whatever-it-was, to launch their attack on Morgan's World. So Flanagan had to make nice; and that's precisely what he did.

"Would you consider—"

[Obscenity from me.]

"Bear in mind that—"

[Another obscenity from me.]

That went on for a while. But Flanagan didn't seem perturbed. He gave up questions, took a bottle of whisky out of his bag. I shook my head. But he produced two glasses and filled them both. I could smell the peaty aroma. I saw from the bottle this was a thousand-year-old single malt from Cambria. The best. Those bottles sell for – well, they're almost priceless. That's what you get for being a legendary hero who saved humanity.

Great single malt.

He pushed a glass across the table. I took a small sip, and felt the warmth seep into my body. I also felt instantly intoxicated. I slammed it back and poured myself a second glass.

Flanagan smiled.

Mellowed by booze, I listened as Flanagan told his tale. How he and Lena came to be still alive, despite their publicly reported deaths[7] and subsequent vastly expensive funerals. It was all he explained, a fake. Carefully planned, superbly executed.

"Why?" I said. "You were rich, famous. The most famous people in the humanverse. Why give all that up?"

"We got bored," Flanagan admitted.

7 This doesn't need a footnote; everyone knows how Flanagan and Lena died on a foolhardy expedition of discovery around the double star of Gemini Plus, when they were caught up in a gravity well and sucked into a fiery death. Some (see Nicholson, and Weber) thought theirs was a deliberate attempt to emulate Icarus's folly in sailing too close to the Sun; and that the whole mission was intended to be a way of achieving a glorious double suicide. But that's a preposterous opinion, which I only quote in order to mock. (And besides, as we now know, they didn't die.) – *Ed.*

"All humanity worshipped you," I pointed out.

"Yeah," he said, dryly.

He thought for a moment. His scarred – sorry, I mean wrinkled – features made him look like a wizened old something-or-other. Something wrinkly and old. Look, find your own metaphor here, okay?

"When I was a young man—" he digressed.

"Just answer the fucking question."

"I had my own rock band. Music was my passion."

"I know." I'd heard the Flanagan Rock Oratorio once. Pretentious shite. Some people should stick to what they're best at. In his case, intergalactic carnage.

"And when I was famous, I started to compose again. I wrote an oratario! Can you believe it? With rock guitar and drums. It was shite."

"I've heard it."

"Shite?"

"Shite," I concurred.

"The reviewers said it was a masterpiece. The greatest piece of music ever written, ever. Beethoven's *oeuvre* was a warthog farting in comparison with this great work by Flanagan. One critic actually said that!"

"No critic ever said that."

"It was implied. So I thought – fuck this. I don't want *sycophancy*."

"Why not?"

"What do you mean, 'why not?'" said Flanagan crossly.

"What's wrong with sycophancy? It beats being treated like shit."

"Only by a narrow margin."

"Oh what would you fucking know?" I snarled.

"I would know," he said stiffly, "as it happens. My generation—"

"Oh Sweet Shiva!"

"My generation suffered," Flanagan insisted, like the mother who starts telling her child all the things that *her* mother used to say, and is appalled to discover she can't stop herself. "It was a—"

"My generation didn't exactly have it soft."

"You have no idea what we—"

"You just don't fucking know what I—"

"What was the question?" said Flanagan, calming himself down. I wanted to slap his smug, grizzled face. But there was something about Flanagan's presence that I found – I don't know – reassuring.

"How and why did you fake your deaths?"

"Why, I've already told you. Or maybe I haven't. Lena and I – we were drifting apart. Nothing in common, except what we'd done together. She was getting really arrogant, and annoying. "

"But you were still the same old humble wonderful guy?"

"Pretty much," he conceded, but in fairness he was smiling. "So I created an expedition. We went off to explore a double star. Our spaceship was sucked into a gravity well[8] and never returned. We'd sent out a mayday message but by then it was too late. That was our story, and the world fell for it.

"And after that, we just travelled. We stayed in space for many years. Then we found a planet, we called it Flanagan. Or rather, I called it Flanagan. She called it Lena. She really is fucking impossible you—"

"So why are you back?"

"Well," he said, "we heard about the war, you see. And Morgan's role in it. And we couldn't resist the challenge. The call, if you like. One last adventure! Before—"

"Before what?"

"Before the next one," said Flanagan. And he laughed, and couldn't stop laughing.

8 As I've already explained. – *Ed.*

"What will you do?" Billy asked.

"Travel," I said. "Find a stellar yacht, point at the stars, see what I see."

"And our baby?"

"There is no baby. It's just – a fucking cell."

Billy flinched.

I was leaving him, by the way. Leaving everyone. Fraser. The mission. Fucking off. I'd had enough. My discharge papers were through, and I no longer cared if the human species lived or died.

Okay? You got a problem with that?

"You do realise," said Billy, "that you could be the only human being left in the entire universe. If this mission of ours fails."

"I've always been the solitary type."

"They really do need you, you know."

"Lena would never accept me."

"Fraser bullied her. She'll accept you."

"I don't care. I really don't care."

"Douglas," said Billy, "is our child. He is NOT just a fucking cell. And the future of humanity really is in your hands. You selfish fucking stupid fucking bitch!"

Billy had only ever sworn at me once before. And he hardly ever raised his voice to me. And he had certainly never criticised me before, and he was clearly criticising me NOW.

It took a lot to get Billy this angry. And that shook me. And made me think twice.

And so, I felt my resolve weaken.

Billy waited patiently. He knew what was coming.

I thought about Lena.

I thought about Douglas.

I thought about that bastard Morgan.

And I sighed. "One last mission?"

There was a pause. And then Billy smiled. And I knew that we were good again. We were pals, again.

"One last mission. Oh and by the way, I'm coming with you," said Billy. And for the first time since I'd known him, there was idealism and passion in his voice. "And if we survive, we'll raise the child together, okay? But we have to do this thing. We have to do it. We have to kill the Devil."

Chapter 13

Let's Kill the Devil

I'd missed, as you know, the final briefing for the Morgan's World Briefing. The Strategic, Political and Historical Overview shit. So I was, to be honest, flying third. But I thought, "Fuck it, I'll catch up as I go along."

So here's all you really need to know for now.

There were five of us, and Flanagan, and Lena.

We hit the ground standing. We were like children, standing in a circle holding hands. Everyone was gripping me *somewhere* – my hand, my arms, even my head. And Quentin had his hands on my shoulders. I was their lucky totem.

This was our sixth flit in a row. We'd skulked into the system, ducking behind metaphorical lampposts, and now we were on the surface of Morgan's Planet.

"You can let go, guys," I said, and they did. All but Quentin. He was still gripping my shoulders.

"Hey, inappropriate touching," I said lightly. But he still held my shoulders. I shrugged to get him off.

"We have a problem," said Fraser.

"Quentin!" screamed Maria. I shoved and rolled my shoulders and broke free.

"Quentin you arsehole," I said, and then I turned to look at him and realised he was dead.

Not just dead. Frozen in place. I waved my hand in front of his eyes. Nothing registered. Fraser manually wound Quentin's face mask down, and he just stared blankly at us. I took off a glove and touched his face. Ice cold. And rock solid.

"He's turned into a statue," I pointed out.

Billy did a vitals scan.

"No brain functions, heart has stopped. He's dead. Organs have solidified. Blood also. Flesh is calcified. Brain is, uh-uh, solid rock. He's, uh, yeah. A statue."

"How come?" said Lena to me, in what I took to be an accusing tone. "I thought you had the lucky touch."

"*You're* alive aren't you?" I said angrily.

"Yes but—"

"It's not magic," I said, boiling with rage; I don't know why, because she did have a point. "It's not fucking magic! It's just luck. Just slightly better – luck."

"Let's move on out," said Flanagan.

"Should we . . . ?" said Maria, patting her gun, and looking at the corpse of Quentin.

"No," said Flanagan. "Let him stay. He died a valiant death, he can be his own memorial."[1]

The air shimmered, and a vast shape appeared, neither real nor unreal, but awesome. Then a second shape. Then a third.

The shimmering stopped. Three Minotaur armoured cars had been teleported to us, each stacked with guns and ammo. We

1 Quentin Crazy Horse Gallifrey. May he rest in peace. – *Ed.*

checked for misflits. Discarded two of the Minotaurs, one of which appeared to be made of an element not known to science. Got in the third vehicle. And the chassis jets fired and we lifted up into the air.

This was a ghastly, ugly planet, at a raw and angry stage of development. The indigenous life was extremophile, and exceedingly nasty. The smell of sulphur filled our lungs, even through the Minotaur's air-con. We flew over fields of mud and shit and slime and green algae-like growths. There were crystalline rocks covered in grey mould, which glistened in the sunlight, when there was sunlight, which wasn't often. Geysers of fire occasionally erupted, spraying mud and sending spatters of tiny swamp-dwelling mites up into the air before they rained, horribly, downwards.

A volcano was erupting in the distance. This was, my brain chip informed me, a common occurrence on this planet. I asked for details of our target and a map scrolled down my visual array.

It had taken an entire year for SNG forces to locate Morgan's home world. Indeed, they would never have found it at all if they hadn't been helped by the flame beasts. But more of that anon.

On the maps, Morgan's World was called X43, and it was considered to be unterraformable because it was subject to wild storms and violent and unpredictable solar flares. But Morgan, cunningly, had made a world here by burrowing *inside*.

And that's how he had evaded capture for so long. Because, from space, there were no signs of sentient life here. No lights. No electromagnetic radiation. In short, none of the traces normally associated with a civilisation. The place looked like exactly what it was: a primordial soup planet, where life was at the earliest stages of evolution.

Oh, and it rained all the time, and lightning constantly flashed like a faulty torch in a dense mist.

We flew through the haze and the rain and over the swamp, all the while preparing for battle.

So, you may be wondering, how come the flame beasts were helping us?

Flanagan explained it to me as we travelled. Making up for the briefings I'd missed.

"The flames date from the dawn of time, and that makes them *strange*," Flanagan said.

I knew that much. "Is it true about the—"

"Oh yeah," said Flanagan, smiling. "They do have a fondness for television soap opera of the human variety. And blues, they love the blues, or some of them do. And there *is* something cool about the way they look and sound. Burning pillars of fire that turn into tumbleweeds of flame. The s-s-s-sssibilants. But they are not our friends. Get that? 'Cause I never got that. I had a flame who I thought was – never mind. That doesn't matter.

"The point is: remember that wasp that landed in your jam at the picnic? You put a glass over it and watched it die?

"That's us, the wasp is us, when the flame beasts turn against us. Which they may do, any minute now."

That's what Flanagan told me, more or less. I forgot to save it to chip, I'm recalling all that from memory. I suspect he swore more. I mean, fuck! That man always swore. He[2]

2 A long rant now follows in the original thought diary, which I've deleted. Among other things, Artemis shares her feelings about Flanagan which are highly conflicted. She was tormented at this time of course because she was sharing a mission with a mother whom she hated. And yet, on this kind of mission, everyone bonds – fear and adrenalin create what has been called an "indissoluble camaraderie". So love and hate were forming a toxic brew in her head. To compound this, Artemis was clearly in awe of Flanagan, as indeed who *wouldn't* be. She tries to express all this in about four pages of disquisition on her own emotional state but reaches no conclusion. And frankly, I take the view that the sooner we get back to shoot-'em-up action the better. Hence my radical edit. – *Ed.*

Picture the scene:[3] the Houses of Parliament in London. Home to the new SNG Government. The President of Humanity, Roger Layton, was making a rare appearance in his seat on the back benches, as the Prime Minister of the Humanverse addressed the House, via holo links with every inhabited planet.

And then the cry went out. Parliament is on fire!

Slow murmuring was followed by hasty panic. An evacuation of the building was ordered and executed. But the sprinkler systems didn't come on. And the Earth QRC reported no trace of actual flame.

And so Roger Layton left the Commons Chamber and walked up the stairs to the river front balcony and saw for himself what was happening.

An infestation of flame beasts! They were hovering above the three Gothic towers of the Palace of Westminster,[4] in a pillar of fire that reached up into the sky and continued, for all anyone knew, to the further reaches of the universe. The river itself blazed with reflected light, in terrifying Turneresque frenzy.[5] And swirling sibilant and sinister sounds emerged, as the pillar of flame began to talk.

And that's when the flame beasts delivered their ultimatum. Once, of course, they knew the beaconspace cameras were rolling, and they had everyone's attention.

Grandstanding or what?

The message was brief, and transmitted in such a way that

3 And now the story continues. Artemis's account is confirmed by Roger Layton himself, who responded fully if soullessly to my twelve page letter of queries about the events of that day. He handwrites his own letters, can you believe that? In tiny and utterly legible actual script. – *Ed.*

4 The Victoria Tower, the Clock Tower, and the Central Tower which is really more a spire. The Palace was built by Pugin and Barry in a Gothic revival style in the nineteenth century. Recent modifications have turned the Clock Tower into a launching tube for small interstellar spacecraft. – *Ed.*

5 A reference to the painting *The Burning of the Houses of Lords and Commons*, 1835 by J.M.W. Turner. – *Ed.*

every word was heard clearly and intimately by the leaders of humanity like a whisssper in the ear.

"Humanity mussst learn to become a civilissssed ssspecies," the flames hissed. (Flanagan described this in general terms; but I subsequently read several eye-witnesss accounts of this event, which is why I have the words verbatim.)

"You mussst desssist from the genocide and murder of other sssentient ssspeciesss," said the flame-entity. "And you mussst punish and remove from power those who have done sssso. Or we ssshall eliminate you all. Thisss we pledge."

Then they ignited the River Thames. It burned all night, with flames that did not scorch. The sight of it was, apparently, extraordinary. Subsequent news reports erroneously described the spectacle – thanks to the work of the SNG propaganda department[6] – as a "Fireworks Display to Celebrate the Freedom of Humanity".[7]

So how did this come about? How did the beneficent flame beasts become the scourges of humanity?

No one knows for sure. Maybe they just got fed up with us?

Now's a good time to remember what happened when the flame beasts declared war on the Bugs, and exterminated *them*.

Such a thing – flame beasts committing genocide – had never occurred before. It was not the flame beast way to wage war on other creatures. They're so damned powerful, there's no point.

But the Bugs posed a threat even to the flame beasts. And that's why they were eradicated.

Wasp, glass, remember?

By this stage, of course, the Galactic Corporation was no more. But the planets run by the Clan Bosses continued to terraform new worlds with utter brutality. Trillions of alien species, including many wonderful sentient creatures, were being

6 The Reconciliation and Rehabilitation Committee has a Public Affairs section which specialises in press manipulation. – *Ed.*

7 Headline in *Human News*, July 14th. – *Ed.*

rendered extinct on a monthly basis, to feed the Bosses' lust for more planets, and more power. They never accepted, you see, that things had to change once Peter Smith was gone.

And so all these Clan bosses – all of them, twenty-five of them originally – had to be killed, or otherwise punished, and removed from power.

And this was the trigger for the Clan Wars. The SNG were *not* the victims. They were the aggressors. They declared war on the *capobastone* and forced them to fight for their very survival. Because that was what the flame beasts had told them to do.

Now, only one *capobastone* remained alive; Morgan, in his many forms. And he too had to die, or be redeemed. But preferably, die.

Otherwise – the End of Days was upon us. Thus the flame beasts had pledged.

I have to admit, this briefing clarified a great many things for me. Up until now, I'd found it hard to comprehend how a liberal wishy-washy democratic regime like the SNG could be so damned effective, and remorseless. I mean, Jeez, these guys even opposed the death penalty! How the fuck did they get to be so good at fighting a fucking *war*?

But now, I got it. I knew why they were so desperate.

And I found it alarming. It made me feel – what can I say?

Things were too big. The stakes were too high. I was tired of fighting. I wanted to go home. I wanted to—

I'm sorry. Ignore me. I always get this way. Just before a battle. Do you know that feeling? Everything is impossible. Nothing will ever be achieved. Life is pointless and we're all going to die and everything, but *everything*, is a complete waste of fucking time.

And then the killing starts, and it's all all right again.

Monsters erupted from the suppurating swamps of Morgan's World and we slew them.

That went on for some considerable time. Most of this continent was TP-blocked, and we were still a long way from our destination. The place where, according to the flame beasts, we would find the real Morgan.

Our Minotaur was like a miniature Caracaras in terms of firepower and the strength of its hull. We sat tense in the cavernous grey-hulled cabin, surrounded by vividly terrifying array images of the hell outside. Fraser was in the pilot's seat, with Lena as co-pilot seated to his right. I was the gunner who had a couch behind them both, and I had my own arrays showing images from the exterior mobile cameras.

And, on these hovering screens, I saw visuals of our own squat beetle of a flying craft, assailed at every moment by gelatinous tendrilled monsters from the ghastly swamps of this planet. All our images were rendered in false colour, since the atmosphere was opaque to human vision; and the swamp creatures themselves were rendered a devilish red, which in no way reflected their real camouflaged appearance.

But it meant they looked like devils attacking a bat-like monster above seas of blinding colour and light; an image out of Dürer as if coloured by Picasso and then infected by the mad visions of El Greco.

And these swamp beasts were remorseless. They clung on to the hull. They spread their oozing slimed tendrils over us and tried to gouge open our ship. They spewed their gases on us, and made the metal blister. We tried flying higher – but these swamp-beasts could hop for miles into the air. And we daren't fly so high we'd register on the radar net.

So we just kept killing them.

All was haze and mists and spouting methane geysers and

darkly clotted clouds and fire-creatures flickering in the sooty atmosphere and volcanoes erupting angrily in the distance and the jellyfish-like swamp beasts leaping up at us and being burned off and falling and splashing back down into the poisonous bubbling morass.

I felt like a hang-glider flying through the intestines of a very fat giant who had indulged in the eating of excrement for many years.

Meanwhile, for much of the time, Lena was staring at me with that lost look of hers. She was, in my view, getting more and more flaky.

Maybe, I even wondered, she was getting too old for this shit.

I stuck my tongue out at her rudely; and she jolted, as if electrocuted.

Brigadier Fraser stood up from his pilot's chair, and stretched his legs.

"Want me to spell you?" asked Flanagan, and Fraser nodded. The two men swapped seats. Fraser sat opposite me. Flanagan steered for a while. I burned some more monsters.

I noticed that Fraser was looking tired. He was old, of course. I didn't know how old. I didn't know much about him, of course, apart from the stories he told of wars fought and victories achieved. He had once, so I gathered, been a professor of Physics. Before war consumed his life.

More monsters. More swamp.

Jay emerged from her catnap and broke open some cans of soda. We all sipped. Fraser retrieved the supplies of chocolate bars. That whiled away a few minutes. Maria did her stretches, and Flanagan snuck a sly glance at her limber athletic body. As, indeed, did I.

Then Jay started telling a story about his first girlfriend. That prompted Flanagan to tell a story about *his* first girlfriend. Things got a little ugly round about then. Lena accused Flanagan of being a womanising fuck. Flanagan retorted by—

Yeah, it was ding-dong all the way from then on, but I tried to tune it out.

And finally, we reached the volcano.

"How about we find another way down?" I asked.

"This is the direct route," said Flanagan.

We soared above the exploding spitting volcano in our bulky Minotaur. Sparks as big as our heads flashed past our craft, leaving trails of fire in their wake. The lava boiled like a pot of fiery gold below us. We hovered above the crater as Jay ran a tomograph analysis of the mantle below the simmering cauldron of red-hot rock.

"An angry world," said Fraser.

"It surely is," said Flanagan, in his Old Testament prophet voice; then he winked to give us confidence.

And then Fraser tipped the Minotaur and we plunged downwards into the boiling lake of lava; like a moth plunging into a candle's flame. Visual arrays showed us our projected path through the hot magma, a route that would lead down to the mantle and beyond. We were using a powerful ion drive to propel us through rock which was molten, and which grew denser and more solid the deeper we descended.

Eventually I began to use energy cannons to burn and blast the rigid plates of planetary crust that were blocking our path. Our arrays tried to make sense of the world outside through false colour displays that showed the flowing rocks of the asthenosphere in blue, the solid substance of the tectonic plates in red, and our craft as a flashing white journeying into places no human craft should ever exist. But blue and red merged, and no images could make sense of the swirling chaos of this planetary subterranean world.

After many terrible minutes had elapsed we breached the

lithosphere and saw our white dot continue on; smashing and blasting a path through into the turbulent depths of this young world.

And down we fell, down into the deepest depths. Fraser was focused; Flanagan was grim. Lena bore an elated look; she clearly loved the danger, and the insanity of our mission.

Jay kept a close eye on the pressure build-up; Maria monitored the engines and our velocity. I kept plasma-blasting anything that looked a potential obstacle; pumping further energy into this hot and volatile inner world.

And finally we were in the planet's outer core; at very nearly the centre of this world. And our arrays started to show us echo-images of the world that had been created within this world; Morgan's secret base.

"Great lair," Flanagan observed. He'd done his homework on our catchphrases.

Our journey to the centre of the planet was a strange and frightening one. We were like a group of deranged mariners sailing off the edge of the earth; or a party of space-travellers insanely attempting to fly *through* the sun. And the Minotaurs were indeed designed to be able to do just that.[8] The walls of our vehicle became translucent so we could see the ductile rock ebb and flow and cling around our hull. But still we moved, tearing a path into the deep interior of this vile nascent planet; the only solid element in an ocean of iron and nickel and sulphur.

And then we saw with false-colour visuals, floating ahead of us – Morgan's World. And it was large, larger than I could have imagined, and almost beyond belief.

For in this Stygian realm beneath the planet's surface Morgan had built a biodome the size of a major city.

Well, why not? The surface was inhospitable and bleak. And

8 I've read the Minotaur manual, and it specifically says, "Do not attempt to drive this vehicle inside the photosphere of a star", implying that some idiot users have attempted to do so. But according to the tech specs, Artemis is quite right. – *Ed*

with biodome technology so highly advanced, and hardglass domes strong enough to withstand the highest of pressures, there was no reason not to live in the depths below.

But how could anyone *bear* to live here? No sun, no air, no solid ground. Just molten horror swirling around the transparent biodome. Like an iceberg made of glass floating in a sea of eerie flame.

"They must have grown it," Flanagan theorised. "A bubble of hardglass, blown and blown and blown, with a fusion-powered bellows powerful enough to fill a planet with atmosphere. Until the dome that dwelled in the planet's core was the size of a Old Earth Conurbation. There must also be a pillar of hardglass reaching to the surface, for access. It's kind of—"

"What?" sneered Lena.

"Marvellous."

"Dumb."

"That human beings can—"

"Totally fucking dumb."

"Ah fuck you, you have no soul," jeered Flanagan.

"I had a soul. You sucked it. Vampire."

"Bitch!"

"Can it," I said wearily.

Fraser met my eye. He was more than a little in awe of Flanagan, I could tell. And he was both puzzled and appalled at the impertinent way Lena spoke to the great man.

We swam or flew or burrowed or slid, whichever it was, through the burning murk towards the dome, still navigating by ultrasonic echo-location. The cabin of the Minotaur was artificially lit, and our headlights shone at full beam, but illuminated nothing. Our velocity was formidable – for without our speed to smash open a tunnel for us through the liquid rock, we were likely to get trapped and die.

"This is not," I said, "one of my more picturesque missions."

"Doppelgängers should be doing this," said Maria.

Flanagan grunted.

"I'm serious!" Maria protested.

"ETA biodome, circa four hours," said Lena.

"Are we sure he's actually in there?" asked Maria.

"No we're not sure," said Flanagan, in the exaggeratedly patient tones a doctor might adopt to a mental patient who thinks he's Adolf Hitler.

"Well what if—"

"SHUT UP," screamed Flanagan.

And for brief moment, I had a flavour of the man behind the legend. Hero or no, he had one hell of a fucking temper.

"Easy, Flanagan," said Lena. She looked old. Flanagan looked old. Maybe the artificial light was less than flattering for multiple-centenarians like them.

I began to think about Douglas. I wondered how he was. I wondered if I'd ever see him again.

My mood began to ebb. I wondered if—

"What's Morgan really like?" asked Billy, casually.

"Better looking than me," said Flanagan sourly.

"How'd you two fall out?" Billy asked.

"Are you all right?" Lena asked me.

I was not all right. I was still thinking about Douglas. I was wondering what would happen if—

I snarled at her. Actually snarled, with a flash of teeth and a gutteral growl. Lena blinked, puzzled, and I turned it into a smile. It felt false as fuck.

What was wrong with me? I felt myself possessed by blind panic; and I fought hard to get my courage back.

"Long story," said Flanagan. He was still talking about himself and Morgan. I realised I'd tuned out for a few moments, lost in terror. This was bad. It was fine to have butterflies BEFORE a mission. But not now. Now when we were—

I took a sip of water. I tried not to think about—

"We've got time," said Billy, nudging Flanagan to tell the tale.

I forced myself back into the present moment. I realised

Billy wasn't meeting my eye. He *knew* I was afraid, that's why he was chatting to Flanagan. Trying to distract me. Trying to distract *them* so they didn't know how shit scared I was. Bless you, Billy.

"Long ugly story," said Flanagan grimly.

"I heard you betrayed him," Billy taunted.

"Who told you that?" snapped Flanagan.

"Navy scuttlebutt. We all thought you were—"

"You were in the Navy?"

"Yeah."

"The Corporation Navy?"

"Fuck yeah. I was your enemy for – well, shitloads of years. That's when I wasn't genociding planets." And Billy grinned, his patent bald evil ugly-fucker grin. It was very provoking. Even I wanted to slap his face and I was his godsdamned *girlfriend*.

Flanagan turned to Lena. "Who picked this guy for our fucking mission?"

"I did, arsewipe," I said.

"He's a fucking war criminal!" Flanagan protested, with genuine rage.

"So are you, technically," I gibed. Families of the many victims of the Last Battle had at one point taken out a class action against Flanagan. It rankled with him.

"Fuck you." Flanagan scowled, revealing his petulant side.

"Fuck you too!" I retorted.

"Now now," said Lena, in what were meant to be calming tones.

"Ah fuck you!"   "Fuck *you*!"

Flanagan and I said, in unison.

"Can we have some civility, please," ordered Fraser. "We are on a mission to save humanity here and—"

"Ah shut up."   "Fuck off."   "Mission to save humanity!"
"Fuck you, Jock!"   "Sweet Shiva!"

All five of us speaking at once. And Fraser glowered.

"I'm the commander of this mission," Flanagan pointed out. "I work best in an atmosphere of dumb insolence."

"Yes but—" Fraser said.

"Nah, nah, nah-nah-nah," said Flanagan, with provocative childishness.

"This is not how I'm used to conducting—"

Flanagan glared; Fraser scowled.

There was a brief hiatus.

Lena conjured up a virtual array and began playing computer solitaire.

Flanagan grunted, clearly delighted to have stamped his lack of authority on things. Then he took out a book – a book! A man after my own heart! – and started to read.

Maria rolled her eyes, expressing her disdain for everyone else in the cabin of the Minotaur, and I think she may have even sighed.

And as for me – my moment of terror was past. Billy's distracting tactics had worked.

Billy met my eye. He winked.

We continued onwards, in silence.

And finally, after some considerable time, we nudged the biodome with our bow.

"Fire cannons," said Flanagan. And we began to burrow a hole in the biodome, using the plasma cannons on tight focus.

It took another long while. But eventually the hardglass began to crack.

And when it cracked, the crack began to spread.

Two hundred miles of impregnable hardglass enclosed Morgan's base. It was impervious to heat and pressure. You could drop a bomb on hardglass and it wouldn't break. But we had state of the art space war cannons installed on our Minotaur, and an array of

Bostock batteries with enough power to run all the TVs in the humanverse for a year which, trust me, is a lot. With technology like that, you can drill through pretty much anything.

So eventually a tiny hole appeared in the hardglass carapace.

We carried on burning. A series of tiny cracks now appeared around the tiny hole.

We carried on burning.

The cracks started to spread and split open. And as the hole enlarged, dribbles of molten outer core began to flow inside the dome. Not quickly. But remorselessly. This was the way planets are forged. The slow movement of objects against each other, eventually generating extraordinary pressures.

There was, in other words, a hole in their glasshouse. And the entire molten planet was *pouring in*.

The flow became a torrent. The crack began to spread. The hardglass began to break apart. Thousands of tonnes of molten planet were spilling into the biodome. Inside, I could vividly imagine the horror as the skies spewed down death, like a monsoon in Hell. Sheets of molten iron and nickel and torrents of burning brimstone would be descending upon the shoppers in their malls and the families in their homes and the diners sipping wine in restaurants or the lovers canoodling in their beds and the soldiers killing time in their barracks. It was a planetary tsunami, *inside* the actual planet.

It was only a matter of time before the entire biodome was filled and clogged with hotter-than-hot core-stuff, and all life within would long before have been boiled and burned to the most ultimate of deaths.

"Let's get out of here," said Flanagan.

However, we couldn't.

The Minotaur was locked in position. The melted rock had thickly clung to us, and the craft was unable to move.

Fraser consulted the Minotaur sensors, and double-checked the manual. Eventually he shrugged. "Looks like we're screwed," he said, less than helpfully in my view.

"Did we know this might happen?" Maria asked.

"Always a possibility," shrugged Flanagan. He looked at me, pointedly.

"What?"

He sighed. "We could do with some good luck. Maybe even an improbable escape?"

"From here?" I laughed.

Then I checked my link with the QRC. Still intact. The nullers were in operation throughout the planet's crust, pointing upwards, preventing all beaconband transmissions from space. But if the QRC could give me the flit coordinates, I might still be able to—

"What can you do, babe?" asked Billy. There was no reproach in his tone. If we died, we died.

"Suit up," I said. And we all raised our helmets and checked our oxygen supplies. Then we gloved off.

"Hold my hands," I said, and held out both hands and they all clasped or touched my bare hands somehow. It felt strange to have Lena's hand on mine.

Then I prayed a silent prayer to Ganesh.

And we teleported out, minus the Minotaur, on to the planetary surface. We landed in a messy ruck. Our warsuits protected us from the bitter cold of the winds; but our hands were bare and we had to struggle to put on space-mitts before our fingers fell off.

Finally the task was done. We breathed sighs of relief, and gave thanks to our gods, those of us who had them.

And then we walked about four hundred miles across treacherous terrain and through vile swamps, until we were out of range of the nullers. It took a long long time.

Finally, we were out of nuller-range; and we flitted all the way back home to the Rock. No misflits. We'd survived the mission with only one fatality.

And Morgan was dead. Or so we hoped. We had no way of telling. All we knew was – *everything* down there was dead.

A week later we got news of another sighting of the real Morgan. The mission had failed.

"Don't take it to heart," Flanagan told me. We were in a bar, just the two of us. The usual drill, for Flanagan: a thousand year malt on the table, one of the many bottles he had pillaged over the years. I had my glass full to the brim, but it tasted like stale peat to me.

"I'm not," I said.

"And don't blame yourself for Quentin's death."

"I don't."

"We have to do this all over again you know."

"I know," I said. "But—"

"What?"

"I can't."

Flanagan waited patiently.

"I'm not a fucking hero," I said. "I never signed up for—" I ran out of words.

"You thought this would be easy?"

"One last mission. That's what Fraser—"

"He was lying."

"How many? How many more?"

"No idea," Flanagan said. "That's how it is." He was looking implacable. He did that very well.

"Shit, Flanagan."

"You're not a quitter."

I shook my head. He was wrong.

"How could you *do* this?" I asked him, desperation in my voice. "All this? Again and again? For so many years?"

Picture the scene: me and Captain Flanagan, the greatest hero in human history, shooting the breeze together! Drinking malt whisky and setting the world to rights! I could hardly believe it.

And all I could do was bust his fucking balls.

"It gets to be a habit," Flanagan said mildly.

"I do," I said, bitterly.

"Do what?"

"Blame myself. For Quentin," I admitted.

Quentin's random death had totally spooked me. It made me think my luck was failing.

"You should, indeed, do so," said Flanagan casually. "It *was* your fault. It's always your fault. Get over it."

That was harsh, I thought, sulkily.

But refreshing. Nothing like a slap in the face to break you out of self-pity mode.

"Yeah, I guess so," I said.

Round about then, that's when I learned the meaning of courage.

Because we did try again. Another planet, another mission. Another Morgan killed, which also turned out to be a cyborg. So we tried again.

Another planet, another mission, another cyborg destroyed, but once again we had failed to kill the real Morgan.

We tried again.

And again.

This continued for some time.

That's courage.

We hit the ground standing.

And I took stock. Maria was dead. Her limbs mutated, and elongated, like a Laocoön. Her chest was crushed by the new body-shape, and she had vomited out her own heart.[9]

Jay was also dead. No outward signs of deformation, but no vitals either.[10]

Andrew, who had replaced Fraser on the last twenty missions, was also dead, with skin inverted and no organs in his flaccid body.[11] Shannon, who had replaced Billy for the last twenty-five missions, was non-viable but put up a fight, so I had to plasma-blast her into oblivion.[12] And Flanagan too was motionless. And when I took his face mask off I could see he was made of – glass. Yeah, that's right. Fucking glass.[13]

Only Lena and me had survived, of the entire Kamikaze Squad.

"Is he gone?" asked Lena.

"Yeah."

Lena didn't say anything for a while but when she spoke her tone was calm.

"You're sure?"

I checked again. "No vitals."

"He's made of glass?"

"He's made of glass," I agreed. There was something magnificent about it. I could see right through Flanagan's face. I could see his crystalline brain inside his translucent skull. He was smiling, I swear he was smiling.

The others had died in equally terrible ways. But only Flanagan had died beautiful.

We didn't try to move him. We didn't even touch him, not so much as a light finger-stroke. But even so his body started to crack.

9 Maria Carelli. May she rest in peace. – *Ed.*

10 Jay Lombardo. He was actually related to me, distantly, on my father's side. May he rest in peace. – *Ed.*

11 Andrew O'Halloran. May he rest in peace. – *Ed.*

12 Shannon Doria. May she rest in peace. – *Ed.*

13 Captain Michael "Mickey" Flanagan, pirate, thief, saviour of humanity. May he rest in peace. – *Ed.*

Flanagan died in a million splinters of glass.

We continued with the mission. Remarkably, we didn't die. But we found no trace of the real Morgan. This mission, too, was a failure. I could tell you more about the specifics of the mission but, well, I'm not going to. Fuck that.

We ported back without revisiting Flanagan's remains. I knew, however, that Lena had taken away a sliver of glass. A fragment of Flanagan's face, the size of a diamond.

Brigadier Fraser didn't believe it at first.

Because Flanagan didn't die. Flanagan *couldn't* die. That fact was at the heart of modern humanity, it was our prevailing myth. No matter what, Flanagan would always prevail!

In fact, even when Flanagan *did* die, after getting sucked in by that double star – no one really believed it. He was still the king who would one day return. As he had! The moment humanity was in deadly peril again, back came Flanagan. He was humanity's greatest hero. Its saviour, no less.

But all that legend stuff is crap. Flanagan was just a man. For a long time, admittedly, he was an astonishingly lucky man, to survive when so many others died.

But then his luck ran out. It happens.

There was a public memorial service for Flanagan, which I did not attend. There were private gatherings of mourners, which I shunned. Speeches were made, and I ignored them.

Then Lena came to see me in my room. Billy made himself absent, with considerable tact. And Lena and I sat and stared at each other for a while.

"Are we friends?" Lena asked, eventually.

"No."

"I thought not."

She was silent a while.

"Will you ever forgive me?" she asked. "For being such a – you know."

"No," I said.

"I thought not." She sounded almost relieved. "Can I offer you some advice?"

"No."

"You don't have to forgive me," said Lena. "But you do have to—"

"Don't give me that fucking cliché!"

"—forgive *yourself*," said Lena.

Cliché or not, it was damned good advice.

All these years, I suddenly realised, I'd been punishing *myself* for what this bitch had done to me. And now she'd given me permission to desist with the self-flagellating. And get on with, well, my life.

Damn, I hate it when other people are smarter about me than *I* am."What the hell," I asked Lena, "do you want from me?"

"I want to hold a wake," said Lena. She was eerily calm. "And mourn the man I loved. And I want you to join me, Artemis. Will you do it?"

I thought about it for a while. And then I shrugged.

"Yeah, what the fuck, why not?" I said.

"Another drink?" I asked.

"Bank on it," said Lena, giggling.

We were the only two left, out of the entire platoon of mourning well-wishers.

It had been a long and disgraceful night. We'd been thrown out of eleven bars by bartenders who didn't recognise Lena. Well how could they? She looked like a whore, of the worst and sluttiest variety. Her raven-black hair had been touched up to remove all hints of grey, and tinted with lurid pink stripes. Her skin was fake-rejuved into an eerie plastic smoothness. She wore lipstick, nail polish, eye paint, facial tattoos, and a low cut dress. She was, all in all, not dressed for mourning.

"Am I embarrassing you?" Lena asked. We were by now in a cabaret club of the sleaziest kind. Naked men were gyrating and Lena was heckling and leering. She was also drinking heavily, very heavily indeed, even by my standards. And she was cramming down drugs, mainly floaters and epiphanies, when she thought I wasn't looking. And even when I was.

It was deeply awful. She was behaving like an evil witch who'd stolen the body of a nubile virgin, and was determined to ruin it before morning ended her spell.

My mother! Did I mention she was my *mother*?

This was gross beyond gross.

"Maybe we should call it a night," I suggested.

"Or maybe I should drink till I puke."

"When did that last happen?" I asked, genuinely curious.

She thought. "Twenty ninety-nine."

"Rejuve, huh?"

"It spoils the experience. I remember—" The memory fled her mind. She had that lost look again.

I tried to reintroduce a mellow mood.

"You want to talk about Flanagan?" I asked gently.

She cackled. "Fuck, no."

"Cool with me."

I sat and festered in silence.

"Okay then. If you're going to *brood*," she sniped.

I brooded a bit more.

"What did you want to know?" she asked.

"What?"

"About Flanagan."

"I don't know," I admitted. "Nothing. Everything. Did he have hidden depths?"

"None."

"Virtues?"

"None."

"Was he nice to you?"

"Never."

"Will you miss him."

"Oh yes. Yes."

Lena looked even more wild. A hunky male dancer came to her and she – look, I'm not even going to repeat it.

Her voice was slurred too by now. She was drinking faster than the fucking rejuve could sober her up.

"He'd appreciate this," Lena said.

"I doubt that," I said sourly.

"He'd want me to—"

She didn't finish the sentence.

"Let me take you to your room," I suggested.

"Leave me. Just leave."

"I'm not leaving you."

"LEAVE ME!" she screamed, and the bouncers came across and I gave them a warning look. But one of them grabbed my arm anyway so I broke his jaw. And—

And that was *twelve* clubs we'd been thrown out of.

"Have you thought—" I said to Lena, a little later, as we walked through the deserted night-time boulevards of the Rock. The sky above us was gunmetal grey. With a flick of a switch, it could be made translucent to reveal the vastness of space behind, but most residents of the Rock found that too spooky. And there were no clouds in this dimly illuminated sky – they vacuum them up every night, to filter for impurities. Oh, and someone had painted a moon on the inside of the biodome, for a gag. It wasn't all that funny really.

"Thought what?" Lena asked.

"You *can* bring people back to life you know. It can be done."

"Voodoo?"

"Cyborging."

"Never," said Lena, in a grey empty monotone.

"I don't blame you," I admitted.

We walked on. It felt like the sort of night where it should have been raining, in a melancholy and atmospheric kind of a way. But on the Rock, the rain came *up* from underground vents, watering the plants and humidifying the air without anyone ever getting wet. Shame, really, it just wasn't the same.

"You can go now," Lena said. "I'm fine from here. Go. I'll drink another glass or two then I'll go back to my room."

"I'll stay. I've got nothing else to do."

We were now walking through the narrower streets of the Rock's residential area. Billy was covering me from a discreet distance, with two surveillance squads. Wherever we staggered, Billy was close behind with his army of bodyguards. Twice, Lena had run out of the back of the club we were in, and Billy had MI'd me her location. Wherever she went, I popped up again. It was really pissing her off at one point during the evening, before she became too drunk to realise what I was doing.

We arrived at her apartment block, and I took her back to her room via the escalator. She threw up in the toilet. Then sobered herself up the old-fashioned way, by having a shower with her clothes on. And I dressed her in her pyjamas and dried her hair and tucked her up in bed.

I waited by her bed for six hours, while she pretended to sleep. Eventually she opened her eyes.

"I'll be fine," she said, weakly. And smiled. "You're so sweet for staying with me. But you can go now. Honest!" And she smiled again. A small, wan, duplicitous smile.

"Give yourself a week," I said grimly.

"I'm sorry?"

"Don't play your fucking games Lena."

"Don't swear at me. I'm your—"

I glared. She shut up.

"A week," I repeated, "Before you kill yourself. If you do it *then*, well. That's your choice. But not tonight. Not tonight. Okay?"

Tears were pouring down her cheeks. "Am I that obvious?"

"Yes."

"I can't live without him."

"Then do another mission. You'll almost certainly die."

"I can't live – even that long. I can't—"

"Look, bitch," I said, and could say no more.

"You want me to live, for *you*?" she said, pleadingly.

"I want you to at least," I said, and the tears were pouring down my cheeks too now, "consider it."

She gave me a sad look.

"If I do, you know. Choose to live," she said carefully, "will you forgive me?"

"For what?"

"For being a bad mother, of course."

I thought about it.

"Hell no," I said.

"Hey, come on!" she protested, startled at my vehemence.

"No!" I insisted.

"Please! Forgive me, and I promise I won't kill myself," Lena wheedled.

I shook my head.

And then she grinned. She actually *grinned*. Though the tears, it looked malign not sweet, but the intention was still a good one.

"You ungrateful slut!" she sneered, theatrically. "You're gonna reject my moral blackmail, huh?" And that sounded more like the old Lena.

"I certainly fucking am."

"Wise," she conceded.

"I thought so."

And then – there was a moment between us.

I'm not sure what sort of moment it was, but it was there. My mother in tears, desperate, suicidal. Me – what? Saving her life.

It was, I guess, a pretty major moment.

"What reason do I actually have to live?" she whispered, after a while. "Seriously, Artemis. I'm not some fucking teenager. I've lived – I can't even remember. Somewhere between one thousand and two thousand years. I just lost the only man I ever loved—"

"You loved Andrei," I pointed out.

"You read my diary then."

"And Tom, the copper. You loved him. And—"

"Look, the thing with Flanagan worked for me. We've been together – can't remember that either. A bunch of years. But I'm tired."

"Then sleep."

"I'm tired of – all this. The fighting. The endless jeopardies. You really think killing Morgan will make the universe a better place?"

"I do."

"Okay then, we'll do it. And then I'll—"

"Don't even say it," I said. "Or think it. Just—"

"What?"

"Live one day at a time."

"Come," said Lena.

"Come where?"

"Into bed. Cuddle me. Stay with me tonight."

I stared at her with horror.

"Are you suggesting we commit lesbian incest?" I asked, appalled.

She roared with laughter.

"Don't be ridiculous," she snorted. "You're too fucking –

young for me. Come on, cuddle your old mum. Wrinkled and withered as I am."

"You certainly are that."

"Wash your mouth out girl."

"Fuck you ginch."

I slept with her all night long.

In the morning I got up and showered and dressed and looked at the sleeping Lena. She was totally wasted. She smelled of booze and puke, despite the late night shower. She was old, very old. Her hair was flecked with grey again, despite the dye. She looked about a million years old.

But she was asleep. And at peace, for a little while.

And she was, fuck it all, my mother. And I – no, I'm not going to utter that ghastly cliché.

I'll give you this much: I hated her less than I had ever done before.

She was snoring. Get that! Snoring. That's how old she was.

I stayed by her bedside until she woke, about eleven hours later. When she saw me she was startled. I could see her trying to work out how the hell she was still alive. And she remembered what had happened. And how I had saved her life.

And then she smiled.

Chapter 14

Never Said goodbye

"This will never work."

"Fuck off."

"We look stupid."

"Get over yourself, woman."

In my hand, I held a pair of lucky dice.

Every army in history has had at least one soldier with a pair of lucky dice.[1] These days, *every* soldier carries 'em. Standard dice. Polyhedral dice. Icon dice. Dice within dice. Before every TP, a soldier will throw his or her lucky dice to determine the outcome. Since there is no consensus on how to read the throw of the dice, you can pretty much decide for yourself what the outcome will be. And if you die, or become horribly distorted or mutated, well, you must have had the *wrong pair* of lucky dice.

Taking the lucky dice off a TP warrior is no easy thing. But we managed it. And now we stood in the Rock's magnificent Star Chamber, where a visual array of every planet in the humanverse sprawled three-dimensionally around us. It was like floating free in the vast and awe-inspiring void of space, but without experiencing the deadly cold, and with helpful captions on all the stars and planets. I turned my back on the star map, tossing the dice from one hand to another. Fraser watched us,

1 Unverifiable, though plausible. – *Ed.*

hiding his anxiety and concern beneath layers of dour Scottish melancholy.

"Good luck, lassies," he said.

Lena snorted at his condescension. Whereas I tried to be more tactful, in recognition of Fraser's role as my mentor and leader:

"Go fuck yourself you four-eyed Jock bastard," I said. And I threw the dice over my shoulder.

They flew through the air and went straight through the virtual star array. I turned. Fraser had noted the points of impact, and was analysing the results.

"Die one," he said, "a black hole in spherical sector D49."

"Not so good"

"And die two?" asked Lena.

"You're not going to believe this," said Fraser.

"I'll believe anything," I said. And it was true. Ever since the nine years, six months and four days, lucky breaks and dumb coincidences have dogged my life. I have come to accept it as normal.

"Just activate the TP," said Lena. "We'll take it from there."

That was just plain stupid!

"Tell me where we're going—" I began to say.

But then we were there.

Cúchulainn.

I should have guessed.

It had the perfect circularity of all coincidences. I was back where I started from. Journey's beginning.

This, however, was wrong. I mean terribly, insupportably wrong.

I mean, just think about it! This is my *life*. It's not a fucking story. The actual lives that actual people live aren't like this. They're – episodic. What you might call picaresque. Things just happen, then other things happen. Whereas stories are—

Sorry, let me tell this the way it happened, okay?

First, me and Lena hit the ground standing and I saw where we were.

And then the shooting started.

But just *before* the shooting started – yeah, my mind was really racing at this point! – I went on to realise that in fact my life *has* been a story. It has a shape, and a purpose. In other words, it has an *author*.

Morgan.

I recognised him at once. Or rather, not quite at once. Not till he spoke my name. But then. I knew him *then*.

I'm aware that I've never mentioned this person before, as someone who appears as a character in my life-story. That's because I didn't know who he really was. And I didn't know, didn't AT ALL realise, that he would be relevant to this tale.

You see, Morgan was my gaoler, in the villa of Baron Lowman, where I was imprisoned. But I knew him then as Henry, because that's what Lowman called him.

Fucking Henry! I didn't even know his (fictitious) surname. He was just a guy, whose name I vaguely knew, who was responsible (on a shift basis, alternating with two other guys) for supervising my internment. And who, from time to time, made me dance. By which I mean, he thought-controlled his remote control and activated my whedon chip, and turned me into a dancing grinning puppet. Just to show me what would happen if I ever dared to fuck around.

Henry wasn't cruel to me though. He was just doing his job. In fact, he tried to be my friend. He brought me treats – food, chocolate, fine clothes – and made sure I always drank the best wine. And he never took advantage – you know what I'm saying. It would have been easy for him to do it, but he never did.

He even offered to help me escape once. But I saw that for the obvious trap it was. I never trusted him, to be honest. Though in fairness, I didn't trust *anyone* by that point.

But within seconds of arriving in Daxox's bar on Cúchulainn, the moment he spoke in fact, I realised that Henry and Hispaniola Morgan are one and the same person.

"Artemis," he said. And that's when I knew.

What a coincidence, huh?

There's more.

Remember, we hit the ground standing and I saw Morgan and he spoke and I recognised him, and I thought all these thoughts, or rather an abbreviated intuitive version of them. But it all happened very fast and there were of course an awful lot of OTHER extraordinary facts to assimilate.

Firstly, we weren't just on Cúchulainn, we were in Laguid. And we weren't just in Laguid, we were in Daxox's club, the Dahlia, where I had spent so many happy and indeed drunken hours. It was the early morning, the club was empty apart from a group of men playing a dice game at a table. The game was – it doesn't matter what the game was! It just struck me as an yet another eerie coincidence. For I'd thrown the dice at random and it had led to me being teleported here, where a game of dice was—

Spooky, huh? Wait till you get to—

No, let me get through this:

As I've explained, the first man I recognised was Morgan, aka Henry. Of course I knew Morgan from his photographs and the film footage of him, but had never made the connection. But when he spoke my name – "Artemis" – in that throaty growl of his, the years came rushing back.

I didn't have time to reminiscence. I was too busy with my sitrep, identifying threats and planning a course of action. Morgan was an obvious danger, he was my deadly enemy and was sitting in a military warsuit, though with the face mask off. Next to him was—

This is where it gets *really* strange.

Next to him was Daxox. Old frog-face. My lover and—

"Glad you could make it," said Baron Lowman, in his usual courtly tones.

Yeah, him.

Because the fourth man was a tubby guy with an eager look, and when he saw Lena he beamed as if she were his long-lost mother. "Lena!" he trilled, and beside me I could hear Lena gulp, literally gulp.

The fourth man, I kid you not, was Peter Smith, aka The Cheo, aka my brother and Lena's son.

The fifth man was Flanagan.

"Lena!" I screamed and I threw myself across the room with guns drawn, firing in mid-air with unerring accuracy. While Lena stood like a fucking fool, gawping.

The first bullet fired by Morgan hit her on the chest, jarring her body armour and shocking her into action. When she moved, she moved fast. Meanwhile, I fired thirty rounds while in a crouching position, rolled and dived, and fired again.

Morgan was the first to die. His warsuit was strong enough to withstand a missile burst, but who the hell wants to play cards with a face mask on? So he was bare-faced, and I had a perfect target and I blew out his brains with my first six shots.

Peter Smith was the cautious sort. He *was* wearing his hardglass mask. I scored six direct hits on his face but all bounced off and by then he had drawn his gun and was shooting back.

Daxox stood no chance. Once she'd got her shit together, Lena engulfed him in plasma fire then fired exploding shells at the fireball. She didn't shoot at anyone else, just Daxox. He too had a hardglass mask but it didn't help him. He burned alive, as the bullets cracked his hermetic seal and the plasma licked outside, then burned within.

Flanagan moved like the wind and shot me when I landed. The impact spun me back and I flipped and landed and fired about fifty shells all of which missed him. He was fast *and* he was graceful, and he really knew how to dodge.

Then Lena popped him with a bullet while he was in mid-sideways-leap, and it threw him off course and he crashed awkwardly to the ground. And she was across the room in four flips and put a limpet-mine on his face mask.

Then she looked at me. I could see her face through the hard-glass. It was an expression of sheer horror.

I leaped towards her and caught her and we teleported twelve feet away. When the bomb blew off Flanagan's head, we were out of range.

"Nice work," I said. The explosion had tumbled Peter Smith off his feet and dazed him. I moved swiftly across and coup-de-grâced him by severing his head with my dagger.

Then we masked off. Sweat was pouring down our faces. Or was it tears?

"Come and see," I said, beckoning to Lena.

"No."

"Come!" I grabbed her by the hand, and dragged her over to Flanagan's dead body. And I put my gun on laser setting and after sixty seconds, I managed to bore a hole in his armour. Then I carved a line down his torso. His body peeled open like a fruit.

"I can't bear to, I can't—" muttered Lena.

"Look," I said. Inside the body of "Flanagan", there was no heart, no lungs. No blood gushed out, no intestines spilled their vile load. It was all silver metal in hermetically sealed units.

"You do understand—" I said.

"I understand," Lena snapped.

"And what this means is—"

"I get all that."

"And this guy," I said. I did the same trick on Morgan's dead body. And his corpse split open to reveal robot organs.

"Cyborg," said Lena.

"I know him," I said, pointing at cyborg-Morgan, and sketching in the history briefly.

Lena got it at once. The implications I mean. She knew my life-story you see. Not from me, from Fraser. But she knew all about what Daxox had done to me. And fear was in her eyes.

"My fault," she said.

"Not your fault," I insisted.

"My fault, all my fault," she said, in tones of utter horror.

And she was right. All the horror of my life. All the terrible things I experienced in the nine years, six months, and four days.

They all happened to me *because of Lena*. And her relationship with Flanagan.

Back up a bit.

What follows is the story of my life, as it really happened. Not the way I *thought* it was happening at the time.

Picture this flashback moment: there I was, an eighteen-year-old idiot, serving in a bar in Gullyfoyle and a guy came in. He was a gangster from Cúchulainn. And he told me tales of what it was like in Laguid, the wildest city in the humanverse.

And in return – well, why wouldn't I? – I told him all about my life on Rebus. And about my dad, Professor McIvor, and my heartless mother who'd abandoned me. And we talked politics too. There was a big galactic war going on round about then. A pirate called Flanagan was hooked up with some relative of the Cheo called Lena Smith. Without FTL or TP, wars were slow protracted things in those days. So we discussed it. Why *wouldn't we?*

So when I went on the run from Gullyfoyle, where did I go? Laguid, of course, capital city of Cúchulainn. The place this hood had just been telling me about . . . Coincidence?

Well, yes. But once I'd made that one random decision, the rest all followed.

Because this gangster now knew my story. And when he got back to Laguid, he told his pals about me. And when I turned up, fencing a hot jewel . . . you get the picture? The story spread.

And then I met Daxox.

Daxox was the boss of the gangster I met on Gullyfoyle, of

course. So he too knew all about me. He also knew about Lena, and her fling with Flanagan, And her affair with McIvor. And the fact that McIvor was my dad, which meant Lena was almost certainly my mother. Because in the days of beaconspace, this stuff is so fucking easy to find out.

And he knew too that I'd stolen the jewel, so he sent his men to kill me knowing that I would kill *them.* Another test. You remember he had that thing about testing me?

The key fact here is that Daxox – though I didn't know it then, I only know it *now* – had an ally, a fellow *capobastone*, called Hispaniola Morgan. Who, for reasons I hadn't yet fathomed, was based on Cúchulainn and not on his home world of Morgan's Planet.[2]

So Morgan too got to know about me, and my history.

Cause, effect. The ripples just never stop.

Morgan knew Flanagan, as you know. And he hated him with a vengeance, but had no way of getting to him. And then along I come . . .

And from that moment on, my life was *authored*.

You know what I'm saying? Morgan pulled the strings. Daxox did all the terrible things he did – because Morgan told him to.

Which means that despite everything, Daxox may actually have loved me. But Morgan was a hard guy to resist. And Morgan wanted to take revenge on Flanagan. Which he did, by punishing *me*.

Back up a little more. Why did Morgan hate Flanagan so much?

The history books say it was because Flanagan was an idealist, appalled at Morgan's massacres. But that's all shit. I knew Flanagan. He was my friend. But fuck me, he was ruthless. And unscrupulous too.

2 Morgan was Daxox's mentor; and the real power behind the throne on Cúchulainn, according to several anonymous sources I have consulted. – *Ed.*

But in the course of their joint adventuring, Flanagan screwed Morgan's wife, Medea – I got this from Lena, it's the truth. Then Morgan found out and killed Medea with his bare hands, in a fit of blind rage. So Flanagan lost his rag and trapped Morgan on a spaceship leaking air. Morgan, somehow, escaped, to the nearby planet of Xavier.

And you know the rest.[3]

Cut to many years later. Morgan sees a chance to take revenge. A girl arrives in his partner's club who is the daughter of Flanagan's latest squeeze. So he arranges for her to become a – and *now* you're with me.

Not quite the same as Morgan getting a chance to fuck over *Lena*, the love of Flanagan's life. But near enough. Psycho logic, yeah?

And that's the story of my life, as far as I've been able to piece it together. I'm just a pawn in the deadly game between Morgan and Flanagan. Eventually, I'm guessing, my dead body would have been sent to Flanagan, with a note explaining who I was, and where I had spent the last ten years. And that, yeah, that would have stung.

It's like Hooperman and Saunders all over again except, of course, Saunders escaped. And that story never had an ending.

And the "author" thing? This is how it worked. Morgan wrote my life as a tragedy. Then I turned it into a revenge drama.

Backstory over.

As we were leaving Daxox's club, we saw two cops arriving, carrying guns.

Both were Morgan.

3 See previous footnote. – *Ed.*

"It's a coup. They've had a fucking planetary coup," I said to Lena.

"Why didn't we know?"

We were out on the street now, making our escape as swiftly yet unobtrusively as we could.

Once we'd got out of the club, Lena had wiped the blood off my face; a smart move because I'd been drenched in it. Then we'd put on our street camouflage clothes and dumped our backpacks and Xenos rifles. But we still had warsuits on beneath our civvies, and our force field generators were strapped to our abdomens. And handguns. We were carrying, between us, an awful lot of handguns.

As we walked, a man bumped into me. It was Peter Smith. Lena stared at him.

"You got a fucking problem?" Smith demanded.

"No problem."

Smith walked on. Lena continued to stare after him.

Three Flanagans walked up to us, talking animatedly. Lena stared at them. They ignored her. But they gave me a long hard appraising look. Followed by a wolf whistle. I smiled appreciatively and walked on. This was freaking me out.

There were plenty of ordinary citizens on the streets too, of course. Market stall owners. Pedestrians. Flybikers. This was the same old Laguid with polluted skies and busy walkways and too much traffic. But everyone we passed had a haunted look.

A holo image on every street corner said: CURFEW IN FORCE. ANYONE FOUND ON THE STREETS AFTER TEN PM WILL BE HUNTED UNTO DEATH. BY AUTHORITY OF HISPANIOLA MORGAN, LORD AND EMPEROR AND POTENTATE OF THIS UNIVERSE.

These old-time villains, they are *so* baroque.

I saw a Daxox, and approached him.

"Do you know me?" I asked.

"I'd like to," he leered.

"What's your name?"

"Daxox," said Daxox.

"You remember me?"

He thought hard. "I fucked you once?" He leered.

"You were great," I assured him.

Lena and I walked on.

"They're not sentient," I said to her.

"Of course they're sentient. They're cyborgs!"

"I mean they're not – not *smart*. They're like apes."

"Degraded copies?"

"Or older copies. Cyborgs go mad, with time."

"There are thousands of the bastards."

"Millions maybe."

A city full of dead people.

A city full of dead people who Lena and I had once, and intimately, known.

It was screwing with my head.

We walked on. Heavily armed Flanagans and Daxoxes stood at every street corner. Heliplanes hovered above, crewed by Peter Smiths, as well as flybuses in which Smith was both the driver and many of the passengers. And Morgans in the bodies of beautiful women strutted along, attracting admiring glances. Though most often the Morgans were male, and possessed of an eerie aura of authority. And the Baron Lowmans too were to be found in many guises – wearing rich robes, or in smart casual jeans and T-shirts flyboarding on the walkways, or in city suits.

And everywhere we went, electronic mosquitoes flocked, gathering data on all street-level activity.

Then one of the soldiers turned, and I could recognise her easily through her hardglass visor.

It was me.

"Identify yourself," said Artemis-soldier. And I couldn't stop myself. I drew my Philos handgun and fired six times at her visor, then grabbed her and threw her and broke her neck.

The cyborg didn't die, she just lay on the ground waddling her legs.

"Run," said Lena, and we ran.

I knew this city so well. I knew every alley and hideout. I knew the clubs and their backdoors and the fire escapes, and the hidden entry ways into the fabricator plants.

We ran and heliplanes hovered overhead and called on us to stop and we ignored them and warning bursts were fired at us. We were masked off, in street clothes, trying to blend in. But the fact we were running like fuck through a city under siege was enough to draw attention to us.

We turned a corner and a squad of six soldiers (mostly Flanagans) saw us and opened fire. We leaped and fired in mid-air, aiming our exploding bullets so they ploughed holes in the sidewalk. The soldiers tumbled over each other and into the pit we'd created. And we ran.

Ran down an alley. Ran through a side door that I unlocked via my Rebus link. Ran inside the illegal manual labour workshop. Human workers were handweaving carpets, their faces pale, their fingers torn with cuts. We ran through as a security guard shouted at us to stop. He drew his gun and fired and I took him down with a bullet to the knee. He fell, cursing misogynistically.

And still we ran. Through the double doors, kicking them open and stepping to the side in case of ambush. A guard shot at us and we leaped up high and clung to the wall with our adhesive shoes and ran past him, catching him a good old kick as we passed by. Then through the red door, up one set of stairs. I blew a hole in the wall and we ran into the next building, the Hunter Refinery. And we ran down the stairs there and out the back to safety and—

Withering plasma fire greeted our emergence and with clothes ablaze we ran back in. Lena and I doused ourselves in flame retardants. Our faces were stinging with the heat. And we were red-cheeked and hot with the effort of the ceaseless running. I nodded, and we took another door that I knew would lead us down to the basement. It did. Once there, we broke open a ventilator shaft and crawled through. It was a long slow wriggle. I thanked my lucky stars I did not have a fat arse! Lena however was not so lucky. (Heh!)

I shoved her through the last few feet, then we collapsed in a heap at the other side.

It was a strange surreal moment – lying on the floor enmeshed and entangled in the limbs and lardy backside (hey! I call it as I see it!) of my own mother.

The moment passed. We got back on our feet, and started running again.

The doors ahead of us were locked and hardmetal sealed. So we put a limpet bomb on the floor and blew a hole in it and jumped through. We did the same for another three floors, and that linked us up to the fibre optic subways beneath the city. We crawled through there on our stomachs, still smelling our own charred flesh from the earlier plasma-blasting, until we emerged in the basement of the Abrox fabricator.

There, we took stock.

"How the fuck," asked Lena, gasping like an old wheezy horse, though I have to admit, she *had* kept up with me, "do we win this war?"

Good question.

I asked Magog.

There were, I learned six hundred thousand cyborgs on this planet, and fifty thousand or so were me.

Or rather, they were robot bodies built in replica of me. Very funny Cyborg-Daxox. Fuck you.

The Flanagan I'd killed had been a warrior. But his mind wasn't the real Flanagan-mind. I was sure of that. Or so I told Lena. In fact I wasn't so sure but—

What the fuck. Let's work on this provisional hypothesis:

Morgan and Daxox have cyborged themselves. And, as a gag, they have created cyborg bodies that are replicas of their enemies and allies. Peter Smith is not the real Smith; he has none of Smith's memories or personality, he just looks like him. In the same way, Flanagan is not the real Flanagan. But Daxox and Morgan – they are the real McCoy. Or rather, the replica real McCoys. Or rather—

It gets tricky doesn't it?

Lena was over her blue funk by now. She too was adamant that we weren't fighting the real Flanagan; and that was a comfort to her, since we'd so recently killed him.

And as we outlined our war strategy, her eyes sparkled and her mood lifted. This was the old Lena. The legendary Lena. I liked her that way.

Picture the scene. There we were, huddled in the basement of a dimly lit fabricator building. Faces flushed, bodies battered, clothes ripped revealing black warsuit armour beneath. Just the two of us, with no means of calling for help, facing an army of half a million or so armed and dangerous cyborgs.

Just the kind of odds that Lena and I both like.

"It's not fucking fair! I know so *much* about you!" I told Lena, angrily.

We'd been in the basement an hour. I was in a reflective mood. And it occurred to me that this would be a good opportunity to bond with my mother.

But instead, I began bitching at her.

"Yeah, you have a problem with that?" she acknowledged, defensively, in response to my accusation.

"It's so damned annoying," I protested. "There's nothing to find out. I've read your thought diary, I know every last thing about you. I know about the freckles. I know about the Kingdom of Alchemy." She rolled her eyes. "I know about all the men. And the drinking. And the drugs. And the game where you stop the heart of the man you're—"

"Wash your mouth out girl."

"Hey, it's in the book!"

"The book should never have been published."

"Yeah, like, you didn't accidentally on purpose—"

"I did not 'accidentally on—'"

"You're just a braggart."

"I was baring my soul."

"Euch, please don't, your soul is vile."

"I agree."

"Now you're being mock-humble."

"Ah, you know that trick?" Lena said, with a mock-sweet smile. She gave as good as she got, this woman, even with her own daughter.

There was a silence, which lasted a little while.

I was working hard, by the way, all this time, fighting the war with the cyborgs. I'll explain how in a moment. But I still had enough headspace to chat. And to enjoy the occasional companionable silence.

"A daughter should never know her mother," I concluded. "There *should* be secrets."

"I have secrets."

"Name one."

Lena thought hard.

"Well, one time Flanagan – hey!"

I laughed.

"Almost gotcha there," I said.

"In your dreams," she retorted, amused.

"Huh."

"I think a daughter should," Lena said, a few moments later.

"Should what?"

"Know. Her mother. Not just as a mother. As a – real person."

I thought about that.

"Maybe," I said.

We were silent again, for a long while.

"We could maybe be friends?" Lena said eventually.

"In your dreams."

"Come on Artemis. Lighten up. Friends?"

"Yes. No. Maybe, if we were in a different life."

"Or if we survive?"

"No hope of that."

"Ah . . ."

Okay. I should maybe clarify my actual strategy here:

I was communing with Magog, you see, all this while, planning our attack.

Lena and I huddled, and talked, and bitched; but the larger part of my consciousness was as one with the quantum brain of the planet's computer. Not, I must admit, conducive to great conversation, but I was doing my best.

I spoke again:

"I'm pregnant you know."

"I know about that," Lena said. "I was told – about that."

"That was my motive for—"

"I know."

"I called the child—"

"Douglas. I know."

"You have spies everywhere, huh?"

"Pretty much. Plus—"

"What?"

"I have Tinbrain in my head."

"Who?"

"Tinbrain is the Earth QRC. The founder quantum computing brain. The rest are really – what would you call it? Subsystems? Clones?"

"Children. Maybe. They're certainly not clones. They're mostly all quite different. The ones I've known anyway."

I already knew this about Lena and Tinbrain. Of course I did, it's in the book. But I should have remembered. She is like me. The only one who is like me. In having a QRC as a – friend.

"If we had a beaconband link, I could talk to Tinbrain now," Lena mused. "And Tinbrain could talk to Magog. And Magog of course is communing with your thoughts on a second by second basis."

My mind whirred, decoding that one.

"You're saying, you'd be able to *read my mind*?"

"Only those thoughts which – yes."

"Even the daydreams?"

"Yes."

"Even the sexual fantasies?"

"Oh yes."

"What kind of mother *are* you?"

"The worst sort," said Lena, and she smiled. Her old wrinkled face smiled. It didn't make her look any younger but—

She did at least look like a mother. MY mother.

"Shall we do this thing?" asked Lena.

"I'm doing it now," I said.

Historical fact:

At the Battle of Agincourt, an army of fifteen hundred British men-at-arms and seven thousand longbowmen faced a formidable French army that stretched as far as the eye could see. In the French army, there were eight thousand men-at-arms, four thousand archers and fifteen hundred crossbowmen in the vanguard alone, with more than twice that number in the rear and on the flanks.[4]

In the Battle of Cúchulainn, however, it was just me and my mum, fighting against a planet full of cyborgs.

Ridiculous isn't it? I thought so, even at the time.

"Are you in?" I asked Lena.

"*I'm in*," she said, in a warm whisper that meant her voice was now inside my head. We had linked brain chips, so she too could access the cybernetic pathways of Magog, this planet's QRC.

I knew Cúchulainn like the back of my hand. In all its wild splendour, and in all its industrial horror. From the Mountains of Marguid to the icy lakes of Garddown. And all across this once-verdant land were the hunched backs of the fabricator planets that spewed out black clouds, turning ore and mud and gas into a staggering superfluity of consumer items. The doppelgänger robots were stored here too, lined up like suits of armour awaiting ghosts to possess and locomote them.

Morgan had of course sundered the beaconband link with Earth, and his cyborgs had no need of doppelgängers. So the chassis of the DRs were unused, and forgotten about.

But now they were *mine*. And so the robots began to stir, controlled jointly by myself and Lena. We grabbed a thousand at a time in the fringes of our consciousness and swept them up. They flew like flocks of soulless birds across the factory lands towards Laguid. They emerged from basement vaults in the city itself, glaring and angry and dusty. They broke out of abandoned factories; they unpacked themselves from storage. And finally, they gathered together on the streets, an army fit to fight the

4 I didn't bother checking all this. I'm sure it's right. – *Ed.*

cyborgs. Five hundred thousand robot shells; controlled by me and Lena.

And then the battle commenced.

Two Artemises, blown up by a missile fired by a seven foot high silver-skinned robot.

A dozen Morgans sundered into pieces by plasma blasts from a flock of flying doppelgängers.

A hundred Flanagans broken in the streets, after a pitched battle with a platoon of humaniform robots who fought naked, but whose bodies could withstand sustained bursts of direct plasma blast.

The Peter Smiths were slain in their thousands. The template mind there was clearly old and slow, for not a single of my doppelgängers was killed by a Peter. Lena, however, refused to kill the Smiths, just as she refused to kill the Flanagans. It made my job all the harder.

But having said that – look, I won't deny it – I was enjoying myself. I was no longer a soldier in an army. I was the entire fucking army!

And Daxox, ah Daxox! He died again and again and again.

Picture the scene: an army in its barracks, enjoying down time. Sipping vintage wine or whisky in the club. Playing pool in the rec room. Swimming, lifting weights, or fucking in palatial bedrooms using to the full the sensory capacities of these cyborg bodies. There are Baron Lowmans galore to be found here. Peter Smiths by the score. Morgans – ah, so many Morgans. Flanagans everywhere you look. And Artemises, too, scattered among them.

And then doppelgänger robots parachute in to the barracks like blossom falling off cherry trees in spring, and a battle royal erupts. Cyborgs and doppelgängers fight hand to hand. Flanagans are blasted with explosive shells. Peter Smiths flee yowling with fear but are gunned down as they run. Morgans are incinerated by plasma bursts or pulverised by exploding bullets. And Baron Lowmans are scattered into pieces, turning the parade grounds into junkyards of cyborg body parts. A massacre.

Many massacres, all over Laguid.

More battles than the mind can conceive, in fact. I fight, I am killed, I fight again. I inhabit a thousand bodies, no ten thousand, no ten times ten thousand. I see citizens screaming with fear as I gun down the cyborgs in the streets. I shoot down heliplanes. And all doppelgänger robots are my allies, for those who I do not possess, are possessed by Lena.

It was like fighting World War III as a computer game, with real fatalities. The scope of it was – well.

I feared at one point that, like my comrades before me in the war of Invasion: Earth, I would never want to leave this hellish but addictive reality.

Morgan used hi-tech on us too of course. Satellites fired energy beams from space. Fighter craft shot us by the million. Missiles erupted among our ranks. But much of the military hardware had the potential to be doppelgänger-controlled. And so time and time again, I stole fighter planes and smart missiles from my foes and sent them back with added hate.

Then some of my doppelgängers broke into the planet's control hub, and disabled the Nullers that kept this system isolated from the rest of humanity.

And so Magog was now able to speak across the vast reaches of space with Tinbrain, the Earth QRC. And the two giant computers joined forces, like whales singing to each other from different oceans. Or like dragons ridden by ants; as Lena and I steered and guided these vast intellects with which we were so indissolubly bonded.

And in the basement of the fabricator building, our bodies twitched and howled and grunted and our limbs flailed, as we slew and slew!

The Battle of Cúchulainn was a strange and a marvellous and a terrible affair. I remember the terror and the beauty of it all. Guns blazing. Missiles exploding. Plasma beams burning. Cyborg skin and organs melting, and their bodies being rent and smashed.

Every hour we rested, for ten minutes, in shifts. For our minds could not take the pressure of possessing so many other minds without respite. So once every hour, I would jerk myself out of the doppelgänger trance, and look around, and see Lena twitching and flailing and shouting.

I tried to sleep in those brief respites but I could not. I was too transfixed with the sight of my aged mother shouting like a mad old crone, as she sent armies of robots into battle and flew missiles and exploded bombs. Each time one of her 'selves' died she shouted in rage, a death cry that chilled my blood. There were many such cries.

Then Lena's voice would be in my head. "*Time in*," she would say and I would re-enter my trance and join her once more. And, I guess, when she took her own respite she seized her chance to look at *me*. Her only daughter. Spasming in frenzy as I killed, as only gods should be able to kill; in many places all at the same time.

No military history has been written of this battle and nor will it ever be. Lena and I kept no records of who died and when and how and what our strategy was. And, quite deliberately, I didn't save the battle record to chip. All I remember is that, at the time, I *seemed* to know what I was doing. I cross-sectioned the globe and marked off each section in my head as I cleansed it of cyborgs. I sent doppelgängers into the sewers and the sub systems and into the fibre-optic tunnels too. I used robot mosquitoes to search for hold-out Flanagans and skulking Peter

Smiths. At one point the enemy even surrendered – I had a message from Daxox offering terms. But I ignored that, of course. Complete victory was the only option I would countenance.

And so it continued. As savage and bitter a doppelgänger war as Invasion: Earth, but far more upclose and personal.

In the process the planet was, I have to admit, wrecked. And there was considerable collateral damage. In other words, innocent civilians died. I couldn't help that. It was not my fault. And they would have died anyway of course. The cyborg way is to turn all human flesh into cyborg, for they honestly think we will prefer it that way.

What else can I say? There was a long, ghastly, extraordinary conflict, but in the end, the robots of Lena and Artemis prevailed.

For there were so many of us. That's how the Corporation had survived for so many years. Its legions of doppelgänger robots were, well, legion.

At Agincourt, the archers turned the tide of battle. Technology defeated martial prowess. But even so, soldiers fought and blades swept and warriors lost their lives.

In this battle, only machines died. Victory was achieved; but not glory.

Let me make that point again; there *was* no fucking glory.

"What are you going to do?" Lena asked me, anxiously.

"Ignore it."

"Can you do that?"

I thought for a while. "No."

One of the few surviving Morgan cyborgs had issued a challenge. He was offering a *mano a mano*. Me and Morgan-cyborg, in single combat, to decide the outcome of the entire battle.

"Why not?"

I thought hard on that one. "It's the way I was raised," I eventually said.

"Raised? On Rebus? By your *father* you mean?" The scorn in her tone was enough to curdle blood.

"My father was the Clan. I am a gangster, Lena. A *capobastone* in blood spilled. It is my code."

"Bullshit."

"I cannot," I said, "refuse a direct challenge."

And it was true. Remember, computers are just machines, which are programmed to behave in certain ways. Whereas humans are—

Yeah. You got it. Same fucking difference.

And so, like a fool. I accepted the challenge. *Capobastone* to *capobastone*, remember, for I had killed the real Daxox, thus acquiring his Clan rank.[5]

Lena was furious with me of course. She didn't understand the whole business of the Clan code. But I'm stubborn. I get it, I guess, from my mother's side.

That's what I told Lena anyway; it's *her* fault I'm such a schmuck.

And so I travelled to the Main Street of Laguid to meet Hispaniola Morgan, in a duel to the death.

Main Street is a boulevard in the centre of Laguid which is wide enough to take thousands of pedestrians at any one time. The walkways are like coloured ribbons here. Children can run the width of the boulevard by leaping from walkway to walkway, as if they were stepping stones, though it's a dangerous business. But now the walkways had been halted. The street was deserted. The sun peeked through black clouds.

5 As recounted earlier. – Ed.

Luckily I have good night vision; in Laguid, you need it in the day.

Lena was three blocks away, in a fortified hotel room, still in communion with Tinbrain and hence Magog, and able to speak to me via MI. She was my back-up in case of a double-cross. But I saw no traces of Flanagans or Daxoxes, or Peter Smiths or Baron Lowmans. Just a single Morgan, as promised, standing in Main Street, waiting for me.

"Lena," said Hispaniola Morgan.

"I am Artemis," I said.

"The challenge was to Lena."

"That wasn't clear."

"It's clear now."

I shrugged. But my spirits soared. Was there a way out for me here?

"*Walk away, Artemis*," said Lena in my head.

"Then the challenge is void," I said.

"I challenge thee," said Morgan, smiling cruelly.

Shit. He was just fucking with me.

"*You can't be serious. Walk away!*"

"Weapons?" I asked.

"Knives," Morgan replied.

I nodded. Up close, and personal, in a knife-fight that would decide the entire war. Everything to play for then. Just the way I like it.

Morgan put his rifle and pistols down on the floor. He took off his helmet. Then he stripped off his warsuit, to reveal he was wearing a Corporation Navy uniform, with a skull and cross-bones sewn on the lapel.

I put down my own guns. Then took off my helmet, stripped off my warsuit. I was wearing black jeans and a black T-shirt. My arms were bare.

I drew my knife.

Morgan drew his knife.

We began, slowly, walking towards each other.

It was a long street. I was alert to snipers. I was on the lookout for heliplanes with missiles. I was prepared for Morgan to try and double-cross me by drawing a concealed gun. I was ready, in short, for anything.

I was barely three feet from Morgan when the mine exploded beneath me. The ground rippled and buckled as if an earthquake had smitten it. It was a bomb that ran the entire length of Main Street – fuck only knows how they'd buried it so well. And my body vanished, engulfed in the inferno.

Morgan smiled.

I tapped him on the shoulder.

The Artemis that died was a holo of course; the real me was waiting in the shadowed area behind a walkway strut for the battle to be over. I had an army of doppelgängers two blocks away, ready to pounce. But for now, it was just me and the cyborg Morgan.

"Hi," I said.

And he turned and looked at me.

And I realised that I could smell him.

I could smell his body odour, the warrior's rank aroma that comes from spending hours or days in a warsuit. I could see sweat beading his brow. I could see the goose bumps on his neck, from the chill wind. I could hear his heart beat. He looked at me and there was a spark of fear in his eyes.

It was Morgan. The real Morgan. What a lucky—

Morgan shot me. I was, of course, in a warsuit; so the bullet bounced off my armour. I fired once, at his face. The bullet went straight through his mouth and out the other side, but didn't explode en route. Blood gouted out, giving him an evil bloody leer. But my second bullet missed, because Morgan was running. And a flock of Smiths and Daxoxes and Lowmans swooped out of the clouds in their black warsuits and began shooting at me, throwing off my aim and, dammit, hitting me.

I gave chase.

This was my city. I knew, as you know, every alley, every building, every cul-de, etc.

And it didn't take long to realise that Morgan was not just running; he was luring me. Leading me to the City Hall, a perfect spot for an ambush. I knew; but I didn't care.

I sprinted down empty motionless walkways, I vaulted walls, I saw him run up the steps to the City Hall main entrance and I allowed the door to open for him.

I ran up the steps, spattered with his blood, and reached the door and paused.

An explosion ripped the door away. Easily predicted. I ran through the smoke. The ambush I'd expected was there. Flanagans and Smiths and Daxoxes lay in wait, hiding behind statuary in this baroque headquarters of the Laguid civil service, firing bullets and energy blasts at me.

"I'll take care of these."

The doors opened again and an army of doppelgänger robots rattled through, silver bodied and with eerie blank faces that somehow all looked like Lena. Bullets and energy beams flew and the cavernous atrium became a war zone. The City Hall was a baroque extravaganza, with glass pilasters and nude mobiles suspended by magnets and, inevitably, a pair of matching pair of statues of Flanagan and Lena, now shattered and cracked with bullet impacts. I ignored the irony of that; and let Lena fight her virtual war with the cyborgs.

Deafened by the gunfire, buffeted by the direct hits upon my body armour, I could still manage to follow a trail of blood with my mask's augmented vision. So I ran into the maelstrom of gunfire and energy blasts and I survived and ran up the stairs to the first floor, where giant tapestries of the founding fathers of Laguid once stood; shredded by the ricochets.

And there, I found Morgan waiting for me.

His movements were uncertain; he was clearly in considerable pain. He was carrying a Philos pistol which one of his cyborgs must have thrown to him. As soon as he saw me, he began to shoot.

It was no contest. I was in a warsuit, he was unarmoured. I

walked towards him, his bullets bouncing off my armour. I could have killed him with a single shot but that wouldn't have been sporting. But his aim, I'll grant you that, was good; he shot me ninety-three times in a small spot in the heart region in the space of a few seconds, and it was a good chance the next bullet would break through and kill me. But still I did not shoot.

When I was close enough, I took the gun off him and crushed it in my hand.

Then I raised my helmet and took it off. I stripped out of my warsuit for the second time. I shook out my arms and took a deep breath. I drew my knife. He drew his knife.

This time was for real. He could smell my sweat; I could smell his. He was gasping, bloodily grinning. "Boss to boss," he said, "*capobastone* to—"

Expecting me to be distracted by his words, Morgan drew a concealed gun from a holster above his arse and fired, in a single fast and effortless movement. I dodged the bullet, came up slashing. I slashed his throat open with my knife.

Then, tiring of the knife stuff, I picked up my own gun and delivered the *coups de grâce* at point-blank range, until his body was a torso with no head.

It was over. Hispaniola Morgan was dead.

Lena and I went to a bar for a drink.

"The battle not the war," I said.

We'd been in the bar all afternoon as the fighting continued to rage outside; our minds still controlling doppelgängers on every spot on the planet.

But by the time we reached the end of the second bottle, Magog told us we had killed the last of our enemies. All the cyborgs were dead. Victory had been achieved.

We both knew, however, that there were still thousands of evil cyborg Hispaniola Morgans left on other planets in the humanverse; up to the usual no fucking good.

But do you know what? That was now someone *else's* problem.

"Battle not the war," Lena echoed. "Isn't that always the way of it?"

We chinked glasses.

It could be years before *all* the Morgans were killed.[6] But, we hoped, the Daxox and Flanagan and Peter Smith and Baron Lowman cyborg bodies had been created more recently. We might have seen the last of *those*.

"Why?" I asked.

"Why what?"

"Why did Morgan hate Flanagan so much?"

That's when she told me the story. Of Morgan's wife Medea, and Flanagan's betrayal of his best friend, and Morgan's subsequent murder of Medea. I'd half guessed it to be honest, so it didn't come as a great reveal.

"That explains a lot," I said, as she reached the end of her tale of treachery and soured friendship.

"Flanagan was never," Lena admitted, "a saint."

I laughed. "No."

"That's why I—"

"Yeah."

"We always—"

"I know."

"He was my—"

"I know he was," I told Lena.

That's Lena, my mother, by the way. Saviour of all humanity. Yeah, *that* Lena. Did I mention she was my mother? I squeezed her hand gently.

We chinked again.

"To Flanagan."

6 And indeed it was. – *Ed.*

"To the old rogue, love of my life, liar, cheat, arsehole, lover, friend, Mickey Flanagan," said Lena.

Her cheeks were damp with tears. I was glad of that. Earlier on, when she would not cry for him – that's when I most feared for her.

"So what next?" I said to Lena.

She drained another whisky and thought.

"I retire," she said, at length. "Find a planet where I can be a grandmother."

From this, I swiftly deduced her cunning plan.

"Near *me*?" I asked.

"If you'll have me."

"I'll try to endure it."

"Artemis—"

"No."

"I just want to—"

"Skip it."

"Do you forgive me? *Now* do you forgive me?"

"Fuck no."

"That'll do."

Lena smiled. She was looking tired. And old, so very old. It was time, I realised, for her to rest.

We left the saloon and walked back down Main Street.

And that's when it happened.

A sniper's bullet whistled through the air, so fast we heard its flight *after* it hit Lena on the face mask. It was a lucky shot, her face mask was already cracked. So the bullet went through and entered her skull and then penetrated into her brain.

And there, it exploded.

I drew my gun and laced the rooftops with bullets. As I did so, I called up an army of doppelgängers who drenched the area with gunfire, and swept the sniper away. The report came back to my MI a few minutes later: the killer had been killed.

It was a cyborg Baron Lowman. Magog had been wrong; we hadn't killed them all. *This* was the last.

I walked back to Lena. Her body was sprawled on the pavement, with her black warsuit armour showing through the rents and gashes in her street clothes. Her face was – gone. I kneeled down, and peered inside her mask, through the gaping hole created by the bullet. I saw nothing but blood and spattered grey tissue. I deduced there was nothing left of her brain. Which means her brainchip was gone too. Her memories. Her updated thought diary. All gone.

Lena was dead. The latest fatality of a long and soulless war.

And I never even got to say goodbye.

Lena Smith

May she rest in peace

extras

www.orbitbooks.net

about the author

This is **Philip Palmer**'s fifth novel for Orbit books; he is also a producer and script editor, and writes for film, television and radio. For further information, visit his website Debatable Spaces (www.philippalmer.net)

Find out more about Philip Palmer and other Orbit authors by registering for the free monthly newsletter at www.orbitbooks.net

if you enjoyed

ARTEMIS

look out for

GERMLINE

by

T. C. McCarthy

ONE
Crank Fire

I'll never forget the smell: human waste, the dead, and rubbing alcohol—the smell of a Pulitzer.

The sergeant looked jumpy as he glanced at my ticket. "*Stars and Stripes*?" I couldn't place the accent. New York, maybe. "You'll be the first."

"First what?"

He laughed as if I had made a joke. "The first civilian reporter wiped on the front line. Nobody from the press has ever been allowed up here, not even you guys. We got plenty of armor, rube. Draw some on your way out and button up." He gestured to a pile of used suits, next to which lay a mountain of undersuits, and on my way over, the sergeant shouted to a corporal who had been relaxing against the wall. "Wake up, Chappy. We got a *reporter* needin' some."

Tired. Empty. I'd seen it before in Shymkent, in frontline troops rotating back for a week or two, barely able to walk, with dark circles under their eyes so they looked like nervous raccoons. Chappy had that look too.

He opened one eye. "Reporter?"

"Yep. *Stripes*."

"Where's your camera?"

I shrugged. "Not allowed one. Security. It's gonna be an audio-only piece."

Chappy frowned, as if I couldn't be a *real* reporter, since I didn't have a holo unit, thought for a moment, and then stood. "If you're going to be the first reporter on the line, I guess we oughta give you something special. What size?"

I knew my size and told him. I'd been through Rube-Hack back in the States; all of us had. The Pentagon called it Basic Battlefield Training, but every grunt I'd met had just laughed at me, and not behind my back. Rube. Babe. Another civilian too stupid to realize that anything was better than Kaz because Kazakhstan was another world, purgatory for those who least deserved it, a vacation for the suicidal, and a novelty for those whose brain chemistry was messed up enough to make them think it would be a cool place to visit. To see firsthand. Only graduates of Rube-Hack thought that last way, actually *wanted* Kaz.

Only reporters.

"*Real* special," he said. Chappy lifted a suit from the pile and dropped it at my feet, then handed me a helmet. Across the back someone had scrawled *forget me not or I'll blow your punk-ass away*. "That guy doesn't need it anymore, got killed before he could suit up, so it's in decent shape."

I tried not to think about it and grabbed an undersuit. "Where's the APC hangar?"

He didn't answer. The man had already slumped against the wall again and didn't bother to open his eyes this time, not even the one.

It took me a few minutes to remember. Sardines. Lips and guts stuffed into a sausage casing. Getting into a suit was hard, like over-packing a suitcase and then trying to close it from the inside. First came the undersuit, a network of hoses and cables. There was one tube that ended in a stretchy latex hood, to be snapped over the end of your you-know-what, and one that ended in a hollow plug (they issued antibacterial lube for *that*), and the plug had a funny belt to keep it from coming out. The alternative was sloshing around in a suit filled with your own waste, and we had been told that on the line you lived in a suit for weeks at a time.

I laughed when it occurred to me that somewhere, you could almost bet on it, there was a certain class of people who didn't mind the plug at all.

Underground meant the jitters. A klick of rock hung overhead so that even though I couldn't see it, I felt its weight crushing down, making the hair on my neck stand straight. These guys *partied* subterrene, prayed for it. You'd recognize it in Shymkent, when you met up with other reporters at the hotel bar and saw Marines—fresh off the line—looking for booze and chicks. Grunts would come in and the waiter would move to seat them on the ground floor and they'd look at him like he was trying to get them killed. They didn't have armor on—it wasn't allowed in Shymkent—so the guys had no defense against heat sensors or motion tracking, and instinct kicked in, reminding them that nothing lived long aboveground. Suddenly they had eyes in the backs of their heads. Line Marines, who until that moment had thought R & R meant safety, began shaking and one or two of them would back against the wall to make sure they couldn't get it from that direction. *How about downstairs? Got anything underground? A basement?* The waiter would realize his mistake then and usher them into the back room to a spiral staircase, into the deep.

The Marines would smile and breathe easy as they pushed to be the first one underground. Not me, though. The underworld was where you buried corpses, and where tunnel collapses guaranteed you'd be dead, sometimes slowly, so I didn't think I could hack it, claustrophobia and all, but didn't have much choice. I wanted the line. Begged for a last chance to prove I could write despite my habit. I even threw a party at the hotel when I found out that I was the only reporter selected for the front, but there was one problem: at the line, everything was down—down and über-tight.

The APC bounced over something on the tunnel floor, and the vehicle's other passenger, a corpsman, grinned. "No shit?" he asked. "A reporter for real?"

I nodded.

"Hell yeah. Check it." I couldn't remember his name but for some reason the corpsman decided to unlock his suit and slip his arm out—what remained of it. Much of the flesh had been replaced by scar tissue so that it looked as though he had been partially eaten by a shark. "Fléchettes. You should do a story on *that*. Got a holo unit?"

"Nah. Not allowed." He gave me the same look as Chappy—*what kind of a reporter are you?*—and it annoyed me because I hadn't been lit lately and was starting to feel a kind of withdrawal, *rough*. I pointed to his arm. "Fléchettes did *that*? I thought they were like needles, porcupine stickers."

"Nah. Pops doesn't use regular fléchettes. Coats 'em with dog shit sometimes, and it's nasty. Hell, a guy can take a couple of fléchette hits and walk away. But not when they've got 'em coated in Baba-Yaga's magic grease. Pops almost cost me the whole thing."

"Pops?"

"Popov. Victor Popovich. The Russians."

He looked about nineteen, but he spoke like he was eighty. You couldn't get used to that, seeing kids half your age, speaking to them, and realizing that in one year, God and war had somehow crammed in decades. Always giving advice as if they knew. They *did* know. Anyone who survived at the line learned more about death than I had ever wanted to know, and as I sat there, the corpsman got that look on his face. *Let me give you some advice ...*

"Don't get shot, rube," he said, "and if you do, there's only one option."

The whine of the APC's turbines swelled as it angled downward, and I had to shout. "Yeah? What?"

"Treat *yourself.*" He pointed his fingers like a pistol and placed them against his temple. The corpsman grinned, as if it was the funniest thing he had ever heard.

Marines in green armor rested against the curved walls of the tunnel and everything seemed slippery. Slick. Their ceramic armor was slick, and the tunnel walls had been melted by a fusion borer so that they shone like the inside of an empty soda can, slick, slick, and double slick. My helmet hung from a strap against my hip and banged with every step, so I felt as though it were a cowbell, calling everyone's attention.

First thing I noticed on the line? Everyone had a beard except me. The Marines stared as though I were a movie star, something out of place, and even though I wore the armor of a subterrener—one of Vulcan's apostles—mine didn't fit quite right, hadn't been scuffed in the right places or buckled just *so* because they all knew the best way, the way a veteran would have suited up. I asked once, in Shymkent, "Hey, Marine, how come you guys all wear beards?" He smiled and reached for his, his smile fading when he realized it had been shaved. The guy even looked around for it, like it fell off or something. "'Cause it keeps the chafing down," he said. "Ever try sleeping and eating with a bucket strapped around your face twenty-four seven?" I hadn't. Early in the war, the Third required their Marines to shave their heads and faces before going on leave—to keep lice from getting it on behind the lines—but here in the underworld the Marines' hair was theirs, a cushion between them and the vision hood that clung tightly but never fit quite right, leaving blisters on anyone bald.

Not having a beard made me unique.

A captain grabbed my arm. "Who the hell are you?"

"Wendell. *Stars and Stripes*, civilian DOD."

"No shit?" The captain looked surprised at first but then smiled. "Who are you hooking up with?"

"Second Battalion, Baker."

"That's us." He slapped me on the back and turned to his men. "Listen up. This here is Wendell, a reporter from the Western world. He'll be joining us on the line, so if you're nice, he might put you in the news vids."

I didn't have the heart to say it again, to tell them that I didn't have a camera and, oh, by the way, I spent most of my time so high that I could barely piece a story together.

"Captain," I said. "Where are we headed?"

"Straight into boredom. You came at the right time. Rumor is that Popov is too tired to push, and we're not going to push him. We'll be taking a siesta just west of Pavlodar, about three klicks north of here, Z minus four klicks. Plenty of rock between us and the plasma."

I had seen a collection of civilian mining equipment in the APC hangar, looking out of place, and wondered. Fusion borers, piping, and conveyors, all of it painted orange with black stripes. Someone had tried to hide it under layers of camouflage netting, like a teenager would hide his stash, just in case Mom didn't buy the *I-don't*-do-*drugs, you-don't*-need-*to-search-my-room* argument.

"What about the gear in the hangar—the mining rigs?" I asked.

A few of the closest Marines had been bantering and fell silent while the captain glared at me. "What rigs?"

"The stuff back in the hangar. Looked like civilian mining stuff."

He turned and headed toward the front of his column. "Keep up, rube. We're not coming back if you get lost."

Land mines. Words were land mines. I wasn't part of the family, wasn't even close to being one of them, and my exposure to the war had so far been limited to jerking off Marines when they stepped off the transport pad in Shymkent, hoping to get a money shot interview, the real deal. *Hey, Lieutenant, what's it like? Got anyone back home you wanna say hi to?* Their looks said it all. Total confusion, like, *Where am I?* We came from two different worlds, and in Shymkent they stepped into mine, where plasma artillery and autonomous ground attack drones were things to be talked about openly—irreverently and without fear so you could prove to the hot AP betty, just arrived in Kaz, that you knew more than she did, and if she let you in those cotton panties, you'd share *everything*. You would, too. But now I was in *their* world, land of the learn-or-get-out-of-the-way-or-die tribe, and didn't know the language.

A Marine corporal explained it to me, or I never would have figured it out.

"Hey, reporter-guy." He fell in beside me as we walked. "Don't ever mention that shit again."

"What'd I say?"

"Mining gear. They don't bring that crap in unless we're making another push, to try and retake the mines. If we recapture them, the engineers come in and dig as much ore as they can before the Russians hit us to grab it back. Back and forth, it's how the world churns."

There were mines of all kinds in Kaz, trace--metal mines *and* land mines. The trace mines were the worst, because they never blew up; they just spun in place like a buzz saw, chewing, and too tempting to let go. Metal. We'd get it from space someday, but bringing it in was still so expensive that whenever someone stumbled across an earth source, usually deep underground, everyone scrambled. Metal was worth fighting over, bartered for with blood and fléchettes. Kaz proved it. Metals, especially rhenium and all the traces, were all the rage, which was the whole reason for our being there in the first place.

I saw an old movie once, in one of those art houses. It was animated, a cartoon, but I can't remember what it was called.

There was a song in it that I'll never forget and one line said it all. "Put your trust in Heavy Metal." Whoever wrote that song must have *seen* Kaz, must have looked far into the beyond.

I needed to get high. The line assignment had come from an old friend, someone corporate who'd taken pity and thought he'd give me one last chance to get out the *old* Oscar, not the one who used to show promise but couldn't even write a sentence now unless he'd just mainlined a cool bing. Somehow, I knew I'd screw this one up too, but I didn't want to *die* doing it.

My first barrage lasted three days. I was so scared that I forgot about my job, never even turning on my voice recorder, the word "Pulitzer" a mirage. Three days of sitting around and trying to watch them, to learn something that might keep me from getting wiped—or at least explain why it was I had wanted this assignment in the first place—and always wondering what would drive me crazy first: the rocks pelting my helmet, not having any drugs, or claustrophobia. Living in a can. The suits had speakers and audio pickups so you could talk without using radio, but I'd never realized before how important it was to *see* someone else. Read his face. You couldn't even nod; it got lost in a suit, same as a shrug. Meaningless.

Ox, the corporal who had educated me about mining gear, was a huge guy from Georgia. Tank big.

"I friggin' hate curried chicken," he said. Ox pulled the feeding tube from a tiny membrane in his helmet and threw a pouch to the ground. "Anyone wanna trade?"

I had some ration packs that I'd gotten off a couple of French guys in Shymkent, and threw one to him.

"What the hell is this? I can't read it."

"It's French. That one is wine-poached salmon."

Ox broke the heat pack at the pouch's bottom. When it was

warm, he stuck the tube through and squeezed. I swore I could almost see his eyes go wide, the *no-friggin'-way* expression on his face.

"Where'd you get *this*?"

"Foreign Legion."

He squeezed the pouch again and didn't stop until it was a wad, all wringed out. "Un-fucking-real. The French get to eat this every day?"

I nodded and then remembered he couldn't see it. "Yeah. And they get booze in their rations. Wine."

"That's it," Ox said. "I'm going AWOL, join up with the Legion. *You,* rube, are welcome in my tunnel."

And just like that, I was in the fold.

Occasionally the Russians lobbed in deep penetrators, and near the end of the second day, one of them detonated, breaking free a massive slab that crushed two Marines instantly. One of their buddies, a private who sat next to them, got splattered with bits of flesh and bone that popped from their armor, like someone had just popped a huge zit. The man screamed and wouldn't stop until a corpsman sedated him, but he kept rocking back and forth, repeating, "I can't find my face." Finally the captain ordered the corpsman to sedate him further, tie him up, and drag the Marine into the rear-area tunnel, where they could pick him up later.

"Good thing they did that," said Ox.

I pulled my knees up to my chest. "Why?"

"I was about to wipe him."

Things returned to normal for a while. Muffled thumps of plasma still shook the ceiling, and suit waste pouches opened automatically to dump human filth on the floor—because someone had been too scared or too lazy to jack into a wall port. *That* was normal for subterrene.

The only flaw in the captain's plan was that eventually the guy who had been sedated came to and picked up where he had left off. Over the coms net, his voice screamed in our ears that he still couldn't find his face, every once in a while adding "the shitheads left me."

Ox picked up his carbine and muttered, "He's dead," but fortunately for both Ox and the crazy guy, a corpsman was close to the tunnel exit and sped off to deactivate the man's communications.

I knew what the crazy guy meant. Ox did too, and that was the problem: nobody wanted to hear it; nobody needed to be reminded that none of us could find our faces. Without being able to touch it, I had begun to wonder if maybe I didn't have one anymore, like it got left behind in my Shymkent hotel so that some half-Mongolian puke could steal it for himself because I had forgotten to leave a big enough tip on the pillow to make stealing not worth it. I *needed* to find my face, knew that it had to be around there somewhere, if I could just take off my helmet for a second.

By the end of the third day, the barrage lifted, and I sat quietly, watching the Marines and feeling like I was the uninvited guest who didn't know what fork to use at dinner, too scared to say anything because my stupidity would show. I'd left my rig in the hotel too, hadn't thought I'd have to go this long without juice, and now I felt the shakes, got that chill, a warning that if I didn't get lit soon, it'd be bad. Even so, nobody moved. Everyone soaked in that stillness, and only an occasional click as the armorer went down the line, checking weapons and suits, broke it. Then the captain slapped the four men closest to him. They stood and moved slowly to a ladder before disappearing through a hole in the ceiling.

"Where they going?" I asked.

Ox checked his carbine for about the hundredth time. "Topside watch."

"Why?"

"'Cause Pops is shifty. Sometimes, when neither of us has a barrage on, he'll try and move in topside."

I shivered, a mental wind that preceded whacked-out thoughts. No way I could deal with all this shit; I wasn't ready. It wasn't what I signed up for; someone else could cover the line, get the first story. My next question proved to me, to everybody, that I was terrified, a rube.

"What about the sentry fields? The bots. Won't they deal with anything topside?"

Ox laughed. "Pops can make magic in his land, and Kaz *is* his land. Sentry bots don't always work."